THE LAST TRAIN

Praise for The Last Train

An unrelenting portrayal of a strong female character driven to dark deeds in a foreign land—and the heart-pounding search to find her.
Publishers Daily Reviews

An absorbing investigation and memorable backdrop put this series launch on the right track.
Kirkus Reviews

For anyone who loves crime and cop novels, or Japanophiles in general, this is a terrific thriller. Fans of Barry Eisler's early novels will find the same satisfactions here.
Blue Ink Review

The Last Train is nothing short of electrifying, a masterpiece that combines action with humor and suspense.
Readers' Favorite

I would definitely recommend it to crime and murder mystery fans, especially those with an interest in Japanese culture.
Online Book Club

Set in Tokyo, this exotic crime thriller is a lightning-fast chase to the finish line that'll leave hearts pounding and pages turning.
Best Thrillers

Written from knowledge *rather than* research, *he knows a lot more than he has any need to tell us...brings the city gloriously to life.*
The Bookbag

...a well written and enticing look into the culture of Tokyo. The story behind Michiko Suzuki is compelling and engaging, you can't help flipping the pages to see what she is going to do next and find out why her victims were chosen.
Literary Titan

While mystery readers will relish the progress of a detective torn between two cultures, it's the reader of Japanese literature who will truly appreciate the depth of background and references that make The Last Train *a standout story.*
Midwest Book Review

...a heartfelt, thoughtful ode to a strange and beautiful city, in the way that so many classic detective novels are. Lyrically written, with plenty of suspense, this a novel that aims to please, and can't really help but do so.

IndieReader

A well-paced and absorbing mystery, with quick action and a look at urban life, theirs is an utterly page-turning adventure.

Foreword Reviews

Gripping and suspenseful, this fast-paced thriller unfolds on the streets of Tokyo, where a clever and cold-blooded killer exacts revenge.

Booklife Prize

The Last Train *by Michael Pronko is a five-star detective read. It is unique, intriguing, and will hook the reader from beginning to end. I highly recommend it to all mystery lovers!*

Reader Views

Praise for Pronko's Writings on Tokyo Life

Motions and Moments: More Essays on Tokyo

Gold Award: *Readers' Favorite Non-Fiction Cultural*
Gold Award: *Travel Writing Global E-Book Awards*
Gold Award: *Non-Fiction Authors Association*
Gold Honoree: *Benjamin Franklin Digital Awards*
Silver Medal: *Independent Publisher Book Awards*
Indie Groundbreaking Book: *Independent Publisher Book Review*
Finalist: *National Indie Excellence Awards*
Finalist: *International Book Awards*
Finalist: *Foreword's Book of the Year Awards*
Finalist: *Independent Author Network*

Pronko is an insightful author capable of seeing a deeper beauty in everything he writes.

SPR Review

...vividly captures the depth and beauty of Tokyo, bringing to life the city and the lifestyle.

Reader's Favorite

This book sparkles and succeeds as a love letter of sorts to Tokyo. The author's writing is a joy to read, with wonderful phrasing and vivid descriptions.

OnlineBookClub.org

This is a memoir to be savored like a fine red wine, crafted with supreme care by a man who clearly has fallen in love with his adopted city.

Publishers Daily Reviews

Each of his essays brought me closer and closer to an appreciation of the complex and complicated place Tokyo is.

Reader's Favorite

Beauty and Chaos: Slices and Morsels of Tokyo Life

Gold Award: *First Place Reader's Favorite Awards 2015*
Gold Award: *eLit Awards 2015*
Silver Award: *eLit Awards 2015*
Gold Award: *Non-Fiction Authors Association 2015*

...a rare gem of exploration that holds the ability to sweep readers into a series of vignettes that penetrate the heart of Tokyo's fast-paced world.

Midwest Book Review

The author's love for the city is evident...he has explored the place and soaked up every small detail about life in Tokyo.

Readers' Favorite

Beauty and Chaos is a spectacular read. The collection is masterful and unique.

SPR Review

These pieces feel flowing and natural, perhaps because many arose simply from walking around, people-watching.

The Bookbag

An elegantly written, precisely observed portrait of a Japanese city and its culture.

Kirkus Reviews

Tokyo's Mystery Deepens: Essays on Tokyo

Gold Award: *eLit Awards 2015*
Silver Award: *eLit Award 2015*

...a rare glimpse of the structure and nature of Tokyo's underlying psyche.

Midwest Book Review

An insider's view of what life is really like in this pulsing, densely populated Asian metropolis.

Luxury Reading Blog

Tokyo's Mystery Deepens plunges into the minuscule details of what it is like to be a Tokyoite.

OnlineBookClub.org

The Last Train
By Michael Pronko
First paperback edition, 2017
ISBN: 978-1-942410-12-6

Typesetting by FormattingExperts.com
Cover Design © 2017 Marco Mancini, www.magnetjazz.net

For more on the Hiroshi series: www.michaelpronko.com
Follow Michael on Twitter: @pronkomichael
Michael's Facebook page: www.facebook.com/pronkoauthor

Also available by Michael Pronko:

Essays on Tokyo Life
Beauty and Chaos: Slices and Morsels of Tokyo Life (2014)
Tokyo's Mystery Deepens: Essays on Tokyo (2014)
Motions and Moments: More Essays on Tokyo (2015)

Also in the Hiroshi Series
Japan Hand
Thai Girl in Tokyo

THE LAST TRAIN

by Michael Pronko

Raked Gravel Press 2017

RAKED
GRAVEL
PRESS

「釜一つあれば茶の湯はなるものを数の道具をもつは愚な」千利休　９７首
If you have one teapot, and can brew your tea in it, that's enough.
Having too many tools is useless.

Sen no Rikyū, *Poem 97*

The water of the fountain ran, the swift river ran, the day ran into
evening, so much life in the city ran into death according to rule, time
and tide waited for no man, the rats were sleeping close together in their
dark holes again, the Fancy Ball was lighted up at supper, all things ran
their course.

Charles Dickens, *A Tale of Two Cities*

Chapter 1

She was as tall as he was, but he was twice as wide and at least a decade, maybe two, older. She held his swaying bodyweight upright with her arm tight around his waist. Her tall, strong limbs prodded him forward along the late-night street—another Tokyo couple after a night out.

His overstuffed suit and rambling walk marked him as a foreigner, and a very drunk one. His knees popped and locked like a cheap robot with rundown batteries. He swayed from the booze inside him, or something more, beyond the fatigue and freedom of Tokyo.

She was sober and focused, nodding absently at his sputtering comments. A long shawl, as thick and black as her hair, fell around her broad shoulders. Her tight summer dress pulled at her trim figure with every stride. Her muscled legs were bare except for the wide leather sashes of her sandals. She was a Tokyo woman, confident, directed and conscious of the city around her.

She pulled him toward the entrance of Tamachi Station away from the nearby warren of bars, eateries and all-night clubs filled with bar hoppers and boozers. She checked her watch, barely noticing the drizzle.

The trains would stop running soon.

Drunken, red-faced Japanese men in groups, or alone with a woman peeled off from one of the hostess bars, ambled along the streets with liquored-up gracefulness. Drunk together at night, they talked loudly and coarsely, acting boisterous and loose, though in the morning they'd return to quiet, meek company mode.

The waiting chauffeurs and taxi drivers parked along the curb smiled to themselves. They could see the poised, pretty woman would have the plump, too-drunk foreigner's money without any more work. He was clearly unable for much more of anything.

The drivers pulled at their uniforms, inhaled their cigarettes, and settled deeper into their patient wait along the curb.

She dragged him forward toward the trains, ignoring their stares.

Near the taxis in front of the station, the first driver in line cranked open the back door. The man swayed toward it, but the woman steered him past without a glance.

Under the glaring lights of the station's vaulted entrance, she appeared even younger and prettier than out in the dark and drizzle. Her face, shrouded by thick hair, was a classic oval. Straight-cut eyelids arched over her strong-boned cheeks and her lips curved deliciously. As they entered the station, she took in the times of departing trains and gauged the distance from ticket machine to platform.

The man's red cheeks, shiny brow and comb-over did not match his chic, European suit. His broad chest and full belly strained against his tie-less, wide-collared shirt, one shirttail flopping out in front. He lurched after her toward the wall of ticket machines, missing a step, then another.

He disentangled his arm from hers and held up his hand in a gallant offer of buying the tickets. She dug in her purse for loose change. He looked up at the sprawling, overhead map of Tokyo train lines glowing like a stained glass window. Neat, bright colors rendered the immense circulatory system of the city into one readable grid, a maze of connections that led everywhere, or nowhere.

The man looked back and forth for a minute, and then twisted toward her in stuttering confusion. She brushed back her hair with her hand and dropped coins in for two tickets. It didn't matter if she got the right price. He tried to make a joke, but she checked the departure board and hurried him through the gate toward the escalator for the silent ride down to the platform.

At the bottom, she steered him around a kiosk shuttered for the night. With his arm clamped in her grip, she walked him down the empty platform toward the end.

An express train shot by. The speeding mass of metal blasted the platform with a whoosh of air and noise that sent him reeling for a couple of sidesteps. Her shawl and hair danced up and around her, but she clutched him tight and kept going.

The yellow-lit windows of the passing train cars were close enough to touch. From inside, images of people safe and snug flashed by, like an old film off its sprockets. Drain channels on the outside of the car spit drops of rain onto the platform. At that speed, the long train passed through in seconds.

Silence and stillness followed.

She checked her watch again. The next express train would arrive in two minutes.

At the dark end of the platform, they stood alone. She propped him against a huge pillar that took up most of the platform, and then she pulled him around to face her, her arms locked on his, keeping him balanced. He leaned forward for a kiss. She gave him her cheek, but his head wobbled too much to kiss her on the first try.

Along the underground sweep of the station, eight other platforms lined up in parallel conformity. On each, a few passengers congregated near the escalators at the center of each platform, fingering text messages, reading tiny paperbacks, or staring off into the night.

If anyone had looked over, they would have seen the foreign man's knees unhinging and his arms swinging. His whole body pinwheeled like a bulky doll, held up only by the strong force of her limbs.

She tugged him over to the yellow warning strips at the platform's edge and squinted down the tunnel at the next express. She could hear it approaching. She craned her neck to see the front lights coming out of the darkness.

She placed her hands just above his elbows and looked into his face. He smiled back giddily and flopped forward, thinking she was going to kiss him again or whisper a sexy secret. Her lips were set as rigid as a Noh mask.

Then, with her left hand, she tugged his wrist down and pried her other hand under his arm. She planted her sandals and took a deep breath.

He looked at her with glassy-eyed confusion, swaying and blinking and nearly asleep.

She could feel the rumble of the train as it sped along the length of the platform toward them.

It was all over in one fluid motion.

In the confusion that followed the long, scared howl cut short by a muffled thump and harsh screech of brakes, no one noticed the woman gliding swiftly up the escalator.

She walked to the exit gate, kneed open the barrier and slipped out.

Behind her, the alarm sounded and uniformed attendants hustled out of the office, careful not to trip as they ran, knowing what to do, but not yet why. Startled passengers stared from the other platforms.

The woman walked with long strides toward the taxis, and the first in line opened its automatic door. She ducked inside and the door closed. The driver pulled off smoothly into the night.

"Yushima Tenjin Shrine," she told the driver.

"Rain's falling harder," the driver said, stealing a glance at her in the rear-view mirror.

"What else can it do?" she said, leaning back for the ride.

Chapter 2

Hiroshi Shimizu's cell phone went off as he stepped out of the elevator onto the open-air walkway outside his apartment building. He
let it buzz in his raincoat pocket as he twirled his umbrella to spin off
the rain. He stopped and looked over the city. No matter how late
he worked this view over Tokyo always made him feel, for a minute,
that another day was over.

And some of the night. It was just past two. The phone stopped
buzzing, but felt heavy in his pocket. The irritating mosquito-buzz
sound was one more thing he needed to change.

His building was eight stories high and sat on a hill whose steep
slope was tiring to climb at the end of a long day. In the morning,
the angle seemed to rush him downhill toward work faster than he
wanted. From below, the city looked gray on gray with the heavy
rain, but once he was eight floors up, the nightscape of Tokyo un-
veiled itself like a glistening dream. All the way to the horizon, the
city's lights flickered white and orange and yellow beneath the grey
shroud of the sky.

The nameplate on his thick metal door needed changing, too. The
clunk of the deadbolt and the creak of rusted hinges welcomed him
home. Inside the door, he toed off his shoes in the genkan entryway:
an in-between space crowded with still-damp shoes, broken umbrellas and used insoles. He pulled the newspapers, three days' worth,
out of the metal door slot and slipped them onto the recycle pile.
Here and there on the tile, dark spots of mold sprang up, feeding on
the dust and humidity.

The phone buzzed again.

Requests from overseas detective bureaus for more information about his reports and cases often came in at night from other time zones. As the de facto liaison between the Tokyo police department and their overseas counterparts, he had to answer. Officially, all he was supposed to do was investigate white-collar crime inside Tokyo, but he ended up working with other countries' police departments more often than not. Crime leapt over boundaries with ease.

Hiroshi gave in and answered. The call was not from overseas, but from Takamatsu who called him as drinking companion and a friendly ear more often than Hiroshi cared for. Takamatsu was lead detective in homicide, which was officially Hiroshi's division. They had nowhere else to put him. Takamatsu was his *senpai* and mentor, and his connection to the rest of the department.

"Let's get a drink another night. I'm tired," Hiroshi said.

"I need your English," Takamatsu said. "Finally, something for you to do."

"You picked up some foreigner?"

"Foreign, yes, but hard to pick up."

"What?"

"Tamachi station. Drink after. You'll need it. This one's messy."

"Messy English?" Hiroshi asked, but Takamatsu hung up.

Something in Takamatsu's voice told him this was more than an excuse for drinking.

Hiroshi draped his wet raincoat over the hall door, deciding whether to ignore Takamatsu's request and get some sleep or go as he knew he should. Officially, he wasn't required to do anything except office work, but Takamatsu kept dragging him to crime scenes and on-site interviews.

Hiroshi had been lucky to land a job where he could use his English and skip most meetings, so he felt obligated to help Takamatsu when asked. Almost always, helping him out just meant joining Takamatsu for a drink. Tokyo's work culture demanded drinking and talking outside normal working hours and working in homicide doubled those demands.

In the living room, a blanket was draped over the sofa. Pizza boxes lay scattered on the coffee table and the kitchen tables. An unreturned sushi delivery tray on the sideboard needed rinsing. His stereo was still on, the blue light glowing on the half-empty book-shelf.

In front of the bookshelf were stacks of ABC International Movers boxes. The boxes flopped open, exposing women's clothes on hang-ers, a hair dryer, Japanese-English/English-Japanese dictionaries. Two empty rolls of packing tape rested on top. He'd forgotten, again, to get more.

On top of one of the boxes rested a photo of him and Linda—his former fiancé—posed together by the Charles River in Boston. They were both dressed in T-shirts and jeans. The well-washed cotton pulled at his broad shoulders and draped her full bosom, their faces smiling like teenagers surprised to find themselves in their 20s. Her big smile dimpled her cheeks and her blond hair hung loose.

In another photo, framed, he and Linda sat on a moss-covered rock in the garden of a Japanese *onsen* hot springs hotel. She smiled self-consciously in a wisteria-patterned yukata robe with bright green obi circling her waist. Next to her in a dragon-and-cloud pat-tern with a dark brown obi, Hiroshi looked like a samurai, square-jawed and serious, his hair hanging long and thick.

He set the photos back in the box, Boston, Tokyo—both lives equally impossible—and dropped his hand into a tangle of kimonos. Linda loved all the black silk with small designs of white or gold forming chrysanthemums, peonies, waves or winding streams. Un-derstated elegance fascinated her after they moved to Tokyo, and she came home with a discreet purchase every other day: kimonos, wood carvings, ceramic cups. But perhaps it was all too understated.

He ruffled the kimonos in the boxes, and flipped over the ugly cardboard top. He was through with women for a while. It was a feeling he'd never had before. He had always been running after them, bored when they liked him, but finally happy to settle in with Linda. Then she gave up on him. Or on Japan, he wasn't sure. Maybe he didn't know how to make the best things in his life last. The job as financial investigator with the homicide branch so far had lasted longer than anything else.

Taking care of white collar crime impressed no one he ever men-tioned it to, since almost no one understood it except the criminals themselves. Blackmail, credit card theft, identity scams, none of it was sexy. Or so Linda said.

He pulled his coat back on, and at the genkan, shoehorned on dry running shoes, unused since Linda left. He grabbed the umbrella with the fewest broken ribs and let the heavy metal door clang shut behind him, dropping the deadbolt with his key.

The elevator clanged open and carried him downstairs.

At the closest intersection, it took time to find a taxi. Buses and trains were no longer running, so taxis were the only way around. He stood in the rain waiting patiently for one to pass by.

Maybe he should give up the detective job and get on a plane to Boston to try working things out with Linda there. It wasn't much of a job, tracking down investment scams, or much of a life drinking with Takamatsu, and standing in the rain to do it.

Everything was a trap if you looked at it closely—the boxes, framed photos, the apartment, his office. Sleeping in the office, on the sofa or waking up to take calls at all hours was like college dorm life, with the feeling that everything in life was still coming and nothing at all was yet settled.

Chapter 3

Hiroshi found Takamatsu standing in the middle of the large hall outside the stationmaster's office, barking at two detectives half his age. They listened, eyes averted in deference, to the flow of commands. The two young detectives, energetic and smooth-faced, scurried off to carry out his orders.

Takamatsu waved his arm to sweep Hiroshi onto the escalator down to the platform, his gold cufflinks catching the light. Takamatsu's elegant suits and silk ties did half his work for him. His way of speaking in the least polite Japanese did the other half.

"These guys are supposed to be finished," said Takamatsu. "But this one took more time."

"Who is supposed to be finished with what?" Hiroshi said, already exasperated.

"The cleanup squad."

"Clean up?"

"Unrecognizable."

"I'm here to recognize someone?"

"A foreigner."

"How do you know if...?" Hiroshi asked.

"Blond hair." Takamatsu lit a cigarette and looked at him. He straightened his cuffs.

"His hair could be dyed blond."

"See, that's why I asked you to come, to fill me in on these things."

They walked along the platform, toward the end.

"The stationmaster's worried about getting the trains going again. Doesn't care about the dead man." Takamatsu shook his head. "Sees them all the time, I guess."

"They have their procedures."

"Same as us."

"Same as anyone."

As they got closer, the breath started getting stuck in Hiroshi's chest and he had to focus to exhale. He had examined dead bodies before, dragged along by Takamatsu to the pathology lab, but the chemical smell and bright lights sanitized the reality. A big white sheet over a washed body kept death covered and clean. As they walked down the platform, Hiroshi's body tightened up.

"Sure seems like a foreigner. Fat. Fancy suit."

"That could be anyone these days. Tokyo's changed," Hiroshi said.

"Yeah? Well, I don't get out much."

"Mended your ways?"

Takamatsu smiled and crushed out his cigarette. "Not enough." He pointed to the "No Smoking" sign on the platform and blew out the last lungful.

They stopped at the far end of the platform.

"English *meishi* shop cards in his pocket," Takamatsu said.

"Plenty of clubs have English cards these days," Hiroshi said. "Lots of people speak English."

"That'll make it easy to find your replacement."

Takamatsu hopped down onto the tracks and Hiroshi followed, each looking down the parallel, metal lines and wondering if the red signal light was enough to stop the trains from speeding into the station. Beyond the station, past the lights, the rails narrowed into the outer darkness.

Takamatsu and Hiroshi had to stretch out their arms for balance over the large chunks of gravel holding the rails and ties in place. The gravel chunks were larger than they appeared from the platform and shifted under each step.

Hiroshi looked back at the train conductors scurrying back and forth on the platform, shouting into hand-held microphones, trying to reorder the schedule.

Staple-shaped iron bars painted bright yellow were sunk into the concrete foundation of the platform to be used as steps or handholds. Beneath the platform was a crawl space just wide enough for a body.

A huge detective with a round head stood in the middle of the tracks. He was bent over, his giant belly hanging like a boulder he was used to carrying, scouring the gravel for clues.

"This is Sakaguchi," Takamatsu said when they got close.

"The sumo wrestler?"

"Ex-sumo wrestler," Sakaguchi replied politely.

"Takamatsu mentioned you," Hiroshi said. "You used to be in homicide."

"I'm helping out," Sakaguchi said. "Temporarily."

"Special call. Like you," Takamatsu said. "Very special."

Sakaguchi's eyes, set deep inside the plump folds of his stoic, moon face, betrayed no emotion, though one of his eyebrows rose just a little. He was used to Takamatsu, too.

The cleanup squad in coveralls looked like puffed spacemen as they bent over the tracks and picked through the gravel with what appeared to be long chopsticks.

As Hiroshi looked closer, he could see them pinch up slivers of tissue, skin and bone and tuck them into clear plastic bags that swung with the rhythm of their work. One of the men stood up and twisted shut his oily, red-stained bag and nestled it inside the large black body bag, thick as a log, resting on the gravel. He shook open a fresh bag and bent back to work.

Sakaguchi's bulk blocked a clearer view of the body bag. The force of the impact had thrown the body three meters beyond the end of the platform to where the body bag was set across the concrete ties that anchored the rails.

Takamatsu steered Hiroshi closer to the body, but Hiroshi looked down at the gravel, and behind him at Sakaguchi. Hiroshi looked away, looked back, turned away.

As they got close to the bag, Hiroshi looked in and stepped back. Through the open zipper, he could see clots of flesh and shredded clothing, a jutting bone and a severed tendon, a gold watch on a hairy arm.

"Where's the train?" Hiroshi asked, looking around for it and breathing deep.

"They had to back it out and reroute it to get ready for the morning rush hour. It's not going anywhere. We'll check it later."

The train conductors watched them work, chatting into their microphones, but said nothing to the detectives. No doubt Takamatsu had already warned them off. It was nearly four, so they had a lot of work to do to reset the precise order of the intricate system, minus the murder weapon train, before the morning rush hour.

"It was an express," said Takamatsu.

"What?" Hiroshi shook his head.

"It shoots through here at top speed. This is the last local stop before Shinagawa."

Hiroshi could hear the click of the giant chopsticks and leaned his arms on the concrete edge of the platform, distracting himself with billboard posters for a cute, teenage boy band and a new, romantic TV drama. In advertisements, everyone smiled and posed, silly with life and music and love.

"One hundred kilometers an hour." Takamatsu said.

"That fast?" Hiroshi said, again reading over the details of the band and the drama.

"That's a lot of metal to be going that fast so close to so much flesh."

Sakaguchi stood beside him, visually scouring the area. He shrugged. "That's about it."

Hiroshi tried to picture where the man would have been standing. The timing to throw a body at just the right moment in front of a speeding train would demand sharp mental focus and plenty of physical strength. A moment too early or too late would mean missing it.

"Could be a suicide," Hiroshi mused, and then wondered if that would be any easier to do.

"A foreigner wouldn't know the train schedules," Takamatsu said.

"Maybe someone told him," Hiroshi offered.

"No foreigner would figure out this was the best place to kill himself. The trains, the times, it takes a bit of planning."

"Maybe he was here by accident?"

"Why was he at the end of the platform?"

Sakaguchi spoke up, "That wide pillar blocks the driver's view."

"Perfect spot for murder," Takamatsu said.

"Looks like suicide to me," Hiroshi said.

12

Takamatsu shook his head. "Japanese are good at suicide, but not foreigners."

"Nobody saw anything?" Hiroshi asked.

"Passengers this time of night tend to be drunk, half-asleep or texting."

"The driver...?"

"Saw a blur and felt the thump. That's it."

"Closed-circuit cameras?"

"The bracket holding the camera drooped. Great shot of the floor. The camera outside showed a foreigner and a tall woman next to him, but just for an instant."

"She was next to him?"

"Behind him. Might be with him. Might not. The shot was from behind."

"So, it's a suicide. Call the embassy." Hiroshi wanted to go home and sleep.

Sakaguchi turned toward Takamatsu with the same unspoken question. His face looked like he could go either way—write it off or dig into it.

"Foreigners don't commit suicide."

Takamatsu turned over a bloodstained chunk of gravel with his shoe. "Not in Tokyo, anyway."

Hiroshi looked down at the stained gravel, wondering if that were true. When it came to foreigners, Hiroshi was never sure if Takamatsu was savvy or prejudiced—or both.

Takamatsu's cell phone rang and Hiroshi took the chance to pull himself up to the platform. He leaned down to pull Takamatsu up by his free hand. Sakaguchi hoisted himself up and onto his feet as if he were the lightest of the three detectives, instead of a man carrying the combined weight of the other two.

At the end of the platform, the police photographer and her assistant worked with relaxed efficiency on the contents of the cadaver's wallet and pockets. Purplish drops pooled in spots on the plastic sheet below the items carefully laid out as if for some gory picnic.

Blood had soaked into the pages of his leather-covered notebook and stained his thick fold of ten-thousand yen bills. An assistant nimbly turned over each item with chopsticks, as the cameraman snapped two shots of each.

Hiroshi leaned down to stare at the small stack of *meishi* name cards. They stank of blood and urine.

"Five are the same," Hiroshi said, twisting his head to read. "Steve Deveaux, Bentley Associates, Consulting and Investing, Nishi-Shinjuku." He looked up at Sakaguchi. "Must be him."

Sakaguchi nodded.

Takamatsu shouted for everyone to finish up. The young detectives double-checked their notebooks and tried to look like they knew what they were doing, glancing around for orders to follow.

The squad on the tracks nestled their plastic bags and long chopsticks into a single large sack, and then zipped it shut. It took six people to hoist the bagged corpse onto the platform, and then on to the trolley. The squad visually checked the area again, pointing at spots one by one with white gloves to run through the checklist in their head.

The squad switched gloves and wiped the outside of the body bag with a clean, white cloth. The crew checked the zipper, sealed it with a plastic tie, plucked the trolley legs to waist height, and rolled it toward the stairs.

As the body bag rolled past them, Takamatsu, Hiroshi, Sakaguchi, and the younger detectives all bowed their heads with their palms together in prayer. Each of the train workers folded their hands and bowed their heads as the body rolled down the platform, into the elevator and out to the waiting ambulance.

Takamatsu nodded the final OK and signaled the stationmaster who started talking excitedly into his walkie-talkie, checking his watch and waving the new printout of the redone schedule. A young worker splashed a bucket of water over the platform and broomed it over the side. He sloshed another bucketful of water over the gravel, but it was not enough, so he went back for more.

"Let's get a drink, huh?" said Takamatsu.

Sakaguchi said, "I have to be in the office before rush hour."

"Those *chikan* train molesters start early?" Takamatsu joked.

Sakaguchi squeezed his eyes to a single line.

"You won't be over there forever," Takamatsu said.

Sakaguchi cleared his throat.

"We'll put the unit back together again. And we'll have some English help next time," Takamatsu gestured toward Hiroshi.

Sakaguchi nodded and walked off to the taxi line. His white shirt, big as a bed sheet, shone over his massive back. He fit himself inside a taxi and was gone.

Hiroshi and Takamatsu walked off into the night toward the small lanes of bars and eateries. Behind them in the station, workers in white gloves hurried to restore order before the first train of the morning.

Chapter 4

Away from the station, Takamatsu lit a cigarette. "That smell," he said inhaling deeply.

Hiroshi tried to keep all his senses in check.

"I know a little place close by here," Takamatsu said.

Hiroshi put up his umbrella.

Takamatsu ignored the rain, and flipped up the collar of his silk jacket.

On the small streets farther from the station, the interior lights of convenience stores and *gyudon* rice-and-meat shops spilled onto the wet pavement like shards of a shattered mirror. A motorcycle shot by. Faint lights glowed from small snack shops and standing bars.

"I guess you're going to dump the contents of his wallet on me?" Hiroshi asked.

"They're all in English. A notebook and some documents, too."

"There are people to do that, you know."

"No one as good as you. Why do you think I got you the job in the first place?"

"Tell me again."

"Crime's globalizing. Hiring you was easier than learning English myself."

"I thought I was hired to drink with you?"

"That, too. There's also his cell phone messages."

"Messages? That'll take ages."

"Think how long it would take me."

"I have a lot of other cases."

"The encryption guys should have the password cracked by morning. They get paid double what we make."

Takamatsu made several turns, each street narrower than the last to where the street was so narrow they had to walk single file, as if already inside.

"It looks like a suicide."

"How things look and how they are..." Takamatsu shrugged.

"I'm supposed to be money transfers, accounting blackmail, investment scams..."

"Yes, yes and chatting with the Interpol guys. Strictly speaking, you are inside the homicide department."

"Eventually, I'll be moved to my own department," Hiroshi sighed and stopped.

Takamatsu turned back to him. "Eventually, but not today. Anyway, we'll soon find he's been killed for money. Money's your area."

"How do you know?"

"A guy like that is all about money."

"A guy like what?"

"Dressed like that with a pretty woman late at night."

"You're not even sure she was with him. And you only saw her for an instant. From behind."

"Every woman in Tokyo looks great from behind."

"Is that the kind of thinking you use to solve cases?"

"You have to think more like a Japanese. You were in America too long." Takamatsu started walking again, turned two more corners, and ducked under an overhanging sign into an even narrower alleyway.

"I've already got extra budget," Takamatsu said, clipped and confident. "First thing I made sure of."

"From where?"

"The up-and-ups want anything with a foreigner solved quick and quiet." Takamatsu stopped and turned back to Hiroshi. "Also, this isn't the first foreigner to end up like this."

"Like what?"

"Killed by a train. There were others."

Hiroshi scoffed. "You think they're connected because they're foreigners?"

"I know so."

"How many others?"

"Depends on how you count."

18

Before Hiroshi could say anything more, Takamatsu grabbed a rough wooden handle jutting out from a wood-paneled wall under a large cedar ball. A section of the wall rolled sideways. It was an opening so low they had to bend over double and sidestep in. When they stood up inside, they were greeted by a booming, "*Irrashaimase!*" from the master, who reached up to turn down the volume on the television. There were no other customers.

Takamatsu apologized with slyly exaggerated excuses for not having come for a long time and introduced Hiroshi to the master with formal language. Hiroshi bowed. Takamatsu hung his jacket on a hook and loosened his tie as if he owned the place. He slicked back his hair, which hung to his collar, and rolled up his sleeves with three crisp folds.

Takamatsu checked his cell phone for messages, took off his watch and slipped them both into his jacket, settling astride one of the large cuts of log topped with thick indigo cushions that served as stools.

From a small warmer, the master drew out two steaming-hot white towels with tongs. After wiping their faces and hands with the towels, Hiroshi un-cricked his back and Takamatsu stretched his neck and shoulders in circling motions.

"You always..." Hiroshi said, but Takamatsu shushed him.

"Now is the time to reflect," he said in a soft voice.

Hiroshi rolled his eyes and let out a sigh. He breathed in and leaned back as if he had just sunk into a hot bath.

The master leaned over the counter to set teensy dishes of pickled vegetables—crinkled and vinegary—on the counter. He fired up one of the small gas burners under a large pot of miso soup and wiped down the wooden cutting board. He cleaned his long sushi knife with a white towel.

The master pulled back a brown curtain over a glass-sided refrigerator filled with *sake* bottles. He pulled out two small chilled glasses from the top shelf and set these on the upper counter inside small, square, cedar wood boxes.

The master shuffled the dozen or so bottles inside the fridge until he found the ones he wanted. Carrying these to the counter, he hoisted the large bottle of cold *sake* and, cradling it in the crook of his arm, poured out the clear, clean liquid. The *sake* flowed gently over the top of the lip of the glass into the box, arousing the aroma of cedar and fresh rice. He poured out *sake* from a different bottle for Hiroshi and placed both bottles on the counter so that each displayed the artful calligraphy of their labels.

They bowed down like penitents to take the first sip without spilling. Then they plucked up the small, thumb-sized glasses for a silent toast before downing the second gulp. Finally, they poured the spillover from the cedar box into the glass, took another sip, and set their half-full glasses back inside the wet cedar boxes.

The master ascertained they were satisfied, glancing up as he set down two small dishes of pickled vegetables, and then he turned back to prepare for whatever they might order.

Hiroshi reached for a pair of chopsticks from a black-lacquered, glass-top box. He pulled apart the wood with a crackle, brushed off the splinters, and held them up in the air for a bite of the pickles.

Seeing the chopsticks in mid-air, the pickles suddenly looked unappetizing. Leaning back, he set his chopsticks down, folded his arms and said, "I don't feel so hungry." He took another sip of *sake* and looked at the rough grain of the wood walls.

Takamatsu looked at Hiroshi's chopsticks, and remembering the chopstick work of the body cleanup squad on the tracks, he left his chopsticks untouched, lit another cigarette and studied the label on the *sake* bottle in front of him.

Chapter 5

Hiroshi pulled open his office door to the lingering smell of disinfectants. The room was large, but windowless, and had been used to store cleaning supplies until cleaning was outsourced to a company. The smell built up every time he closed the door for long and greeted him when he came back to the room, located between two floors of the back stairwell in the Central Police Agency Second Annex.

Despite the smell, and the isolation, he felt comfortable, as if the room were another skin. Two large desks, plenty of shelf space, and a small chair that unfolded out into a comfortable-enough futon mattress took up most of the room. The centerpiece of the room was his coffee machine, which he used all day and most of the night.

Takamatsu's chief, Hiroshi's chief as well, told him that conversations in English with overseas police departments would be impossible in the regular offices. So, the chief requisitioned the room to give Hiroshi his own workspace. His exile from the bustling homicide department in the main building, with its unaired smell of tobacco and nervous sweat, was a boon. He was the only detective at any level to have his own office—the ultimate Tokyo luxury.

When he took the job, in a bid to support Linda and himself, he skipped most of the regular training and went straight to work using his English and the accounting degree he acquired in the States. The former financial detective, hopelessly disorganized and barely competent in English, quit, or was fired, and Takamatsu—an old family friend he barely remembered—got him the job.

Linda hated Hiroshi's job once it became clear the temporary police job he took to support them was going to be full-time plus overtime. She had taken a job teaching English, which she felt was beneath her. It was exhausting and led her all over the city, moving all day from company to company, while Hiroshi was stuck in his office.

Her photo came up on his smartphone the next morning by accident. Every time one of her pictures appeared, when he pressed a wrong button, or looked for something else, he thought of Linda's departure. They were waiting for her flight at Narita Airport sitting silently on chairs in the departure lobby when he got a work call. The last words she said to him were, "Turn that fucking thing off."

She was back in Boston, their relationship turned off. Hiroshi was not good at turning anything off. He stayed at the job.

Hiroshi's basic unit inside the large homicide department was, so far, just Hiroshi. His office was quiet enough that he could talk with people all over the world, anytime he needed, and he could even take a nap whenever he felt like it. He could sleep overnight in his office, too, which, after Linda left he did more and more. He took long walks in the city by himself in the middle of the day. It cleared his head and gave him a chance to work through the details. He got used to the solitude.

Hiroshi spent most of his time tracking down foreigners who absconded with business profits, refused to pay child support, defaulted on loans, ripped off elderly investors or fled ongoing investigations. He worked more closely with his counterparts in London, Paris, New York, and Hong Kong than with anyone in homicide. It was safe and clean work, entirely different from the work at the train station the night before.

The possibility of extraditing the people he investigated back to Japan was remote, since Japan had few such treaties with other countries. Those countries didn't want to send their nationals to Japan, even with a lot of evidence. So, with most cases, Hiroshi satisfied himself by letting his work add to their cases. He rarely saw anyone caught or prosecuted. It felt like playing long-distance chess, with a stalemate every time: warrant issued, pending arrest, filed with the court, no trial.

He never imagined he would love pulling apart the tangles of a Ponzi scheme, dismantling an investment pyramid, or unmasking the subtleties of embezzlement cases. He would become so immersed in the scamming techniques, he would lose track of time. Linda accused him of being obsessive-compulsive, and he knew she was right.

The rest of the time she accused him of drinking too much, something that also emerged after a few months into the job, but was the first time in his life he drank much at all. When all the detectives worked together to track someone or seize evidence under search warrant, it was hard to beg off from drinking afterwards. He'd lost most of his Japanese groupthink over the years in Boston, but back in Tokyo, he felt the need to keep good relations, which meant accepting the obligation of drinking with the other detectives.

Coming home late, and none too sober, was not a cultural practice Linda adapted to. She would be waiting at the door in one of her kimonos, calmly, quietly demanding an apology or explanation or something she could get angry at. Hiroshi could never find the right way to explain where he'd been or why. That he had to work and the work involved drinking with colleagues was such a basic Japanese concept, he couldn't put it into words. Linda would demand an explanation, not get one, and then storm off to bed to get some sleep before dawn.

Often, he wasn't drinking, but the time difference calling overseas investigators meant he had to stay at work late. He couldn't explain that to her, either.

Hiroshi could understand now how her loneliness piled up with boredom at teaching and the pressure of adapting to a new culture. He knew she felt the oppressiveness of being a woman in Japan—especially a foreign woman—so much so that the pressure pushed her to action, and she left. When she did, she handed the loneliness to him.

* * *

Hiroshi cranked up the coffee grinder, tired after being out so late with Takamatsu the night before. The taste of the *sake* lingered in his mouth. The loud grind of the machine helped wake him up and restore his energy.

The files from Takamatsu were already on his desk. Another folder contained a printout from the text messages on the victim's cell phone, but it was hard to read, with numbers and symbols riddling the messages. He would have to use a yellow highlighter to get through the mess.

He flipped through the body photos as fast as he could and closed the folder.

He popped the DVD of the train station's camera footage in his computer. The first two seconds showed a large man listing drunkenly beside a woman—nothing more.

A second image showed the escalator, but the camera was aimed at the opposite escalator, and only captured the back of the head of the man and the woman. She was tall, with long black hair and dark-colored clothing—maybe with him or maybe not.

After a scramble of dead time, the next shot caught the man's slip-ons—soft leather, designer brand—and the sashes from her sandals, wrapped around her legs. After that, there was only the platform.

Photos of the contents of the dead man's wallet showed all the *meishi* shop cards from high-priced restaurants in Azabu, Daikanyama and Ginza, credit cards and ATM bankcards from Tokyo Mitsubishi UFJ Bank and from Mizuho Bank. The *meishi* cards formed a trail of people he met and shops and restaurants he went to and wanted to remember. The foreigner shopped for himself and probably lived alone, evidenced by well-worn discount point cards for coffee, CDs, DVD rentals, bread, and two up-market grocery stores, Kinokuniya and National Azabu.

The last photos from the wallet were *meishi* from clubs in Roppongi. Hiroshi guessed they were exclusive hostess clubs because of the names—Pink Rose, Enjoy, Ransom, White Leather—quite a collection. People at the clubs would remember the dead man clearly, but would not talk. People at the stores would talk, but not remember him.

Like most foreign executives, the dead man probably lived a comfortable life, especially with the "hardship pay" foreign companies dished out. If he committed suicide, he hadn't gone on a mad spending spree before the end. The hundred thousand yen, in cash, now soaked with dried blood, would have covered a big night out in Roppongi. His bankbook showed the usual automatic payments, in and out.

Hiroshi's cell phone rang again.

"Hai? Yes?"

"Takamatsu said you should attend a funeral, at Yushima Tenjin Shrine. Not far from Ochanomizu station." It was one of the secretaries, but he wasn't sure which one. He didn't recognize her voice.

"Takamatsu told me to tell you. The funeral is for, I don't know how to pronounce it, Steve Deveaux or something, the guy hit by the train last night," she said.

"I'll meet him there?"

"He said it's better if you go alone."

"Why isn't he going?" Hiroshi asked.

"He said it will be in English," she said. "He has some photos he wants you to take with you, to see if they show up at the funeral."

"Who?"

"Acquaintances of the deceased, I guess."

"Why doesn't Takamatsu check these people out?"

"He said to tell you, though I hate to even repeat this, but he thinks all foreigners look alike."

Hiroshi let out a sigh. "Where are the photos?"

"I'll bring them over in a few minutes. I want to get out of the office and the long walk over to your place is a good chance to escape."

"What does he want me to do at the funeral?"

"He said you'd know."

"Well, I don't know."

"He also said to meet him tonight at Roppongi."

"For what?"

"You'll have to ask him. But I can guess," her voice held no hint of amusement.

"Tell Takamatsu he owes me."

"He owes everybody," she said.

Chapter 6

After morning meditation, the young priest sweeping the grounds at Yushima Tenjin Shrine was surprised to see a tall, young woman sitting alone, staring at the main building as the sun came up. The warmth of a cloudless day eased into the temple's plum trees and the sun dried the curved slate roofs, the air crisp and fresh after the heavy rain.

When she noticed him watching her, she walked to the front gate where water trickled into a stone basin from a brass dragon spout. With a long-handled scoop, she poured water over her hands. She had entered the grounds hours earlier, but sat down without the ritual purification, content to be alone in the early morning quiet of the shrine.

The young priest glanced at her intermittently as he swept the dark brown, still-wet leaves with his dry straw broom. While he had removed himself from worldly interests, he could not help but notice how poised and intense she was, even across the spacious courtyard.

Without a glance at him sweeping, she walked to a small side hall where the temple shop had trays filled with small folded sutras, bright portable *omamori* charms. She selected an *ema*, a small wooden plaque with a silk cord and a painted picture of a horse, on which to write her request to the gods.

No one was behind the counter in the shop yet, so she slipped the money into the slot of a locked box and took the small wood board over to a bench in the middle of the courtyard. She pulled a felt-tip pen from her purse and began to write in neat lines from top to bottom, right to left:

Kamisama, Kigan. My supplication, Lord. Please let his soul go free and not wander. Protect me from others and from myself. Purify my actions with your wisdom and power. Nature takes its course and only the half-living follow unnatural paths. The rest still needs to be done. Take care of their souls.

As she wrote, she watched the ink soak into the plaque's grain, soft as wooden flesh. She walked to a tall rack from which dangled hundreds of similar plaques. Each one held a heartfelt plea for a cure from a disease, for a husband, for easy childbirth, for world peace. Most asked to pass the university entrance exam. Each one was suspended in the morning breeze, tied up with red cords along taut wires that stretched between worn, wood posts.

She found a space for hers, for his, reaching under the row of other plaques to tie her words carefully in the middle. She brushed a row of plaques, which swayed and clacked, then quieted and stilled.

She turned from the *ema* and walked down the long steps toward the thick, old posts that marked the front entrance. She walked to the main street and caught a taxi to Omotesando for the rest of the morning's business.

* * *

She got out of the taxi in front of the Tokyo-Mitsubishi-UFJ Bank on Omotesando Boulevard—Tokyo's Champs-Elysees—and stood waiting on the wide, tree-shaded sidewalk for the bank to open. She looked through dark sunglasses at her outlined reflection in the shiny-clean, two-story bank window. Her broad shoulders were draped in a gauze-thin blouse and her hips set snug in a tight skirt. Moving behind her reflection, she could see the passing reflections of women, and a few men, walking back and forth on the one sunny morning in the middle of rainy season.

The other women, out for the day with former classmates or their husband's colleagues' wives, glided by in flowery Milanese and frilly Parisian fashions. Their outfits were well matched and they matched each other. They were well-raised and well-schooled at women's universities, after which they worked for a few years before quitting to get married, have children and focusing on the levers of power at home while their husbands worked at climbing the ladder in big companies or government posts.

The women's passing reflections reminded her how different she was from them. They enjoyed the area around Omotesando with its refined pleasures—the boutiques, art galleries, starred restaurants and beauty care centers—as if it were their birthright. They seemed encircled by their luxury, satisfied with the pleasant encompassing. She and the women had only the morning sidewalk in common.

At opening time, she stepped over toward the door when an employee set aside the "please wait" sign, reset the automatic doors and bowed deeply to the first customer of the day—her. She walked briskly to the number machine in the bank's atrium and took her number—"one." Her tall, fit figure looked thinner in the cavernous interior of the bank.

She leaned on the counter to fill in the forms for the renewal of money transfers and automatic deposits as seriously and conscientiously as she had written the *ema* at the shrine. She took out her *hanko*, her personal seal, and set her red-inked mark, "Suzuki," into the correct oval on the forms.

When her number popped up, she folded her long legs to the side as she sat down in front of the counter cubicle, set her sunglasses on top of her head and looked straight at the clerk, a middle-aged woman in the bank's uniform, who quickly looked away as she took the forms, muttering in the politest Japanese, "Please wait. This will just take a minute. Please take a seat and we'll call your name."

She sighed, stood up and moved toward the sofa chairs, sat down, and idly surveyed the dappled marble that lined the floors, columns and walls of the bank. A few other customers wandered in and took numbers.

"Michiko Suzuki," the clerk called out. Michiko came over and sat back down in the same chair as before. Clearing her throat and looking at the imposing woman before her, the clerk said, "I'm extremely sorry, but we cannot send an automatic renewal notice to an overseas address."

"Could you please call the manager for me?" she asked.

"Yes, of course," the clerk answered, bowing deeply and scampering off.

The manager, a pasty-faced man with a comb-over, smiled a practiced smile as he noticed the silver and gold lines across her account book that signaled she was a preferred customer.

Michiko said, "I will be overseas for an extended time. However, your renewal for automatic payments must be resubmitted every year, so I would like to have the renewal notice done automatically."

He frowned, looked at the amount in her account, and tightened his lips. "Please wait a minute," he said, and hurried back to his desk to make a phone call.

Michiko remained seated and watched the comb-over manager talk while the uniformed clerk stood nervously to the side. After a few minutes, he called for another clerk to bring another form, which he looked at as he listened on the phone. He hung up and hurried over.

"We can allow an extension of one time period," the manager said, resetting his thin hair with his fingers. "So a total of two years. However, we would ask that you return in person at the end of that time to renew. Would that be acceptable to you?"

"It's better than one year," Michiko said.

"Thank you very much. This is your name here? Michiko Suzuki?"

"Yes."

"I understand," the manager said, averting his eyes from Michiko's stare. The manager told the uniformed clerk, who nodded uncomfortably, following orders, how to fill in the form. Michiko watched her closely.

"When will the automatic transfer be complete?" Michiko asked.

"It will take three working days."

"Can that be expedited?"

"I am very sorry, but the banks in Switzerland require a day to process and a day to send, plus there is a time difference and we need to get the bank manager's approval."

Michiko stared at the woman.

The clerk cleared her throat. "We will have an online system introduced in the fall."

"I won't be here then. That's why I'm doing this now," Michiko said.

"Yes, I'm sorry. I understand," the clerk bowed her head again.

Michiko tucked the receipts carefully into her black leather purse, zipped it tight and hoisted it onto her shoulder. Her footfalls echoed against the marble walls as she walked out to the shady boulevard.

Outside, Michiko followed her reflection in the large windows of the elegant shops, before refocusing her eyes to study the interiors of each. Inside one shop, the glass shelves, well-placed mirrors, and sparse racks made the items on sale appear small works of art in themselves.

At Mizuho Bank, Michiko followed the same procedure as at Tokyo-Mitsubishi-UFJ Bank. The clerks there said nothing about foreign bank transfers being a problem. From there, she set up regular international money transfers to be picked up at European locations every month.

At the Postal Savings Bank, she filled in several forms to finalize regular automatic transfers to the address of a factory in Kawasaki, and to a fruit and vegetable stand, also in Kawasaki. From the one new account she had, she entered the password from her notebook and then automatically transferred all the money to her old Postal Savings account.

The rest of that morning's errands could be finished in a few hours.

The other things she had to do before she left would take time, effort and attention.

Chapter 7

Michiko's black sunglasses let her check out or ignore whatever she liked as she walked toward the travel agency. Arrangements could be made online, but she preferred going in person. She preferred leaving a human—not a digital—trail, if she had to leave one at all.

Her regular agent—a young man with spiky, dyed, and oiled hair—hopped up as soon as he saw Michiko climbing the stairs. He straightened his wide white collar and tight-fitting suit and waved her toward a partitioned area curtained by potted bamboo.

"Suzuki san, good morning. I have everything ready for you, and I am sure this time, it will be to your complete satisfaction."

She pulled her sunglasses on top of her head and stared into his eyes. The young man looked down and ran his hand over his head. He managed a practiced smile and signaled for tea before excusing himself.

* * *

The first time Michiko went overseas, she was seventeen. She was fascinated with the tickets, her first passport, the airplane and the airport. Everyone was going somewhere. The airplane felt like an amusement park ride that was slow at first, with only the clouds outside, but opened into an exotic wonderland.

She had moved out of her father's place and was living with Reiko, her best friend since childhood, in a small, shared apartment near Yoyogi-Uehara. It was close enough to where they worked to get a taxi home, far enough to be affordable. One of the men from one of the clubs invited her. He would pay for the whole trip.

Reiko was more excited than Michiko about the trip, and the man, but mostly the trip. Reiko was never jealous of Michiko. They were too close and Michiko was always ahead. Reiko fluffed around picking out the outfits for Michiko to wear at the beach resort in Hawaii, a different bikini for each day, a different outfit for each dinner.

"Men notice, even if they don't say anything," Reiko lectured her, though she only read about these things in magazines. She wanted to be sure that Michiko would not embarrass herself with a more experienced man on her first trip outside Japan.

While he played golf all morning, Michiko went swimming and wandered the resort shops. After lunch, they had sex all afternoon, and then he went to another meeting over cocktails. She wasn't sure where, but didn't really care. They ate late over candlelight, looking out at the Pacific Ocean. Michiko had never seen such large portions of grilled fish or such large glasses for cocktails.

By the end of the week, Michiko longed to go back to Tokyo. The fishing boat tour, volcano trip and waterfall hike were all very beautiful, but there was too much nature. She was relieved, after they went their separate ways at Narita, to see Tokyo's skyline at night. Later, after she started traveling to European cities, she never went to another resort.

The travel agent returned, followed by a receptionist carrying two small glasses of cold tea. She set each glass gingerly on the table and bowed in retreat. The travel agent opened up the folder with the travel arrangements.

"I have a flight for two on the 20th and another single seat on the 22nd, business class, as you requested," he said, handing over the itinerary and tickets.

Michiko looked at the thick wad of tickets.

"Of course, we will not be able to secure a refund for you if you don't use them. It's only two days from now and..."

"I'm not concerned about refunds. I'm concerned about options," she replied. "I'm not sure I can get everything done in time for the 20th. You understand?"

"Yes, yes, of course, I understand. Many of our clients have tight schedules that make it necessary to set up multiple bookings."

"My schedule is tight and uncertain." Michiko reached to pick up the tickets but the young man politely slipped them into an envelope with the Fly A Way agency logo. He folded and smoothed it neatly before handing it to her.

She stood, pulling down her sunglasses and he followed her to the door where he bowed again as her broad shoulders and long hair disappeared down the industrial-chic stairs.

"No trouble this time," he said to the receptionist, and went back to work.

* * *

From Aoyama Boulevard, Michiko walked past the Omotesando crossing and turned down a narrow side street between two rows of buildings and into an inner courtyard with two floors of small, neat shops. She walked up the small staircase to a perfume boutique.

A wave of aromas wafted out as the saleswoman purred a soft, "Irrashaimase! Welcome!"

Michiko dug in her purse for a bubble-wrapped package in a clear plastic bag. She handed it to the saleswoman, who took it gently with a bow.

"Did you want the Lotus Royale or Lotus Supreme?"

"I want the same one as last time."

"That maker has divided the Lotus into several types now, but the Supreme is closest to the one before."

"I want the one before exactly as it was."

The saleswoman stopped and said, "I will check in the back to see if there is another bottle left. If not, I can ask them to special mix it for you?"

Michiko frowned and the salesclerk hurried to the back.

Michiko checked out a counter of green-tinted hand-blown glass with sample strips. She sniffed them until she found one she liked and rubbed a drop on her wrist, inhaling after it warmed up on her skin.

The saleswoman came back out smiling.

"One last bottle of the same lotus scent. I am so sorry they changed it. I liked the old one, too."

"You wore the old one also?" Michiko asked.

"Oh no, I can't afford it. I liked the smell when I tried it out for customers here in the shop," the saleswoman said quickly. "Can I fill the bottle for you the same as before?"

"Yes," Michiko said, nodding at the package. The woman took the bubble wrap off of the diamond glass perfume bottle and held it up in her hands.

"Was this your mother's?" the saleswoman asked, running her finger over a chip in the glass.

"Why do you ask that?"

"I'm sorry. It's none of my business. It's just that a bottle of this quality seems special."

"It is special," she answered.

"I'll take it to the back and fill it up for you."

* * *

When she first ran away from home as a girl, Michiko jammed as many of her mother's things in a bag as would fit: the perfume bottle and her mother's blouses, her school books and the leftover bag of candies her mother had sucked on as the cancer ate her up.

That first time, she hid in an abandoned factory until the police found her. She wrapped herself up, shivering in the dark and thought about what she could have done to stop her mother from dying. She felt it was her fault, for not being a good girl.

The policeman, who found her late in the evening, didn't scold her but sat with her on the ratty old tatami mat on which Michiko had hunkered down.

"Everyone is worried about you," he said to her in a soft voice.

She nodded, choking back tears.

"I knew your mother, too. She was quite a woman," he said. He'd worked in the same district for years. "It's so sad she had to go so soon."

Michiko sniffled.

"Let's get some ice cream on the way home. What do you think?"

Michiko nodded yes, and the policeman helped her up.

At the gates of her father's small factory, all the workers—twenty sweaty machinists and metalworkers—let out a cheer when the policeman walked into view, holding Michiko in one arm and carrying the bag with the other.

The men, seeing her pretty little face safe at home, lit cigarettes and laughed with relief. The boss's little girl was all right. They had stopped work that afternoon to scour the neighborhood for her in their coveralls and towel-wrapped heads. They would have to pull an all-nighter to finish the large order by the next day's deadline.

Michiko dropped the last of her ice cream in the gravel-covered parking lot and apologized with a cute bow for worrying them. She knew about work even at that age. The workers lifted her onto their shoulders and danced her around until she giggled. When her father returned, he sighed and lit a cigarette. They looked each other in the eyes before her father apologized to the policeman and took her bag and passed it to Michiko.

Then, she allowed herself to be led upstairs by one of the older workers, Uncle Ono. He was almost too old to work, and had a bad back from lifting too much over the years. From then on, he would look after Michiko when her father was too busy, which was almost always.

Tired and hungry from her ordeal, and still cold, Michiko's bag slipped from her grasp and fell down the metal stairs, chipping her mother's perfume bottle inside. Hearing the crack, Michiko zipped open the top and pulled the bottle out in one hand and a chipped-off piece in the other, trying to fit them back together like pieces of a puzzle.

Tears came to her eyes as she squeezed one hand around the chip and the other around the bottle. The sharp chipped glass cut into her small fingers and blood filled her little palm as she pounded up the stairs to the rooms where they lived above her father's factory.

* * *

"Here you are. Just as you like it. And I have a new perfume I think you might like." The saleswoman's cheerful voice startled Michiko out of her reverie. The saleswoman wiped down the beaded glass with a soft cloth and wrapped the bottle in bubble wrap. "It's a new scent perfect for your classic looks."

"Classic looks?"

37

"I mean your face is lovely in a traditional Japanese way. Do you ever wear kimono?"

"Never."

The saleswoman pulled out a sampler bottle. "The base aroma is Chinese star jasmine, but grown in Japan. To me, it smells of nectarines and peaches, with a hint of jasmine. It's made only when the crop is right, sometimes only once every three years."

Michiko took off her sunglasses and brushed her thick hair to the side. The saleswoman leaned forward to place a drop behind Michiko's ear and motioned for her to rub it in just a little.

"Just the right accent for your looks!"

"What's it called?" Michiko asked.

" 'La Petite Mort', made by a French company but very Japanese."

"Interesting name," Michiko smiled. "But the scent is a little strong for a funeral."

"Are you going now?" The saleswoman asked, a little startled.

"Yes."

The saleswoman reached under the counter for a damp hand towel wrapped in plastic. "This will take the scent away."

Michiko pulled the plastic off, unfolded it and wiped the scent away, then cleaned her hands.

The saleswoman walked her to the door.

Chapter 8

Stepping under the wooden torii archway of the shrine where Steve Deveaux's funeral was being held, Hiroshi frightened a few crows waiting for leftovers near the gate. They flapped up into the gray sky, squawks lingering in the damp air. His feet crunched on the wet gravel as he walked to the stone font to rinse his hands and shake them dry before entering the grounds.

He looked up at the temple design soaring skyward. The roof was made of gray slate and all the walls, beams and woodwork were painted black. Lights for the funeral cast glimmers along the beams and pillars, which were wet from the evening drizzle.

A pop song spilled out from the main hall, the bouncing bass line and bright vocals sounding phony in the ancient shrine, sadder than silence would have been.

Hiroshi noticed a woman sitting alone on a far-off bench along a walkway whose narrow roof encircled the main courtyard. It was hard to make out her face as the drizzle grew heavier and droplets fell from the dingy canopies and slate roofs.

Chairs were set outside under faded white canopies, under which a few people sat on folding chairs, their legs pulled in to stay dry. Dozens more were seated reverently inside the main hall on *zabuton* floor cushions facing the altar. Hiroshi could see them through the wood-framed, rippled-glass front doors of the hall.

It had been a long time since he'd attended a funeral. When he lived in Boston, he'd missed the funeral of his grandmother and of a college friend. His parents' funerals had been long before, when he was too young to do anything but follow directions. A chain of funeral memories seemed to encircle him and weigh him down as he sat on a folded chair under the canopy.

He pulled out the photos Takamatsu had sent him of Deveaux's former colleagues at Bentley Associates: an older woman in a well-tailored business suit, prim with a passport smile, and another of a young man who was model-handsome, much younger than the deceased, with a perfect smile only American dental work could produce.

On the back of the photos were their names: Barbara Harris-Mitford, Mark Whitlock. The wind blew drops of rain onto them, which Hiroshi wiped off, and tucked back in his pocket. He wondered why Takamatsu had sent printed photos rather than digital, but Takamatsu had always been old-school. Hiroshi could only see the backs of heads at a distance through the rain, so it didn't much matter.

Inside, a man in a business suit was giving a speech in Japanese. That was followed by a eulogy in English. Hiroshi could not hear either very well from outside the glass, as the patter of rain on the plastic canopy grew louder. After the speeches, another pop song started and those inside the hall began getting up. Someone rose to help a woman from the front row, weak from grief, stand and walk toward Steve Deveaux's urn. A line formed behind her.

Other people, a little confused by the protocol, stood up and walked toward the urn next to the dead man's photo, paying their respects. Each lit incense and placed it in front of the altar, the urn and the photo. Each in turn walked out of the temple hall and huddled under the closest canopy, chatting in small circles and glancing at the rain.

Hiroshi wondered about the next gathering, where everyone could eat and drink and console each other, but no one made a move. Hiroshi could see no other place for coming together.

As people talked, the business types in black suits and black ties fiddled absently with the umbrellas in their hands. Hiroshi repositioned himself to confirm the two colleagues were present, but he couldn't tell from that distance.

He remembered the solitary woman on the other side of the courtyard, turning around to be sure she was still there. She sat motionless on a bench under the roof of the walkway, staring at the ceremony

40

without moving. Three monks stood under the roof of the wooden walkway near the main shrine, watching the funeral from afar.

The wind blew fine drops of rain under the canopy and people started to put up their umbrellas and hurry their conversations. What was Hiroshi going to tell Takamatsu? He felt as useless as the closed-circuit camera that captured nothing at the train station.

He knew he should talk to the woman and to Steve's colleagues, but instead, he put up his umbrella and walked to the racks of *ema*. He brushed the wooden pentangles with his hand. They swayed, pendulums of action and reaction. His eyes glided over the anxieties, hopes and desires inked on the soft wood, a few of the outer ones already blurring where the rain hit them.

* * *

When Linda first arrived to live with him in Japan, she loved going to temples and shrines. She had asked him question after question about what everything meant, but he could hardly answer. He'd never gone to shrines or temples, even at New Year. He appreciated their beauty, and they were great places to visit together, mainly because she was so interested. Little by little, he started reading about shrines just to answer her questions.

Once she discovered all the things to do at each place—buy *omamori* protective amulets, get an *omikuji* fortune told, have a sutra written, or put prayers on the *ema*—she wanted to do it all. She had quite a collection of *omamori* at home and left *ema* at each of the temples they visited. She wrote some alone, too, hiding them on the back racks without letting him see.

Hiroshi had never even thought of going to a church in America. He'd insisted it was all superstition manipulated to make money. Linda argued for the deep spiritual beauty of the places. He accused her of romanticizing the orient as exotic and "other." She accused him of overcompensating with rationality and therefore missing the beauty.

They were both right—and both wrong—Hiroshi realized, now, too late.

When she left, he felt like he had been dropped off a ledge. From the grand, sweeping view of Japan they had together, he fell into an up-close encounter with a culture and society he no longer felt part of. He could no longer look at Japan through her eyes. He had to look through his own.

* * *

Near the main shrine, the three monks—one old and two young—stood impassive in their robes, shaved heads unmoving, hands folded respectfully over prayer beads. The taller and older of the three, his large bald head catching the courtyard lights, watched the proceedings with unmoving eyes and statuesque equanimity.

At the main front gate, the mourners were all passing under the torii and getting into taxis. Someone held an umbrella over the collapsing woman from the front row and helped her into a taxi. Others climbed in after discussing where they should sit. Another taxi pulled up, took four more passengers in, and pulled off.

Hiroshi put up his umbrella and started to walk over, but he knew it would be too late, and he had no idea what Takamatsu wanted him to ask.

The last few mourners stood talking under large black umbrellas. Many of them were foreigners. Hiroshi could tell from the way they stood and moved. But just as many were Japanese, bowing politely and nodding. When the last taxi left, stillness fell over the shrine.

Hiroshi glanced back at the monks, envying them their serenity. He glanced over at the woman, still sitting there, and wondered at her composure and her distance. He would go speak with her after he went inside. He could pay his respects to the deceased and see what the funeral might offer in the way of insight into his life. Nothing, he guessed.

The two young monks hurried out in the rain to fold and stack the chairs. Hiroshi walked to the room set up for Steve Deveaux inside the shrine.

He took off his shoes at the bottom of the wooden stairs, put his umbrella in the worn umbrella rack and climbed up to the inner altar. Inside, a photo of Steve was placed in the middle, surrounded by bottles of whiskey and *sake*, a few cigars, piles of oranges and flowers, and many books and cards.

Hiroshi lit several sticks of incense, bowed three times and placed them in the smoldering forest of incense. He looked at the large black and white photo of Deveaux and wondered how long ago that photo had been taken. In the photo, Steve looked handsome and cocky, his eyes and smile brimming with confidence and enthusiasm.

Judging from the body bag, though, he must have packed on a lot of weight over the years in Tokyo. The city's life must have added—and extracted—its load right up to his final battering. Staring at the photo, Hiroshi wondered how someone with all the energy that photo displayed could end up where he did. Hiroshi bowed to the photo again and left.

At the bottom of the stairs, Hiroshi pulled on his shoes and opened his umbrella. He headed across the courtyard but the lone woman was gone. He looked toward where she had been sitting then back again, and around the courtyard, but could see her nowhere. She must have slipped out very quickly.

The older monk stood calmly under the eaves of the shrine, while the two young monks, their shaved heads dripping rain onto their thick brown robes, clacked the unused chairs together in neat stacks on a metal cart.

"You have a lot of funerals?" Hiroshi asked them.

"Every day," one answered, reaching for another chair.

"Foreigners?"

"Not often," said the other, slapping the chairs together on the cart with a clank.

Hiroshi nodded and looked around the empty space. "Must be a lot of cleaning up here."

"That's all we do," said the other monk, tossing the last chair up on top and catching it before it slipped off the other side.

"Aging population," the other said.

"This one wasn't so old," Hiroshi said.

Hiroshi saw the head monk by the back wall placidly waiting without moving, his large bald head gleaming even as the evening darkened around the black-painted shrine. He envied the monk's strength in the face of solitude, and wished he could do the same.

At the front gate, there were no taxis along the empty street in either direction, and the rain began to fall more heavily. He waited a minute, hoping another taxi would drive by, but none did. He started walking away from the shrine and the smell of incense turned to the smell of pure, clear rain.

He had several hours before meeting Takamatsu to start the rounds of Roppongi nightclubs. Walking through the back streets would clear his head and give him some exercise. He could only connect things in his mind when he was away from the computer, walking the city by himself far enough from the data to let it assemble itself into the patterns he needed to put a case together. Only for this case, he didn't have much data.

As the downpour thudded onto the nylon of his umbrella and the wet soaked into his socks, he wondered whether the queasy, unsettled feeling he got from all these funerals accumulated somewhere inside to become a strength, or just another kind of weakness.

Chapter 9

Roppongi pulsed and glowed. Lighted signs listing the clubs inside zipped up the sides of buildings from sidewalk to rooftop. The names shouted over each other—Black Moon, Abrazos, Kingdom Come, Patpong Alibi, ManZoku, Balibago Den. The overhead writing in all the Japanese scripts, *romaji, hiragana, katakana* and *kanji* blurred with foreign words into a crossword puzzle of decadence and desire. Light cascaded out of these mini-marquees that climbed the buildings like electric ivy.

On the sidewalk, waist-high signs on rollers for restaurants, clubs and bars jutted out into the flow of pedestrian traffic. African doormen in tuxedos boomed out baritone invitations. Teensy dyed-blond girls with dimpled, lipsticked smiles in clinging dresses handed out leaflets. In Roppongi, no taste, need, pleasure or curiosity was left un-catered to.

People streamed out of subway exits, slid out of taxis, and stepped off bus after bus. Hordes of office workers in dull gray pants and dark skirts blocked corners, shouting directions into their cell phones to those yet to arrive. Fashion-conscious hipsters, mini-skirted amateurs, and yakuza wannabes walked to their favorite places to play, eat, drink, or work. The night sidewalk their only point of overlap, everyone was out for a good time in their own way. To arrive in Roppongi was to feel a little high already.

Hiroshi gave himself over to the rush. He zigzagged through the crowd convening outside Almond Coffee, one of the most popular meeting points. Before their undercover research at the clubs, Hiroshi wanted to fill his stomach with ramen noodles, a foundation to soak up the alcohol. Certain counters, standing bars and all trains welcomed single people, allowing Hiroshi to always find someplace he could feel comfortably alone. He had his places to eat and drink all over the city.

His favorite spot was in a half-floor-down basement that specialized in spicy miso-flavored ramen. A small, hand-lettered sign covered in Saran Wrap pointed down the oily stairs. Ramen was what he missed most during the years he studied in Boston. His father took him for ramen—the one thing they did together after his mother died. Ramen was more than hangover prevention; it restored him to himself.

Inside, the shop was humid from the constantly boiling water for the noodles and the simmering broth that made the air deliciously sour and salty. He tucked a thousand yen note into the vending machine by the door for tickets for miso ramen, dumplings and a small bowl of rice. He handed the tickets to the chef and stared at the TV on the wall. The comedy programs were all the same to him, laughing *talento* celebrities overacting a hollow sense of fun—not unlike Roppongi itself.

The cook one-handed his bowl of noodles over the counter and turned back to the cutting board. Hiroshi alternated slurps of thick, chewy noodles with spoonfuls of salty broth. Between glances at the pseudo-comedy show, he tucked in bites of rice sprinkled with *furikake* flakes of seaweed, dried fish, and sesame seed.

The cook set a small plate of fried dumplings on the counter and Hiroshi pulled it to the lower counter. Once the dumplings had cooled a little, he dipped them one by one into a mixture of soy sauce, vinegar, and hot oil, heavy on the vinegar.

It would be another hour before Takamatsu arrived to begin their rounds. In his mind, he could hear Takamatsu's banter already. Until then, Hiroshi wanted to enjoy the beauty of a ramen meal, sitting quietly in his own interior world.

* * *

By seven in the evening, the coffee shop, "Les Chats Gris," was full of bar hostesses flipping through glossy magazines, drinking coffee, chain smoking, and tapping messages on bejeweled cell phones. Quaint photos of Paris adorned the shop's mock-French interior.

The Paris in the photos—where passionate lovers kissed, wise beret-wearing men smoked and jaunty boys paraded huge baguettes—felt like the urban opposite of Roppongi.

The hostesses dressed in sexy outfits with low necklines and open backs. Their tanned, young bodies were draped in sheer tops and short skirts that puffed or clung or glittered, depending on their club's atmosphere. Many wore one-piece dresses with coiled necklaces across their collarbones. High-tech bras lifted and molded their breasts into alluring shapes.

The afternoon spent at hair salons, layering the well-teased curls and pinioning them with gleaming barrettes, was conspicuous. Their cheeks, canvases of pastel colors sharpened by the thick mascara and dark eyeliner above, appeared to need constant upkeep, as they repeatedly touched up their faces in fold-out mirrors kept ever-ready in their purses.

Most hostesses smoked, pulling cigarettes from designer cases and lighting them with expensive lighters. Several women recognized each other by nodding, and a few sat together chatting. To not receive a call or two was an embarrassment. When their phones buzzed to life, they covered the mouthpiece with long, sparkly nails, keeping whispers unheard, but on full display.

In the middle of the coffee shop, Michiko sat alone. She was dressed in all black, her hair newly dyed chestnut brown with blond streaks. Over her shoulders hung a thick, black shawl, as intricately knotted as chain mail. Unlike the others, she hunched over her table working, her long straight hair falling around her like a curtain. She knew a few of the hostesses. Many of them, like her, had been coming to the coffee shop for years, but she acknowledged no one.

She worked back and forth, using two smartphones, several notebooks, and a ledger book propped upright on her leather bag. She wrote in careful, neat lines from top to bottom, in traditional style, and used a ruler to keep the columns of numbers in line.

Numbers came so easily to her, she was accused of cheating on her math exams the last year she bothered going to high school. She didn't know why it was easy; her mother and father had barely finished junior high. Years later, she took a night class in accounting, but quit because it was so simple. Her own accountant, a dour man, who handled only complicated accounts like hers, had taught her more.

Over the years, she had also gleaned a lot from talking with men about the actualities of making, keeping track of and investing money. Appearing confused, but interested elicited lectures in financial management and tricks of the money trade. She mastered what the men said about money as completely as she had the convivial fictions of hostess talk. When the money started coming in, she knew what to do with it.

More hostesses, getting ready for the night's work, crowded the shop. Several latecomers eyed the open chair beside Michiko, but they all sat elsewhere.

One young hostess with a round, pleasant face and a figure so full and plump she had to twist sideways and suck in to maneuver through the densely packed chairs, pushed in to find a seat. She seemed new to hostessing or only part-time. As she tiptoed behind Michiko, her purse slipped from her shoulder and swung down, hitting Michiko square in her back.

Michiko erupted out of her chair, her arms taut and ready at her sides.

Startled, the plump woman lost her balance and landed sideways on the next table. Her high heels scrambled for purchase like a cat on ice. Her skirt hiked up to her underwear and her coffee cup clattered to the floor. The other hostesses recoiled in their chairs, yanking up their anklet-adorned legs.

A couple of women asked in high, plaintive voices, "*Daijobu desu ka*? Are you OK?"

Others let out an unhappy, "Waaa!"

A waiter in black tie and vest scurried over to help, promising to bring a new cup of coffee for her. Another woman reached out with an arm to steady the fallen woman, as she righted herself and pulled her dress back in place.

Michiko drew in a full breath and calmed down. A splash of coffee had landed on her account book and Michiko wiped it off with her handkerchief, which she tossed on the table.

The plump woman stood up, brushed herself off and laughed, ready to apologize and forget it.

Michiko glared, towering over the scene, the tendons in her arms and hands visible beneath her skin, her shoulders set back and her legs in a ready stance.

The plump woman laughed again, and bowed in apology to Michiko.

Everyone breathed a collective sigh of relief, but Michiko failed to acknowledge the apology. So, the plump woman bowed again, more stiffly, straightened her tight-packed one-piece, and carried her shame and stained dress to the bathroom.

Michiko folded shut her notebooks, fingered off her cell phones and dropped them in her bag. All eyes were on her as she straightened her black dress, swung her bag over her shoulder and headed for the door without a glance to either side.

Michiko was going to work that evening, too. She had come there for years, but was tired of these hostess hangouts. The coffee shops in Europe were another thing altogether. She had to go change for her alibi of being at work before she finished the evening's plan.

Chapter 10

Hiroshi walked the back streets past the cheaper hostess clubs with garish front door colors and glitzy photos of women in coy poses. Other clubs took the opposite approach, arousing curiosity with a single elegant character in dark red. In Roppongi, understated simplicity was just as inviting as open arms.

Hiroshi finally found the club—the Venus de Milo. Hiroshi nodded to the men in suits, hair oil and biceps at the door and walked up the marble-lined entryway, a red carpet underfoot. At the top of the curving stairway was a full-size copy of the Venus de Milo, gleaming white beneath bright spotlights.

Takamatsu was not there yet, and Hiroshi hesitated to go in without him. But the mama-san—a large woman in a sequined gown with thick, upswept hair—spoke to two of the women congregated at the back comparing outfits. They dutifully walked over with graceful steps. Once they took his arms, Hiroshi could not back out, so he followed them to a sofa. There were no other customers. It was too early.

The room, drenched in a russet glow from soft purple sofas and maroon carpeting, was large, separated into discrete areas with patterned glass dividers, large potted plants and tall gauze curtains that swept down from the high ceiling.

At points around the walls were positioned Venus de Milo busts on pedestals. Spotlights under the smaller replicas of the famous sculpture cast upswept shadows over their classic features.

Hiroshi was about to start talking with the two women when Takamatsu blustered in, drawing everyone's attention. When it was clear Takamatsu would be joining them, one of the women unfolded her long legs and moved to escort him over.

The two hostesses, both dressed in tight silk dresses with low necklines, welcomed Hiroshi and Takamatsu by leaning toward them with deep-throated coos, settling the men into place. Before the conversation got going, a bottle of whiskey arrived with a bucket of ice, bottled spring water, and glasses.

"First time here?" the hostesses asked, brushing their hair back and settling onto the sofa beside Hiroshi and Takamatsu, boy-girl, boy-girl.

Takamatsu said, "Yes, but not the last." He looked at the two girls with a face that displayed desire without any filter or restraint.

"I'm Miki and that's Shiho," the shorter of the two said.

"I'm Suzuki and that's Sato." Hiroshi made a mental note to remember his cover name, though the girls would remember it better than he would. The girls had their working names, so why shouldn't the guys? Miki leaned forward to mix the whiskey, weak yellow for the women and strong brown for the men.

Miki had straight, jet-black hair and almond-shaped eyelids. Her eyes veered politely sideways, attentive, but never connecting. Her smooth hands and manicured fingernails handled the bottle, drink stirrer and ice tongs with practiced poise. Each time she moved, the bright yellow squares on her tight, red dress contorted delectably.

Shiho, in an all-black dress, sat forward with her eyes on Hiroshi. Her long body sank deep into the soft cushions. She smiled with such directness that Hiroshi felt a gratifying bolt of desire. He snuck a glance at Shiho's shapely legs as she reseated herself and pulled her dress into place.

Takamatsu raised his glass for a toast, everyone singing out, "*Kanpai!* Cheers!" together as one.

Takamatsu took off his jacket, and a waiter came to take it, patting it to be sure he didn't forget his cell phone before hanging up the jacket. Takamatsu rolled up his sleeves in three perfect folds and shook out cigarettes for the girls. Only Miki smoked.

"You've got the good girl," Takamatsu said. "We smokers stick together. Bad habits lead to more bad habits, right?"

"I hope so." Miki laughed and bounced on the sofa. She drew deep on her cigarette and held it up as she blew out, waiting to see if Takamatsu would take the conversational reins.

"You're attractive, you two," Takamatsu said.

"Let's not talk about us. Let's talk about you. What do you do?" Miki asked.

Takamatsu answered, "Business."

"What kind of business?"

"Foreign investment," Takamatsu said.

Hiroshi squirmed, unsure of whether he could act like a business-man.

"What does that mean?" Miki asked, Shiho listening quietly.

"It's mostly just talk and trust. If you talk the right way, you get their trust and make the sale."

"That sounds like what we do," Miki laughed.

"It is, indeed. But I like talk after work, too, if you know what I mean," he said, laughing a little too loudly.

"So do we," said Miki, squirming on the sofa. "Tell us something interesting about work!"

To Hiroshi, Shiho seemed more beautiful the quieter she re-mained. He thought of Linda, and then he quit thinking of her and just let his eyes roam over the strong curves of Shiho's shoulders and breasts and waist. When she leaned back on the sofa, she caught his eyes, and then she looked away with a girlish tilt of her head.

Her chestnut brown, blond-streaked hair billowed thick and long over her shoulders. If all her gestures were practiced, they were practiced to perfection. As she uncrossed and re-crossed her legs, her hose rustled and whispered. When she caught him staring, she looked away and smiled. She liked to be looked at, or was used to it.

Takamatsu launched into a story: "We made a killing today. We took these foreigners on a complicated trade. Foreigners think our English isn't good, but we know how to make money, we Japanese, right?"

"All in a day's work," Hiroshi said, trying to act confident. "I deal with foreign companies most of the time, but I hate them."

"So, you must speak English?"

"A little."

"Can you teach us?" asked Miki, her eyes wide in anticipation.

"I'd love to," Takamatsu chimed in. Hiroshi laughed, since he knew Takamatsu could only sputter a few words in a row.

"Why don't you like foreigners?" asked Shiho, with a frown.

Takamatsu shook his head. "They're changing the business environment. They bring in Western practices—like transparent accounting—that disrupt the old connections."

Hiroshi was amazed at Takamatsu's ability to fabricate—to lie—so convincingly.

Takamatsu continued: "They want a contract for everything, and pay lawyers to write them up. In the old days, Japanese business ran on trust. Not much of that left."

"I know what you mean," said Miki, pouring a second round of drinks for everyone.

"I hope you don't get any foreign devils in here."

"We do."

"Are they troublesome?"

"Mama-san is strict, so we switch around among ourselves if there's ever a problem. This is the best club I've ever worked in," said Miki.

Shiho nodded as if it wasn't, necessarily, the best one for her.

"I'm taking an English class now," said Miki. "I want to work in a place with more foreigners if I can."

Miki set her hand on Takamatsu's shoulder.

"Foreigners?" Shiho said, finding her voice at last. "They tend to want one thing. And it's not conversation."

Everyone laughed.

Miki said, "Nothing wrong with that," bringing another wave of laughter.

"I meant money," Shiho said, not laughing.

"One gets the other!" Miki said.

"That's the same in every country," Takamatsu said, leaning in closer to whisper to Miki. She giggled as she listened, putting her hand over her mouth and huddling forward.

Takamatsu leaned over to Hiroshi with a mock-quiet whisper, "Divide and conquer," in terribly accented English. That left Hiroshi and Shiho to talk.

It had been a long time since Hiroshi had bantered with a woman in Japanese. He had hardly spoken to a woman since Linda left. He knew this was all an act, but it was a successful one. He felt as if Shiho were sister, mother, confidante, colleague, and lover all at once. Being attended to—paid for or not—was its own kind of pleasure.

Sensing Hiroshi's hesitation, Shiho started to talk. She loved to travel, had been to Paris, New York, and most resort spots around Southeast Asia, with, Hiroshi guessed, different men. She liked onsen hot springs resorts and—premature though it was—Hiroshi asked her to go with him to one sometime.

Shiho smiled a disappointed smile and said, "I wish I had met you before."

Before Hiroshi could say anything more, Takamatsu gave him a serious look and waved his watch at him.

"We have the two most beautiful women in Roppongi right here," Takamatsu said, "But we still have business to do. Our boss is waiting for us."

"I thought you were the boss?" Miki said.

"I am, but we still have a meeting. Could we buy you girls a drink later?"

"The mama-san is a little short-handed tonight, so we can't leave her right now. One of the girls quit yesterday, and another didn't come back from vacation yet."

Takamatsu tapped his cell phone so his phone number displayed on the screen and said, "You can contact me here. We need to go."

"Where do you go after work? Can we meet you there?" asked Hiroshi.

"Miki goes to the David Lounge every night," Shiho said.

Miki twisted away. "Men have to be accompanied in there," she said with a restrained, angry smile at Shiho, who had obviously hit a nerve. "Shiho's leaving soon on vacation."

They turned to look at her.

"Just for a while," Shiho said, her eyes darting at Miki, angry at the divulgence.

"Where are you going?" Hiroshi asked.

"Just a short trip abroad."

"Never mind, we'll come back another night." Takamatsu said.

Takamatsu stood up to settle the bill. The two women helped Hiroshi, who let them walk him—one on each side—to the door. The mama-san got down from her perch at the bar and came over to ask if everything was okay, since they were leaving so early.

Takamatsu assured her everything was fine, that they had a meeting, but that they would return again soon. The two women walked with the two men down the carpeted stairway under the gaze of Venus de Milo.

When Takamatsu and Hiroshi got to the street, the two women stood politely on the bottom step, folded their hands at their waists with their high heels formally together.

As Hiroshi and Takamatsu started away, the two women bowed, and waved their hands bye-bye like high school girls until Hiroshi and Takamatsu were out of sight around the corner.

Chapter 11

When they were out of earshot, Hiroshi said, "Now, what did we get out of that?"

"We're warming up. Getting in character," Takamatsu said, using badly pronounced English for the last phrase.

Hiroshi shook his head.

"Thanks for sticking me with the bill," Takamatsu said, once they were out of earshot.

"I thought you had a budget?"

"I'm in trouble with the department accountant already."

"I can't believe you talked them into paying for this."

"It was the foreign aspect that got them. Loss of face. They want this over."

"Did you tell them we'd be going to hostess clubs?"

"I mentioned the suspect was a hostess, yes."

"We're looking for a tall woman with long hair who might be a hostess? That narrows it down to a million suspects in Tokyo."

"Don't be so pessimistic. You have to shake the tree."

"There're too many trees." Hiroshi gestured at the clubs in all directions.

"What did you think of those two?" Takamatsu asked.

"Typical hostesses. Not murderers."

"The tall one, yours, was not unlike the video clip."

"Like I said, a million women look like the video clip."

"We're checking all the clubs in his wallet. That's logical, isn't it?"

"In a way."

"In a drunken way," Takamatsu laughed.

"The whiskey is strong."

"Washes the American-ness out of you. Makes you a real Japanese again."

Barkers and doormen stepped halfway in front of Hiroshi and Takamatsu, trying to corral them and get them to come inside, which meant that at least Hiroshi and Takamatsu knew their disguises as non-detectives were working. From one club to the next, came price lists, discount coupons, photos of women, and lists of options.

"You should have left it as a suicide," Hiroshi said.

"And miss all this fun?" Takamatsu laughed.

The streets had become clogged with middle-aged men in wobbling groups deciding where to go, like it was their rightful purpose in life to get drunk with young women whose companionship drew exorbitant prices. Touts from nearby clubs circled them with discount offers and enticing patter.

"I forgot to tell you," Takamatsu said. "The American ambassador made an unofficial inquiry this morning."

"Really? Do they always inquire about dead citizens?"

"No. That's the problem."

"Was Deveaux important?"

Takamatsu stopped to read his leather-covered notepad.

"Where's the David Lounge?"

"*What's* the David Lounge is the question."

"The Tulip is close by here. Let's try that first."

They walked down a small, connecting lane that led back to the main street, toward Azabu. The club was two blocks down in a large building covered with brown tile. A long list of drinking spots, clubs and bars were listed on the building's front directory. The Tulip was on the twelfth floor. The clean, well-kept elevator had a security camera and a tidy atmosphere. Such an efficient, organized building in Roppongi meant yakuza ownership.

They got off on the twelfth floor and entered a darkened hallway with the entrance to the Tulip on the left. Hiroshi and Takamatsu both stopped still. On the right, a small brass plaque on the wall had "David Lounge" inscribed in small, tight alphabet script. The name hadn't been on the signboard downstairs.

They couldn't get into the David Lounge if the hostesses took their dates there, and anyway, the lounge wouldn't be open until later, after the hostess bars closed—so they decided to try The Tulip.

The bartender looked up as they entered, but said nothing. Instead, he went back to chipping at a palm-sized ball of ice he rotated in his left hand.

The bar had one black marble bar top with a half-dozen low stools. The end of the bar curved to the right around toward the front wall, with space for two more stools. Floor-to-ceiling doors, for storage most likely, took up the left wall. The back shelves were lined with immaculate rows of select, expensive liquors and a green-glowing stereo system.

The silent bartender wore a tieless tuxedo vest with a fresh purple tulip pinned to the lapel. His face was pale, with cheeks sunk in dark ravines down each side. The light from below the bar shone upwards, highlighting his skeletal features and casting a shadow of his lanky body on the glass shelves behind.

Hiroshi put on the drunk act. "So, this is the place Suzuki's always raving about?" he said a little too loudly, nodding in approval to the bartender, who kept working silently, tossing the ice ball in his hand to find the next spot to flake off.

They sat down and Hiroshi ordered two single malt whiskies, neat.

The bartender put the ice ball in the freezer and moved off to retrieve the drinks. He placed the two whiskey glasses and a small glass bowl of peanuts on the counter in front of them before retrieving his ice ball and pick.

Takamatsu looked around for a hook to hang his jacket, but seeing none, folded it and set it on the stool next to him. He rolled up his sleeves in three crisp folds while Hiroshi tried to get comfortable on the cushioned stool.

Takamatsu started to talk about his past lovers. At first, Hiroshi thought Takamatsu was making up the stories, but gradually he realized they were probably real. True or not, Takamatsu was a great storyteller, and Hiroshi was a natural listener. Takamatsu detailed the women, though edited the most intimate details: this girl from a club last year, another from when he was training but met again by accident, one he met on a case last year. Hiroshi never asked about Takamatsu's wife and kids, and Takamatsu never mentioned them.

Meanwhile, the tall, pale bartender kept up the constant rhythmic sculpting of the ice ball. After checking to see if it fit in a highball glass, he placed it in the freezer, pulled out a fresh rectangle of ice, and started chipping a new ball.

A muted buzzer sounded, and the bartender pulled open a small window on the back wall and retrieved an order. He turned away as he hunched over to mix the drinks, and then set them on a rolling tray that disappeared inside the wall.

"What's that? Giving the wall a drink?" joked Takamatsu.

The bartender glanced at him and went back to the ice ball, chipping with irritating regularity.

Takamatsu gossiped about department people, being careful not to say anything that would flag them as detectives, but the quiet jazz and cold, watery whiskey was making Hiroshi sleepy. Takamatsu never seemed to get drunk or tired. Hiroshi was both.

"Not busy tonight," Takamatsu shouted to the bartender, who paused for a second to shrug.

"Never any women in here?" The bartender shrugged again, not missing a beat on the now-rounder ball.

Takamatsu put out his cigarette and nodded at the bartender, who put away his half-finished ice ball in the freezer and got their bill. Hiroshi paid and they left. In the hallway, they both looked at the elevator camera without a word.

At the building entrance, they stopped short. A heavy rain had started while they were inside. Neither of them had brought umbrellas. They waited at the door to see if the rain would lighten.

"Those two whiskies at The Tulip were more than the whole tab at the Venus de Milo," said Hiroshi. "I should have paid for the first one."

"I'll see if I can get some more funds."

"We didn't find much, did we?" Hiroshi said.

"If we find his route, we'll find whoever killed him."

"And if we don't?"

"We keep coming back until we do," Takamatsu added. "I have to give the chief something to tell the embassy soon."

"It'd be nice to see that elevator tape," Hiroshi said.

"And get inside the David Lounge."

"That ice pick was driving me crazy."

"I wanted to snatch it out of his hand."

Takamatsu looked around the entrance area for an umbrella stand from which to "borrow" an umbrella, but he couldn't find one. When they gave up on the rain slowing, they pinched their collars around their necks and quit talking as they ran through the rain toward the nearest subway station.

Chapter 12

Michiko had a key to Takayuki Shibuya's place, and let herself in silently. She set her umbrella in the stand, shaking off the rain. It was pouring outside. In the genkan, several pairs of men's designer running shoes surrounded a single pair of women's leather pumps.

The apartment was disordered, the designer furniture misaligned and littered with convenience store and shopping bags, jackets, and a rack of video cameras, monitors, LED lights, reflectors, and tripods. A row of DVD players lined up next to stacks of homemade DVDs.

She walked in her socks through the living room past the small kitchen area to the door of the bedroom and pushed it open. Shibuya was sprawled across the double bed. She could not see his face, only the dark-tanned flesh on his back and his spiky, dyed blond-brown hair. Two bright gold chains snaked across the tan flesh of his shoulder blades.

Shibuya's inability to get beyond holding court in a game center and living like a twenty-year-old infuriated her even more than his inability to manage money. She had been carrying him for years, and it was time to stop. She knew what she had to do and knew where Shibuya kept the money.

Beneath his smoker's snore and the cyclic hum-rattle-hum of the air conditioner, she heard another light breathing rhythm. Beside him in bed she saw the curved outline of a thin girl under the sheets.

She was as darkly tanned as Shibuya and one small breast with a tiny nipple poked out from under a sleeveless T-shirt. Her thin hip stretched into a thinner waist, and her long leg hung over the edge of the bed.

The plain white shirt, blue tie, white socks and plaid skirt folded neatly on the chair beside the bed indicated the girl was still in high school—or pretended to be. Or maybe the folded outfit was just a prop for a video shoot.

Michiko leaned back, thinking. She had expected Shibuya to be alone. A dozen years ago, it had been Michiko there in bed.

* * *

Her best friend Reiko met Shibuya first. Reiko's father used to work at Michiko's father's factory, but he drank too much and disappeared. Reiko's mother watched TV all day, pouring out glass after glass of *shochu* from a big plastic container. When she was sober enough to walk, she played pachinko, losing what little money the family had.

Reiko started coming home with Michiko after school to eat and do homework, and then, she just moved in. It was okay with Michiko's father, who worked overtime and felt guilty not spending more time with Michiko. The apartment above the metal workshop her father owned had room for another bed, and the workers made a bed frame from leftover metal for her.

Reiko met Shibuya one day when she skipped class and went downtown by herself. She was always ahead, socially and sexually, of Michiko. She had a way with boys that drew them to her, at school and on the street. Her sassy manner, full-body curves, and self-possession were hard not to notice. When she started using make-up, she looked ten years older. Michiko soon followed.

When Michiko's father found out they were running off to young people's hangouts in the teen worlds of Harajuku and Shibuya, he was furious. He started popping upstairs from the workshop—his clothing, hair, face and hands covered in metal dust—to be sure they were doing their homework. They found ways to sneak out anyway. So, he brought in one of Michiko's cousins, Natsumi, an older girl from their ancestral hometown, to keep an eye on them.

Natsumi had just graduated from high school when she moved in, and she knew how to do laundry, shopping, and housework. Michiko's father said Natsumi was her cousin. But Natsumi was evasive when Michiko asked more about the family connections. It was complicated, the relations from her mother and father's hometown.

The workers made another bed frame to hold Natsumi's futon and another study desk that fit next to Michiko's and Reiko's. The three of the girls shared clothes, since Natsumi, older by three years, was not much taller. Michiko went from being alone to having two sisters.

They suddenly had lots of things to do, eating and talking together, and shopping on the weekends. The two housemates kept Michiko from brooding over her mother's death. At the home shrine, they rang the bell and lit incense for Michiko's mother; they had all lost something.

Michiko's father came up the stairs from the factory for late dinners, sometimes not until 10:30 or 11:00. He was busier in the factory than ever before. She tried to stay awake long enough to talk with him a little when he looked in to their room late at night after work. Father and daughter whispered about everything while Reiko and Natsumi slept.

* * *

Michiko toed Shibuya's leg, but got no response. She kicked his knee and he flipped around to a sitting position, snatching at his leg, looking confused. He gasped seeing her standing above him, but said nothing.

The girl lying next to Shibuya lifted her head and scrambled back toward the head of the bed, clutching a pillow with her shiny, long fingernails. She blinked at Michiko with huge, long eyelashes that glittered in the dim light. A dark-blue bird tattoo swooped across her right breast. The girl's body, cooked red-brown at a tanning salon, glowed in the dimness.

Shibuya rubbed his knee and frowned, breathing out heavily. He pushed back his long, layered hair.

"Pretty," Michiko said, nodding toward the girl, her voice loud and husky in the smallness of the room.

"Yeah, she is," he answered, fumbling around for his boxer shorts.

"Tall, too."

"About your height."

"Coincidence."

65

Shibuya grunted and got out of bed as Michiko and the girl stared at each other.

Shibuya pulled his shorts over his bony waist. He started to say something to the girl, but then decided not to, and followed Michiko out of the room.

In the bathroom, he stood on the toilet, pushed up a ceiling panel, and reached inside. He pulled down three packets of ten thousand yen notes stashed inside zip lock bags and handed them to her. She hefted them to feel the weight and tucked them inside her bag. He reached up for three more and stepped back onto the tile floor. He looked older in the bathroom light, his skin wrinkled from tanning, the gold necklaces looped unevenly over the tendons and collarbones around his neck.

"I thought you left already," he said. "You didn't call."

"I called. You didn't answer." She weighed the additional stacks after he handed them to her and gave him a questioning look.

"That's all of it," he said. "Really." He pushed his hands through his hair.

She smiled at him.

He nodded.

She slapped him hard, just short of his ear.

He held his spot, but said nothing.

"I'm not gone yet."

"Check your records," he said. "You're always so careful."

"I have to be." She nodded her head toward the bedroom, "Back to videos again?"

"There's no money in that anymore."

"High school girls?"

"No, something less complicated."

"How long will it take to get that up and running?"

"It already is."

"And the girl there?"

"Look, I like her, all right?"

"Films well, does she?"

"It's not that."

"Settling down?"

"Maybe. Finally."

Michiko slapped him again.

Holding his cheek, Shibuya held her eyes for a moment, and then looked away.

Michiko tucked the last packet of bills into her bag, considering whether to slap him one more time. Finally, she said, "Maybe you should go back to work? Just while I'm gone."

"I told you, it's coming."

"When?"

"I just need to collect what people owe me."

"You better do that. Or you'll collect what's owed you."

He nodded, his eyes turned downwards.

She shook her head, pulling her bag now loaded with the money over her shoulder. "Shibuya-kun, when are you going to grow up?"

He nodded, looking away, tight-jawed.

"When are you leaving?" he asked.

"Just a couple of loose ends to tie up."

"I'll drive you to the airport."

"Did you get your license back?"

"No, but I got my car back."

"I can get there on my own." She nodded, as if having come to some new decision. "But, you know, let's go out one more time, for old time's sake. Tomorrow night? The David?"

He nodded OK. His eyes searched back and forth over the tile floor for something that was not there.

Outside the door to the bedroom, she paused to look down at the girl in the bed. Their eyes met for a moment, until the younger girl turned away, blinking her absurdly long eyelashes.

When the young girl finally mustered the courage to say something, Michiko was gone, leaving behind only the scent of lotus perfume.

* * *

After Natsumi found a boyfriend, she started taking Reiko and Michiko with her to Shibuya, Harajuku and Shinjuku, the very places her father did not want the girls to go. Natsumi started spending more time with her boyfriend, leaving Reiko and Michiko to walk around on their own.

67

Sometimes, they sang karaoke with boys they met, or talked over green tea and red adzuki bean desserts. They ate crepes filled with ice cream, strawberry sauce and whipped cream until they felt sick. They went with the boys to small restaurants where they ate okonomiyaki pizza-pancakes filled with shrimp, pork, and cabbage, and slathered with sweet sauce, mayonnaise, and crinkly, curling bonito fish flakes.

After they ate, they went to karaoke parlors in Shibuya's tall buildings, which were so thin the girls could barely fit in the elevators. Michiko was good at winning prizes in the game centers, and she and Reiko made a good team, manipulating the mechanical arm of the glassed-in, UFO-catcher machine that dropped cute stuffed animals through the prize hole.

It was in one of those game centers that Reiko met Shibuya. Reiko met him alone several times. They had done it, Reiko whispered one night, and she and Natsumi giggled. Shibuya was older and knew how to talk to girls, but Reiko soon lost interest. Michiko started to meet Shibuya, occasionally, and then more and more often. It was the first time Michiko ever felt more attracted to a live person than the boys in the posters on her bedroom wall.

At first, Shibuya always had lots of money and he told Michiko and Reiko how they could make lots of money themselves. Pretty soon, Shibuya was arranging dates for them and Michiko and Reiko had more money than she could hide. When her father discovered the money, it took him a couple of weeks to find Shibuya in the confusing teen world he hung out in. But when he did, he and two other workers beat Shibuya to a pulp.

After that, Uncle Ono started coming up from the factory floor all the time to check on all three girls. Michiko's father watched her more closely than ever.

A couple years later, when Michiko was kicked out of school and decided to run away, Shibuya didn't want to get beat up again. But eventually, he reluctantly took her in.

In time, she took him in.

Chapter 13

The phone rang and Hiroshi clawed in the direction of the sound, pulling himself off the sofa where he landed a few hours before. The rough weave of the fabric had imprinted itself on his cheek, making it feel raw. His head felt bloated with unmetabolized whiskey.

"*Moshi moshi.* Hello?"

"This is Sakaguchi."

"Sakaguchi?"

"We met on the tracks the other day."

"The sumo wrestler."

"Former sumo wrestler."

"What...?" Hiroshi's hangover made it hard to hear.

"I hate to ask, but we need your English. Takamatsu said I should call."

"He's quick to volunteer my services."

"There're two English speakers we need help with. Could you come down?"

"It'll be an hour."

"Aren't you in your office?"

"No, at home. I was out with Takamatsu last night."

"You must be hungover."

"Badly. Where are you exactly?"

"Interrogation rooms near the chikan section. Main building. Take your time. I'll get them something to eat."

Hiroshi had nothing to do with the recently formed chikan office that dealt with train gropers, molesters, window peepers, exhibitionists, and underwear thieves, but the stories circulated like jokes without a punch line.

69

Hiroshi started piecing together his return home—noodles at a *yattai* night street stall, a taxi driver who spoke phrases in a hundred languages, stumbling over the unsent boxes, collapsing onto the sofa. He looked around anxiously for his wallet and cell phone. Reassured he hadn't lost them, he kicked into hangover autopilot, doing simple, concrete things in order.

* * *

From the main building's pale, tiled corridor, the door of the interrogation room opened to reveal a large foreign man sitting at a table with his arms crossed. His barrel chest and large belly terraced up to a thick jaw, red face and bald head.

Across the table Sakaguchi seemed even bigger in the low-ceilinged room, his tree-trunk limbs and kettledrum belly hanging easily on his two-meter frame. He leaned back when Hiroshi arrived and nodded him back into the hall with a thrust of his full-moon face.

"My English is all textbook stuff and this guy has a thick accent. The girl speaks too fast."

"She's a foreigner?" Hiroshi asked.

"Half, I guess. She won't say a word in Japanese, but her mother's Japanese."

"So what's the deal?"

"The high school girl dragged this Russian off the train shouting, 'Chikan.' The Russian didn't even know the word meant train groper. He claims he did nothing. The girl quit talking. They've been here since rush hour."

Hiroshi thought for a minute. "Let me talk to Mikhail Gorbachev first."

The large Russian-looking man acknowledged him with a sullen nod.

"My name is Hiroshi Shimizu. Did you get some coffee?"

"I have coffee at my office."

"And where is your office?"

"I explained it several times. He is not speak English."

"Could you start once again? I need to hear it directly."

"Are you in charge here?"

"I am now."

"What is your rank?"

"Look, whatever my rank is, I have to translate for you. So, I need to hear it all again."

The Russian man took a big breath and exhaled loudly. "I am riding to my office on train. That little monster/schoolgirl grab me and start shouting, 'Chikan, chikan.' I do not know this word and think she need help. That's why I am getting off train. To help. Then, I am trying helping her and she is saying, 'Money, money,' in English. She say, if I give money, she forget. I refuse to give. We have serious criminal in Russia, so I not afraid of little girl."

"Did you explain that?"

"Station attendants grab me. She try run away." He leaned back and folded his arms across his chest.

"And you didn't bump her or touch her in any way?"

"Everyone bumping and touching in rush hour. Same in Moscow."

"And you say she asked you in English?"

"Yes, English. What country have schoolgirl like this? I ask you."

"OK, if you would please drink your coffee and calm down, I'll see what she has to say."

Hiroshi stepped outside with Sakaguchi. Switching to Japanese, Hiroshi asked Sakaguchi which story he believed.

"I believe the man. The real chikan enjoy being caught. The more perverted they are, the more they love the whole drama. After being sent over here, I listened to a lot of these little creeps. This Russian seems all right."

"Did you call his office?"

"It all checked out. He works for an import-export firm, like he said, a Russian outfit that's completely aboveboard."

"And what about the girl?"

"Her mother is very upset. The girl seems to understand Japanese, but refuses to speak anything but English. Pulled in before, let go without a record. None of the juvenile people remember anything, so it couldn't have been too serious."

"Let me talk to her," Hiroshi said.

In the other interrogation room, a woman in a designer trench coat was leaning over a girl in a high school sailor-girl uniform. Two bowls of just-eaten noodles were neatly stacked at the edge of the table.

Hiroshi paused at the doorway.

The mother looked up with eyes as glassy and wild as a horse. She wiped the tears from her dainty face with her palms. Hiroshi fumbled in his pocket for a packet of tissues. The mother wiped her eyes and handed the handkerchief to her daughter, who wiped hers without looking up. Hiroshi could barely see her face inside the wall of long hair. The daughter had the same elegant, aquiline nose and curving lips as her mother, but she had a fuller nose, bigger eyes and almost-plump cheeks. Her shoulders were too big for her school uniform.

Hiroshi dug into his pocket for his name card. The mother bowed gently and reached to take it from him, her eyes averted down, toward the card. After reading it, she placed it on the table in front of her, and squared her shoulders to speak.

"My name is Sanae Atsuki, and this is my daughter Yukari," she said in a soft, cracking voice with another slight bow forward. "I am so very sorry for this disturbance. Yukari has something she would like to say."

Yukari brushed back her hair and in flawless English said, "I'm not sorry really. I just have to say so."

Her mother growled, "Speak Japanese."

Hiroshi intervened in English. "That's wonderful English. Perfect pronunciation. How did your English become so good?"

"How did yours?" said Yukari, tilting her head to stare at him with wet, wide eyes.

"Well, I went to school in New York when I was very young and I went to college in Boston," said Hiroshi, in a matter-of-fact tone.

Sakaguchi came into the room quietly as an overfed cat, but as conspicuous as a sumo wrestler.

"That's what I wanted to do, stay in America, but my mom made me come back here."

Sanae leaned forward to speak in Japanese. "Her father and I felt it was best for her to not forget being Japanese. Now she refuses to speak anything but English."

Yukari said, "The real reason we came back was them. I loved my high school there."

Sanae frowned, and said, "We had trouble in our marriage. The only person that adapted well to America was Yukari. Too well, perhaps. My husband is, was, American."

"He died?"

"Divorced."

Hiroshi leaned back in his chair. "So, this is not the first time to get in trouble."

"It's that guy she got caught up with. This punk kid. He's the one that should be arrested, not Yukari. I've tried to keep them apart, but I can't watch her every minute. He took money from Yukari. He tried to get money from me."

Hiroshi put on his soothing voice, "Can you tell me about this guy?"

Yukari started to tear up, but stopped herself. "He was nice to me at first. We hung out. School in Japan is so boring, and stupid. The teachers hated me because I was good at English. I skipped class because I did no work and still got perfect marks."

"So, what did you do when you skipped class?"

Yukari dropped her head and breathed in. Her mother looked away. She spoke slowly. "I hooked up with foreigners. You know, *enjo kosai*, paid dates. Foreigners paid more. I didn't do it many times, but I got caught," she said shrugging her shoulders. "Anyway, it's no different from my mom. She used to work as a hostess. That's how she met my dad."

Sanae blushed crimson and covered her mouth.

Hiroshi nodded, his eyes downcast politely.

"Anyway, I stopped that. The train thing seemed easier, and a lot less yucky."

Sanae let out an exasperated breath.

Hiroshi interrupted. "Have you reported this guy?"

"I have and no one did anything," said Sanae.

"Well, maybe, Yukari, you won't mind telling us where we can find him?"

Yukari silently stared at the table.

"Where can we find this guy?" Sakaguchi asked, stepping closer to the table.

Yukari sat silently.

"Tell them, Yukari. We'll see about going back to the States, I promise you. Just tell them where he is. We just talked about this."

Yukari looked down, her hair over her face.

Finally, shifting in her chair, she said in a soft voice, "He's at the game center every day."

"Which game center?" asked Hiroshi.

"In Shibuya, near the 109 building, up that side street to the left from Hachiko Square."

"And what's his family name?"

"Shibuya."

"First name."

"Takayuki."

"Easy to remember. Shibuya in Shibuya," Sakaguchi growled.

"Do you have a photo of him in your cell phone?" Hiroshi asked.

Yukari spun through the photos on her phone until she found one. Hiroshi and Sakaguchi leaned down to look and memorize the face.

"So, that guy on the train didn't really do anything?" Hiroshi asked.

Yukari shook her head, no, side-to-side American style.

"And Shibuya does that with other girls, too? Not just you?"

"He does more things, too."

"What kind of things?"

"Everything."

Hiroshi caught Sakaguchi's eye and changed to a friendlier tone. "Listen, Yukari, I had a hard time adjusting when I came back."

"I totally failed to adjust," Yukari said, chuckling sadly and puffing her cheeks before sighing.

"These things you're doing hurt others, and hurt yourself, too," Hiroshi said.

Yukari nodded her head, yes, she understood. "Can we go?" Yukari asked. "I won't...," she stopped mid-sentence. She leaned over and hugged her mother, who patted her back to comfort her much larger daughter.

"Yes," Sakaguchi said, relieved. "You can go."

Sanae and Yukari bowed deeply in apology as they gathered themselves and got up.

"You have my card," Hiroshi said. "If there's anything else, call anytime."

74

Sanae looked at Hiroshi's meishi again, tucked it into her purse and put her arm around her daughter's shoulders.

Sakaguchi opened the door for them and Hiroshi watched them walk down the hall.

"I'll tell Mikhail Gorbachev he can leave," Sakaguchi said. "Want to join us? We can always use a hand."

"For what?"

"Shibuya in Shibuya. Have you back by lunch."

"I've already wasted the morning."

"Takamatsu said you hole up in your office all alone. This will be a good chance for hands-on training."

"I've got a full workload today."

"You have to learn the other side of what we do. The car's on its way."

Chapter 14

The three officers waiting in the police parking lot wore sunglasses and suit jackets that fit tightly over their bulky frames. Their faces were as round and plump as Sakaguchi's.

"Are these guys sumo wrestlers too?" Hiroshi asked Sakaguchi.

"Sugamo was, but Ueno and Osaki did rugby."

"Rugby?"

"Pays better," one of them said, and they all laughed.

"Pays differently," another said, and they laughed again.

Hiroshi could not tell if they were joking or not.

"That's Sugamo driving, and this is Osaki and Ueno."

"I don't usually go out of the office," Hiroshi said.

"Good exercise," Sakaguchi said. "Takamatsu said you got in on your English. We got in on our size."

Osaki held the back door open for Hiroshi.

"Actually, I didn't take the martial arts training when I started," Hiroshi said.

They all stopped, each with one leg in the car.

Hiroshi looked embarrassed. "I studied kendo at university, so the head of my dojo wrote a letter for me."

They mentally re-planned the attack positions, and reset expectations.

* * *

The Shibuya streets were packed with shoppers roaming from large department stores to small shops to boutiques to specialty stores. Racks of clothes, shoes, jewelry, and eyeglasses spilled out onto the sidewalks as if shopping could never be contained. The automatic doors of ATM plazas inhaled and exhaled people for cash withdrawals. Karaoke places rose stories overhead. Advertising images danced across giant TV screens. Four-story-high posters of singers and celebrities smiled impossibly wide, too-cheery smiles.

Young people squatted on stoops and curbs munching cream-filled crepes, sugary hamburgers, and consuming plastic-bottled drinks and palm-size bags of nibbles. They clustered in groups to reconfirm themselves with every purchase and text message, sinking into the anxiety-soothing haze of teenage consumerism. Shibuya held them tight in its grip of teenage fun.

"Hiroshi, be careful until we get them down on the floor," Sakaguchi said. "Ueno back there got sliced, when was it?"

"Couple years ago," Sugamo said. His greased-back hair missed only the sumo wrestler topknot.

Osaki leaned forward, around Hiroshi. "That high school girl, right?"

Ueno grunted. Everyone held back a laugh. They all had earthy Osaka accents like Sakaguchi.

Sakaguchi turned his head around and said, "Good you have plenty of bowls of *chanpon* rice porridge between you and your vitals."

"A moment of inattention; six months to heal." Ueno patted his belly and looked out the window.

Sakaguchi said, "You should have rushed her with an *uwatenagi* overhand throw."

Ueno pushed back his long, oiled hair and said, "I should have felt her up like Osaka would have. She had the blade inside her underwear."

Osaka, the youngest and leanest of the group, said, "I never felt up any of those girls. They just kept claiming that."

"Oh, right, because you're so handsome," Sugamo said, leaning back from the steering wheel. "They stab me and flirt with you."

Everyone laughed.

"Does that happen often?" Hiroshi asked, serious.

Everyone looked at him.

"Knives?" Hiroshi asked.

"These days, every time," Sakaguchi said.

Sugamo parked across the street from the game center. They all got out of the vehicle with quick purpose, leaving Sugamo waiting at the wheel of the car.

Ueno and Osaki looked even larger in the juvenile universe of Shibuya, and out of place in their stiff, unfashionable suit coats. They hurried across the street ahead of Sakaguchi and Hiroshi. Sakaguchi stepped to the side of the building to see if there was another exit. Then, they plunged into the blast and blur of the game center arcade.

Squeals, shouts, bells, gunshots, and theme music blared from the games. High school students in uniforms wielded laser guns, punched attack buttons, and fisted joysticks with manic energy. The boys' shirts fell loose, and their pants were slung low on their thin waists. The girls hiked up the pleats of their sailor uniforms to expose the skin of their thighs.

In back, a circle of young punks skulked in one corner, their white shirts unbuttoned under off-the-rack suits. They stood around as if they ran the place, as they probably did.

Ueno and Osaki disappeared around the machines on either side of the middle row of games. Sakaguchi headed straight for the group. Hiroshi hung back. He had never actually used his kendo outside a dojo.

One of the boys in the group noticed Sakaguchi and muttered a warning in a low voice. The others positioned themselves for a fight. Sakaguchi kicked the closest kid's leg out from under him, sending him down hard, the back of his head smacking a video machine.

Hiroshi hurried to catch up and put his shoe on the kid's shoulder so he couldn't get up, and made sure the kid didn't have a knife.

Sakaguchi was looking at the other guys standing in a defensive half-circle.

No one moved.

Sakaguchi cleared his throat. "The moron lying on the ground isn't Takayuki Shibuya. So, which one of you is?"

The group tensed, defiantly quiet.

Hiroshi guessed which one was Shibuya, though they looked very much the same: tanned skin, flyaway hair, and gold chains around their necks. Hiroshi readied himself to kick whichever one of them needed it. Out of the corner of his eye, he caught sight of Ueno and Osaki coming down the outside aisles.

"Those of us with real jobs have this different sense of time. We don't like to wait. We have things to do."

The group stood quietly.

Then, as if by a predetermined signal, the one Hiroshi guessed was Shibuya bolted for the door. Sakaguchi lunged after him, but two other punks grasped at his thick arms long enough to let Shibuya get a step ahead.

Hiroshi grabbed the arm of the kid closest to him and twisted. The boy dropped to the floor. Sakaguchi flung the other kid against a game machine and shot after Shibuya, Osaki right behind.

Ueno punched the third kid's cheek before he could even move and then put a hand on the kid's shoulder to ease him down to the floor. The kid put both hands over his bleeding nose and tear-blinded eyes and slumped to the floor.

Customers looked over from their fantasy worlds, but they just kept playing. With three of the boys corralled on the floor, Hiroshi looked over at Ueno for guidance. Ueno shoved each of the guys they pinned down again, but seeing that they weren't a threat, he nodded at Hiroshi and walked off toward the door.

Hiroshi, thinking of the knife, looked back at the trio, who were picking themselves up. They showed no sign of doing anything.

Outside, Sakaguchi and Osaki were holding the ringleader—Shibuya—who made a break for it, against the outside wall of the game center, arms pinned behind his back. The other detective patted him down and took his cell phone and money roll from Shibuya's pockets.

The detectives frog-marched Shibuya across the street to the car. Sakaguchi caught his breath and said, "Shibuya-kun, I have a feeling you're the kind of young man who likes to go driving. Am I right?"

Shibuya squirmed and flailed at his arm, breathing deeply with his eyes shut. His right shoulder was out of its socket, limp and useless at his side.

Sakaguchi frowned and nodded to let him go. Sugamo grabbed Shibuya's wrist and Osaki held the kid around his scrawny chest. Shibuya moved to the side without a word, shuddering.

Sugamo leaned back into a steady, even pull, and Shibuya's arm popped back into its socket with a loud, bony click.

"Better?"

Shibuya nodded, relieved in spite of his tough attitude. He tested his shoulder.

"Let's drive a bit. It'll relax you."

Hiroshi wondered how everyone would fit, but they squeezed in with Shibuya in back and Hiroshi in front. With Sugamo at the wheel, they drove quietly through the shopping streets for a few minutes, and then pulled up onto the expressway.

As soon as they merged into the traffic, Sakaguchi leaned over the seat and cracked Shibuya across the face with his palm. Shibuya pulled his hands up, ready to block the next blow.

"That's for kicking me on the way out of the game center. Do that again and I'll rip your arm all the way off. When I come to talk to you, you talk. Understand?"

Shibuya leaned back and nodded.

Sakaguchi backhanded him again. The sound was loud in the tight space of the car.

"Speak up!"

"Hai. Yes."

"You organized high school girls to extort money out of men on the morning train, right?"

Shibuya nodded.

"Speak up!"

"Hai."

"And you're going to move into another line of work from now on, right?"

Shibuya hesitated, but then nodded again and muttered, "Hai."

"So, who are you giving this money to?"

"I have debts," said Shibuya.

"To...?"

"Different people."

"Let's stick to names, places, amounts, OK?"

Shibuya nodded but said nothing.

"You're making my afternoon difficult. Who?"

"A woman."

"Yeah? Sounds interesting."

81

One of the detectives shifted into the inflamed shoulder socket on Shibuya's sore side, making Shibuya contort in pain.

"A hostess," Shibuya said. "Works in Roppongi."

"Which club?"

"For special tastes."

"What kind of tastes?"

"For hostesses to relax after work."

"Was it the David Lounge?" Hiroshi asked, turning back toward him.

Shibuya looked up at him in the rearview mirror. "Not there. A different place called The Tulip—other side of Roppongi."

Hiroshi said nothing. Could there be a second club? It was unlikely. It must be the same. He could tell Shibuya was lying, since the two clubs were next to each other—not on opposite sides of Roppongi. He would get in there with Takamatsu when they went back to Roppongi.

"And the debts?" Sakaguchi asked.

"She loaned me money."

"And she organized you to do this?"

"She doesn't know."

"How much do you owe her?"

"A lot."

"A sharp businessman like you? Your tough friends know that?"

Shibuya shook his head.

"What's her name?"

"Michiko."

"That's her real name?"

"Yes."

"What's her family name?"

"I don't know."

"You don't know much. What's she look like?"

"Haven't seen her in a while."

"A while?"

"A while."

"She can't have changed that much?"

"She changes that much."

Osaki shifted his weight onto Shibuya's shoulder.

He twisted in pain, before he said, "She's tall, big shoulders, long hair, trim figure."

"That's half of Tokyo."

"She's strong. Fit. Muscular."

"You're not strong enough to take on a girl?" Ueno asked.

"Sounds like my kind of woman. What's her number?" Sakaguchi asked and nodded to the detective on the unhurt shoulder side.

He held up Shibuya's cell phone. Shibuya sighed.

"What's it under?" asked Sakaguchi as the detective clicked through the numbers.

"She's not in there," Shibuya said.

"Come on," Sakaguchi said, as if talking to a child.

"Really. I don't know her number. She calls me. Nothing ever happens around her she hasn't thought of."

"You must have saved one of her calls."

"She doesn't have caller ID."

Osaki scrolled through the numbers, the recent calls and missed calls, but there was nothing. He held up the screen to Shibuya and asked, "This your home address?"

Shibuya nodded.

He copied it into his notebook. "We might want to come visit you sometime."

Sakaguchi leaned over the seat. "Shibuya, where does the money really go?"

"Like I said, it's all just to her."

"*Chinpira* punks like you are too stupid to operate on their own."

"I make it how I want and pay her back little by little."

"That's it? You don't help her out other ways?"

"I owe her a lot of money."

"Maybe we should keep the whole thing?" Sakaguchi said, waving the cell phone.

Shibuya leaned back in exasperation. He had too many valuable photos and addresses on there.

Sakaguchi rolled down the front window, twisted the phone in his hand until it snapped in two, and then gave it a light backhand toss out the window where it bounced and shattered against the shoulder of the expressway.

They drove on to the next exit and pulled under the expressway onto side streets lined with manufacturing companies, distribution centers, and vacated blocks of buildings. Under an overhead highway and train line, they pulled into a deserted car park.

Osaki got out, and Ueno shoved Shibuya toward the door. Clutching his shoulder, he slowly got out of the car, ready for whatever was to come, eyes closed, shuddering slightly.

Osaki snorted at him and slid back in the car.

Sugamo pulled off, circled once around Shibuya standing alone in the wide, empty space clutching his arm awkwardly by his side amid the tall clumps of weeds springing up through the concrete.

Sugamo headed back to the small streets.

"I'm a little hungry after that workout," said Sakaguchi. "What about some ramen noodles? I know a good place close by here. Old sumo guy runs it."

"When is Takamatsu putting the unit back together?" Sugamo asked.

"Soon, he said," Sakaguchi answered. "And Hiroshi here will join us, too."

Sugamo, Ueno, and Osaki all nodded their approval.

Chapter 15

West Shinjuku gleamed like a vain architect's dream. Functional, systematic, efficient—it was a business conception of spatial order unlike the organic chaos of old Tokyo. On the sunny side of the skyscrapers, the banks of windows ricocheted splinters of sunlight back and forth between buildings rising dizzying stories into the air. Opposite the sun, the massive buildings threw shadows over the grid of straight roads and neat walkways below. Global hotel chains and offices for conglomerates bullied aside the standing bars and cheap eateries that once dotted the area, though a few noodle shops and discount stores hung on at the feet of the skyscrapers.

Michiko walked past the office workers returning in reluctant waves to their sky-world cubicles after lunch. Small clusters of women in pastel uniforms giggled, clutching wallets and cell phones. Men with serious faces left their ties tucked into their shirts to keep them from falling into noodle bowls or oily plates of fried rice.

Michiko walked to the front desk of the lobby of the 60-story NS building. Her loose summer blouse, layered skirt, and long hair flowed behind her, tousled by the wind. At the reception counter, she dropped her heavy bag like a schoolgirl and asked the receptionist to call Mark Whitlock at Bentley Associates and say Michiko was here to see him.

The receptionist smiled formally, dialing the number, her mouth covered politely. Michiko looked down on the receptionist's white pillbox hat until she hung up, bowed and pointed with a white-gloved hand toward sofas across the atrium.

A few minutes later, Mark Whitlock bounded out of the elevator and across the atrium, as athletic as a college student, but dressed for a mid-level position. He looked around for Michiko, and then aimed his thick blond hair and expensive suit toward where she stood near the windows.

She pulled her sunglasses on top of her head, amused at his curt, stiff manner. He stopped an arms-length from her.

"Not much of a welcome," Michiko said.

"I told you not to come by here," Mark hissed. "Especially not now."

"I thought you might take a break?"

"Steve killed himself, and you still—"

Michiko nodded her head and looked away.

"Did you talk to him recently?" Mark asked.

Michiko shook her head, no.

"The money for the new branch in Bangkok is missing."

"Sounds complicated," Michiko said.

"No one has a clue where it went," Mark's voice rose to where it echoed off the panes of glass. He quieted himself.

"You need a break," Michiko said, catching his eyes and holding them.

"I'll be working straight through to tomorrow morning."

"You need to recharge."

He looked at her and sighed.

She raised her eyebrows with a question.

He sighed again, unable to resist her, as always. "I'll go upstairs and make some excuse to Barbara. Tell her I think I know where the money went. That's all she cares about."

"Good, then," Michiko smiled.

"Give me 20 minutes. You going to wait here?"

Michiko nodded yes.

Mark went back across the lobby shaking his head. He pressed the elevator button, rocking on his heels as he looked at her back across the huge atrium.

When he got into the elevator, Michiko texted Reiko. "We're still on for tomorrow. Just a couple more things to do before I go. See you tomorrow, xxoo!"

Reiko was the only person she wanted—rather than needed—to say goodbye to.

The first time they ran away together, Michiko sent Reiko out front with the picnic bags and told her to wait under the back pylons beneath the apartment above the factory. Michiko left by the back window, clambering down the struts of the iron scaffolding in back of their apartment, dropping down next to the barrels of used oil.

They hurried along the canal-side footpath to an abandoned factory not far from home and squeezed inside between bent strips of rusted siding. After a minute, their eyes adjusted to the dark, and they climbed up to a landing situated above what was once a workshop that hummed with well-oiled lathes and die-casting machines. If they tried to have a picnic in the open, at a park or by the river, someone would see them and tell her father.

"This is creepy," Reiko said. "There's no one here."

"My dad said people are the only thing to be afraid of—and only some of them," Michiko said.

Reiko looked around, and Michiko smiled. "It is a little dark in here, but that makes it fun."

They settled onto empty pallets, spreading a blanket and opening a pink umbrella for atmosphere. They squirted on perfume from Michiko's mother's perfume bottle and ate onigiri rice balls in between sips of juice.

They'd just begun a new card game when the front metal door rattled open and light sliced through the dusty air.

Michiko put her arm around Reiko, pressing a finger to her lips. They rolled over onto their tummies and inched to the edge of the landing.

Michiko saw five of her father's employees in coveralls, sleeves rolled up and towels tied around their heads. She almost called out to them, thinking they were looking for her, but then she saw another man in a torn suit and ripped shirt. Three of the factory workers held long-handled wrenches in their hands and pushed him inside.

The man in the suit looked like he was drunk or asleep, and he was missing one of his shoes. She knew from his punch-permed hair and clothes that he was not a worker from another factory—and he wasn't the representative from the big company either. The five workers surrounded the man.

The man held up one hand and shimmied to his knees. He clutched his throat as he answered the workers' questions. Michiko could only catch some of their cut-down verb forms and harsh country dialect.

The five men looked at each other, as the punch-permed man leaned over with one hand on the ground.

After a long silence, one of the five men nodded.

Then, one of the workers she liked the most kicked the man in the head. The man fell flat on the factory floor and didn't move.

Michiko squeezed Reiko, who was trembling. They tucked their heads down so they couldn't see.

But they still heard the non-metallic sound of flesh being pummeled on the floor below.

When it fell silent, they looked over the edge. The workers picked up the man and set him on a thick quilt used to cushion machinery. They hoisted the heavy, folded quilt in to the back of the van outside.

They did a quick scissors-paper-stone to decide who would drive and who would ride shotgun. Two of them drove off, leaving the other three standing quietly in the shafts of dusty light.

Reiko drew herself up to her knees, clearly terrified and confused. Her knee hit a bucket, which clonked against another bucket. Michiko snatched at her friend, her elbow hitting a crumpled box of bolts whose contents spilled out with a clatter.

The three men started and turned toward the landing, shouting in their country dialect. One darted up the ladder with several quick pulls, wrench in hand.

He stopped short when he saw Michiko and Reiko, and their blankets and backpacks and picnic lunch. He stared at them for a long time.

"We were having a picnic," Michiko said.

The stillness filled the room, as the remaining men looked up at the worker on the ladder. He looked down at them and back at the girls.

Finally, he said, "Get your stuff and go home."

At home, Michiko's father stood by the upstairs door between the office and their rooms. His brown-gray face and stocky body filled the doorway. He didn't say anything, wiping his face with the small, white towel hanging around the back of his neck. Michiko could smell fish cooking and rice boiling for dinner.

Eventually, her father said, "Why don't you two girls take a bath?"

The two girls walked up the stairs then without another word.

After they'd slipped into the bath together, and had soaped up, Reiko asked Michiko, "Are we in trouble?"

"We'll see," Michiko said. "It's only the first time for you, but it's the second time for me." They dried off and changed into soft clothes before going to the living room for dinner.

Her father's cousin, Uncle Ono, was setting the fish, rice, pickles, and miso soup onto the table. To Michiko, Uncle Ono's short height made it seem as if he understood things from a child's height. When Michiko asked her father why Uncle Ono was so short, he only said, "Size doesn't matter when someone like Uncle Ono explodes."

After a first bite of rice, Michiko asked her father, "Why did they beat up that man? Did they take him to a hospital?"

Her father finished chewing, but kept his chopsticks in his hand. He wiped himself with his white neck towel and considered her. "He was a bad businessman."

Reiko, as always, watched wordlessly as Michiko and her father spoke.

"He wanted us to give him money."

"I thought the other businesses gave you money and you gave them the cranks and gears and casings?" Michiko knew the words for machine parts because she played with them before her mother got sick and couldn't pack them anymore.

"That's how it usually works, yes. But this man—with his friends—was a different kind of businessman," he said, putting fish in his mouth with his chopsticks, then carefully pulling out the small bones one by one.

"It was like you said to do if boys tried to bully me at school? Don't listen."

"Yes, it's like that. Only sometimes, not listening isn't enough. You can't give people something for nothing." He eyed Michiko. "Do you understand?"

"I think I do," she said, but it took a long time for her to fully understand what he meant.

* * *

Mark came out of the elevators, his hands tucking his cell phone into the inner pocket of his light blue summer jacket. He swept her with an outstretched arm toward the revolving doors.

As they left, Michiko thought she saw the same man who appeared at Steve's funeral. She couldn't see him through the rain and the dusk that day, but too much coincidence was not good. He stared at her then and was staring at her now. She quickly put her sunglasses over her eyes and let her hair fall around her face. She thought about stopping to take a photo of him, but let it go.

Outside on the wide sidewalk leading toward Shinjuku Station, Mark put his arm around Michiko, until they got to the other, northeast, side, where the streets got quieter. On the other side of a thick stone wall that shielded the entrance for privacy, a small fountain trickled water into a basin with a potted lotus beneath a palm tree that crowded the entry.

Mark fumbled for his money as Michiko surveyed the pictures of the rooms. He slipped a 10,000-yen note into the machine, and she leaned forward to press the button for a two-hour rental of the best room whose photo showed an ornate, red satin and gold-lined interior called, "Bedroom from Versailles."

He placed his arm around her shoulders when they got into the elevator, kissing her as the doors shut. He laughed when she slipped her arm around his waist and she pressed him against her hip, reminding herself of his weight.

Chapter 16

At the 60-story NS Building where Bentley Associates had its office, the downstairs receptionist found Hiroshi's name on the appointment list and, with her white gloves, pointed him toward the elevators. She bowed until her white pillbox hat was pointing right at him.

Takamatsu talked Hiroshi into going to Bentley because Hiroshi's English was so good, and because the first detective who went found nothing to help the case. Hiroshi complained his own cases were being postponed while he worked on Takamatsu's. Takamatsu said all cases were shared.

Hiroshi got out on the fortieth floor at Bentley Associates, and two women stood up from behind the reception desk. One of them led Hiroshi along a hallway lined by polished wood doors and floor-to-ceiling glass walls. As they approached each office, the tinted smart glass frosted over to keep each office private. After they passed by, the privacy glass automatically returned to its transparent state. The thick carpet whispered underfoot.

This is where I should have been employed, Hiroshi thought to himself. Every international company in the world needs accountants. Huge office, great view, high salary, less work, safer work—he might have been able to keep Linda with him in Japan. Straight accountancy was so much easier than illegal books. Investment scams made for exhausting work. You had to really think—and think differently.

Several hallways led to another reception area with another desk identical to the one in front. The first receptionist bowed deeply and returned the way she had come. The new receptionist stood up and smiled. She was in her twenties, with full, round cheeks that fit well with her bobbed hair and earthy blouse.

"Please come this way," said the young woman in English. She was warmer than the formal receptionist from the front desk, and acted corporate enough, but radiated the carefree energy of someone whose real life was outside of work.

"Oh, you speak English?" Hiroshi asked.

"The official language of Bentley is English and Mr. Deveaux speaks, I mean, spoke almost no Japanese," she said, looking straight into Hiroshi's eyes. "I was told you would speak English."

"Who said that?" asked Hiroshi.

"Our director, Mrs. Barbara Harris-Mitford."

"Steve's boss?"

"Everyone's boss."

"Do you mind if I have a look at Mr. Deveaux's things?"

"Mrs. Harris-Mitford said to let you do as you liked. The company has been through them already."

The earthy secretary pushed open the door to Steve's office and leaned back to let Hiroshi by, before allowing the door to shut behind them.

Hiroshi sat down at Steve's desk. Its leather top had a computer but not much else. Shelves along the wall held potted plants, a couple of thick file folders, and a few knick-knacks from different Asian countries. The office was large, with huge windows overlooking Tokyo's sprawl. It felt as if someone had once worked there long ago.

"Steve, I mean, Mr. Deveaux, was going to transfer to Bangkok, so he was winding down the office here," the secretary said.

"Were you going with him to Bangkok?" Hiroshi pulled open the desk drawers, noting that they'd already been cleaned out.

"They offered me the chance to go. But I have my life here."

"Was he a hard worker? You called him 'Steve,' I guess?"

"Yes, I call Japanese by their title and foreigners by their first name. Funny, eh? Steve was hard-working. He often stayed late."

"Was he looking forward to Bangkok?"

"Yes. He got back some of his old fire."

"He lost it?"

"Not lost, but he had a woman problem. And a drinking problem."

"Related?" Hiroshi said.

"Maybe, but he got rid of both when Bangkok came up."

Hiroshi thumbed through several folders on the shelves, just business plans, for Bangkok, it looked like—not even a schedule or calendar. It was good that Bentley didn't get into his pants pockets before the detectives did, or there would have been nothing left there, either.

"The woman problem was a wife or girlfriend or...?"

She suppressed a giggle. "He went to hostess clubs in Roppongi."

"Did they call here?"

"That wouldn't happen with Japanese men, so I was surprised when, at first, they called the office."

"He was rich."

"And unmarried," she said.

Hiroshi got down on his knees to explore under the large wooden desk. He glanced up for anything that might be taped underneath. There was nothing.

"You know...?" Hiroshi shouted from beneath the desk.

"Yes?"

"I really need to know the name of the hostess that called most often."

She paused before answering and then said, "There was one named Michiko. It's my name, too, so I remember. Maybe it was just the name she used at the club."

"Did you ever see her in person?"

"No, but I recognized her voice. She stopped calling for a long time, and then called a few times recently."

"Did you make reservations for him to go anywhere?"

"Yes, of course."

"Do you remember where?"

"Many places."

"Could you make a list for me? You can send it to me later."

"OK."

Hiroshi looked through the drawer of pens, paperclips and random office stuff. "Did Steve seem depressed?"

"Not enough to—" She looked down at the carpet.

Sitting back in Steve's chair, Hiroshi looked straight at her. "What do you think happened?"

"They said it was an accident."

"Was he the type to kill himself?"

"No one is. Are they?"

"Maybe not."

"He was self-centered," she said. "But most Americans are."

"Too self-centered to commit suicide?"

"He wouldn't have done that. He wasn't the type."

"I was also going to talk with one of the other employees, Mark Whitlock," said Hiroshi.

"Yes, he's expecting you. Mark and Steve worked together. I'll call him." She dialed Mark's line from the desk phone, but got no answer. A little surprised, she bowed before returning to her desk down the hall.

While she was gone, the fortieth floor gave Hiroshi a view of the sky changing color as a typhoon pushed toward Tokyo, the buildings, streets, rivers, parks, and canals below, all distant as a postcard.

The secretary named Michiko stepped back into the room and said, "It seems Mark is out of his office."

"I had an appointment."

"I'll call Barbara," she said.

When she hung up after talking to Barbara, she led him down the hallway to a conference table in an empty meeting room, and bowed before leaving.

He sat in one of the chairs that surrounded the twenty-person table. The table's intricate inlaid pattern, polished to perfection, reflected his face back to him as a glossy silhouette. He looked outside at the greenish darkening of the sky.

"I'm quite sorry that Mark is out of the office. He knew you were coming, but things come up unexpectedly in our business," Barbara Harris-Mitford said as she entered and closed the door. "I'm Barbara."

Hiroshi stood up and handed his meishi to her. The same secretary, Michiko, brought in two cups of coffee and left with another bow.

Barbara was a tall, serious woman with ample hips, but a fit, quick, and formal manner. She gave the impression of being personable to expedite business, but not because it came naturally. As they sat down, she reached for her name card case in her dark-blue business suit.

94

Hiroshi said, "I can meet with Mark later if you can have him contact me. If Steve's death was not suicide and not an accident, he must be careful, too."

"Are you suggesting that his death is connected with the company?" Barbara asked, touching her coffee cup but not drinking.

"That's one possibility."

"I thought the police decided it was suicide."

"What was the reaction here at the firm?"

"We were all just stunned, Mr. Shimizu."

"Please call me Hiroshi. I'm used to first names. Can you think of anything that was out of the ordinary in the days, or weeks before his death?"

"We try not to interfere with employees' personal lives, but he was a bit of a character."

"How do you mean?"

"Well, he lived the life."

"Most Japanese companies do a lot of socializing with clients. Was that part of his work here?"

"It was, yes, but he went above and beyond that."

"Nightlife?"

"He drank too much. Last year, he took time off for rehab, and came back on form. All I ask of an employee is to perform well at work. He did that—even half in the bag."

"But he performed badly outside work?" Hiroshi asked.

"We have quite a large consulting section largely through his good efforts. He was quite good at what he does. Did." She paused. "I still can't believe it."

"What was he working on the week of his death?"

"He was collecting information about purchases of unused and underused land."

"Here, or in Bangkok?"

"Here. He worked hard here, to the end, even though he was starting things for the new branch in Bangkok."

"If he was so good, why let him go to Bangkok?"

"Very simple. Steve built us up from the ground floor here. Always the right people and the right investments. We wanted him to do the same again."

"He would be in charge of a large budget then?"

"His entertainment expenses were legend, but every employee needs some indulgence."

"I meant budget for setting up the office."

Barbara thought for a minute and said, "Suffice it to say that a new office involves a very large initial outlay." Hiroshi realized only then that Barbara was older and more in control than she first appeared to be.

"Was there anyone you could think of who could benefit from his death?"

"We are a business that handles information about investing in property. That's not usually dangerous, is it?"

"What about his personal life?"

"Mark can perhaps fill you in on that."

"Are there records of his expenses?"

"We have a rather soft accounting system for things like that, frankly."

"I won't tell the tax office, but it would help to get an idea of his day-to-day."

"I'll try to get those to you."

"Who did he work with most closely?"

"Mark was set to take over Steve's client base here in Tokyo."

"Mark's name was the most often called from Steve's cell phone," said Hiroshi, pausing and waiting. "Yours was the second most often called."

Barbara nodded coolly. "As his direct boss, that shouldn't be a surprise, should it?"

"He called repeatedly the days before he died."

"Endless, last minute details about Bangkok."

"But he was still working on things in Tokyo, you said?"

"He was a worker."

"Were his personal finances in order?"

"He had an ex-wife, if that's what you mean. We were not sure who to contact, actually."

"Was there any cash anywhere?"

"Cash? American taxes for citizens abroad are complicated. Britain is easier—but we all shelter where we can."

"Was he the kind of person to commit suicide?"

"Definitely not. I tried to convince the other detective who came here of that, but he seemed reluctant to listen. Perhaps suicides are less trouble."

"They are, perhaps, when they're true."

Hiroshi and Barbara looked out the window at the looming clouds, their coffee cold and untouched.

Chapter 17

Not far from the love hotels of Shinjuku, a small tangle of back alleys rebuffed the glow from Shinjuku's neon-peppered streets. The alleys huddled tight along the train tracks converging on Shinjuku Station. The *yakitori* stands and *tachinomi* bars, their odd-angled braces and slapdash crossbeams trembled with each passing train.

Gusts of typhoon rain dripped off the ramshackle gutters and sluiced through rusted pipes onto the woven rice-straw mats slung over the alleys. Grizzled men and dough-faced women worked tirelessly all night serving shochu distilled rice liquor, cold bottles of beer, and small plates of food.

Michiko and Mark sat at the oily counter of a yakitori place at the end of the alley. Shadows fell from the single bulb dangling over the grill counter. Michiko sat up straight sipping a tepid glass of shochu. Mark leaned heavily on the counter. He roused himself to brush his thick blond hair out of his glassy eyes, an empty glass in front of him.

Michiko checked her cell phone for the schedule of trains and then settled their bill, hoisting up Mark and—half-holding, half-stumbling—guided him out the door. At the end of the alley, she leaned him against a wooden pillar as she dug into her bag for her umbrella. He was tall and hard to balance, but she maneuvered him to an underpass beneath the tracks. In the rainy night air, she'd begun to sweat with his added weight.

Near the exit, Mark suddenly stirred and shouted, "Michiko, I love you!"

"We need to hurry," she said, and kept peg-legging him forward, step by step. She checked her cell phone again and shook it as if that would give her a little more time. They could catch the last local train and ride it two stations away to a quieter station where the last express of the night would speed through without stopping.

Out of the underpass, toward the station, people walked briskly in one homeward-bound herd. Women skittered on stiletto heels, men swung briefcases, and shoppers bounced along with bags in both hands. Michiko moved Mark through the crowds as quickly as she could, irritated that Shinjuku always had too many people.

Inside the station, everyone searched for train passes or spare coins, looking up at the electronic departures board. Lovers hugged shyly in corners, and groups of friends made promises in goodbye clusters. All of them watched the time.

She maneuvered Mark close to the entrance and dug around in her purse for her pass. Then she pulled his wallet out of his pants. "Where's your pass?" she yelled at him. She dug into his pockets, but he just pulled a silent-movie, no-idea face. He wobbled forward and back.

Deep-voiced train announcements boomed through the underground passageways. People sprinted toward the gate, frantically checking overhead to be sure their train had not left yet. Michiko hurried to the ticket machines, dropped in coins, and pressed a button. It didn't matter what ticket she got; any ticket would get them through the gate.

A large sign dangled from a chain across the Keio line entrance, blocking entry. A conductor with a megaphone announced a "human incident"—the euphemism for a suicide. A handwritten scrawl on a whiteboard recommended alternative platforms for the lines that were still running.

She scowled at the conductor blocking their entry, but he was too busy to notice. She pulled out her cell phone to check the other train lines.

"I think I'm drunk," Mark stammered, smiling. "What did we drink?"

She pulled him forward toward the Shinjuku south exit. There was still an Odakyu Line train, if they could make it.

"Michiko?" Mark said into her ear. "I need to sleep."

"Soon," she answered, scrolling through the online train schedule and yanking him along by his upper arm. If she could make it, the

Odakyu Line would take them one station away to a less crowded platform where one last express came through.

She wove through the underground passageway, dodging passengers who were deciding whether to run for it, keep drinking, crash out in a capsule hotel, or pay for a taxi home.

She pulled Mark closer, against her body to keep him walking toward the gate as he slowed down, but she needed another ticket for him.

He ran a hand through his blond hair and smiled at her. "Michiko?" The bright lights from the ticket machines shone down on him like a beacon. "I need to lie down."

"Soon," was all she said as she put his ticket into the machine. She looked up at the overhead departure board and saw the train's light wink off and disappear from the list. She stamped her foot.

"Isn't there another local?" she shouted at the conductor.

He turned around to look at the board. "Train service finished," it flashed in polite Japanese.

"Not tonight," he said. "I'm very sorry."

She twisted Mark's arm until he shouted, "Ow!" They took an escalator down to another deserted underground walkway that led away from the station, the walkway storefronts all shuttered. His knees locked and unlocked until they got to a steep stairway that ascended almost two stories to street level. Mark could barely make it up the first step, much less the second.

"Where are we going?" He asked, obediently wobbling upward.

"Come on." She got behind and pushed him. She would have to help him up concrete step-by-concrete step, all the way to the top.

Halfway up, Mark wailed, "I'm so tired." There was no one in the long stairwell below. She kept shoving him upward.

Near street level, she balanced him against the handrail and hurried ahead to the top landing, looking down at him as he struggled toward her.

When he was three steps from the top, she set her body and took a deep breath.

Mark appeared surprised to find himself near the night air of the street. "Almost there," he giggled.

Michiko closed her eyes in concentration.

When she opened them, she noticed, on the periphery, a line of people waiting for taxis across the street. They were facing in her direction, scanning the street in both directions for the next taxis.

She was furious.

From the other direction, a group of business people—men and women together—hurried through the rain toward the exit/entrance, clutching black umbrellas and chattering, red-faced and amiable.

Mark stepped forward, but it was too late. There were too many people. She shouldn't have mixed it so strong. It all could have worked out, and she could have been taking a taxi to the shrine already.

She spun her umbrella, too angry to think clearly, while the drunken office workers took down their umbrellas and headed around Mark down the stairs, their drunken banter echoing in the steep stairwell.

"Made it," Mark said, pleased with himself. He stuck his hand out to feel the heavy rain outside the small glass awning. Michiko grabbed him and pushed him into the rain. He got soaked in an instant, sobering him slightly before she covered him with her umbrella. He wiped the rain from his face as she steered him down a small lane that curved back toward the station.

"Where are we going?" Mark asked.

A taxi eased along the lane, straight toward them, heading for the taxi line. Without warning, Michiko stepped in front of the taxi. It jerked to a stop. She clutched her hands together and pulled in her shoulders imploring the driver with cutesy, girlish gestures.

The driver shook his head, "no," through the windshield wipers and pointed toward the taxi line.

She twisted her body like a schoolgirl to beg him again, catching his eye and smiling.

He looked away, but when she got to the side window, pointing at Mark's condition and gesturing, "Please," the driver opened the back door.

She pushed Mark inside, leaned in and tossed a 10,000-yen note at the driver as she gave him the address, repeating it twice. To both of the men's surprise, she stepped back from the taxi.

Mark twisted, confused, trying to see her face through the fogged-over rear window, but she'd already walked away, her umbrella covering her, until she was lost in the rainy dark.

Chapter 18

"Where do you want to start?" Takamatsu asked Hiroshi, reading his notebook in the light of a convenience store a block from the Roppongi crossing. "We have a choice between Pata-Pata, Backside, Golden Showers, Man-zoku, Roomful of Mirrors or Sanctum Sanctorum?"

"They each sound awful in their own special way," Hiroshi said, ignoring Takamatsu's horse-snort laugh.

"The David Lounge is what we want. Some girl from one of these clubs will escort us in."

"Start at the top then—the Pata-Pata."

They wandered across the four-way crosswalk and headed toward Azabu, Takamatsu checking the map the secretaries printed out for them.

"Sakaguchi was impressed," Takamatsu said, "with how you handled yourself."

"I didn't get stabbed. Why's he working over there in the chikan squad anyway?"

"He took the blame for a screw-up. Budget money. It wasn't his fault."

"Whose fault was it?"

"What did you find at the dead man's company?" Takamatsu asked.

"Steve's company seemed upfront. But then, so do all the front companies."

"They all look good until they don't. Like women."

"Not everything's about women," Hiroshi said.

"That's where you're wrong." Takamatsu cut left onto a small, downhill street, heading toward an area of small bars. Takamatsu looked up at the wall of a building for the small blue street address tag. They had to backtrack. "I asked around. Seems Bentley Associates is a little too good at getting ahead of the competition."

"What do you mean?"

"They have the right information before everyone else."

"How would they get that?"

"Steal it or buy it."

"Where would they do that?"

Takamatsu stopped and spread his arms open wide.

"Here? In Roppongi?" Hiroshi looked around.

"When booze is flowing, secrets spill." Takamatsu chuckled. "All the girls have to do is listen."

"Girls?"

"Hostesses, companions, masseuses, 'delivery health girls'—whatever they call themselves. A couple years ago, during my leave—"

"Your suspension."

"I worked part-time, consulting at a company. Spying, basically. I followed employees to see where leaks happened."

"Information leaks?"

"Any kind of edge on new products, real estate sales, mergers, corporate strategy, is crucial."

"Crucial for...?"

"Making money. And saving face. Not knowing is the worst embarrassment."

"I thought we were investigating a murder."

"There's no such thing as a murder." Takamatsu walked on a few steps and then turned back and said, "It paid better, too."

"Why did you come back then?"

"Safer as a detective. They play rough in the corporate world."

"So, you think our dead guy was a corporate spy?"

"Information is the real currency of Japan," Takamatsu said.

"I thought you said it was real estate?"

"Information always comes first."

Takamatsu stopped in front of a small sign by a back staircase. "Here we are. Pata-Pata, first show, ten nightly."

A large wooden door opened to a bald-headed bouncer standing alone in a curtained area the size of a closet. He looked Takamatsu and Hiroshi over and asked how they knew the place.

"Steve," said Takamatsu. Whether the bouncer actually knew Steve or the name just sounded right, he waved them in.

A rotating spotlight wandered over the stage. Two girls in eye-patch bikinis and high heels danced listlessly. A young girl, topless, led them toward a second row seat. The girl leaned forward as she set the menu on their table, her breasts at eye level.

"You won't need plastic covers in these seats. I'll be back with your drinks in a second." She pirouetted away on high heels.

"Plastic covers?" Hiroshi wondered aloud.

Once their eyes adjusted to the dark, they could see the place was full of customers. Near-naked women in high heels walked to and fro delivering drinks. Their small, firm breasts swayed as they set down drinks, picked up empties and paraded their flesh.

"You've got to get back out there," Takamatsu said, his eyes following a waitress walking by.

"I will," Hiroshi said, taking a drink.

"You can't let one woman unman you."

"I know," Hiroshi said, drinking deeply from the iced whiskey.

A shout erupted from the crowd. Two nude women strode from the back of the bar. Spotlights hit the stage. The dancing girls were gone, and waitresses pulled back a tarp to reveal a huge pit of gray mud sunk into the stage. Men in the front row giggled, pulling a long sheet of plastic up to their necks.

A nude, black woman with large breasts swayed back and forth for the crowd. Everyone clapped wildly. A second woman—Japanese with a full, round body, a surprisingly thin waist and weightlifter arms and shoulders—took the stage with her hands raised over her head.

Takamatsu laughed and Hiroshi couldn't help it. He laughed, too. The crowd and noise and drinks and the unabashed nakedness was intoxicating.

The girls squared off and went right to it. They leapt into the knee-deep pit of mud, locked each other around the shoulders, the crowd whooping as one. Tables of drunken salarymen were already out of their chairs hooting till they were red in the face.

The women toyed with the crowd. They faked judo throws and karate chops. They slogged in and grappled in the wet grayness. They positioned their breasts like weapons, wiggled their asses against the plastic, and humped each other, finally slathering handfuls of mud onto the long plastic sheet under which the front row cowered in titillation.

"How's that!" shouted Takamatsu.

"Unbelievable!" Hiroshi agreed, his eyes riveted by the spectacle.

The match ended when the women came together in a muddy embrace, kissing.

As they came down off the stage, one drunkard leapt up and blocked the path of the women wrestlers. The black woman, used to it all, grabbed him in a full-body hug that sent the crowd into collective spasms. The man spun around proudly dripping mud from his white shirt and tie. His friends gave him a standing ovation.

The crowd quieted with fresh drinks. Hiroshi noticed that every table had an identical bottle of whiskey, ice cubes, water pitcher, tongs, and drink stirrer.

Takamatsu waved for the waitress. When she came over, he whispered in her ear. She shook her head, no, but leaned down to listen as Takamatsu continued, her breasts bobbing in front of his face. Finally, smiling, she leaned back, focused on Takamatsu, and shook her head again, no. She set the bill on the table, and Takamatsu pushed it over to Hiroshi.

Hiroshi looked at the bill and said, "They must've been wrestling in pure silver!"

Takamatsu took a look. "That puts a crimp in our investigations."

Takamatsu flipped cash onto the table, and a large bald man in a soft black suit came over to collect it.

"Everything okay this evening, gentlemen?" the man asked, in a gruff rumble.

"Great," said Takamatsu. "It's all right to bring foreign clients next time?"

"We take credit cards," answered the man, tucking the money into a thick, black leather waist pouch inside his suit. He escorted them out, handing them a flyer from a stack at the door. "Here's our monthly calendar of events."

108

Outside on the sidewalk, Takamatsu said, "Golden Showers was next on the list."

"What's that?"

"The girls urinate. That's the golden shower. It costs double if you want it on you."

Hiroshi contemplated this with drunken curiosity. "Kind of a pervert," Hiroshi said at last.

"Who?"

"The dead guy."

"He's not a pervert now. He's dead."

Hiroshi nodded. "What's after that?"

Takamatsu looked it over for a minute: "Roomful of Mirrors."

"It has to be cheaper than fresh urine!"

"Let's hope." Takamatsu charged ahead. "Still, it's Roppongi genius to turn girl piss into profit."

The front entranceway of Roomful of Mirrors had a signboard featuring photos of the girls inside. At the door, a young man wearing a tuxedo waved them in through a mirrored wall that turned out to be a sliding door.

The interior had mirrors covering every surface. Beams of blue, green, red, orange, purple, and yellow light reflected off of tables and plastic-covered sofas dotted with small mirrors. Wall mirrors were set at various angles, all visual sense of up and down was lost, reflection and reality reversed. Only the tug of gravity kept everyone upright.

Naked girls in high heels, thongs and barrettes, danced on alcove stages and small platforms hanging from the ceiling, while others ambled among the tables. Their bodies were covered in pasted-on glitter from which sparkles changed colors as they moved.

Takamatsu and Hiroshi stood stunned for a minute before two girls came over to lead them to a sofa. The men flopped down next to the naked, friendly and twinkling women.

"What's your name?" the woman next to Takamatsu asked.

"Uh, Mizoguchi," stuttered Takamatsu, "And that's Sato."

"Where have you been tonight?"

"A lot of places," Hiroshi stammered. He felt drunk already.

Takamatsu lit cigarettes for the girls, "And what're your names?"

They leaned back to inhale, which lifted up their breasts.

Hiroshi stared.

"Yoko from Osaka and Yoko from Sapporo."

"Easy to remember."

"You have to remember the city."

Takamatsu laughed. Hiroshi felt strange sitting with two naked women who acted as if everything were normal. He couldn't remember ever just sitting with a naked woman he didn't know; he remembered lying down, having sex, showering, but never sitting casually on a sofa. Could one of these women be capable of pushing a man in front of a train?

A whiskey bottle appeared with four glasses, ice cubes and bottled water. Takamatsu's Yoko bobbed up to mix the drinks, strong for the boys and weak for the girls. Hiroshi wondered how strong the whiskies were and how many the girls drank each night.

"This is a nice club," said Hiroshi.

"They keep it too cold," said Hiroshi's Yoko.

Takamatsu's Yoko said, "I'm shivering by the end of the night."

"You need to be warmed up," leered Takamatsu.

"Ooohhh, you're right!" both Yokos laughed. Takamatsu rolled up his sleeves and let his hand drop onto her thigh.

"You work every night?"

"We're part-time."

"Do you have a day job?"

"Sort of," they laughed again. "That's part-time, too!"

"Where do you work?" they asked.

Takamatsu quickly leaned forward. "We're in foreign trade. So, we're just checking this place out to see if it's good to bring customers."

"We have foreigners here all the time," said Hiroshi's girl.

"You do?"

"They always get more embarrassed. It's fun!"

"I guess they would," said Takamatsu. "Wouldn't they?"

"Maybe it's because they never bathe together like in Japanese families?"

"One time, this guy kept choking on his drink. It was so funny. So inhibited, the foreign guys."

"Until they get you in a room!" They both laughed at this.

110

Takamatsu took over the drink mixing. He handed two tumblers to the Yokos who eyed them to be sure they were not too strong. Takamatsu, knowing their stay-sober game, laughed. The girls poured more water in theirs when Takamatsu leaned back to light a cigarette.

"You like working here?" asked Hiroshi.

The Yokos looked confused at the question.

"I used to work as an office lady, but this pays better."

The other Yoko said, "The last place I worked the customers could paint our bodies with Day-Glo paint that lit up under black lights."

"What?" Hiroshi blurted, stifling a laugh.

"They had brushes or used their hands and covered our bodies with glowing colors. It was a mess at the end of the night. We had to really scrub in the shower. You can't believe where the paint would end up," she said.

"And they always painted your nipples. It was caked on there by the end of the night, and hurt!" Both Yokos touched their breasts and laughed.

They had more drinks and paired off to chat.

At last, Takamatsu said, "Well, girls, we must get going. What time do you get off? We'll take you out for a meal later, what do you say?"

The girls hesitated. "There's a strict no dating policy," they both said.

"It's not a date. It's dinner."

They both giggled.

"No need to tell anyone. It's just dinner," Takamatsu insisted.

They squirmed in their seats and whispered to each other.

"Give us your number. We'll call you when we're done. We get off at one or one-thirty."

Takamatsu smiled and wrote out his and Hiroshi's numbers on two pieces of paper—one for each girl. "Put this someplace safe!" he said.

They giggled, and tucked them inside the front of their thongs. When he peered down where they tucked them, Hiroshi noticed that the thongs actually had a small inner pocket. Maybe for tips, he wondered.

"What are your real names?"

"I'm Mina."

"I'm Sae."

"We'll take you to a nice meal."

The girls bowed deeply, their breasts bobbing as they stood up to walk them out through the maze of mirrors. At the mirrored door, the two girls waved good-bye. The cashier/doorman took the money from Takamatsu and handed him a discount coupon for the next visit.

Outside on the street, Hiroshi said, "It's a little strange, isn't it?"

"What?"

"Sitting with naked girls. It's more about power than sex."

"That's why it costs so much," Takamatsu said. "The clothed ones were more expensive."

"Will they call?" asked Hiroshi.

"They're our only bet for getting inside the David Lounge."

The men walked to an all-night book store to get out of the rain and stood reading under the bright lights with other customers, all of them seeming to be waiting for someone or something.

Just after one, Takamatsu's phone rang, and he nodded happily into his phone, rolling down his carefully folded sleeves and shooting his cuffs into place.

"We're on," he said from the aisle across from Hiroshi, who put his magazine back onto the rack.

Chapter 19

Hiroshi's eyes refused to open at the first buzz of his cell phone. He elbowed himself up and reached for its jittering body in the pocket of his jacket, which was flung over a chair, under his crumpled pants. He only had to lean over as the room had just enough space for a double bed and a chair.

He tried to cobble together what happened the night before—dinner, drinks, dancing, kissing, what-was-her-name, Mina, fumbling with clothes, fumbling with condoms. Nothing sharpened to believability in his mind.

He pushed back the nausea and answered his cell phone.

"Hai?"

He held it a ways from his ear, but Takamatsu's voice came through, "Where did you go?"

"Good question."

"You and Mina took off."

"We did?"

"I can understand why."

"Weren't you with—what was her name?"

"Doesn't matter."

"Did you find anything?"

"I have a surprise for you here."

"Where's 'here'?"

"Your office. Where you usually are—except today."

"I'm on my way. Did you get in to the David?" Hiroshi asked.

Takamatsu hung up.

Hiroshi flopped back onto the bed. He recognized the love hotel décor from his college days. Cheap red velvet upholstery, mirrors

113

on the ceiling and walls giving the illusion of a bigger room. He remembered they ate a big meal and drank a lot of wine in an Italian place. Wine on top of whiskey. He looked at himself in the ceiling mirror. The mirror framed his solitude and the hangover hung it to the wall. When had she left?

He remembered fleeting bits of sex—the first since Linda—her reflection in the mirror when he opened his eyes. He felt her still. He threw his legs over the edge of the bed and went to the bathroom, turned on the light, turned it off, turned the water very hot and let the shower jumpstart his body. His eyeballs felt like they were roasted in salt.

* * *

Outside he hailed a cab. His clothes were still damp from the rain. His socks were sodden. He suddenly panicked, thinking he had lost his wallet. He slapped his pockets and found his wallet, then panicked it would be empty. He opened it and everything was still there. Had he paid for anything? Had she paid for it all?

She was pretty when she relaxed, gorgeous in the shower, almost as tall as he was, and easy inside her own body. Did he get her number or she, his? He had not been so drunk since Linda left, when he had been drunk every night for weeks.

Mina had been lively, active, pushing him onto the bed, pulling at his clothes, whipping hers off in a kind of dance, dragging him into the shower and back out again, whipping him with a towel, thumping him with one of the pillows. She knew how to enjoy herself—something Hiroshi had forgotten.

He could remember bits and pieces: her looking down on him from above, grinding into him, using him—slowly, repeatedly, methodically. Mina had known what she wanted and got it. Hiroshi wondered if he had, too.

He hurried into his office before anyone could see him. He kept a clean shirt, underwear and socks in a file cabinet drawer. He was unwrapping the plastic from a dry-cleaned shirt when a woman he'd never seen before walked in.

She let out a surprised, "Oh!" and almost dropped her armload of folders. She juggled them to keep them from tumbling to the floor.

She gaped at his naked chest—hairier than most Japanese men—and his unbuttoned pants.

She set the folders on the desk and turned away, but didn't retreat. Working with homicide detectives, she thought she had heard it all. Now she could say she had seen it all.

Hiroshi turned away from her, talking over his shoulder. "Excuse me," he said, as he worked buttons. It was an effort; he felt like even his fingers were hungover. "What—"

"I'm sorry," she said, "I'm Kido. Akiko."

Hiroshi shook his head, confused.

"Didn't Takamatsu tell you? Your new assistant?" Akiko said, speaking to the wall.

"Guess he wanted to surprise me."

"He succeeded, it seems."

"I'm, well, you know who I am, I guess. Hiroshi Shimizu. Please call me Hiroshi."

Akiko was like a setter on a volleyball team: sturdy and solid. Most Japanese would consider her plump the way her body rounded out her knee-length skirt and tight-knit top. But she was narrow in the waist and had a thin face with wide, brown eyes.

"Please call me Akiko," she said, bowing to the wall.

"I usually dress at home."

"But not always?"

"Not today."

Hiroshi tucked in his shirt and zipped his pants up with as much dignity as he could muster.

"I brought the folders from Takamatsu," she said, trying to decide whether to say more, or wait for him, or just stand there.

"I usually don't come in so late," he said, adjusting his belt, and then, finally straightening up and turning toward her. Sensing him dressed now, Akiko stole a glance.

They both looked down at his bare feet.

He reached for a pair of fresh socks from the file drawer and sat down at his desk to pull them on. He rolled up his damp clothes from the night before, bundling them into the ripped-open dry cleaning bag.

"Was Takamatsu here?"

"He was, but he left. He said for you to go ahead and solve the case and he'd be down in an hour." Her face had lovely, crescent-shaped dimples. Her eyes were wider than most Japanese woman, which reminded him of Linda's. Her hair was dyed light brown and cut squarely along the ends.

"I decided to put my desk here. Is that all right?" she asked. That was what was different. He was too hungover to notice the desk on the way in.

"That's about the only space left," Hiroshi said. They both sat down and started to arrange things on their desks in silence.

"How is Takamatsu paying you?" Hiroshi asked in a serious tone.

"What do you mean?" she said, cocking her head.

"I mean, well, Takamatsu got money from somewhere."

"I came over from administration, if that's what you're asking." A note of indignation slipped into her voice.

"I'm sorry. It doesn't matter. I, we, I could use your help."

"Apparently."

"Do you speak English?"

"I went to Ohio State for four years."

"What did you study?"

"Sociology," she said. "Listen, is this an interview? Maybe you don't need—"

"No, just—look, it's not an interview. I'm not used to having to apologize when I come in to work."

"Do you come in like this every morning?"

"Did Takamatsu say what you would be doing?"

"Look, I can probably still get moved back."

"That wasn't what I meant." Hiroshi wished Takamatsu had said something about her. "I'm just not used to having anyone else around. I just—"

Akiko looked around his office, hoping for the best. It was a small office with just one detective and she was used to being in a big room with dozens of them. She thought it would be a nice change, but now, she wasn't so sure. She stopped herself from sighing by asking, "Are there any other files you need now? Or just these?"

Hiroshi thought for a minute, self-consciously doing one last shirt button. "I requested a list of train suicides. Could you check on that?"

"It's there in the pile." She leaned back with a little bounce.

"If you could search the databases to find out how many suicides were reported, and where they were, I want to check them against the railway reports."

"I'll start someone on that. What else?" She leaned over her desk to write on a notepad.

"There's a list of places the dead man went in one of the files. Find out who owns those places and whatever else you can," said Hiroshi.

"Do you want information or scuttlebutt?"

"Both."

She picked up the files, raised her eyebrows and asked, "Anything else?"

"I, I mean, we, want to see where the trails of information and money cross."

"Where would those trails start?"

"I don't know, but they have to start somewhere."

Akiko wondered what she was supposed to say back to that. Usually, detectives were brimming with confidence and clear directions.

"Do you drink coffee?" Hiroshi asked.

"Yes, I'll go get some. What—"

"No, I want to make it for you. I have a good coffee maker." He said, nodding toward the shelf that held a gleaming red Italian coffee maker.

"Oh, well, OK, yes, I love coffee." She was so used to getting detectives tea, she'd stopped thinking about it. Having coffee made for her would at least make the new arrangement tolerable.

"I don't trust anyone else with it," he said. "And I don't trust anyone who doesn't like coffee. Hope you like it strong?"

"Very strong."

"Even better."

"I'll take these folders over and be back in a few minutes."

"Coffee'll be ready by the time you get back."

She returned after a few seconds. "Does it smell like disinfectant in here?"

Hiroshi looked up and started to explain about the room having been storage and the lack of windows, but Akiko cut him off.

"I'll get a fan from maintenance," Akiko said, and left.

Hiroshi sat back with a pad of paper and put his feet up on the desk. He closed his eyes while the hangover bloated his thoughts with confusion, guilt, nausea, and irritation. He hadn't asked for anyone to come help him. Takamatsu was a pain. He hadn't even thought of using a fan to get the smell out, though he'd start letting it run all night.

The foreigners whose scams he tracked always left a trail. It was like they couldn't help themselves. Many of them got caught only because they wanted to stick their tongues out at the authorities. To find them was a process of finding the right thread and then pulling it, pulling it hard.

Chapter 20

"You're dressed," Akiko said with brisk confidence, arranging the folders in her hands for his easy reading. "You are isolated over here. It's a bit of a walk."

"You'll soon find that's a good thing."

"Here are the reports on suicides. Last year there were over 2,000 suicides at train stations in Japan," she read, "And over 30,000 suicides for the year."

Hiroshi whistled. "That many?"

"One suicide every fifteen minutes. Five or six a day by train."

"We just need the foreigners. And just on trains."

"They have some of those noted, but it might include Koreans and Chinese. I'll call the office of statistics to see how they count them and whether they have specific records for foreigners."

"Maybe it's faster to call the embassies. Start with the Western embassies, but be careful what you say. The last thing we want to do is stir up trouble. Unless it helps."

"You want to line up the times and dates and places, right?"

"Yes. Details in order turn into patterns."

She got up again, but Hiroshi said, "Coffee's ready. Hope you like it black?"

"It's not dessert," she said. "I'll be back in a minute." Akiko looked at the coffee, smiled and walked off.

Hiroshi stared after her. He looked at his door, which was usually closed. She'd left it open. It was going to take some getting used to, having someone in the office. He would have to think of what to ask her to do, to stop doing everything himself. He couldn't think with her going in and out and asking questions all the time. He would have to take longer walks by himself.

Hiroshi poured himself a cup of coffee and leaned back in his chair and shut his eyes. He could picture the dead man, Steve, and his younger colleague, Mark, walking the streets of Roppongi, cocky, loose, proud. He imagined them in the Venus de Milo, laughing a little too loudly, lightly intimidated by the women's cultivated sexiness, but attracted to their seeming acquiescence, their exoticism. Most foreigners, like Japanese, could never imagine that the corporate secrets they let slip so carelessly could be bought and sold.

Why hadn't Steve taken a taxi or stayed at a love hotel? Why had he been in the train station at all? There could be only one reason. Takamatsu was right. Why push a man, or rather, flip him in front of a train? If the killer was able to make money from Steve's information, why stop the flow of valuable info? Why not string him along? Even if Steve had moved to Bangkok, he'd still have been helpful. Maybe money wasn't the issue—or maybe it was only part of the issue?

Takamatsu knocked as he walked straight in to Hiroshi's office.

"Got it all figured out?" he said, heading for the coffee machine.

"Almost, until you interrupted."

Takamatsu flipped a tied bundle of files onto his desk and poured himself a cup of coffee. "How's Kido-san? Cute, eh? Smart, too."

"She's only going to get in the way."

Takamatsu shook his head. "You'll see she's a lot more help than you think."

"I do my best thinking alone."

"You can talk it through with her before thinking alone. I have twenty detectives in my office over in the main building," Takamatsu said, laughing. "You should learn to think in public, like a Japanese."

"Did you get into the David?" Hiroshi asked.

Takamatsu nodded, yes. "Did you break your dry spell?"

Hiroshi frowned.

"I can tell that means yes," Takamatsu said, sipping his coffee, and then looking for sugar and creamer.

"Black only," Hiroshi said.

Takamatsu sighed. "The David didn't have much. Hostesses, their dates, drinks. So, I started thinking it might just be a suicide. Too hard to prove otherwise."

"You did?" Hiroshi sat forward, confused.

"I did. But when I got to the office this morning, I got called to administration. The chief introduced me to the head of the American Chamber of Commerce, the PR Division Head for Japan Railways, and the new chief of detectives. I hadn't met the new chief in person before. He just came over from the Justice Ministry. Total bureaucrat."

"You talked to all three? All together?"

"I got talked to. I didn't say a word. They told me to find out who did it and make sure nothing leaks to the press. If the media gets this, it'll be murdered foreigners, unsafe trains, and incompetent cops."

"A triumvirate of failures."

"A trium-what?"

"Three failures."

"Ah, a triple play."

They drank their coffee in silence.

After a while, Takamatsu said, "The good news was they said, 'spare no expense.'"

"Can't we announce it's a suicide to buy more time?"

"Better to say nothing. Dead foreigners make Japanese officials nervous. And dangerous trains make everyone nervous."

"Kido-san's checking on the suicides. There must be other suicides that weren't suicides. Let's look again at the girl in the video, maybe we can go from there."

"What video?" asked Akiko, walking in.

"Kido-san, our angel of investigation!" Takamatsu got up and bowed dramatically.

"Takamatsu, you might have told Hiroshi I was coming," Akiko said.

"Where's the fun in that?" Takamatsu smirked. "Show her the video," he commanded.

Hiroshi cued the video up on his computer. "It's only a few blurry seconds, but let's look again. Since we're under orders."

Hiroshi let Akiko sit in his chair to watch the video clip as he poured her a cup of coffee.

Akiko watched and then rewound the snippet of video and let it play again. "Look how she walks, with dignity, but also with training. Her clothes are not off the rack. They're from a boutique. Ginza or Aoyama," Akiko said.

"So, she's rich?" Hiroshi said.

"Or knows someone who's rich. And she's definitely with him," Akiko said.

"How can you tell?" Takamatsu asked her.

"The way she almost reaches for him when he wobbles—right there!" She pointed at a spot in the video as Takamatsu and Hiroshi bent in to look. "That's not what a woman would do with a stranger or a casual friend."

"But she doesn't touch him."

"Doesn't matter. You can see she moves to touch him. Watch." Akiko backed up the video and let it run. "There. And her hair has an unusual cut. Most hostesses have curlicues and piled layers. Hers is more tasteful, meaning more expensive. She uses professional treatments, antioxidants, proteins and vitamins. See the way it shimmers? Her regular hairdresser might recognize her from behind. Her hair looks dyed, too."

"Looks black to me."

"Hers is blacker than black. It's dyed."

Takamatsu was, for once, quieted.

Hiroshi waited for more.

Akiko continued, "She's a meter eighty. Seventy, seventy-five kilos. She works out. A lot. Look at her legs—there. She stands more like a man, legs apart. Athlete or martial arts. Her lace-up sandals shouldn't be too hard to find. Designers like that sell at only one or two boutiques."

"What does her face look like?" Takamatsu said, joking. The video angle was only from behind.

"A woman like that is gorgeous."

"How can you tell?"

"You can just tell," Akiko said, shrugging her shoulders.

"Every woman in Tokyo looks great from behind!" Takamatsu laughed.

Akiko growled her exasperation with him and said, "It's not so hard to flip a man if he isn't expecting it. And no man ever expects it from a really attractive woman."

Takamatsu and Hiroshi cleared their throats and watched as Akiko played it back again, watching to the end.

Akiko continued: "The suicide reports from Japan Railways will be here this afternoon. The police reports mentioned an interview with the train drivers not included in the final railway report. I'll find the drivers. They'll be worth talking to."

Takamatsu and Hiroshi paused, waiting to see if she was finished.

"As for motive," continued Akiko, "If it's a woman killing a man, I can think of a million reasons."

Chapter 21

Michiko walked beneath the raised highway that divided her old neighborhood from the new apartment complexes closer to Kawasaki Station. The matching beige apartment buildings looked like toy boxes dropped at random by a massive child. Newly planted flower beds and trees propped up with struts dotted the fitted-brick walkways and rolled-out grass turf.

Housewives hung out futons over the railings of identical balconies, a patchwork of bedding up and down the buildings. The whomp-whomp of futon-beaters reverberated through the air, the housewives thrashing out dust and sweat and clumps of stuffing along with frustration.

From the other side of the sound-insulated highway, the metallic-sulfur stench from thousands of small factories and foundries, most now abandoned, steered Michiko home. The farther she got from the stylish apartments, the older and more used everything became.

The older Kawasaki residents, rough and robust, had mostly retired, died, or moved away, replaced by pale office workers and their soft, uncertain families. The area became a place to sleep, not to make things. Thriving factories became boxed-in bedrooms.

Michiko stopped at the shrine nearest her home. With the "*taifu ikka*"—the fresh, clean air after a typhoon, the sky seemed high and far away over the shrine grounds. The main pillars of the building had started to soften and decay. Only the gravel and tamped earth resisted. Incense from morning visitors smoldered in the large urn by the main building.

She was startled at how much the old cherry trees had spread and grown, the branches now drooping under their own weight.

With the years, their shapes had grown fuller and thicker, the bark coarser. One or two had been cut down, damaged in storms—but they looked somehow wiser and more beautiful than ever. She and Reiko waited for her father, his last year, under the trees, to have a *hanami*. Michiko stopped at the spot.

* * *

Reiko and Michiko got to the shrine early to set up the plastic tarp. They set out the rice balls, tea, *senbei* rice crackers, and, for him, beer. In April, when the year's orders were just coming in, her father could get away for a few hours to go for a meal, a walk, and cherry blossom viewing party.

Reiko and Michiko chatted as the blossoms fell and dotted the grounds white and pink, with a dash of dark pink from one of the trees. While waiting, they tried not to nibble everything, checking on the beer to be sure it was still cold. They played a card game and used cherry blossoms as point markers, giggling when petals blew away in the breeze, ruining their count.

When one of the workers came to get them, Michiko was furious. She packed up the rice balls, tea, and cakes they had laid out and stormed home. Michiko charged up the stairs to demand an explanation for why her father broke his promise.

The factory workers, with bandages, slings and ice packs on their heads, were in the midst of a heated discussion. Michiko saw the bandage around her father's arm but she still shouted, "You promised to come."

The workers looked down. They had been encouraging him to spend more time with his daughter, taking on extra tasks to free up time, and telling him a boss was entitled. But that day, things had gone awry.

Her father spoke calmly, "We'll go tomorrow."

"I don't want to go tomorrow," Michiko said, staring at him, her face red with anger.

Her father waited for her storm to pass, while the workers kept their eyes averted.

Finally, Michiko stomped off through the door into their living quarters. Reiko, as always, followed dutifully behind.

Later that night, Michiko's father came to her room. Reiko was asleep, but Michiko was still reading by the light on her study desk. When he sat on the edge of her bed, she pretended to ignore him.

"You're just like your mother—beautiful, smart and hot-tempered. Her family was a samurai family. I told you before. Do you remember?"

Michiko nodded slightly, but kept reading her book.

"I want to explain what happened. I think you are old enough. We lost our contract to the big company. We had to give up our long-time small contracts to take the bigger one. But now, that big company cut back, so we don't have either the small ones or the big one."

Michiko listened but still did not speak.

"And you remember the other bad businessman? The one you saw in the factory that day you ran away? Well, his friends came back. They pressured us to take new contracts." He fiddled with the bandage, readjusting the stretchy wrap around his forearm. "We refused, but they insisted. Some of the workers had enough, so a fight started. I had to stop it. That's why I couldn't come today. I was looking forward to the *hanami* just as much as you."

Michiko looked down at her book.

"We're going to go again, okay? I promise."

Michiko kept the promise to her mother not to cry.

"Are you okay?" she asked, tears starting.

Her father held his arm up. "I just hurt my arm a little. It's okay. I can work."

"Before mother died, she said I had to take care of you," Michiko said, looking over at a sleeping Reiko so he could not see her face. "But I don't know how."

"You're doing a very good job," her father said, ignoring her sniffles.

"I'm going to start aikido."

"Are you?"

"To help."

"Help?"

"In case," Michiko said.

127

She walked around the outer balcony of the shrine, its floorboards creaking. She stopped by the open shutters in the back where the fox statues that had scared her when she was a little girl were lined up along the stone wall in back. Then, she continued around and went down the stairs to the wooden votive *ema* plaques.

She pulled a new one from the stand, and placed her coin in the payment box. She pulled a pen from her purse and wrote on the wood carefully.

Kamisama, Kigan. Protect me. Help me to get my tasks done, so I can leave. Help me to do them right. Grant me a safe journey. I can't keep going on my own. I have to keep going. I'm almost ready to go.

She hung it on one of the higher racks. It would be burned with the others during the fire ceremony in a month's time.

Two blocks from the shrine, Michiko stopped to look at her old aikido dojo. The martial arts training hall now leaned to the side, the wood mildewed and termite-eaten. The hours she spent there learning from Sato sensei after the failed *hanami* taught her more than just self-defense.

* * *

"Balance is everything," Sato sensei said on the first day. He made her stand on one leg, then the other, then stand leaning forward, and then leaning back. She kept falling over, catching herself with her other foot, or her hand, asking him how to do it right. He said nothing but made her practice landing and rolling and blocking and dodging. He never smiled, but spoke in a voice that rose from inner depths. "You try too hard," he said.

She practiced until she could do whatever it was he showed her. He never scolded or praised, only showed her and advised her. After the first few months, she never asked for an explanation and never again tried too hard.

"Timing is everything," he said, and by then she knew better than to ask why. She worked on the timing of punches, throws, joint locks, escapes, blocks, reverses, twists, until time was inside her. Aikido was about the inside, no matter what happened outside.

When she won her first contest, she carried the trophy to Sato sensei. He put her trophy on a shelf and worked her harder than ever, though she had planned to take the day off. Sato sensei did not look like he had much power in his tiny frame. His long gray hair and lanky posture made him look older than he was, but one circular sweep of his hand could topple Michiko to the mats, hard and quick.

After each of the contests she won, he followed the same routine, working her to exhaustion. Whenever she felt she was at last truly ready for the workout, Sato sensei showed her she was not, dropping her to the mat in a new way. The floor became her friend, just as he had said. "There is always more to master," he told her when she could try no more.

Years later, after Michiko had stopped aikido for a long time, she showed up again at the dojo. Sato sensei took her back as if she had never left, and helped her to gradually reestablish the form she had lost. He gave her more intense instruction as an adult, much of which she spent on the tatami mats where he dumped her, just as he had when she was a teenager. He sensed she needed to burn something out, and burn in something new. He didn't ask her what it was. He just kept pushing her past her limits, a place she liked to—or had to—be.

* * *

She pushed aside the memory of his funeral—which she paid for since he had no family other than his students—and wondered if Sato sensei would appreciate the irony of his dojo training hall crumbling, though his lessons endured. The irony was similar for her father.

She walked over a footbridge of welded beams just wide enough for a handcart, one of many that crossed the long canal. Kudzu vines and water reeds overran the banks, and a trickle of water pooled here and there, dribbling on, reluctantly.

Both sides of the street were lined with two- or three-story structures of corrugated metal bolted onto I-bar frames. Long chains, thick as an arm, dangled across front doors, the locks rusted shut. A few gave well-oiled evidence of recent use, for storage, not production.

Her father had always taken her for walks all over the area, so she knew everyone. Back then, the entire area was a cacophony of manufacturing. Now, it was silent.

Even the *koban* police box had been moved. She hated the place and had walked on the other side of the street for years after her father died.

She remembered sitting in the front chair across from the local policeman, explaining over and over to them and refusing to cry. She came all the way in from the city in a taxi and spent the morning and the next day there after her father was hit by a car and killed. The detectives didn't listen to her because she was dressed in a slinky one-piece and was made up like a model.

Her father had been drunk, the policemen said. He stumbled in front of the car, they said. Michiko explained to the police that was impossible. He seldom drank and never to excess. She demanded an investigation.

The investigators never found the hit-and-run driver. She was sure they hadn't looked too hard.

After that, Michiko divided her time between her apartment in Roppongi and her old room, trying to sort out who was owed what. She discovered a trail of what looked like bad decisions, but her accountant in Akasaka—after she got him to go over the paperwork—told her the debt was probably forced on her father. The workers knew almost nothing about the factory's budgets or how her father handled the money. But they offered to work without pay until it was all cleared up. Uncle Ono knew even less about the debts.

Little by little, the workers found other jobs. Michiko tried her best to restart the factory, collect the little they were owed and postpone any of the bills she could. But without her father there to arrange new contracts, no new ones came in. Eventually, all that was left was Uncle Ono and a mountain of debt.

She walked up the steel grate steps, stooping under the low ceiling, to the second-floor office. Metal desks were pushed together in the middle of the room. Along the back wall was a row of filing cabinets and glass-fronted bookshelves holding record-keeping logs, spiral notebooks, and file boxes.

From the window over the factory floor, she looked down at the press drills, precision lathes, spray guns, and belt sanders. Seeing

Uncle Ono working on the machines calmed her. He was so short he had to get up on tiptoes to reach the ball-end handles of some machines, but his wiry, pointed energy pulled them down with ease. Out of habit more than expectation, he kept the machines running, polishing the drill presses and making sure oil was worked into the points of friction on the grinder, thread roller and lathes, even though orders no longer came in.

Michiko walked down the narrow hall to her childhood room. The room was packed tight with three beds, a study desk, two chests of drawers and a small closet fashioned from pipes. She dug in the drawers for an oversized T-shirt and pulled it on, dropping her other clothes in a pile on the pink shag rug.

She sat on the edge of the bed, looking at her study desk. Its upper shelf held English dictionaries, textbooks and French self-study books, practice guides for college entrance exams, and brightly-colored preparation folders. On a small bookshelf, matching sets of manga in serial order were lined up next to novels in alphabetical order.

The walls held a poster of Hide, her favorite singer, and Disney movie posters for Mulan, Cinderella and Pocahontas. A small box, covered in red washi paper held earrings, necklaces and bracelets, expensive gold she got as presents from clients mixed in with plastic junk she bought herself when she was young. She dug out a hair tie and spritzed perfume on the maroon pillow and futon to mask the mustiness.

Her collection of *kokeshi* dolls—wooden, woman-shaped spindles with black hair and eyes and red lips and kimono—were arrayed on a shelf over her bed. The workers who specialized in lathe work from Miyagi and Akita made hundreds of these dolls for her, each a different height and width. Goddesses of the lathe, they formed a protective forest above her bed. With the gentle rumble of the workshop lathe and the soothing lotus perfume on her pillow, she fell deep asleep.

Chapter 22

For a moment, Hiroshi could see the eyes of the driver staring straight ahead before the train blurred into a flash and shot on. The whoosh of the massive steel, solid as a building, blasted a wall of air that made him step back to brace himself. The express train was so close he could touch it. And it was gone, though its slipstream sucked him a step toward the tracks and let him go.

After a few minutes, the local slowed alongside the platform. Hiroshi got on the front car, right behind the driver's cabin. The doors shut, and he looked in. The driver's hand rested on a silver accelerator lever that eased the train forward at a steady pace. On the driver's control panel, the speedometer and pressure gauge sprang and climbed. An old-style, wind-up train watch set firmly in a frame ticked the minutes between stations.

The train picked up speed, and overhead wires, fencerows, piles of gravel, and sidetracked maintenance cars slipped by. Hiroshi blinked, focused and refocused on fleeting buildings, billboards, sidewalks, and streets. The speed gauge trembled at 80 kilometers an hour, not as fast as an express, but fast enough.

When the train came to a stop in Chiba, Hiroshi phoned Akiko from the platform. She had left a message. As he listened to it, he couldn't help but notice the many passengers two short steps from the edge of the platform. After being down on the tracks to see Steve's body, the yellow warning line—a row of raised-bump tiles—seemed useless to warn anyone of anything.

"I was looking through the matching list of Japanese suicides. One of them seemed different," Akiko said.

"Different how?"

"The family hired a lawyer to keep the case open."

"Were they wealthy?"

"What does that matter?"

"Insurance."

"Their life insurance paid."

"Even though it was ruled a suicide?"

"Their insurance covered every cause of death."

"They must be rich."

"Denenchofu address."

"Very rich."

"Want me to set up a visit?"

"Tell them it's urgent. I'll go there after I talk to the driver."

The neighborhood where the driver lived was east of Tokyo in Chiba, in a modest area of broad streets and huge apartment buildings. Hiroshi followed the numbers painted on the top right hand corners of the buildings. The rain returned, a swift invasion of gray.

The wife of the driver bowed at the door. She spoke in soft Japanese phrases, taking his umbrella and handing him a dry towel to wipe off the rain. In the living room, the driver, Torigai, rose from a low wood table and bowed deeply.

Hiroshi handed the driver his *meishi* name card as they settled onto flat *zabuton* pillows on the tatami and exchanged formal greetings.

Torigai was in his late fifties, with a wrinkled face and a burly body. His arms were folded across his chest in permanent resignation, and his head looked as if it had been bald forever.

The window was open to a garden with well-trimmed trees arching over a pond rimmed with moss-covered rocks. The rain fell on the green garden and splashed into the pond's surface.

On one side of the room, a TV sat atop a knee-high bookcase next to a *tokonoma* alcove with a ceramic vase and a scroll of calligraphy. Hiroshi could not read the fluid black characters, but the knotty wood of the pillar made him want to run his hands over its smooth, furrowed grain.

Torigai's wife knelt to pour tea for Hiroshi and then for her husband, moving fluidly from the table to the kitchen after setting out *senbei* rice crackers on a cherry bark tray.

"That must be a *shidarezakura* weeping cherry tree out there," said Hiroshi.

"I planted it when we first moved in twenty-five years ago. The apartment rules forbid gardening by tenants, so I snuck out in the middle of the night. The gardeners took care of it after that and never said a word," chuckled Torigai.

"It's the perfect view from this room. Did you do the calligraphy?"

"Years ago. I'll take it up again when I retire. Or when I'm fired."

"You've been driving trains for twenty-five years?"

"Thirty-five. I drove on other lines ten years before that."

"That's impressive."

"No, just the opposite. Most drivers get promoted or find better jobs. I'm just stubborn."

"So, politics is as bad for drivers as for detectives."

"And the stakes are lower."

Torigai sipped his tea.

"After the national railway was privatized, driver schedules were compacted."

"Layoffs?"

"Pay reductions. They scheduled overtime, which was where we made our real money. They added longer commutes and more paperwork, all unpaid."

"That was after privatization?"

"In the '90s. I organized the drivers to file a written complaint."

"Did it work?"

"It worked to put me on their blacklist."

The doorbell sounded, and Torigai's wife shuffled past them from the kitchen to answer it.

"There was a blacklist?"

"The union structure changed during the '90s. The new managers wanted to boost efficiency and cut costs. All they know how to do. The only way to do that was to take it out of us."

"The man who fell in front of your train last week—"

"It wasn't my train." Torigai said.

"But your name was on the..."

"Yes, it was."

"But you weren't the driver?"

"No, he was," Torigai nodded at a man in his late thirties being led in by Torigai's wife. He was unusually tall and thin with long limbs waving awkwardly around the small room. He bowed jerkily before sitting down—as if out of practice—and pushed his thick, oily hair away from his face.

"This is Tada," Torigai said.

Hiroshi bowed and passed Tada a name card. Tada bowed, his head lowered for a long time.

Torigai said, "Tada was driving."

Hiroshi again settled on the *zabuton* cushion as Torigai's wife offered Tada tea. She poured him a cup and went back to the kitchen.

"I don't have a name card anymore," Tada said in a thin, dry voice. "You're going to ask me about the guy I killed?"

Torigai interrupted. "You didn't kill him. You were doing your job."

"I killed him," Tada insisted.

"Killing involves motive, intention, action. There are very strict rules about that," Hiroshi said.

"I feel like I killed him," he said, jiggling his leg.

Hiroshi cleared his throat. "It must be upsetting."

Tada said, "It makes an incredible sound. His body cracked the window."

Torigai lifted his chin to encourage Tada to keep going.

Tada fidgeted with his hands and continued, "The mind fills in all sorts of things, just to make a complete picture, I learned, so I can never be sure if it really happened the way I remember. I'm sure, though, that his feet were in the air."

"His feet?" asked Hiroshi.

"What was, *was*, my therapist taught me. That means to accept, but it doesn't mean to forget. His feet were in the air. That wasn't put in the report. I didn't even write the report. Someone else did."

"So, the name signed on the driver's form was forged?" Hiroshi asked.

Tada looked at Torigai, who cleared his throat and answered, "Yes."

"Who forged it?"

Torigai said, "Tada was officially on leave. If you have any, well, psychological issues, you can take medical leave, but your salary is docked. But since there are not enough drivers, some people go on overtime. So, what happens is the drivers on leave take a shift from time to time and sign the name of a driver who is not on leave. We split up the money after. The company turns a blind eye because they save money by not hiring new drivers. It's easy to cover up."

"Unless there's a suicide."

"It wasn't a suicide," Tada intervened. "I've been over it in my head so many times. I go to therapy to talk about it. I'm better now that I don't replay the scene so often. That can drive you crazy. It DID drive me crazy," Tada laughed and choked and took a hurried drink of tea. He waved his hand over his mouth, sucking in air to cool the burn of too-hot tea.

"Why do you think it was not suicide?" Hiroshi asked.

"There was a woman on the platform with the man. I could not see clearly because there's a wall there at the end of the platform. But I did see the way she looked as the body hurtled through the air. She did not have a look of surprise or shock."

"What was her look?"

"Concentration. Calm and focused."

They all took a sip of tea.

Hiroshi continued: "And you remember that distinctly?"

Tada nodded his head vigorously. "I remember it because I had another so-called suicide. That's why I was on leave in the first place. The first one got to me unconsciously. At least this time, it's conscious trauma."

"When was that?"

"March 15th, 11:15, Musashi-Kosugi station, one away from Kawasaki. The case number is 974218," Tada recited.

Hiroshi took out his notebook and jotted down the details. "Thank you. That's very helpful."

"Is it?" Tada asked with sudden earnestness.

"Yes, very much. What do you remember from this time?"

Tada took a sip of tea, remembering to blow over it first. He set the teacup on the table and picked up the wooden coaster, turning it in his hands as he spoke. "I was always working on the late shift, which makes it difficult for me to meet people and find friends. But you get used to things. I saw the body flying in front of the train.

I saw her face. I stopped the train. I saw the dead body on the tracks and looked back at the people on the platform." Tada swallowed.

"Take your time, Tada. There's no hurry," Torigai said with a fatherly voice.

Tada nodded, took several deep breaths, and continued flipping the coaster in his hands. "A man and a woman walking down the platform turned to look at a tall woman with long hair walking away. I wouldn't have noticed her at all, but they stared after her. I was so panicked I couldn't move. The man punched the emergency call button. I sat down on a bench, and my life was over."

Hiroshi asked, "The woman you saw was the woman walking away?"

"It was front and back, but it was her."

Hiroshi nodded, wondering if he could be believed, or if Takamatsu and the others would believe him.

"The strangest thing was people were angry." Tada said, setting the coaster back on the table.

"Angry? At what?" Hiroshi asked.

"At being delayed. I was standing there, in shock, a normal reaction in those situations, my therapist tells me, but most people complained about not getting home on time."

"Do you remember anything else about that woman?"

"She walked forcefully."

"Forcefully?"

"You could tell she was strong."

"And the couple?"

"They claimed they did not see what happened," Torigai said.

"Was that in the report?" Hiroshi asked.

"No, they were foreigners on vacation. The train investigators took them out of the final report," Torigai said.

Tada spoke up again, "Also, she didn't push him. She flipped him. Her height, hair, sandals—" Tada's voice got higher and faster.

"She wore sandals?"

"I could see them when she got on the escalator. And she wore all black, too and—"

Torigai said, "Tada-san, calm down."

"OK, yes, give me a minute." He breathed in, closed his eyes, focused on breathing, found some inner point of calm and then opened his eyes.

Hiroshi turned to Torigai. "So, you signed the paper for the shift."

"We shouldn't even be telling you this," Torigai said.

"Why are you, then?"

Torigai said, "You should know the truth. That's why you came, isn't it?"

Hiroshi looked out at the garden.

Chapter 23

On the way back to the station, Hiroshi called Akiko, one hand holding his umbrella and the other on the cell phone. "Can you check one suicide: March 15, 11:15, Musashi-Kosugi station. The case number is 974218."

"Give me a minute," she said. Hiroshi could hear her shuffling through papers. "Hey, that's the one I was just talking about."

"The rich people in Denenchofu?"

"Yes. Wakayama is the name. I called them already and they seemed eager to talk with you."

"Did you hear from Takamatsu?"

"No."

"He's the one telling me how important it is to talk with the drivers and the victim's families. Now, he's disappeared?"

"He trusts you," Akiko said.

"I'm not sure it's mutual."

"I found one more thing. Several of the suicides worked in real estate."

Hiroshi stopped in his tracks. "How many?"

"Some were in consulting or investment companies, joint ventures—I'll count and cross-reference them."

"Did Wakayama do business with Bentley Associates?"

"Let me check. Wakayama was listed as an advisor to Bentley."

"It seems his widow might have a lot to say."

"By the way, Wakayama's daughter was an actress."

"Really?"

"She was famous for a few years, but attempted suicide. She spoke about it to the press. Broke the taboo. It was in all the papers."

141

"Not by train?"

"No, pills. There's a photo of her at Cannes. Stunning. Watch yourself!" Akiko laughed.

"I watch myself too much," Hiroshi said, though he was thinking just the opposite.

*   *   *

Getting off the subway at Denenchofu Station, Hiroshi cringed at the deafening tremors of the train inside the enclosed tunnel. The more he thought about the frail body of Steve—and the frail bodies of all these humans—the bigger and heavier the trains seemed, and the smaller and closer the stations. Walking along the platform felt like walking beside a busy highway. He hurried up the escalator to the relative safety of the taxis.

The Wakayama's Denenchofu house was in a neighborhood of houses hidden by high walls of layered, sculpted rock. One of the few planned areas of Tokyo, Denenchofu's small parks punctuated the neighborhood's layout at regular intervals. The taxi driver checked his dashboard's computerized navigation map and pulled onto a quiet street with no sidewalks.

Larger and larger gates blocked the entrances to the neighborhood's many compounds until the taxi stopped at an entryway with no number or name.

"Is this it?" Hiroshi asked the driver.

"It must be," the driver said. "Do you want me to wait?"

"No, I'm sure you're right," Hiroshi said and paid and got out. He pressed the button on a wall panel. A light flashed and the thick gate rolled back, allowing Hiroshi inside. The gate quickly closed behind him.

He followed a stone pathway through the large garden, breathing in the rich, moist air. A light mist drifted over the fountain bamboo, flowering shrubs, and dragon beard grass. Small maple trees pruned in soft, swaying layers punctuated the green with dark red leaves. At the top of the path, the wood timber frames and flat rock walls of the house emerged, as if from the soil.

At the door, a woman in her early sixties with gray hair in a tight bun and a woman in her mid-thirties—her hair long and unbound—

bowed deeply in unison. Obviously mother and daughter, both women dressed in loose, cotton clothes. When the daughter looked up she was, as Akiko warned him, stunning.

"So sorry to bother you," said Hiroshi, handing over his meishi with a bow. They stood in the largest genkan entryway he had ever seen—as big as his living room.

"Please come in," both of the women said in unison.

"We are happy to have the chance to talk, again, about this. I'm Wakayama, and this is my daughter, Sumiko."

They were both tall with big shoulders, fine features and an elegant way of moving. They led him along a hallway of black stone adorned with modern woodblock prints and tea ceremony bowls on inset shelves.

The ceiling of the living room was two stories high at the back and sloped gently down to large windows looking out on craggy rocks and spiny shrubs nestled into raked waves of white-gray pebbles. One flat rock jutted in under the glass, making the rock garden feel as if it were a part of the room.

Wakayama's widow settled on a sofa-chair and gestured Hiroshi to sit across from her. The daughter, Sumiko, came in with a lacquered tray holding three ceramic cups and a matching pot. Serving coffee, her motions displayed the natural elegance of tea ceremony.

Hiroshi took a polite sip of his coffee, unsure where to begin. "I'm sure it's painful to have to talk about your husband's, your father's, passing."

The mother asked, "Have there been any new developments?"

Hiroshi sat forward. "I'm investigating a death similar to your husband's that happened a few days ago. Would you mind if I asked about your relationship with your husband at the time of his death?"

The mother took a deep breath and Sumiko looked down, pausing to consider. "The insurance company investigators asked me that, too. My husband and I were estranged, but without any animosity. My daughter's career was in full swing and I spent more time with her. He must have felt abandoned by us."

"Estranged?"

"We were not angry at each other, not even considering divorce. We talked every day. We just lived separate lives. We became friends, at last, in middle age."

"What was he busy with?"

"Everything. My husband overworked. He never slowed down," she said.

"Did he have any special projects or—"

"Apartment complexes in Kawasaki, advising companies, many things."

"Real estate mainly?"

"Yes. Except for a hostess club, of all things."

"Do you know the name?"

"I'll find it for you. We never talked business."

"Does Bentley Associates sound familiar?"

"Only because the insurance investigators told me the name was in his schedule that week."

"He never got a chance to enjoy his success," Sumiko, the daughter, said. "I guess I learned 'all work, no play' from him."

"What was your father's reaction to your career?"

"When I ran into trouble, he was there. Maybe that's why I ran into trouble."

"When Sumiko went into the hospital, he found the best doctors. He was there every day. But at home, he started buying expensive wines, high-end stereo equipment—"

"For you?"

"For all of us, I guess. Money was the language he spoke."

Sumiko said, "When I got out of the hospital, he gave me an Aston-Martin. I didn't want to drive it. I just wanted to feel better. But it was a gesture."

"He suddenly wanted the best of everything. Enjoyed spending money for the first time."

Hiroshi cleared his throat and said, "The money came from his investments?"

Mother and daughter looked at each other.

Sumiko said, "We don't really know."

"My husband had lots of secrets."

"What kind of secrets?"

"Money and women. What other secrets could there be? He had mistresses, lovers, whatever you want to call them."

Sumiko stiffened. "I saw him one time with someone. In Roppongi. By accident."

Hiroshi asked, "What did she look like?"

Sumiko said, "She looked like me."

Hiroshi took in her face and eyes.

The mother said, "Well, it doesn't matter now, does it?"

"No, it doesn't," Sumiko said. "I was in Roppongi, late at night. I was trying to go out more—part of my recovery. She was younger than me, dressed in black, with long hair. She was a woman men would desire. I followed them."

"Where did they go?"

"They wandered the streets for a while," Sumiko said.

Hiroshi pulled out his cell phone and a map of Roppongi. "Can you tell me exactly where?"

Sumiko leaned over the small cell phone screen. "It was about here that I saw them," she said, pointing with her finger. The place was near the David Lounge. "They walked for a while, discussing something. And then my father put his arm around the woman and they walked off."

"My husband started going to hostess clubs after he built his first apartment building. He said he had to go where business was conducted."

"When did you see him?" Hiroshi asked Sumiko.

"A week before he was killed," Sumiko said.

"If I had just said something to him, confronted him then—" Sumiko put her fist on her forehead. Her mother rubbed her shoulder.

"I'm sorry to upset you with all of this," Hiroshi said. "I'm sure it's been difficult."

"Mostly, it's been strange, but then my husband was always a bit strange," she said. "He left a huge amount of money. It was my inheritance that got him into business, but he turned it into much, much more. I found out from the accountant, he bought apartments in Paris, Hong Kong, Bali. I don't know if it was for retirement or a savvy investment, or for that woman. He never said a word. Such a strange man."

"Would you have a list of his purchases from that year?"

"The accountant would." She paused, working over it again in her mind. "His accountant told me all this. He told me my husband left everything to Sumiko and me."

145

"There were no loans or losses or missing money?"

"He probably left money for that woman, but the accountant spared me the details. I wouldn't begrudge him that. Life's so short, and my husband always had to prove himself. He was a charming man, handsome, and lively when we were young, and then, when we got older, he just wasn't around."

Hiroshi paused for a minute. "Would you mind if I contacted the accountant?"

"We don't use him anymore. I use my own accountant."

"It would be good to talk with him," Hiroshi insisted.

"Can you get his address?" she asked her daughter. Sumiko left and quickly returned with a name card and copied the information out on a piece of paper for Hiroshi.

"Why are you so sure your husband didn't commit suicide?" Hiroshi asked.

"I know he didn't. The man from the train company came all the way here, but he refused to listen. He told me all widows refused to believe their husbands killed themselves." She snorted in anger.

"So, they came here to offer condolences?"

"No, to give me a bill."

"A bill? For what?"

"For expenses incurred."

"What expenses?"

"For cleaning up the body and delaying the trains."

"Families are charged for the cleanup?" Hiroshi asked, his coffee cup held midair.

"I had no proof. There were no witnesses. What could I do? It wasn't about money, but about knowing what really happened. I hired a private detective, but he found nothing. It might have been an accident, but it wasn't suicide."

Hiroshi nodded and sipped his coffee. The garden was as well-designed as the ones he and Linda had seen in Kyoto. "I've taken up enough of your time," he said and gathered his things.

At the genkan, Hiroshi pried on his shoes with a long, lacquered shoehorn. "I'm sorry to bring up bad memories." Hiroshi bowed.

As he picked up his umbrella, the mother said, "My daughter is calling a taxi for you. It will be at the gate in a few minutes. I'll call

146

the accountant and let him know you're coming. We want to know the truth—whatever it is."

Hiroshi bowed again, umbrella overhead, and walked carefully along the stone walkway downhill through the garden. The rain kept up a constant patter on the leaves lining both sides of the stone path.

Chapter 24

Ryo Shibata sat at the large worktable in the middle of his photography studio examining vintage photographs of Japan. He loved the old, sepia-tinted world glowing with life and vitality. The hand-tinted kimonos, faded-pink cherry trees, and soft-red lanterns fascinated him. The old technologies—albumen, silver and collodion—kept the old world alive better than all the top-of-the-line equipment and digital gimmicks he had at his command.

Recently, he could no longer look at his own photographs and had no interest in taking new ones. He only wanted to look at vintage photos. He bought them obsessively online and from dealers and old shops. Collecting old photos felt more meaningful than taking new ones. The bemused stares and natural poses were more intriguing, more human, than the narcissistic cell phone cameras that seemed to erase the meaning from people, places and events.

He tucked his graying shoulder-length hair behind his ears and got up from the stool for another single malt scotch.

Catching a reflection at the window from the corner of his eye, he squinted at the glass door of his studio to find Michiko staring in at him. He watched her as she pushed the door open and walked in.

"I thought you left already?" he said, letting his glasses drop to his chest.

"I haven't told you goodbye yet," she said, her voice husky and deep.

"I'm honored to be on the list," he said, brushing back his thick hair. "But it concerns me who else might be on the list."

"You always worry," Michiko said, walking her fingers, slowly, toward him along the large worktable.

"When are you leaving?" Shibata asked. "Do you want a drink?"

"Soon and no."

"I figured you'd tell me where to send it once you got there." He massaged his goatee without taking his eyes off her. The room was backlit by small spotlights aimed at the photos hanging on the concrete walls. An overhead work lamp splashed light over the worktable and onto the floor.

"What are you working on? A new show?"

"Vintage photos. Edo period. I've got quite a collection now," Shibata said, pouring himself a drink and waving the bottle at her.

She shook her head no. "They're not your photos, though, are they?"

"Yes and no."

"More no."

"When are you leaving? You didn't answer."

"Tomorrow, if I can finish things. Two days later, if I can't."

He took a sip of the scotch and watched her.

"I like old photographs," she said, gazing at them laid out in unfinished rows.

"I'll get what you came for," he said, taking another sip.

She watched as he went to a squat, green security cabinet, spun the combination wheel, and inserted the key he kept on another chain around his neck.

He pulled out a half dozen envelopes filled with ten thousand yen notes and set them on the worktable. He re-locked the cabinet.

"Is that where you keep your most valuable photographs?"

"And the most expensive scotch. I got paid in scotch for some special photos."

"Special?"

He shrugged and arranged the envelopes into a stack. He tucked the edges of the envelopes around them in crisp origami folds. When he finished, he slid them toward her across the worktable and said, "Here's one way to say goodbye."

"There are lots of others," Michiko said.

He leaned back in his tall ergonomic stool, and studied Michiko, while she riffled through the money. When she was done she did the calculations in her head as she looked around the room. Behind him, a shelf filled with large, glossy photography books ran under a row of louvered skylights.

"Recording all this?"

Shibata shrugged. He kept small cameras, just under the skylights, running all the time. He backed up the video files every day. "I'll delete them later."

"Not too much later, I hope." Michiko pulled out a black leather duffle bag with a wide strap and started placing the envelopes inside.

Shibata watched her, thinking what a subject she had been, and still could be. He had taken so many photos of her, each one special. Other models had no interior to capture, but Michiko had always been unfathomable, his camera never getting close to touching what was deep inside.

"You should have told me what you were going to do," he said.

"If I did that, would you have gone?"

"No," he said, pulling at his loose, open-necked shirt. "I wouldn't have gone."

"That's why I didn't tell you."

They stared at each other, both dressed in black. Only their faces caught the light.

"Did you delete them?" she asked.

"Not yet."

"Keeping them as insurance?"

"Insurance against what?" Shibata said, standing up. "And I thought we agreed to work clean."

"I was cleaning."

He looked at her.

She looked back.

"If you're leaving," Shibata said, "why did you even—"

"I wanted you to know."

"I already knew," he said.

"That's your photographer's eye. You can see inside people."

"Everyone except you."

She adjusted the money in her bag and zipped it tight, running her hands over the outside. When she was done, she turned to his wall of portraits, rows of black and white photos of nude women. He made some of them famous, and made a lot of money for himself.

151

"Don't you ever get tired of nude women?" she asked, studying the photos.

"They are beauty itself," he said, taking a step toward her.

"Don't you get tired of beauty?"

"I like all kinds of beauty, like these older photos. But that's just a different kind of beauty. Women are—"

"Is this one me?" Michiko pointed to one in the middle of the wall and looked back at Shibata.

"You never look like you in the photos."

"Am I supposed to look like me?"

"It's good when you do," he said.

"I was so young."

"You're still young."

In the photo, Michiko sat with her arms around her knees, her face covered by her hair and her breasts hanging full from her broad shoulders, making shadows beside shadows. Her fingers stretched down to play with her toes, pulling them apart.

"The secret language of the body. Just like you always said," Michiko said and ran her finger over her own photo.

He had told her during the shoots that the most everyday gestures were the most erotic. "You never smiled in any photo I ever took. That's the only one you even look playful."

"Except for the real playful ones?"

Shibata shrugged. "I wish I had just one genuine smile."

"Is that your last request? Take one now?"

"You should go if you're going," he said.

"You want me to thank you again?"

"You'd still be in Kobe if it wasn't for me."

"If it wasn't for you, I would never have been dragged down there."

Shibata ran his hand through his long hair and twisted his glasses.

"I have to finish what I started. What they started."

"No, you don't. You can just walk away."

"I am walking away from Kobe. Instead, I'm going to Paris."

"Paris?"

"They take their mistresses shopping. They don't bring much security."

"That's why you're going abroad?"

"Why did you think?"

"I thought you were going to live, to change, to—"

"I am, but first, I must get this done!"

Shibata looked at her calmly. "There are limits to everything. I've reached mine."

"No limit to their money."

"You got some of that. Let the rest go. Why beg for trouble?"

"I don't think of it as trouble. I think of it as justice."

"Your anger will catch up with you." Shibata stood up.

She turned back to the wall of photos. She pointed at hers and said, "Can you take down this photo of me?"

"It's a great photo."

"I don't want it up there," she said in a firmer voice.

"OK, I'll take it down. Throw it out. Tear it up. Burn it. Whatever."

"And the other photos of me, too? I don't want to end up like those Edo period photos, an unknown face staring at the camera from another time."

"I'll get rid of them," he said, gazing over her now matured, but still youthful hair, body and face, so full of anger and energy—so full of life—as photo-ready to him as ever.

She picked up the bag, redistributed the weight inside. "I have to go. I have another appointment tonight."

"Another?" He looked at her across the worktable.

"Are you worried about me?" she asked.

"No, I'm worried about me. They'll come after me, too." He looked in her eyes and tried to read her, but failed, searched for the right thing to say, and came up with silence.

She hoisted the heavy bag on her shoulder.

He took a big breath, and asked, "Where are you going after Paris?"

"Why not come and see?" she said, pausing at the open door. And then she smiled the smile he always wanted to catch in a photo, but never could.

Chapter 25

Shibuya had spent the day collecting what debts he could. Most of the hostesses and AV idol wannabes he managed could only give him designer bags, jeweled lighters, dangling earrings and expensive hair clips. They had no cash, or said they didn't.

He stuffed all these unwanted presents from customers into one big Louis Vuitton bag and headed to the pawnshop in an old ferro-concrete two-story house near Roppongi. He didn't want Michiko to wake him in the middle of the night again before she left.

The pawnshop garden was lined with a maze of statues and garden decorations, numbered tags dangling from everything. From outside, he could hear the fierce barking of the Japanese Tosa fighting hounds the pawnbroker, Ikeda, and his son kept. He looked up at the first surveillance camera and waited patiently in front of the bollards until the security gate rolled aside and let him in.

The neatly arranged shelves paraded Fendi bags, Prada perfumes, Valentino dresses, Cartier necklaces, and Armani and Gucci everythings. The long line of hostesses waiting in line up to the window made him exhale in exasperation. He dropped the Louis Vuitton bag on the floor and pulled out his cell phone.

The Tosa hounds' barks blasted out from behind the protective glass and echoed through the low-ceilinged room. The girl just ahead of Shibuya in line flipped her long blond hair around her almost-cute face and asked, "They can't get out, can they?" The dogs' low growls sounded like motorcycles revving.

"There's a door, I'm sure," Shibuya answered without looking up from his cell phone.

"I'm afraid of dogs." She clutched her cell phone with delicate fingers topped by long, thickly lacquered, white and pink fingernails. "How long will this line take?"

Shibuya looked up. "It's not usually like this."

"I was told it was quick here."

"It is when there isn't a line," Shibuya answered. "After midnight is rush hour here. What are you cashing in?"

"Just some stupid purse. This guy brings me a present every week. I never get much at the pawnshops in Akasaka. One of the girls told me to try here."

They stepped forward in line.

"This is the best pawnshop in Roppongi. I've been coming here for years." Shibuya could hardly find her eyes inside the dark-pink eye shadow and glitter powder on her cheeks. The dogs barked again, and the girl pulled her pink-silver shawl tight around her shoulders.

"I don't like those dogs," she said.

"Why don't I give you something for it and you can take off?"

"How much?" she said, holding up the bag. "Is this brand famous?"

"Marc Jacobs? Not so famous," Shibuya lied, pretending not to even look at it.

"I was hoping for twenty thousand yen."

"No way. You can stand in line and see, though."

The dogs barked again, and her shoulders scrunched together as she crossed her arms. "How much then?"

"I'll give you ten thousand. But be careful. There're cameras everywhere in here."

The dogs barked again and she handed the bag to him. Shibuya took a ten thousand yen note and gave it to her with his hand out of sight, against his thigh.

"Thanks. You saved me," the girl whispered and hurried away.

The next girl in front of him smiled through bright purple lip gloss outlined in black. "I heard hosts get really expensive presents. More than we get."

"I wish that were true," Shibuya said, not looking up from his cell phone. Her perfume was too strong and Shibuya turned away. There were still five women ahead of him.

Behind the Plexiglass window, the pawnbroker's son, Ikeda had a plump face with drooping eyelids and thick folds of dark brown flesh that wrinkled and unwrinkled as he looked over the goods, picking up each one and eyeing them carefully for telltale details. He wore a short-sleeve Hawaiian shirt throughout the year. A large Tosa sat beside him, staring up at Shibuya.

Shibuya smiled at the dog and held up the Marc Jacobs bag. "Here's the big ticket item!"

Ikeda looked at him without a word and pulled open the large thru-wall drawer. Shibuya put the stuff inside, and Ikeda pulled it to his side of the glass.

"Twenty thousand yen on the Jacobs bag."

"Twenty-five."

"Twenty-two, but I'm going to look carefully at this other stuff."

"You won't find any knock-offs in here," Shibuya said, calmly checking his cell phone. Ikeda wrote out the tickets and slid them through the currency tray. Shibuya picked up the total and said, "You're joking!"

"Times are tough," Ikeda said. "I can't move half of what I get these days. A couple of yours are knock-offs. You have to watch that. Not everyone will buy something fake anymore. It's not the bubble years."

"What about this chain?" Shibuya said, holding up the chains around his neck.

"Chains are one thing I have too many of."

Shibuya signed the receipt, folded the money into his pants' pocket, and hurried. He scurried through the garden and stepped out to peer both ways down the street.

He paused at the entrance to the garden, his elbow resting on a weatherworn Jizo statue, stolen—no doubt—from a temple, by someone really desperate.

Shibuya was careful to tuck the notes in two places—the interior of his vest and the inside waistband of his pants in a special pocket. After slipping on his loose, summer jacket, he was startled to hear Michiko's husky voice behind him.

"Did you get enough to take me out?" she asked, taking his arm.

"Were you following me?" Shibuya asked. He looked around to see where she had come from.

157

"It's been so long since we had a drink together, just the two of us."

Shibuya gathered himself and said, "I'll buy you a sayonara drink. Would you like that?"

"You were always my favorite," she said.

He gave her a kiss on her neck. "Aren't I still?"

"Where should we go?" she asked. "Dancing? That couples club? Or maybe that blue bird tattoo girl has worn you out?"

"I have plenty of energy," Shibuya said, taking her arm.

"Then, let's have some fun."

"Just one drink. I have to check on some girls."

Michiko smacked his shoulder, hard.

He jumped from the pain and clutched his arm. He didn't want to explain being picked up by the cops and having his shoulder pulled out of socket, so he just said, "Okay, okay, two drinks."

Michiko smacked his shoulder again.

Shibuya stopped and grabbed his arm. "Don't do that. My shoulder is killing me."

"Did something happen?"

"Not exactly."

"One of those older women hurt you tying you up?"

"Just a sore shoulder. I collected some debts like I told you. I have some of your money."

"Let's forget about that for tonight. I'm leaving, so it doesn't matter."

Shibuya stopped and asked, "You can give me more time for the rest?"

"All the time in the world," Michiko said.

"Really?"

"You'll never pay it all back anyway, will you?"

Shibuya looked embarrassed.

"Let's go spend what you have there and call it even," Michiko said, pulling him on. "I need to let off a little steam."

Their steps started to sync as they got under the lights and heard the bustle of the main streets of Roppongi. She kept a hand on him.

"Let's go to the David," she shouted, like a schoolgirl, holding both her hands out toward him in invitation. "We can dance."

"I don't want to go there," he answered, stopping and growling at her. "You know why."

"Please? For old times' sake?" She stopped and came back to him, putting her hands on his hips.

"Let's go someplace else."

"Let's stop by the David, just for a few minutes, and then you can take me to one of your favorite spots. What about that place in Ebisu?"

Shibuya nodded his head, okay, and took her arm.

* * *

Inside the David, the action was already in full swing.

"I'm going to go wash my hands," Michiko said.

"I'll be at the bar," Shibuya answered.

The early evening jazz and J-pop had given way to wild Latin club music. The bar was packed with women in tight full-body dresses and stiletto heels. The escorts and hosts and boyfriends were dressed in light summer suits, shirtfronts open to reveal tanned, hairless chests draped with gold necklaces.

The women dancing in the middle circled their fists up at the ceiling to the heavy Latin beat, crouching down, thighs stretching, hips pumping, shaking their work stress away.

The bartenders made drinks as fast as they got the orders, straining ice-filled shakers into frosted glasses, silver ice tongs and drink stirrers flashing in the spinning lights, no time to re-cap the bottles of wine and champagne.

Michiko, her hair spilling down her back, squeezed next to Shibuya at the bar. She handed her purse to the bartender for safekeeping in a cabinet above the bar. She ordered drinks and surveyed the throbbing, dancing crowd.

After their first cocktails, Michiko pushed Shibuya out to the middle of the dance floor. She moved effortlessly, loosely. The music jumped to a faster, funkier tempo, and the whole club moved as one.

Ceiling lights at the corners circled over the crowd, exposing lightning glimpses of long, bare necks, sturdy calves and slender, pretty arms all moving in time to the music. As if searching for someone or something, the lights roved over their drunk-silly smiles and lusty, let-loose eyes.

The room warmed up and the air was mingled with perfume, cigarettes, aftershave and expensive liquor. The dancing heated up everyone's personal scent. Shibuya stretched his shoulders and breathed in Michiko's lotus perfume.

A pile of jackets began to form at the end of the bar. A young guy, too drunk to work the buttons, yanked off his shirt and tossed it in the air, exposing his lean muscles and deep tan to the loud whoops of women who danced over to run their fingers over his sweaty skin. They shimmied their bodies at him to get him to dance more wildly, and when he did, they laughed and danced away.

Two women ripped the pants off a boy who seemed to be just out of high school. He laughed and went with it, kicking his shoes off to whoops of approval. Standing in black designer underwear and socks, he swung his body in circles as the women screamed girlishly and slapped his round butt cheeks as he circled by. A woman fell on top of him and pinned him against the bar, the frenzied crowd egging her on.

Some of the women, with their dates or with each other, slumped against the walls in deep, private clinches, their faces pumping kisses, hands working each other's bodies, everyone writhing to the heavy beat of the music.

On the dance floor, Shibuya moved against Michiko, putting his hand on her hips. She ordered another drink for him by nodding at the bartender. They wriggled over to the bar, and Shibuya slurped it down. "That's three drinks," he said, holding up the empty glass.

She snuggled up to him, putting her arm around his thin waist, gently kissing his neck, saying, "Let's get out of here."

"Where to?" Shibuya asked.

"What about a big breakfast?"

"It's about time."

Michiko checked her watch. "We can just catch the first train if we hurry."

Chapter 26

Out the north exit of Kichijoji Station, Hiroshi opened his umbrella and hurried past the traffic circle toward a pedestrian shopping street. He was late and could not remember the directions. He stopped to scroll through his phone but kept walking as he scanned the long row of narrow shops—packed in like giant books on a shelf—for the coffee mill statue he was supposed to find.

There was no giant coffee mill statue, so he dropped his umbrella in the stand outside the coffee place that looked like it should have a statue and walked down the steep stairs into the basement, hoping he was right.

In the calm space of the coffee shop, she was even more beautiful than he remembered. She was a petite woman, with fine features. Hiroshi watched her as she tucked the book she was reading into her bag and waved to him from a corner table.

Sanae Atsuki, the mother of the girl, Yukari, caught for trying to shake down the Russian guy on the train, didn't look old enough to have a daughter in her last year of high school.

Hiroshi asked, "Where's the coffee mill?"

"It disappeared!" she said, laughing. Her hair was pulled back into a thick, flat ponytail. "I almost called you, but I thought, well, you're a detective!"

"I used the detective technique called a wild guess," said Hiroshi.

"Is that how you do it?"

"More often than not."

Jazz streamed from large speakers in the corner of the room, and they both smiled at the waitress who brought a menu made of Japanese paper glued to a thick wooden board.

161

"I didn't know if there were regulations about this," Sanae said.

"About what? Drinking coffee?"

"About meeting...um—"

"Innocent people?"

"I didn't feel innocent that day in the station."

"You were, and so was your daughter, Yukari, more or less."

She brushed her ponytail in nervous strokes and looked at him as if for the first time.

"When are you leaving?"

"A couple days."

"So soon? How..."

"When we got home that day, I told Yukari to start packing."

"I'll bet she was thrilled."

"She was, but funny thing, as soon as I said let's go to America, she started speaking in Japanese again. She even dyed her hair back to natural black." Sanae shook her head and rolled her eyes.

Hiroshi chuckled.

"She was right, though. There's nothing for her here. For me either. Her school here is terrible. I don't want her to waste her life like I did."

"You didn't waste your life. You're still young."

"Kids always win one way or another."

"And you. You're ready to go back?"

Sanae shrugged her shoulders. "I guess I am. I'll have to be."

At the police station with her daughter, she'd been crushed by shame and worry, but now, across the table, she opened up. Her face flowered with inflection and attention. Hiroshi tried to look at her without her noticing. Sanae tried not to notice him looking.

Their cappuccinos arrived. The barista had put brown smiley faces into the foam, one with long hair and a feminine face and the other with a man's face.

"Look at these!" Hiroshi said.

"What are these?" Sanae blushed and giggled.

They hesitated to sip them and ruin the faces. They looked over at the barista who was intent on the next order.

Sanai took a breath and said, "The reason I invited you was to thank you for saving Yukari. She insisted I call you."

"I'm glad you did."

"If you hadn't been there—"

"Nothing would have happened. It was okay."

"She's had so much trouble. I finally realized she was crying for help. I wasn't listening because, well, I wasn't listening."

"America will be a fresh start. For you both."

She took another sip and recomposed herself. "The green card's been the best part of the marriage."

"Where's your husband from?"

"New York."

"That's a good place."

"It would have been."

"If...?"

"If my husband treated me like I imagined American men would."

"What do you mean?"

"He had this image of me as exotic and passive."

"And beautiful."

"Looks don't count for much in the end, though, do they?"

She sipped from the top of the foam head figure floating on the coffee.

"I was so young when I got married, and Yukari came along right away. We tried things in the States for a while. The problem wasn't the country or the language; it was us."

"Where did you meet?"

"I was working as a hostess. He was a customer. Simple as that."

"Things like that are never simple."

Sanae hummed her agreement. "I had two sisters and two brothers. So, if I was going to pay tuition at a two-year women's college, I had to work. The hostess club paid best."

"There's no shame in that."

"I feel ashamed of using him. If I was whatever I was to him, he was a ticket out for me. I wanted things to be better for Yukari."

"They will be."

Sanae looked up. "Will they?"

He hummed "yes" deep in his throat and sipped from the outline in his foam.

"But what about you? You must meet a lot of people as a detective."

"I met you."

163

Sanae blushed.

Hiroshi continued. "My work is pretty routine. Phone calls, files and emails. I can go for days without seeing anyone face to face."

"That sounds, well, inhuman."

As if in response, his cell phone buzzed. Hiroshi reached down and turned it off. "Things have changed the past couple days."

"You met someone?"

"What? No, no, just at work. More time out of the office. I was living with someone, but she went back to the States."

"So, you had an international relationship, too?"

"Same as you, but in reverse. She was American. It was difficult."

"It's like speaking two different languages at once."

"Japanese and English, you mean?"

"No, two different languages of the heart."

"Four different languages total."

"And none of them connect."

They slipped into an intimate quiet.

"Any chance of saving your relationship?" Sanae asked.

"None whatsoever," said Hiroshi, and they laughed again, exhaling loudly in unison.

"Me, neither. Now, it's all down to money." Sanae giggled.

They both slurped the last little pools of foam at the bottom of their cups.

"What are you going to do in the States?"

"Getting Yukari into college is first. Maybe I'll also take a few courses."

"What kind of courses?"

"I only finished two years of school—and barely that."

"You learned English."

"That was easy."

"And the other language? Of the heart."

"I'm still studying that one. I'm learning a lot from Yukari."

Hiroshi hummed deep in his throat.

Sanae swished her cup around, trying to get the foam to liquefy for one more sip.

"Listen, I've got to get back to work," he said, checking his cell phone. "Uh oh, urgent text message. Several, actually."

"Yukari will be happy to know we talked. She's been pestering me to call you."

"I'm glad you did."

Sanae snatched the check, insisting on paying and holding the check behind her back as they argued good-naturedly over who would pay.

It was the first time he had gone out with a woman since Linda. The other night didn't count, not only because he was too drunk to remember it, but because he'd felt more alone afterwards.

They climbed the narrow, twisting stairs back to the shopping arcade, Hiroshi watching the back-and-forth of her hips right at eye level from a few steps below, her thighs and hips twisting deliciously in her tight jeans.

At the top of the stairs, his phone rang again. "I really have to go," he said, tamping down the text messages from Sakaguchi and Akiko with his thumb.

Sanae took her umbrella from the stand.

Hiroshi searched the umbrellas in the stand. "Mine's gone!"

"Was it an expensive one?"

"No, cheap convenience store one."

Sanae laughed and said, "Why don't you just take someone else's?"

"I can't do that."

"Stealing umbrellas is an accepted Tokyo custom," she laughed. "Even for detectives."

"I can't do that," he said, laughing and again ruffling through the umbrellas.

"Well, here, take mine. I have to go shopping anyway."

"I'm just going to the station."

"My contribution to the anti-crime effort."

Hiroshi turned the designer umbrella over in his hands awkwardly, "I'll return it."

"Please do."

She stepped forward and gave him an American hug, which he returned—his favorite American custom—and after looking in each other's eyes again, they walked off in opposite directions.

Chapter 27

Hiroshi saw Sakaguchi from the end of the hospital hallway, his round, human girth a sharp contrast with the pushcarts, supply trays, and medical equipment along the white walls. Ueno, the other sumo wrestler from the outing to Shibuya, sat in a chair at the far end of the hall.

Hiroshi walked down the long hall wondering which room he was in. The intensive care ward was quiet. Waiting families slumped in chairs inside the rooms, nurses walking briskly back and forth. Small shaded windows opened into each of the rooms.

"You're back in homicide?" he asked Sakaguchi.

Sakaguchi nodded, yes. "Enough of those chikan perverts."

"So?" Hiroshi nodded toward the hospital room.

"He's in pretty bad shape," said Sakaguchi, his bass voice a whisper. "He was stable enough for me to talk with him for a minute, but he needs surgery for swelling or fluid or something on his brain."

"Where did they find him?" Hiroshi asked.

"Right below the bridge near Ebisu station. Hit the electric wires on the way down. Burned him, but bounced him to the side of the tracks. Ueno got there just after the ambulance. Thought we had another one."

"He was luckier than the others."

"Drugged with the same thing they found in that foreigner..."

"Steve?"

"Foreigner's names all sound alike."

"What time did it happen?"

"First train, about four-thirty this morning."

A nurse came out to the supply cart. Hiroshi asked her, "Can we talk to him?"

"We need to get him prepped," she said, looking through the cart and making notes on a clipboard chart.

"He may have valuable information," Hiroshi said.

"He's sleeping, so you will have to wait until he comes out of surgery."

"It's urgent."

"This is a hospital, not an interrogation room," she snapped, looking up from the supply cart.

Sakaguchi looked around her into the room.

"It might save someone's life," Hiroshi said.

"I'll ask the doctor." She folded the chart closed and walked off shaking her head.

"You made more headway than I did," Sakaguchi whispered.

Hiroshi and Sakaguchi walked down to where Ueno was sitting in a chair at the end of the hall. There wasn't much to say.

At the other end of the hallway, a tall woman with long hair, wearing a white mask over the lower half of her face, got off the elevator and peered into the first room on the floor. Hiroshi pulled Sakaguchi into an open door. Ueno let his head droop to appear to be asleep in the chair.

"Do you think that's her?" Hiroshi whispered.

Sakaguchi nodded his head, maybe.

"Coming to finish her work?"

"Let's wait and see what she does. Peek out."

Hiroshi peeked out for a second to see her looking into the rooms one by one. She carried a big, heavy bag. "If she heard he was still alive..."

"...we might catch her in the act."

When she found Shibuya's room, she slipped inside without a sound.

Sakaguchi and Hiroshi took off toward the room she went in, scrambling around the supply carts. Ueno followed them at a trot.

Sakaguchi got into the room first and pinned her against the wall with both arms behind her back.

On the bed, wrapped in bandages and full of IVs, his arm in a sling and both legs elevated, Takayuki Shibuya, the punk they beat up outside the game arcade and took for a ride, was very much awake.

Sakaguchi levered his full weight against the masked woman, but she brought her thick platform shoe down hard on top of his foot. He yanked his foot back and cursed, but did not let go.

Hiroshi pulled the heavy bag from her shoulder, as Ueno grabbed her right arm. She swung her elbow free, catching Ueno in the ribs. He huffed, but held on.

She raked the sole of her platform shoes down Ueno's shin and stomped on his foot. He yowled and Hiroshi reached in and pushed her neck tight against the wall.

She pushed again for a weak point to wriggle out an arm or leg to strike again, but they held her tight. She kept struggling, so they pushed her harder against the wall.

"Quit moving or we'll really take you down," Hiroshi shouted.

"Leave her alone," Shibuya shouted from the bed. "Stop! Please stop!"

Hearing his voice, she stopped squirming and let herself go slack.

Hiroshi and Ueno loosened their grips, but Sakaguchi held one arm behind her as she turned around.

She was pretty and young with silver-flecked eyelashes and multi-colored fingernails that matched the indigo blue of her one-piece tube dress. Her hair fell over her dark-tanned face and tears dripped from her eyes onto a blue bird tattoo swooping across her small, firm breast.

"That's my girlfriend!" Shibuya choked out, his voice garbled as if he bit his tongue.

"Your what?" Hiroshi said.

"My girlfriend," he said, in a rasping voice. "She's not the one who did this."

Hiroshi looked at the girl's face and frowned. Ueno released her and stepped back. As soon as he did, she went to Shibuya and settled her head onto his chest.

"Ouch!" he squirmed and she pulled up and put her hand on his cheek, lightly stroking the bandages that framed his face.

"How old is this girl?" Sakaguchi demanded.

"Old enough," Shibuya answered, his voice thick and slow. She kissed his forehead. He shifted his arm cast, and took her hand in his. Swollen, red-purple bruises covered his thin arm, bony shoulder, and face.

169

A nurse and a doctor rushed into the room. "What's going on in here?" the nurse demanded.

"You're not supposed to be in here," the doctor said.

"It's OK," said Hiroshi.

"Who's this?" demanded the nurse. "It's not visiting hours."

"She's with me," Shibuya gurgled.

Hiroshi turned to the doctor. "We need to talk with this guy now. Other lives are at stake."

The doctor said, "He should have gotten his anesthetic by now. He needs to have the pressure relieved in his skull. Right away." He checked his watch.

The nurse checked the tubes and wires going into and out of Shibuya. Yellowish fluid leaked through his bandages. She scowled and stomped out.

The anesthetist came and pulled back in surprise at so many people in the room. The doctor waved him in and pushed the detectives and the girl into the hall.

"What's your name?" Hiroshi asked the girl.

"My name's Arisa Nagatani."

"Where do you live?"

She nodded toward Shibuya.

"With him? Where do your parents live?"

"My parents kicked me out."

"What high school do you go to?"

"I haven't been to school in a year," she answered. The tears welled, washing eyelash sparkles down her tan cheek.

"How old are you?" Sakaguchi asked the girl.

"Seventeen," she said, wiping her nose and dabbing her eyes.

"Should we call juvenile?" Sakaguchi asked.

Hiroshi sighed, "There's no law about visiting hospitals."

Sakaguchi had enough. He took the girl by the arm back to Shibuya's bedside.

The doctor and anesthetist started to protest, but Shibuya pushed the girl right next to Shibuya. "Tell us what happened or we call juvenile."

Arisa reached for Shibuya's hand and held it tight.

The anesthetist said, "You've only got a minute or two before he's totally out."

"Were you at the David Lounge last night?" Hiroshi asked Shibuya.

Shibuya's eyes opened wide, but were glassy and distant. Shibuya gestured and grunted, "yes."

"You took the wrong date home? Or you just slipped off the bridge?" Hiroshi demanded.

"Bridge?" Shibuya spoke in jagged tones.

"The one you dropped from onto the train tracks."

Shibuya shook his head, drifting off. His lip was split and it was an effort to use his mouth.

"Who were you with? You must remember that."

Shibuya turned to Arisa. "She was following me. I had to go with her."

Arisa nodded and put the back of her hand to her dripping nose and said, "It doesn't matter. As long as you're OK."

"Who was it?" Hiroshi insisted.

"A woman named Michiko."

"Michiko what?"

"Suzuki."

"Is that the woman you said you owed money to?"

"Yes."

"You worked together."

"I was her manager."

"And now?"

Shibuya closed his eyes.

The doctor intervened, "That's enough. He's going for surgery."

Shibuya breathed in and woke back up a little. As he opened his mouth, Hiroshi could see a couple of teeth missing and his tongue had a dark-red gash. Hiroshi had to lean down to hear him mumble, "She was gone for a year. Came back. Cherry blossom season. Wouldn't say anything. She looked haunted."

The doctor tried to stop any more questions and Sakaguchi tried to move the girl toward the door, but she clung to Shibuya's hand and the railing.

Shibuya coughed and started again. "She needed a place to store money. Phone, cards, bank accounts."

"And you got those for her?"

Shibuya nodded, yes.

"What do you remember?" Hiroshi asked.

"Dancing."

"With her? At the David Lounge?"

Shibuya nodded, yes, in drugged surprise.

"What time was that?" Hiroshi asked.

Shibuya shrugged. "There's a photographer and an accountant." His voice grew cracked and faint.

Hiroshi leaned down. "Where do we find her?"

"I don't know. They don't know either."

"Where's her family?"

"Kawasaki. Factory area."

"How do we find it?"

Shibuya mumbled faintly, "She's leaving, or left."

"Leaving?"

"If she finds out I'm still alive—" he said as his eyes shut. They didn't flitter back open again.

Two nurses came in and shooed everyone into the hallway.

"He'll make good bait," Sakaguchi said.

"If he makes it through the surgery," Hiroshi said.

"Even if he doesn't," Sakaguchi said.

Arisa wiped the sparkles and mascara washing down her face and looked at the detectives standing next to her in the antiseptic corridor, her knees unsteady on her high platform shoes.

When they rolled Shibuya out of the room on the gurney, they paused for a second as Arisa grabbed at her boyfriend's hand and leaned over him, tears pouring down.

Hiroshi pulled her away and they stood watching Shibuya being rolled off toward the operating rooms.

Arisa took a few steps after him, her tall figure slender and delicate in the empty frame of the quiet corridor. Then, with her head hanging down, she started to weep, slowly collapsing into a crouch so low her hair spilled around her onto the floor.

Chapter 28

Akiko shouted when Hiroshi and Sakaguchi walked into the office. "You know what I had to listen to this morning?"

"Coffee?" Hiroshi headed straight for the coffee machine.

"I haven't had time for a cup all morning. Too busy fending off everyone asking for you," Akiko said, coming around the side of her desk.

Sakaguchi said, "Just tea. Sumo habit."

Akiko growled.

The coffee grinder rasped loudly, drawing her out. Hiroshi kept his finger on the switch and turned an ear to Akiko, showing he couldn't hear.

She tried to talk over the grinder with a hand on her hip, the other hand waving a thick folder.

"Done?" Akiko asked after the grinding stopped.

Hiroshi nodded.

Sakaguchi looked back and forth.

Akiko waved the file again. "You know who stopped by?"

"To my office? No one ever has before," Hiroshi said, as the water started to boil.

"Three people. The head of homicide, a representative from the Railway Technical Research Institute—whatever that is—and a bureaucrat from the Ministry of Land, Infrastructure, Transport, and Tourism," Akiko said. "You know what kind of people they are?"

"Insistent, powerful."

"Bullying, irritating," Sakaguchi added.

"And angry, at you and Takamatsu," Akiko said.

"No word from him?" Sakaguchi asked.

"Nothing," Akiko said, her voice polite in answer to Sakaguchi. She raised her voice at Hiroshi. "I made elaborate excuses and apologized again and again."

"Your *keigo* polite Japanese is better than mine anyway," Hiroshi said.

"It probably is, but that's not the point."

"What is the point? They want this solved quickly and quietly." Hiroshi checked on the coffee. The boiling water gurgled and trickled through the coffee grounds. "Murder's noisier than embezzlement."

"I don't think they care about that. They just want to be sure not to scare commuters. If the trains seem dangerous—"

"The trains are dangerous. Obviously."

"They do not want trains to appear to be deadly weapons," she said.

Hiroshi continued, "Forty million people a day ride the trains and subways in Tokyo."

Sakaguchi interrupted. "And very few die. It's a good record."

"The international element is what has them spooked."

"Because he was American?"

"Because several were foreigners." Akiko waved the folder in front of him.

"Several?" Sakaguchi asked.

Hiroshi took the folder from her and opened it.

"I'll go get Sakaguchi some tea," Akiko said. "I don't mind getting it for him."

She walked out, but then stuck her head back in the door. "Oh, and by the way, a representative from the American embassy will be stopping by with the chief of homicide in a half hour or so." She waltzed off to get tea.

Hiroshi looked at his watch and then at Sakaguchi. "We better get out of here before they arrive."

"Maybe I'm not so glad to be off chikan duty," Sakaguchi said. "It's all so cut and dried over there."

Hiroshi flipped through the folder, and closed it with a sigh.

"Anything?"

"Accidents or murder, hard to say," Hiroshi said. "At least we know her name,"

"We know a name," Sakaguchi said.

"Yesterday, I found out the drivers of the trains are not the real drivers. They use each other's names to divide overtime pay."

"We used to do that in the Osaka police force, too," Sakaguchi said.

"The woman might also have killed at least one Japanese," Hiroshi said. "I talked with the widow of a man named Wakayama who had ties to Bentley and Associates. He had lots of investments in land, always with timing that was a little bit too good."

Hiroshi poured a cup of coffee for himself and for Akiko.

Akiko came back in with a can of tea for Sakaguchi. It looked teensy in his thick-fingered paws.

"How do land investments tie in to the homicides?" Sakaguchi asked. "And why a train?"

Akiko said, "Everyone who died either owned and managed buildings or bought and sold land. Several other such foreigners appeared to have committed suicide."

"You found that yesterday?" Hiroshi asked.

"What do you think I've been texting you about?" Akiko said. "I collected it there." She pointed to the folder Hiroshi had read and put down on his desk.

Hiroshi sipped his coffee.

Akiko sighed. "I called Steve's ex-wife in America, too."

"What did she say?"

"She said he was, and I quote, a 'scumbag.'" Akiko used the English word.

"What does that mean?" Sakaguchi asked.

Hiroshi explained graphically. The explanation sounded cruder in Japanese, but Sakaguchi chuckled.

"She said his alimony payments stopped, so she turned it over to the courts to get an income withholding. But he failed to file taxes in America."

"He was working here," Sakaguchi said.

"Americans have to file taxes both in the country of residence and in the States," Hiroshi said.

"Because he didn't file for two years, there was nothing she could do since Japan never signed a treaty with other countries," Akiko said.

"How did you find all this out?" Sakaguchi asked.

"Typed in a question and hit search."

"Still, that doesn't mean he didn't have the money," Hiroshi said.

"How much would it be? A couple of buildings?" Sakaguchi asked.

"Billions of yen, just to build a small one," Akiko said.

"Money for construction companies, architectural firms, a lot of different payments. If you get contracts prearranged, you get a good cut."

"With high rent, you make a lot, too," Akiko said.

"Rich people can't lose in Tokyo," Sakaguchi said.

"Unless they end up in front of a train," Akiko said.

"The problem is," Hiroshi said, "Many buildings weren't turning much profit when vacancy rates slipped. So, competition for the best locations increased."

"That raised the price for information," Akiko said.

"Information about what?" Sakaguchi asked.

Hiroshi said, "Our girl found out secrets and sold them."

"Sold them?" Akiko looked confused.

The phone rang and Akiko answered, speaking in her politest Japanese, before hanging up. "The chief's on his way with the embassy rep."

"We better go," Hiroshi said, grabbing his coat and an umbrella.

Sakaguchi stood ready at the door.

Akiko said, "I'll find some excuse, but where are you going?"

"To talk to Wakayama's accountant," Hiroshi said.

Sakaguchi said, "I'll try to find Takamatsu."

"You want the building purchase contracts?" Akiko said.

Hiroshi nodded "yes" to Akiko and followed Sakaguchi out the door. "Meet me in Roppongi later. If we go in circles long enough—"

Akiko sat down and got into the reports, preparing an excuse for when the chief and the embassy rep arrived.

Chapter 29

The accountant's office was a long walk from Akasaka station. The buildings got older and squatter the farther Hiroshi walked. Walking time from the nearest station—noted in minutes—was a basic part of directions—and of rents—in Tokyo. This was more of a taxi ride away, Hiroshi realized too late. By the time he got to the lime-green building on a backstreet, Hiroshi's shirt felt as wet and sticky as a washrag.

The accountant's building had a front bed for plants with nothing growing in it. Tiles were missing from the walls and the lobby was just wide enough for a person to turn around. Unlike the other businesses on the half-empty directory, Sono Accountancy was written in both English and Japanese.

The elevator arrived with a long creak ending in a dull thunk. Hiroshi checked the elevator inspection date as he rode slowly up.

Sono's door had beveled glass set in thick wood with his name hand-painted on the glass in English and Japanese. Hiroshi knocked, and a soft, startled voice asked him to come in.

A thirty-something woman, hair pulled back above round, thick-framed glasses, looked curiously at Hiroshi as he poked his head around the door. She was sitting at a desk with a blanket over her lap. Behind her were two rows of cubicles made from mismatched partitions. The room was cold as a refrigerator.

"I'm Detective Shimizu. I called."

She looked at him.

"Just a minute."

She flipped a shawl off her shoulders and took a blanket from her lap. She walked between the patchwork partitions and leaned down

177

to whisper to someone in the last cubicle. The room was silent except for the hum of the air conditioner on full blast. Hiroshi shivered in his sweat-damp shirt.

"Please come this way," the receptionist said. He followed her to an area whose dingy, cloth-covered dividers enclosed a laminated wood coffee table with four low sofa chairs. The fluorescent lights in the ceiling cast an anemic, yellow light over the room. One flickering bulb in back made the room twitch nervously.

Hiroshi sat down, and in a minute, the secretary returned with a cup of green tea. Tea spilled into the saucer, and would drip if he picked it up, so he let it sit.

The accountant, Sono, wore a plain white shirt and red-blue tie that dangled when he made a perfunctory bow. Hiroshi handed over his meishi. The man didn't offer his, but sat down, pulling up his pant legs and shirtsleeves in clockwise order and looked at Hiroshi's meishi on the table in front of him. Deep wrinkles flexed over his thin face. He seemed used to talking with people, but not as if he liked it.

"I'm happy to help," Sono said, "but I've been over this before."

"The case with Wakayama is closed. However, info about him might help us with a new case."

Sono called to the secretary/receptionist, "Bring the Wakayama files."

"It's not about what's in those files exactly."

"Then what do you need to know?"

She brought in two thick files, and placed them on the coffee table in front of Sono. He opened one and then the other, bending back the fold of each with both hands until they gave out a loud crack.

"All the accounts are here, so what do you need?"

"Mostly I need background on Wakayama."

"Background? I work with numbers. I'm an accountant."

"So am I."

Sono looked at him, a bit confused.

Hiroshi leaned forward. "His wife didn't believe he committed suicide. What do you think?"

"I'm not a psychologist." He took off his glasses and opened and closed the temples. "Is there something about his investments you need to know?"

178

"Was he good at investing?"

"He made three real estate purchases that were highly profitable. They were old buildings he resold for large gains. I'd say he was very good."

"Where was the real estate?"

"One was near Tokyo University—an old student dormitory— another was an apartment building in Takanawa, and the third was in Kawasaki. All those areas were being developed."

"He bought them only a short time before he sold them?"

"They were turnarounds. The time frame was short."

"So, he had help?"

"Help?"

"He had advance information."

Sono cleared his throat. "Real estate investing is all about having the right information."

Hiroshi shrugged that off. "Would his wife have benefited if it was murder?"

"She did not retain my services, so it's no concern of mine, but it seems strange she wanted to keep the case open."

"She wanted to know the truth."

"He made money. He died."

"His wife said he was sending money to a woman?"

"Several women, in fact. I didn't think I needed to tell her everything, so I reduced the number to one. She didn't seem interested in the details."

"I am, though. How many exactly?"

"Two large regular payments and three occasional ones."

"Bank transfers to five different women?"

"He also withdrew cash."

"Were any of the recipients named Michiko Suzuki?"

Sono paused and slowly turned over several pages in the folder. "Anyone can open a bank account in any name."

"It could have been the same woman with different names on the accounts, then?"

"Possibly. They often do that, those women."

"Those women?"

"*Mizu shobai*, the water trade. Hostesses, call girls, companions, AV actresses."

"Do you handle accounts for them also?"

Sono said, "I have handled accounting for them sometimes, yes. They know how to make money, but also how to spend it. The more they make, the more they end up in debt. A few have taken my advice." He eyed Hiroshi as if that was more information than he usually extended to anyone.

"Was Michiko Suzuki one of them?"

He looked down at the Wakayama files. "I'd have to check my files. Her name doesn't ring a bell."

"Are you sure the payments from Wakayama didn't all go to the same woman?"

"I don't track down who is on the receiving end of bank transfers."

"That must make things easier."

Sono frowned. "Covering one's tracks on paper is not complicated." He again peeled his glasses off, working its hinge back and forth steadily. "Nor is it illegal."

The room was too cold for Hiroshi's shirt to dry. It clung to his skin. He looked at the sporadic blinking lightbulb. "Wakayama's wife said he invested in a hostess club."

"And lost the entire investment."

"Lost it?"

"The club went bankrupt."

"What happened?"

"Bad management, few customers, bad location, the usual, I suppose."

"The bankruptcy was a way of laundering other gains?"

"Sometimes a bankruptcy is used that way, I've heard, but Wakayama was not that type."

"That was right before his death?"

"A few months before."

"Could you give me the exact date?"

Sono paused, and then flipped through the two files, running his fingers through a spreadsheet and a timeline. "Two weeks before. Fourteen days exactly."

"Did he take out a lot of cash before he died?"

"I put a certain amount in his account every month."

"How much? Roughly?"

"He roughly took out as much in cash as he paid in bank transfers."

"I can request the accounts formally if that's better."

"You're welcome to do so," Sono said, shrugging and neatening the files.

"Where did that cash go?"

"The point of cash is you can't trace it."

"And you said you handle these women's accounts, too?"

The light bulb that needed changing flicked jumpy shadows and sizzled softly.

"Not those same women, but others. I already gave the police all the records. And the insurance company, too. They're more careful than the police."

"What's your impression of Wakayama's cash flow?"

"I don't deal in impressions, detective."

"Did he like to spend money?"

"He had it to spend."

"Any thoughts on his relationships to these women?"

"It's not something we discussed. Like other men of his generation, he no doubt considered the attentions of young women another benefit of working hard."

Sono called to his secretary for cigarettes, offered one to Hiroshi, who waved it off. As Sono lit up, he held his elbow in his other hand and observed Hiroshi closely. His secretary came in with an ashtray.

Hiroshi pulled his chilled shirt from where it stuck to his back and sat forward.

"What happened to the other businesses?" Hiroshi continued. "His wife mentioned there were many."

"He owned stakes in many businesses."

"Could you give me the list?"

"He cashed in and cashed out a lot over the years."

"I need the list."

"It would take time. I can send it to you," he picked up Hiroshi's name card. "To this address?"

"He had good information about other companies, too?"

"He knew where to invest."

"You liquidated the percentage ownerships in almost all the businesses after his death."

"His wife asked me to do that."

"Who bought most of the shares?"

"It's not shares like stocks, just a portion of the business." He looked down at the folder and flipped through several pages. "Most of them were bought by a company called Bentley Associates. They're located in West Shinjuku."

"In fact, the dead man I'm investigating worked there."

Sono leaned back on the sofa, and then leaned forward to tap off his cigarette ash. "That's a coincidence worth investigating."

"Let me just ask again, did it seem like Wakayama wanted to kill himself?"

"Wakayama was an old-style businessman—shrewd and confident. He sent presents to everyone twice a year and had a lot of contacts. He knew how to chat for a long time before asking a business question. He wouldn't know how to be depressed."

"That's a dying breed." Hiroshi leaned forward in his chair. "Thank you for your time."

"I wish the investigation had been done correctly the first time."

"Just one more thing," Hiroshi said, as an afterthought. "Wakayama's case may be connected to another, similar case. Anyone involved in either one is an accessory to both. Murder is different from money laundering. With murder, two is much more than one plus one."

Sono stood as Hiroshi left, but let Hiroshi see himself out. When he sat down again, he finished his cigarette slowly and then ground out the butt in the ashtray until the filter was reduced to tiny, smoke-brown splinters.

Chapter 30

Akasaka to Shinjuku was not far. Hiroshi exited onto a balcony that looked down over the passengers coursing through the west exit. Akiko told him that every day more than three million people passed through Shinjuku Station.

Could that be possible, he wondered, so many people through one station? What would one more—or one less—human being matter among all these others? The place was a shrine to mobility, efficiency and work, an overflowing offering of humanity.

Hiroshi moved into the stream of brisk-walking people making their way toward the skyscrapers of West Shinjuku. He found the basement lobby of the NS Building from the underground passageway, safe from the heavy rain aboveground. He waited a long time for the elevator that took him up to the 40th floor, to Bentley Associates.

In the reception lobby, he waited by a huge window dripping with condensation. It obscured the view of nearby buildings and turned the lights and traffic forty stories below into twinkling dots of blurry color.

The same secretary that showed him Steve's office during his first visit came out to meet him. She looked earthy and radiant in that stiff corporate entryway.

"Back again?" she asked, looking at him directly, her face not a mask like other secretaries.

"It always takes more visits than you think," Hiroshi said. "I need to talk to Barbara Harris-Mitford again, and to Mark Whitlock. He was out the last time I came."

"Barbara is expecting you, but things are in a bit of an uproar to-day," she said, leading him to a meeting room down the hall. The privacy glass frosted automatically as they passed, blocking Hiroshi's view inside.

"Uproar?" Hiroshi asked.

Steve's former secretary switched to English. "Some money went missing!" She pulled a face of surprise and concern.

"Is that right?" Hiroshi said in English.

"I'm quitting in two weeks," she said, and then dropped to a whisper. "So, I don't really care."

She showed him to the same meeting room with the twenty-person table, the lacquered inlaid wood gleaming from the soft lights above.

"What are you going to do?" Hiroshi asked.

"I'm going to Australia," she said. "A classmate opened a flower shop in Sydney. I'm going to work there!"

"Sounds exciting."

"Sun, wine, cheap rent."

"Three of life's essentials." Hiroshi handed her his card. "Call me after your last day here. We can celebrate!"

"That would be nice," she said.

This is getting easier, he thought to himself.

She slipped his card into the hip pocket of her summer skirt. "My name's Shiho, by the way."

"Shiho. I'm Hiroshi."

She hesitated a minute and returned to polite, corporate Japanese, "Barbara will be in shortly. I'll bring some coffee."

"I also need to talk to Mark Whitlock."

"Mark? Didn't they tell you?" Her brows came together over her round face. "He's taken a leave from the company."

"Where can I contact him?"

"He's on emergency leave."

"Emergency?"

"Family emergency."

"Where is he now?"

"I booked a ticket for him back to the States."

"When does his flight leave?"

"This afternoon."

"What time?"

"Is this important?" she asked.

"Very," Hiroshi said.

She hesitated. "Well, I'm leaving anyway. I'll go get his flight info. But don't tell Barbara. Company policy is not to hand out that kind of information."

"Understood," Hiroshi said.

Hiroshi looked out the window at the rain. Its staccato rhythm on the glass echoed in the large, empty meeting room.

Shiho returned with a printout of his departure. He would have to hurry to get to Narita airport in time.

"Barbara's coming right now," she whispered. Hiroshi folded the flight information and stuffed it into his jacket pocket as Barbara walked in the door.

"Detective Shimizu? What can I help you with today?" said Barbara, plopping down a stack of file folders and a leather portfolio.

Her manner was even brisker than before and her blue linen business suit tighter and trimmer. She exuded the air of a woman used to being listened to, not questioned.

"I just had a few more questions."

"I hope I can help." Barbara waved him toward a seat and nodded to Shiho to bring coffee.

"Our investigation has expanded. So, we need to know the specific companies that Steve worked with."

"I'm afraid that would be impossible," Barbara said. "Those firms are ones that took years to establish relations with."

"It would be strictly confidential."

"Nothing is ever completely confidential. We can't lose their trust just because you can't find any leads."

"To have him dead must have shaken everyone's trust."

"It certainly did. The loss is professional as well as personal."

"We can get a court order if necessary."

"That takes a lot of time in Japan."

"The process can be sped up. You don't want that."

Barbara nodded and said, "I'll see what I can do."

"Did you have any hint Steve was being blackmailed?"

"Pressure is common in the kind of business we do."

"Blackmail is common?"

"I would not call it blackmail. I would call it pressure. A business like ours always engages conflict."

"Just like detective work, then."

"Except you don't make money from it," Barbara pointed out.

Hiroshi thought of how poor his pay was, and how much he would make at a company like Bentley.

Hiroshi pulled out his cell phone and scrolled to a document Akiko had found for him. "I have a copy of a filing by Mitsutoki Corporation against Bentley for theft of information."

"That was last year. It was bogus. It was resolved."

"Was Steve involved in that?"

"Yes and no."

"What kind of information was that? Corporate spying, I know, is the norm. That's not my concern. I still need to find out why someone wanted to kill him."

Barbara stared at Hiroshi and then out the rain-spattered window. "Do you know much about doing business in Japan, Detective, and how hard it is for foreign businesses to break into the Japanese market?"

"I know it could drive a company or an individual to extremes."

"Extremes?" Barbara smirked and looked away. "The central fact of the Asian business world is that connections and information are essential. Our company is about success. Though his methods were controversial, his track record was stellar. I did not ask him details. Neither was he forthcoming."

"His methods were in a gray area."

"Methods do not show up on quarterly reports."

"Neither do deaths."

Barbara put her fingers together in front of her. The table was so highly polished it reflected her hands like a mirror. "Our company has a strict business ethics code. Codes do not always work. That's the Asian business environment."

"It's better for you and the company that this be solved."

She paused and then continued, "If I knew who might be involved, if I even had a clue, I would tell you. Before Steve died, he was training Mark to take over his work. That is why it was such a surprise what happened. He seemed already out of the fray."

"Did Bentley ever facilitate investment in Kawasaki?"

"Kawasaki? I think we helped negotiate a building contract there years ago, but I couldn't tell you details without looking. Steve was the kind of guy who would remember."

"We need the names of the companies Steve worked with. And I need to talk with Mark."

"I can give you one, but not the other. Mark has taken a leave from the company."

"I thought he was taking over for Steve?"

"He had a family emergency."

"Is his leave permanent?"

"More or less."

"More him and less the company or—"

"More or less on both sides, mutually."

"Is his departure connected to the missing funds?"

Barbara did not betray a hint of surprise. "I see you do your homework."

"Being a detective is nothing but homework," Hiroshi said. "The only thing I could not find is whether it was Steve or Mark who lost the funds."

"I wish I knew," Barbara said, speaking in a voice that Hiroshi, for the first time, found honest.

Her honesty turned them both quiet. The rain slapped against the huge windows of the room.

"I'll have the personnel office bring you Mark's contact information," Barbara said, standing and gathering her files and portfolio.

"I'm in a bit of a hurry," Hiroshi said, standing up.

"Aren't we all?" Barbara pointed him toward reception. "I'll have it sent to your office."

Hiroshi hurried along the hallway with the window glass frosting each office he passed wondering, after the shilly-shally of the accountant and the executive, if anything meaningful ever got accomplished in offices at all.

If he ran through the underground passageway back to the station, he could just catch the express from Shinjuku and get to Narita in time to catch Mark at the airport.

Chapter 31

Once he got down to the underground exit of the building, Hiroshi took off at a sprint, slowing and sidestepping and speeding up to dodge people in the crowd. He swiped his train pass to get inside and headed for the Narita Airport Express platform down two flights of stairs, up an escalator, at the far end of a long platform.

He got there just as the doors opened and the alarm sounded for the brief few seconds it took to let on people and their luggage. He hopped on and the door slid shut.

Hiroshi waited for the conductor in the space between the cars, showed his badge, and got a ticket for a seat. The conductor carefully deducted 150 yen from his train pass and calculated the new fare on his handheld ticket machine.

Hiroshi called Akiko.

"Can you find the number for the Narita liaison officer?"

"You're going all the way out there?" Akiko asked.

"Mark's leaving in an hour and a half and it's an hour out there."

"Do you want me to have them stop him?"

"I don't want to tip him off. Just find out where I can get through security. Text me, can you?"

Hiroshi found his seat, but the Chinese tourists in the other three seats had huge bags, and he could not stretch his legs out. They kept talking, loudly, but he closed his eyes and soon dozed off for the hour to the airport.

He was first off the train at Narita, hurrying through security and up the escalators to the departure lounge. The plainclothes officer was waiting near the travel insurance and exchange counters right where Akiko said he would be. The officer gave him a security card to put around his neck and asked, "Do you have a gun?"

"No," said Hiroshi. "Will we make it?"

"Maybe," the officer said. Boarding would start in twenty minutes. A sign said Mark's gate was twenty minutes away, but that was on foot.

When they got to the gate, the plainclothes officer separated from him but kept a close eye on him. Hiroshi walked back and forth in the boarding area, and then into the airport bar. A guy with blond hair was staring up at the baseball game on TV. Hiroshi went up to him.

"Mark Whitlock?"

He looked up at Hiroshi and said, "Who are you?"

"I'm detective Hiroshi Shimizu of Tokyo Homicide."

"Oh, shit," he said and threw his hot dog onto the plate. "I knew it."

"What did you know?"

"Barbara would send someone after me," he said, taking a big swig from his beer. "She's a vindictive bitch."

"She didn't send me. If anything, she covered for you. I need to ask you about Steve Deveaux."

"You were the guy scheduled to interview me at Bentley?"

"That's me."

"I don't know anything."

"Did you know you were next on the list?"

"What list?"

"Can we find a quieter place?" Hiroshi said.

Mark took a final swallow of beer and rubbed the foam off his lips with the back of his hand. He caught the bartender's eye and circled his finger over the beer and hot dog with the practiced motion of someone who spent a lot of time in bars. He paid in dollars and followed Hiroshi to a row of empty chairs at an unused gate. The airport security officer waited at a distance.

"What's the reason for your emergency leave?"

"Leave? Who said that? Barbara? I quit."

"You quit?"

"They accused me—"

"Of stealing the funds for the start-up in Thailand?"

190

"How did you know that? Barbara wanted that hushed up."

"You were next on that list, too."

"What's with all the lists?" Mark said, sitting on the edge of his chair.

"Where did the money go?"

"Are you investigating the money or the murder?"

"There would not be a murder without the money."

Mark shook his head. "I don't know where it went. I'm not an accountant. It was there one day and gone the next. Steve did everything—budget, accounts, and research—the whole thing. I just know how to talk to people."

"He was grooming you to take over his spot when he left, right?"

"He told me some things, but not everything. Honestly, I couldn't cut it. Too many reports. Too much schmoozing. Too many meetings. I first came to Japan to be a model."

Hiroshi looked at his chiseled features, casual chic jacket and studied-rumpled shirt. He should have stuck with modeling, Hiroshi thought.

"So, who do you think killed him? Was it a woman?"

Mark looked at Hiroshi. "Why do you ask that?"

"Was it?"

"I don't know," he looked away and shook his head. "Steve had many women. Some were business contacts."

"Paid for."

"He had money to pay. I never had to pay."

"I need your help here."

"He had many women who gave him information."

"Any regular ones?"

"Some more than others."

"They gave him information?"

"And more. But he wasn't one to talk about sex. Fortunately."

"They gave him information he could use to help Bentley."

"He called it 're-gifting.' He was always joking."

"How would I find the women he re-gifted information from?"

"I don't know," Mark said, brushing back his hair and looking up at the departure board.

"The woman Steve had before—beautiful, strong, and special—you had a relationship with her, too, right?"

Mark nodded his head, yes, and looked down in silence. "I'd rather not talk about it."

Hiroshi said, "It's much safer for you if you get on this plane, but we can take you to a passport control room or downtown where we can hold you for twenty days."

Mark sat up. "If I tell you, it can't get back to me."

"You're leaving, right?"

"They wouldn't let me quit. They're going to keep paying part of my salary."

"To keep you working?"

"To keep the confidentiality agreements. I have to keep certain things secret as long as they pay me. I'll find a lawyer in the States."

"As long as you have secrets, you'll be next."

Mark took a breath, twisted his mouth to the side. "Why do you think I'm leaving?"

"If we don't find her, she'll find you. Even in the States."

Mark looked at the crowds milling around in the waiting area, wondering if his hunch was right. It seemed to be.

"There's no need to say how I found out. I just need to know," Hiroshi said.

Mark twisted his shoulders. "There's a coffee shop called Les Chats Gris. Steve went there when he needed to get a hold of them."

"Hostesses?"

"Ones who had information."

"How did he pay them?"

"He never explained that. They had the information ready for him at the café always."

"You have names and photos, I'm sure." Mark knew all about Steve and the woman, just as he guessed.

Mark pulled his cell phone out and clicked through the photos. Finally, he held up a photo of himself with his arms around two Japanese women. One was tall with long hair, her eyes covered by sunglasses and the other was short and cute with a ripe, plump face. The tall woman stood rigid and unsmiling, but the short one had her arm around Mark, laughing.

"Where was this taken?"

"A club in Roppongi."

"What's the name?"

"The Venus de Milo."

Hiroshi showed Mark the screen of his cell phone, "Here's my text address. Send that photo to me right now."

Looking at the address, Mark clicked the buttons to attach the photo and send it, looking up as he heard his boarding call announcement. "That's my flight," Mark said.

"You never felt threatened by her?"

"What do you mean?" Mark asked. "She's just a woman."

"You never ended up too drunk with her?"

Mark shook his head, thinking. "Yes, twice."

"Once recently?"

Mark reluctantly nodded his head, yes, looking confused, starting to connect the dots Hiroshi was drawing for him.

"She drugged you," Hiroshi said.

"What? No way!"

"She uses Rohypnol."

"Ro-what? What's that?"

"It's called the date rape drug in America because victims lose consciousness and cannot remember clearly what happens. She used it to weaken men before she threw them in front of trains."

"Whoa! What are you talking about? Steve was...what men?"

"That woman, the taller one, killed Steve."

"No way. Steve's death was an accident. He often drank too much."

"He was helped along by Rohypnol. We found it in Steve's blood during the autopsy. And in another victim, too."

Mark sat up and shook his head. "I can't—"

"You better believe it."

"Both times I ended up a lot drunker than I expected, but—"

"And you were with her both times?"

Mark nodded, yes. Hiroshi could see he was chipping away at his denial.

"Steve set you up with her?"

"In a way, I guess. He knew her, but with us, with her and me, it was...different," Mark said, shaking his head. "I can't believe...she would—"

"What? Kill someone?"

"Drug me and—"

193

"Her name was Michiko, right?"

Mark leaned back. "How did you know?"

Hiroshi checked his cell phone and opened the photo Mark had just sent him. The sunglasses covered half her face, and the flash solarized them, but it was a better image than the black and white closed circuit security cameras.

"Tell me who the short one in the photo is."

"She's her friend, Reiko. They grew up together. They're like sisters."

"Where can I find them?"

"Good question. Michiko always found me. She didn't even give me her phone number. I posted her a LINE message, but she opened and closed chat rooms all the time."

"Can you give me the ones you have?"

"I—" Mark sighed. "Here," he said and gave Hiroshi the LINE names. "She has a million names, though, so she won't accept your connect request."

"I'll try anyway," Hiroshi said. "And where can we find Reiko?"

"Les Chats Gris. But she only goes there certain nights."

"We'll give it a shot," Hiroshi said.

Mark stood up.

"You're lucky to be alive, you know?"

Mark nodded and gathered his travel bag. He shook his head still confused. "She—"

"—was so beautiful?"

"Yeah! I mean who would think a woman like that—"

"—could kill someone?"

"I'll never understand women, or Asia, or business," Mark said.

"Maybe leave them alone for a while."

"That's what I plan on doing." Mark shook his head. "Tokyo's a strange, lonely, wacko place. I won't miss it. If I could tell you all the weird shit that happened to me here—"

Hiroshi half listened as they walked toward the gate.

"I'm outta here." Mark said, saluting with his boarding pass, and getting in line for the boarding gate.

Hiroshi watched him go, and after Mark walked down the boarding tunnel, he mumbled, "Bon voyage."

Heading back toward the express train into Tokyo, Hiroshi emailed the new photo of Michiko to Akiko, asking her to get clear copies printed.

The plainclothes officer came back over to Hiroshi. "Did you get what you needed?"

"Made some lucky guesses."

"Those always help."

Hiroshi called Sakaguchi. "Can you meet me in an hour?"

"In Roppongi?"

"How did you know?"

"Need extra weight?"

"Sumo weight."

"We'll meet you in Roppongi at nine."

He called Takamatsu again, but there was no answer.

Chapter 32

Sono heard the doorbell and was surprised when he didn't hear his secretary's voice. Seconds later, he looked up to find Michiko towering over the entryway to his cubicle, her black outfit refusing the glare of the accountancy office lights.

He folded shut the double-entry account book, ground out his cigarette in the overflowing ashtray and said, "Please call before you come."

"If I needed to call, I wouldn't come at all," she said.

His secretary brought the files and set them down on the table in the back cubicle. Michiko took off her sunglasses, pushed back her hair, and pulled out her account books. Sono followed her in to the cubicle.

In the small kitchenette, the secretary started preparing two cups of green tea. The greenish-yellow flicker from a fluorescent light, twitching and buzzing along the length of bulb, cast shadows across Sono's creviced smoker's face.

"I thought you were leaving?" he said.

"Day after tomorrow," she said. "Just a couple of loose ends left."

He looked at her closely, lit a cigarette, and opened the top account book. "I wouldn't call this a loose end."

"That's right," she said. "It's under control."

As the secretary set the cups out, tea spilled over into the two saucers. Sono gave the secretary a weary glance, but she kept her eyes down and went back to her desk.

"When your father's factory is paid off, what are you going to do with it? Sell it? You should have sold it before."

"I wanted to make a point."

"You won't even be here to see the point made."

"The point is I have sentimental reasons, a belief in the old economy. And Uncle Ono is still there."

"Other properties will hold value better."

"I have those, too. But Kawasaki will grow and when it does, I'll be ready. There has to be something better than more apartment buildings," she said. "And can you put out that cigarette?"

Sono looked at his cigarette. "I didn't know it bothered you." He stabbed the cigarette out in the ashtray and set it on top of a gray-metal cabinet behind him.

A thread of smoke still rose from the ashtray. Michiko looked at the smoke, then at Sono. He reached back and ground out the cigarette firmly.

"And can you turn down the air-conditioning?"

He called for his secretary, who came out with a lap blanket over her shoulders and turned it down. "Land for apartments is where we make the most."

"Those factories can become apartment buildings, but not before I say so," Michiko said, examining the books line by line.

"How do you know that? Same guy as before?"

"I look and I listen."

"You can manage all that from overseas?"

"That's why I have you here."

"I'll send the last payment after you tell me you're gone, OK?"

Michiko pulled out the envelopes of cash from Shibata the photographer and set them carefully on the table.

He shook his head. "I told you not to bring cash to the office."

"I didn't know it bothered you," she said, without looking up from the ledger lines as she entered the amounts in her book.

Sono carried the packs of money to a black safe in the back of his office, bending down to stack them inside. He closed the heavy door, set the handle and spun the tumblers.

Sono nodded, "Any questions on this one?"

"Let's go on to the next." She pulled out the next account book in her stack.

He pushed his green and red book across to her. She opened it, straightened her glasses and began copying its figures into her account book.

"If you put all this on a computer, it would be easier," she chided him.

"If I put it on a computer, it would be easier for someone else to access it."

"You can encrypt things these days."

"It is encrypted. Only I know how to read these," Sono said.

"And now I know, too," Michiko said. They pulled out the next account book from the stack at the same time.

After checking it, she folded it shut with the string place-mark left neatly on the last completed page. She took off her reading glasses.

"You should stop seeing anyone from Bentley," he said, fingering his cigarette pack.

"I won't be talking to them again."

"They know your name."

"Who?"

"A detective."

"Which name?"

"The one on the factory and most of the accounts."

"He knew my name before he came in or by the time he left?"

They locked eyes. He pulled his cigarette pack from his pocket and then put it back.

Michiko said, "That's why I'm keeping those videos. They arrest people for what you like to do. And those they arrest are made examples of. You want me to send copies again?"

"There's no need for that," he said, leaning back and frowning.

"You used to like to re-watch them," she snickered.

"I destroyed all the ones you sent."

"I hope so. They were so young; you wouldn't need much of a trial."

Sono sipped his tea and resettled himself, tapping the account books on the table between them.

"It didn't bother you to tell them about me."

"They beat that information out of me. I was in the hospital for a month."

"A month? I was gone a year." Michiko stared down at the blurring figures on the pages as the memories came back clear and sharp.

* * *

The morning that year started, Michiko made the mistake of telling Shibata to wait outside while she withdrew money from an account in her name in Roppongi. The bank teller, used to large cash withdrawals, did not blink an eye but reached across the counter to help Michiko place the money in each envelope before Michiko set them in her black leather duffel bag.

Shibata waited across the street from the bank with the photos and mailing envelopes. He smoked and dug around in his camera bag, checking again, anxious to get everything done. They had tickets for an early evening flight out of Narita.

He looked up and saw it all happen at a distance: Four guys in black suits and sunglasses grabbed Michiko outside the bank and forced her into a car. They were not robbing her. He could see the smile on one of them at the weight of her duffel bag.

Shibata was in good shape then and he took off across the street, but traffic was too heavy to get across six lanes in time. They would beat him senseless, he knew, but he ran across anyway, hoping to at least delay them. All four of the men had hands on her as passersby scurried out of the way.

He dodged cars, watching Michiko struggle and land a few kicks before they shoved her into the back seat. A car grazed Shibata's knee before he got to the sidewalk. He ran at full speed, but when he got to the car all he could do was slap its trunk as it sped away.

He yelled and ran and threw his bag at them, hearing the cameras inside smash, but hoping they'd stop and come back for him, drag him inside with her.

* * *

When the car stopped, Michiko tried to peer out of the bag over her head as they pushed her out of the back seat. After standing up beside the car, they pulled the bag off her head in what appeared to be the private garage of an apartment building. Large black SUVs filled the few spaces and the door to an elevator was the only way out she could see. The four men started to walk her toward the door.

Michiko swung her leg into the stomach of one of the guys, flooring him. He looked surprised and embarrassed lying on the pavement and heaving for breath.

She cracked the wrist of a fat guy in a black suit closest to her. He dropped to his knees, snatching at his wrist and letting out a scream. She kneed him in the jaw, slamming his head back into the side panel of the car, and he was out.

The other two, more wary, came around the car from both sides. Michiko braced herself to take them down, but the man she had first kicked in the stomach snatched her legs. She lost her balance as the man who had been driving jabbed a stun gun into her ribs. She toppled over, falling hard onto the concrete floor of the parking garage.

The other man came from the other side and jolted her with another few seconds of pain from a second stun gun. She bucked and rolled and then quit moving.

The two men dove on top of her and slipped plastic cuffs around her wrists and ankles. She roused herself and tried to kick them, but they hit her again and again with their open palms until she stopped.

They picked her up from the pavement and carried her to the elevator that took them up to penthouse where they kept her for a few weeks.

After that, she didn't know where she was. A few months later, she didn't care where or what she was.

* * *

Michiko took a sharp breath and sipped the tea, despite the dripping, to calm herself. Only the flickering, buzzing bulb disturbed the silence.

Sensing Michiko was not focusing on the accounts, Sono said, "What happened before was an accident."

"An accident?" Michiko stopped and looked up from the books, holding her pen in the air.

"It was more than that. I understand. Risk is part of doing business."

"Part of business?"

"There's always risk. It won't happen again."

201

"You're right it won't." Michiko looked back at the account figures.

"I've never told you everything."

"You never explained how they found out."

"I never knew. Look, I don't tell anyone everything. That's why this works. But we need someone like the Bentley guy to blame. Now, he's gone."

"I'll be gone, too, so it doesn't really matter. The building site in Roppongi I told you about—"

"That information was valuable. Look what they paid us. But with that guy gone, our insurance is gone, too."

"He took the blame with him. That's better insurance."

Sono let go a phlegmy cough.

He was used to days of silence, broken up by short meetings with clients or brief phone calls. He could wait on her as long as she wanted, but he had no idea what she wanted. He took off his glasses and worked the hinge back and forth in his hand.

Michiko folded the account books and pushed his back to him.

Sono took the books back. "You don't tell me everything, either. That's also why this works."

"You keep saying that."

"Can I give you some advice about accounts in Europe?" Sono asked.

"Go ahead," she said, arranging things in her bag.

"Banks in Europe are more cautious than here, so be careful about large amounts of cash. Do not keep changing the password and account numbers. That brings suspicion. If you remove a regular amount each month, it is less likely to draw attention."

"I know all this," Michiko said.

"I'm just trying to be sure you do."

"When will you send the payment to Switzerland?"

"Once you're settled there. You'll have to move it quickly. But wait until I tell you."

"I don't want any accounts to get frozen again."

"We have this all set. The information is already passed on to both parties. They'll fight it out. We get our cut from both. We move the money bit by bit."

She looked at him, considering how hard it would be to manage all this without him. He knew what he was doing, but never let her know. Until she could get to Paris and finish things, she still needed him.

"Enjoy Europe. You deserve a rest. Until your flight, just stay out of trouble."

She stood up from the table and looked down at him. "What are you talking about?"

He folded his arms across his chest. "It's just a phrase."

"It's the wrong phrase," she said and pulled down her sunglasses.

He sat still, listening as her footfalls receded along the row of partitions and the front door clicked shut.

He lit a cigarette and inhaled deeply. Despite the deep, lung-filling smoke, he could still smell the perfume she'd left in her wake.

Chapter 33

Sakaguchi was waiting in front of the Almond Coffee Shop. His huge bulk drew stares. Everyone wanted to ask if he was a sumo wrestler, but nobody did.

Groups of people circled along the sidewalk discussing where to go next, their faces flushed and limbs loose after a first round of food and drink. People chatted into cell phones as if conversing with voices in their heads.

"Where're the other guys?" asked Hiroshi.

"Ueno and Osaki are following us. Don't look around. Works better that way. Where's Takamatsu?"

"I don't know."

"He'll turn up."

"He'd better. What's his wife think? Did you ever meet her?" Hiroshi asked. They walked down the crowded sidewalk.

"No. You?"

"He never mentions her."

"Maybe she takes care of the house. He brings in the money."

"That'd never work with an American woman."

"How long did you spend over there?"

"Too long maybe."

"Ever think of going back?"

"Sometimes. All the time. And you?"

"Not to Osaka, but I'd go back to sumo. It's tougher, but more predictable."

Hiroshi laughed. "Are you married?"

"With a face like mine?"

Hiroshi drew back and looked at him. "Must have sent fear into your opponents."

"There aren't any women my size anyway," Sakaguchi said.

Hiroshi laughed. "Might find someone tonight."

"Roppongi is the last place I'd look."

They walked down the main street past girls in shiny tops and short skirts handing out glossy pamphlets. Bouncers in tuxedos called out their club's offerings. Well-dressed businessmen strode on the balls of their feet and black-clad young hipsters swung along sober and glib.

"What landed you in the chikan section really?"

"Money."

"Something went missing?"

"No, just the opposite. Takamatsu ended up with too much."

"How could that happen?"

"That's what the chief of homicide wanted to know."

"Well?"

"He got it as part of an investigation. Not the best part."

"He got it from where?"

"I didn't ask, exactly," Sakaguchi said. "Anyway, they split up our unit. That was before you came."

Hiroshi stopped and looked up at a second story window. Lace curtains half-covered an ironwork array of cute, gray cats and curlicued letters for Les Chats Gris.

Hiroshi flashed Sakaguchi the photo he got from Mark at the airport.

"This the girl? Wait, Akiko forwarded it to me, too." Sakaguchi fumbled with his cell phone until he brought up the picture. "The short one, right?"

"The tall one's the one we want. The short one will take us to her."

Sakaguchi followed Hiroshi up the steep stairs inside. Outside the door, Sakaguchi stopped at a stack of boxes resting on the landing—a fire code violation. The boxes and his body blocked the exit.

Hiroshi pulled open the door to face a dozen women who looked up from magazines, cell phones and conversations. He breathed in the thick blend of smoke and perfume and pretended to look at the photos of Paris on the walls, while scanning the women dressed in tight, stylish dresses their hair swirling in carefully coiffed designs.

Some feigned indifference, while others started to leave. Since he was the only man in the room, and everyone was a hostess, Hiroshi would have to be a stalker, jilted lover, or a cop. They paid their bills and sashayed out. In the hallway on the landing, they had to make themselves small to squeeze by Sakaguchi as they fled.

Hiroshi scanned the room for Reiko, Michiko's friend in Mark's photo. She, or someone very much like her, was sitting by the cat-covered window. She looked older than in the photo, her hair dyed a blond that arched over her head in neat, thick plaits. She turned the pages of a glossy magazine, glancing at her cell phone screen as an incoming message lit it up.

Hiroshi checked the photo in his cell phone again to be sure it was Reiko and walked over to her table.

"Mind if I sit down?"

Reiko kept looking through her magazine.

Hiroshi said, "You're Reiko, right?"

Reiko put her cell phone in her purse, carefully, without looking up from her fashion magazine and asked, "And you are?"

"A friend of Michiko's."

"I don't think so."

"I want to ask you a few questions," he said in a low voice. She finally looked up at him, and the blue-tinted contacts in her eyes surprised him. The combination of Japanese face with blond hair and blue eyes gave her an exotic prettiness, amplified by thick blue eyeliner. Her eyelashes ended in small, blue feathers pasted to her skin.

"This is not a good place to talk," she said, noticing the exodus of women.

"Where is?"

"No place, really."

"I can start speaking louder." Hiroshi set down his cell phone with the photo of Reiko, Michiko and Mark in front of her.

She stood up, twisting her hips and pulling the gold chain of her white leather purse over her shoulder. "I have to go to the women's room first."

"I'll wait out front."

Hiroshi walked out and told Sakaguchi to stay where he was. They waited for her in the hallway.

When Reiko finally came out and saw Sakaguchi outside, she scoffed and walked downstairs, frowning at Hiroshi, who fell in beside her. Sakaguchi followed.

"So, what do you want to know?" she asked, adjusting her purse.

"Where's Michiko?"

"Paris, London, Milan, I'm not sure."

"Where is she exactly?"

"She loves to go abroad. I'm a bit of a homebody."

"Let's get a drink. My treat," Hiroshi offered, stopping in the busy sidewalk.

"I'm supposed to be at work at ten," Reiko said, checking her watch.

"You can be a little late."

"All right, follow me," she said and led them to a side street where she pulled back the thick metal door. One long counter and several short tables crowded the back of a long, narrow room. A row of retro yellow lamps along the counter illuminated the leather upholstery of the seating and the thick wood of the tables. Jazz played quietly. One man sat along the counter sipping whiskey. Reiko walked to a back table.

"I guess you're the kind of girl who likes martinis?" Hiroshi said, sitting next to her.

"I guess you're the kind of guy who asks dumb questions?"

Sakaguchi sat on a nearby stool.

"Two martinis," Hiroshi said to the bartender after Sakaguchi shook his head no. Hiroshi searched past the make-up and tinted contact lenses for her eyes. She lit a cigarette with a diamond-lined gold lighter. Her long, square-filed fingernails, teensy green and pink flowers pasted in the centers, clicked around the stem of the martini glass.

"So, Michiko and you went to school together?"

"Until she got kicked out."

"For what?"

"For wearing her skirt too short. Michiko was smart, but she couldn't follow rules."

"And you did?"

"No, but no one noticed me. Everyone noticed her."

"Sounds like a strict school."

"Not strict, just stupid."

"When was that?"

"Ages ago."

"So, Michiko was a good student?"

"She won an English speech contest, but the next day she forgot to take out her earrings and lower her skirt when she came onto the school grounds. So, they kicked her out."

"For a short dress?"

Reiko smoked deeply and slowly. "A boy and I smashed the glass case and took her speech trophy to give her. That's when I got kicked out!"

"So, you didn't finish high school?"

"What for? Michiko and I made a lot of money back then. We were so young. She still makes a lot."

"Where is Michiko now?"

"I told you. She left. For Europe."

"Any idea where in Europe?"

Reiko laughed, shook her head, and lit another cigarette.

"She went by herself?"

"She always goes by herself."

"She speaks English?"

"And French. She worked at clubs with foreigners. Almost married one once. But in the end, he turned out to be like most men." Reiko laughed. "Another martini?"

Hiroshi waved at the bartender for two more.

"Why are you so interested in Michiko?"

"We just want to talk with her."

"We haven't really been in touch recently."

"But you know she's in Europe?"

The bartender brought over the drinks, looking nervously at Sakaguchi not drinking, and set them down on the table in front of Hiroshi and Reiko, who took the last swallow of her first martini and started on the second.

"When was this photo taken?" He again showed her the photo of her with Michiko and Mark.

"Seems like another lifetime."

"Your family is also from Kawasaki."

Reiko frowned, lit another cigarette. "They died, my mom and dad."

"I'm sorry."

"This killed them," she said, holding up her martini glass. "Michiko's father let me live with them."

"What about Michiko's parents? Are they still living?"

"Her mother died when she was young. I barely remember her except we baked cookies. She had really long hair and nice perfume. Her dad was killed in an accident. But it wasn't an accident. Everyone loved him. Especially Michiko."

"You must go back often?" Hiroshi asked Reiko.

"To light incense for my parents, and Michiko's, at Obon festival every August. After the factories were cheated out of their land and the place was buried in apartment buildings, there's no other reason to go."

"Where did she live exactly?"

She sighed, finished her martini. "There's nothing there anymore."

"So, how do I get in touch with Michiko?"

"You can't. She gets in touch with you."

"Can you tell her we have to talk to her?"

"She probably already knows that."

"Can you give me your number, so I don't have to bother you at the coffee shop again?"

She frowned and sighed but wrote it out for him on a paper coaster.

Hiroshi dialed the number to be sure it worked.

Reiko looked at him when her cell phone rang and shook her head. "Don't trust me?" She typed in "cute cop guy" in English to save his number in her address book. "I have to go. I'm one of the older ones at my club now, so I help the mama-san with the new girls. It's busy."

"Why don't you open your own place?"

"I'm planning on it. With Michiko's help. She was always good at making and saving. I'm just good at spending." She laughed at her own joke.

She pulled a large folding mirror out of her white leather purse, adjusted her hair, and straightened her top. She stood up and said, "Michiko's never done anything wrong. It's the system that's wrong."

Reiko finished the last sip of her martini, raised her eyebrows in thanks, and walked out.

Sakaguchi stood up and walked over. "Should we follow her?"

"I first want to see if anyone around here recognizes the faces from these photos."

"And if they don't?"

"We go to Kawasaki."

Chapter 34

At Man-zoku, Hiroshi walked to the doorman, who looked like he was barely a teenager, and showed him the photos of Steve, Mark, Michiko, Reiko, and a few distracters. The kid shook his head as Hiroshi flipped to the photo of Michiko and asked again. The kid shook his head, looked away, his hands shuffling discount cards he was supposed to hand out to passersby.

Sakaguchi stepped closer and cleared his throat.

The kid spit on the sidewalk.

Before it hit the ground, Sakaguchi had him on tiptoe by his arm and was hustling the kid around the side of the building. Sakaguchi was about to crack the kid's face, but Hiroshi held up a restraining hand.

"Whatever loyalty you have to this club, you better think clearly," Sakaguchi said.

The kid didn't resist, waiting it out with his eyes down. "It costs," he said, looking sideways at Sakaguchi.

Sakaguchi shook the kid like a rag doll. "We don't pay for information. We put people in jail until they give us information."

The kid looked at the photos and sighed. "I've never seen the people in those photos."

"Look again."

The kid looked again. "I worked here two years, never saw them."

"Look again."

Hiroshi showed them again.

"All foreigners look the same. The women change their looks all the time."

Sakaguchi let go of the kid. "You keep your eyes open. We'll be back."

The kid straightened his jacket and walked back to his spot on the sidewalk, acting tough. The same scenario played out at the next three clubs: Pata-Pata, Backside, and Sanctum Sanctorum.

Before Hiroshi and Sakaguchi got to the Venus de Milo, Hiroshi's phone buzzed.

"Takamatsu?" Sakaguchi asked when Hiroshi hung up.

"No, our friend Shibuya," Hiroshi said.

"He didn't make it?"

"The anesthetic, apparently."

"He had too much on top of the drug?"

"The doctors weren't clear, but something like that."

"Add that to Michiko's list. What about the girl? Call her parents?"

"Her parents were probably the problem. We can bring her in later," Hiroshi said.

"Seems like she can fend for herself all right," Sakaguchi said.

The bouncers at the Venus de Milo were older and more experienced. They stepped out to the cars pulling up to the curb, opened the doors and greeted the regulars by name. In between, the doormen chatted with each other as if they owned the street.

Hiroshi said, "This is where Steve came all the time. I came here with Takamatsu."

Sakaguchi said, "Let's not waste time, then."

Sakaguchi stepped ahead of Hiroshi to the doorman standing in front of a fake Venus de Milo. Before Hiroshi could get a word out, the bouncer shoved Sakaguchi in the chest.

Sakaguchi kneed him in the thigh and grabbed his hair. Twisting the bouncer's head and arm, Sakaguchi pushed him over the back of a Mercedes Benz with tinted windows.

Immediately, a man with a slicked-back ponytail and leather gloves shot out of the drivers' side of the Mercedes, glaring. Sakaguchi pointed at him in caution, and frog-marched the doorman around the side of the building.

Ueno, who had been following them, hurried from across the street, stepped in front of the ponytailed chauffeur and said something too low for Hiroshi to hear. Hiroshi followed Sakaguchi—who had the bouncer's head locked in his thick arms—into the alley and heard the Mercedes Benz door shut with a heavy swoosh.

Sakaguchi twisted the doorman's head, tumbling him backward over two large, blue plastic trash bins, which collapsed with a plastic crackle. Sakaguchi picked him up and pushed his face against the brick of the wall.

"Look closely and don't make a mistake," hissed Sakaguchi.

Hiroshi pulled the photos out, flipping them one by one before the doorman's angry face. For light, Hiroshi then pulled out his cell phone and used the glow from the screen. The doorman gave no response.

"Look again," said Sakaguchi, pushing until the bins caved in, and trash spilling over their shoes.

This time, the doorman nodded at Steve's photo, and then at Mark's photo.

Hiroshi asked, "They came here often?"

Before the doorman could answer, a tall man in a black suit, black shirt, and thin, black tie stepped into the alley. He was older and thinner than the doorman. His long, round face took in the scene. Two more men stood behind him at the entrance to the alley, both of them holding long, thin knives along their thighs.

The thin man spoke in a calm, clear voice. "That is one of my employees."

"We need information," said Hiroshi.

"You are disrupting our business operations."

"It won't take long. Unless you want it to," said Sakaguchi.

The man glowered, his face pale and expressionless.

"You're the owner?" Hiroshi asked.

"Let's say I'm the manager."

"Well, why not tell your employee to answer our questions, so you can get back to business?" Hiroshi said.

The man stared at Hiroshi.

"If you'd like us to send the media here, there's always some reporter looking for a scoop." Hiroshi had learned this threat from Takamatsu. "We could go through your books, too, send in a crew."

The manager considered this.

At that moment, Hiroshi noticed, with relief, Ueno and Osaki standing behind the men with the knives. Behind them was the ponytailed chauffeur of the Benz.

"All we need to know is how often two foreigners came to the club and which of the hostesses they favored."

After a pause, the manager nodded to the doorman who was still bent over the trash bins. "Tell them what they need to know. There are always more women."

Sakaguchi released his grip, letting the doorman stand up and brush the garbage off his shoes and pant cuffs. Hiroshi again held up the photos.

"What about this guy?" said Hiroshi, holding the photo of Steve.

"The guy used to come in all the time."

"And this guy?" The photo was of Mark.

"Sometimes."

"How often?"

"Once every couple days. I don't know."

"How often exactly?"

"Every day sometimes. Then gone for a week. It depended."

"And this guy?" Hiroshi held up a photo of Wakayama, the rich real estate speculator.

"Yes. That guy, too. Often."

"They were together?"

"Yes, but that was a year ago. I heard he died."

"They both died. Same girls every time?"

"I'm outside. I don't know who they talk to. I just call the taxis."

"You see them get into taxis, right?"

"Limos."

"What did the girls look like, if you don't know their names?"

"Attractive. Sophisticated."

Sakaguchi took a step toward him and he spoke more quickly.

"Tall, strong, confident. Everything—hair, dress, make-up, changed all the time. You know how they are. Fashion trend of the moment."

Hiroshi held up the photo of Mark with Michiko and Reiko.

"The tall one comes only on special occasions. The other quit. They had other girls sometimes, too."

"What was the tall one's name?"

"I don't know any of their names."

"Did you go out with them?"

The doorman snorted. "They go out with their own guys."

"Not with a doorman?"

The doorman rubbed his wrist. "There are photos in the hallway."

Ueno, the biggest of all of them, walked up the stairs of the club entrance and ripped the frame board of photos of the hostesses off the wall. He pushed through the two guys holding knives and carried the board back into the alley.

In the photos, twenty or thirty women with startled half-smiles, pale from a too-bright flash, stared out at them. The doorman pointed at one—which Hiroshi plucked out of its inner frame, then at another.

"Any others?"

"The tall woman's photo isn't there. Maybe the mama-san took it down. I haven't seen her in a long time."

"She look like this?" Sakaguchi jammed a cropped photo of Michiko in sunglasses in front of the doorman.

"That looks like a thousand girls in Tokyo," the doorman said. "Even the one in your cell phone could be anybody."

Ueno tossed the photo board onto the trash. Hiroshi put the photos in his pocket.

The men holding knives put them away inside their long coats, and then stood with their arms ready.

Sakaguchi and Hiroshi straightened their jackets and walked out of the alley.

"If you need information, you should ask politely," the manager said as they passed.

"That was polite," Sakaguchi said.

Before Sakaguchi and Hiroshi got to the street, the manager turned to them and said, "If it's a hostess you need, I can arrange one for you."

The three detectives stopped.

The manager continued, "They'll tell any story, take the blame and do the time. It gets them out of debt, gets your case closed. Everyone's happy."

Hiroshi turned to look at the manager and said, "It's too late for happy."

"Never too late," the man said. "Plenty of other cops do that. It's not as expensive as you might think."

Hiroshi's cell phone rang.

"It's Takamatsu."

Chapter 35

The hallways were long and quiet and well-marked. Neither Hiroshi nor Sakaguchi spoke as they walked to the south wing elevators, one large and one for personnel only. The gurney-sized elevator moved at a ponderous crawl. The inside smelled of disinfectant.

At the tenth floor, they were directed down a long hallway of private rooms. In a chair at the end, a plainclothes guard looked up from his manga and recognizing Sakaguchi, motioned with his chin to the room.

"Where's Sugamo?" Sakaguchi asked.

"Went for more coffee." Several empty cans of vending machine coffee rested on the table beside him.

Hiroshi walked into the room, pulled back the curtain and reeled back.

Fluids oozed through a tangle of tubes taped in place. Velcro straps circled the man's arms and air casts covered his lower legs. IV drips dangled from above and a rack of monitors hummed. Two flexible tubes wormed into the man's mouth. The bed was tilted up at an angle, so that his head, bandaged, flopped a little to the side.

Hiroshi and Sakaguchi stood there for a few, shocked minutes, the machines burbling and pulsing.

Sakaguchi grunted and leaned away.

After checking the name to be sure it was him, Hiroshi sighed deeply. He could hardly recognized Takamatsu underneath it all. He stepped forward to touch a small open patch of Takamatsu's forearm. There was no response, only the rhythmic sound of the monitors indicating life.

"He must have found our girl," Sakaguchi said.

Sugamo came in. "He's been here a while, but they couldn't ID him. No wallet, no cell phone, nothing. It took them hours to figure out who he was. I got here as soon as I could and called you."

"When did they bring him in?" Sakaguchi asked.

"The train station called it in and the ambulance brought him here to the ER, so a few hours ago at least," Sugamo said.

"Did someone tell his wife?" Hiroshi asked.

"She was here, but went home to check on the children. Said she'd be back in a while."

Hiroshi murmured, "I'll stay here and wait for her to return."

Sakaguchi said, "Sugamo, you might as well go home. Be back after you sleep. On your way out, tell Osaki to come up here. He's in the lobby. Tell the guy across the hall to be back late morning."

They stared down at Takamatsu. Most of his body's functions had been externalized. He was breathing on his own, but fluids, pain and oxygen were all taken care of by machines. Dark bruises and scraped-raw skin were visible through the bandages and tape.

A nurse with a large folder came into the room, startling Hiroshi and Sakaguchi both. Hiroshi asked her, "When will he wake up?"

The nurse busied herself in her cart, "Not until the gamma hydroxybutyric acid filters out of his body."

"What's that?"

"The date rape drug."

"Rohypnol, you mean?"

"That's a benzodiazepine. This has the same effect, but it's a little stronger, and colorless and tasteless. He had a very large dose."

"How large?"

"It could have killed him. The alcohol made it worse. He had a large dose of that, too."

Hiroshi and Sakaguchi listened to her as attentively as school boys.

"No internal bleeding, fortunately. Two broken ribs, a broken collarbone, and a broken forearm. His legs are OK." She arranged the medicine and supplies in the cart and made notes. "He was lucky."

"What time was he given the drug?"

"Hard to say. Are you a family member?"

"Colleague. Detective."

"So, talk to the doctor. They start their rounds at six." She checked all the equipment again and walked out.

Sakaguchi said, "You sure you want to stay? I don't mind."

"I want to be here when he wakes up," Hiroshi said. "And talk with the doctors."

"Get some sleep. You could use some."

"I could use a lot."

"I'll be back in a few hours." Sakaguchi looked at Takamatsu again, shook his head and walked out.

Hiroshi was left to stare down at the comatose Takamatsu. He flopped into a small chair in an alcove by the window, a few steps from the bed.

It was just like Takamatsu to go it alone, stubborn bastard, always so sure of himself, always doing things his way. If Takamatsu had only called to say where he was going and why, Hiroshi might have been there. Who had he found, he wondered? Did he find her or find someone or something else—stop thinking, Hiroshi told himself. Takamatsu would explain it all when he woke up.

Hiroshi pulled a chair over for his feet, took off his shoes, and closed his eyes, trying to quiet the thoughts ping-ponging inside his head. He turned on his side toward the window, slung his jacket over his shoulders, and let his exhaustion carry him into a deep sleep.

* * *

Something in the rhythmic beeping of the monitors shifted and Hiroshi blinked his eyes open. His neck hurt. He wrapped his arms around himself and pulled his jacket over his shoulders, wondering if there was a blanket somewhere. He was too tired to get up to ask the nurses, so he hunkered back down.

Before he fell back asleep, the rhythm of the monitors slipped offbeat again. He rolled over and saw a woman in a beige dress slip out the door.

Must be his wife, he thought and rocked himself halfway up. He found his shoes and stood up. He had never met Takamatsu's wife before, and in his mind he was formulating what to say to her in his mind. Hiroshi tried to shake the fatigue out of his head, squinting to refocus his eyes.

He walked stiffly out to talk with Takamatsu's wife. Outside the room, he saw her walking down the hallway. Strange, he thought, still dazed. He watched as she turned to look into the nurses' station, and the light hit her for a moment.

She wore a gauze mask and a big floppy hat. She was tall with long hair, and moved easily, as if she did yoga classes all day in whatever suburb of Tokyo Takamatsu owned a house, or was it an apartment. Hiroshi didn't have any idea.

Hiroshi wondered where the woman was going. Had she been standing there for long while he slept? He could see her waiting at the elevator at the end of the hall. He started to wake up, walking quickly, and then jogging toward her.

A nurse exiting the station nearly collided with him.

"Who was that?" Hiroshi asked the nurse.

He saw the woman get on the elevator and disappear.

"You're the detective," said the nurse said, continuing on her way.

Hiroshi stopped her. "Is the small elevator faster than the large one?"

"Much faster," she said.

"You have the keys?"

"Yes."

"I need you to open it for me."

She shook her head. "Police are always so much trouble," she said and dug in her pocket for the keys, walking briskly ahead of Hiroshi. She keyed the small elevator and waited until it arrived, then leaned in, put the key in and asked, "Where to?"

"Lobby, I guess," Hiroshi said.

She pressed "L" and let him go.

Hiroshi rode down. A couple of young doctors got on at the sixth floor, and, at the fourth, two nurses got on. Hiroshi pressed the "close door" button repeatedly. The doctors and nurses stared at him in silence.

In the lobby, Hiroshi ran back toward the main entrance and dialed Osaki.

Osaki sounded as groggy as Hiroshi had been before a shot of adrenaline woke him up.

"I think she came to the room," Hiroshi said. "I'm going after her."

"Where are you?"

"Lobby."

"I'll be down," Osaki said.

"No, stay there—" Hiroshi barked, but the phone clicked and the line went dead. Who knew if Osaki heard him? Hiroshi didn't have time to find out. He hustled out to the drop-off circle and asked the guard in charge of traffic, "Did you see a tall woman with a mask and floppy hat?"

The guard said, "I don't look closely."

"The last few minutes?"

The guard shook his head indifferently. "I'm sorry, I don't really look."

"Is there another door out of the hospital?"

"This is the main door."

Hiroshi looked around stupidly. She was too young to be Takamatsu's wife—unless she was in spectacular shape. If she were, he would have bragged about it. Hiroshi stepped out from under the eaves into the gray rain, looking at the bicycle parking area and the bus stop and cursing himself.

On the opposite side of the street, far down, past the end of the hospital, he caught a glimpse of a woman walking quickly. The umbrella blocked her, so it could be anyone or it could be her. He stayed on the hospital side of the street and picked up his pace to close the distance. He wiped the wet off his forehead and felt the rain soak into his shoulders.

The street wound downhill and spilled into a lane of small wood-framed shops with old rusting signs and sliding glass front doors, a pocket of the city unchanged for decades.

She apparently knew her way and walked at a steady speed.

The raindrops fell heavier. Hiroshi wiped his eyes. He passed a bus stop and saw a clear, vinyl umbrella with a broken stretcher and bent ribs hanging on a rail. He snatched it and slid it halfway open.

She turned into the large courtyard of a shrine and walked across the gravel toward the main shrine building. Hiroshi slipped inside the courtyard after her, turning down a long, covered walkway that led away from the main shrine.

The woman, still covered by the wide umbrella, threw a few coins into the collection box, rang the large bell with a rope, and clapped her hands twice before bowing her head in prayer. She stepped down from the screen-covered inner shrine and stood still, looking straight ahead into the shrine, its interior hidden behind long hanging screens.

Hiroshi stepped behind the small stone pagodas, near a huge pine tree with spreading branches propped up by wood supports. The half-working umbrella spared him from the rain.

The woman dropped a coin in the donation box for one of the wooden *ema* prayer plaques left out for after-hours purchase. She pulled a pen from her purse and wrote for a long time. When she finished, she walked to the large upright frame where hundreds of *ema* hung in tightly packed rows under a thatched roof.

With his head down, Hiroshi scooted across the back area, around to the other side of the courtyard, where the woman couldn't see him.

When he looked back again, she was gone.

He searched the courtyard carefully, looking from different directions. There was nowhere to hide in the courtyard. She was just gone.

He ran around the main shrine building and then to the front gate. She would have had to run hard over the gravel to get to the gate, but he heard no crunch.

He snooped cautiously around the tree and, as he passed the racks of hundreds and hundreds of *ema*, he stopped. He found her *ema* on the top right. Raindrops plunked down splattering the ink.

Kamisama, Kigan. I had a moment of weakness and I felt human again. Thank you for that. Let me leave this city of pain, this city of men. I'll let you punish those who deserve it, save those who need saving. Please, transport me safely, away, from this, from here, never to return.

He let the *ema* swing back with a clack and looked around again wondering how she managed to just disappear.

He dropped the broken umbrella and started running back the way he came. Just outside the gate, he met Osaki.

"Where is she?" Osaki demanded.

"I lost her," Hiroshi said.

"She can't have gone far."

"That might be far enough," Hiroshi said. "Who's with Taka-matsu?"

"No one."

"Takamatsu's all alone?"

Hiroshi grabbed Osaki's shoulder and spun him around as he took off at a sprint back for the hospital.

Chapter 36

Osaki outweighed Hiroshi by double, but ran twice as fast. Osaki looked back once, and then went ahead at a sprint.

At the hospital, Hiroshi, soaked with rain and sweat, bounded up the stairway to the entrance and rushed across the lobby toward the elevator. Hiroshi pushed into the small elevator and flipped open his badge, telling the doctors and nurses not to press any other floors. He jammed his thumb on the close door button.

On the tenth floor, Hiroshi rushed past the nurse's station toward Takamatsu's room. Spinning into the room with his left hand on the doorframe, Hiroshi bumped smack into Osaki. Osaki didn't budge.

Hiroshi looked around his shoulders to see a woman leaning over the bed, holding Takamatsu's barely lifted hand, her long hair draped like a canopy over his bandaged, pincushioned body. She glared at them, her eyes red, her hair tangled.

As Hiroshi caught his breath, he could see that this woman was shorter, rounder, older, and in different clothes than the tall, masked woman who had entered the room not an hour earlier. This woman wiped her cheeks with the back of her hand and straightened herself. She was about to speak when Takamatsu groaned.

They all turned to him.

"Awake finally," she said.

Takamatsu craned his neck to look at each of them, using only one eye. The other was swollen shut, the skin red and puffy. He waved his hand and in a voice that sounded nothing like his regular booming bravado, managed to croak out, "Hiroshi, Osaki, my wife."

"I'm Hiroshi Shimizu," Hiroshi managed, finally, and bowed deeply to her, since it was the first time they had met. "I'm pleased to meet you, but I wish it were under different circumstances."

Takamatsu's wife bowed and turned back to Takamatsu. "You're supposed to be asleep," she admonished her husband, pulling his sheet up, and folding it back at his shoulders.

Takamatsu's voice was a distant whisper, barely able to squeak out his answer. "Sleep sounds nice." One side of his face quivered as if he was trying to smile.

"Could you let us talk a minute?" Hiroshi asked Takamatsu's wife in polite Japanese. She ran her palms over her eyes, nodded OK, and stepped outside.

Hiroshi looked into Takamatsu's still-open eye. It was also swollen, next to his blue, bruised nose, but not completely shut. "Anything to avoid having a drink with me, huh?" said Hiroshi, swallowing hard.

Takamatsu swallowed, the effort obviously causing him pain. "Just a little hangover," Takamatsu's shriveled voice was so faint Hiroshi had to lean over to catch it.

"You feel like talking?"

"Let's get it over with," said Takamatsu shifting his weight and moving his shoulders slightly. "Morphine drip?"

Hiroshi pressed the button, but nothing came out. The timer clearly showed that it was too soon for another dose. Hiroshi kept pressing the button anyway, and said, "I'll tell you what happened, then you squeeze my hand once when I'm on track, and twice when I'm off, OK?"

Hiroshi took his hand and Takamatsu grasped his just enough to make Hiroshi notice.

"The night we separated you found her in the David, right?"

Takamatsu squeezed once.

"You figured you'd do it on your own. I'm not sure why."

Takamatsu croaked, then squeezed once.

"You went to eat with her and to another club."

Takamatsu squeezed.

"So, the place you picked—"

He squeezed twice.

"She picked."

Takamatsu tried to look around at the drip. Hiroshi pushed the button again, but nothing came out.

"Was it on the list?"

Yes, he squeezed.

Hiroshi continued narrating for him. "You toast with small *sake* glasses. You suck yours down in a gulp. Small dishes, lacquer chopsticks. You eat, as does she, in small bites, talking in between."

Takamatsu squeezed and coughed.

"She's asking you detailed questions about family, your job, your life. You give her tidbits from past cases and past affairs. You make her laugh."

Takamatsu tried to talk, swallowed, and managed to say, "She never laughs."

"The talk gets freer, and you forget to call me. Then you look for a chance to take a break, but your phone is off or doesn't work inside the place."

Yes.

"Your eyes can't pull away from her. More *sake*. You decide she's the one."

Yes.

"Her face was more stunning up close, but icy and distant, a perfect mask. Can you remember her face?"

Yes.

Hiroshi continued, "She took you back to the David Lounge, right?"

Yes.

"You knew what would happen because you knew it was her."

Yes.

Takamatsu nodded at the morphine drip. Hiroshi pushed it, sending a small flow through the tube and a wave of comfort through Takamatsu. He eased into his pillow.

Hiroshi waited until Takamatsu came back and started again, "Then—"

But Takamatsu squeezed his hand twice. He swallowed and tried hard to bring his voice out. "I...twisting in the air," he whispered, out of breath by the end. Takamatsu picked his head off the pillow. Bloodstains and yellow fluid covered the depression where his head was.

"Go slow, OK?" Hiroshi said. "That was her here, earlier wasn't it?"

Takamatsu drifted away. The machines tracked the weakened rhythm of his life. His usual swagger, vitality and glimmering eyes were buried deep under the morphine. Hiroshi waited. In a few minutes, his eyes opened and he managed to squeeze Hiroshi's hand a little.

"There's more," Takamatsu said, his voice clearer. "Tell Sakaguchi...it's her. He...remember her—"

Hiroshi leaned close to hear, waiting to see if he had more. His voice was too weak to catch all his words.

"Before...another case. She...information."

"It's OK. Why don't you rest?" Hiroshi said.

Takamatsu fought against the pain and the pull of the morphine. "We bought information...sold...she helped—"

"What information? About companies' investments, building projects, future plans?"

Yes, Takamatsu squeezed, trying to find his voice again.

Seeing him struggle, Hiroshi said, "Take it easy. There's no hurry now."

Takamatsu continued. "...tipped off chief...too much money...she was...smart...set us up—"

"The information was connected to Bentley?"

Takamatsu nodded.

"That's why you wanted me to go there. Wakayama laundered the cash, losing on real estate to get it clean." Hiroshi pushed the button for the morphine drip, but nothing came out.

Yes, Takamatsu squeezed.

"When was that? A few years ago?"

Yes.

"But you recognized her again?"

Yes.

"So, she's more than just a purveyor of information. She has other things going on?"

Yes.

It was getting to be an effort to tell if Takamatsu was really squeezing, yes, or not. His grip was almost gone.

"How did you find her yesterday?" Hiroshi asked, leaning over Takamatsu's maroon, swollen lips.

"She found me," Takamatsu managed.

"And she lugged you to the platform from the David Lounge, and then you were in the air with the train barreling right at you?"

Takamatsu groaned from deep inside. Hiroshi knew it was a groan of pain, but also a groan of humiliation and shame too profound for even the morphine to touch. Takamatsu's pride would be decimated after his go-it-alone approach, and unethical and unauthorized techniques failed, nearly costing him his life.

Hiroshi stood up. "Rest now."

Takamatsu squeezed again, several times it felt like, and said, "My wife—."

Hiroshi walked to the door and looked for Takamatsu's wife. She was folded into herself, seated on a chair, staring listlessly at the floor. When she saw him, she got up and came into Takamatsu's room. She reached into her bag and pulled out a large manila envelope that was ripped open at one end.

"What's this?" Hiroshi asked.

"I hired a private investigator to follow him," Takamatsu's wife said. "I needed photos for the divorce lawyer."

Hiroshi opened the envelope and pulled out black and white prints of Takamatsu with Michiko. Many of the shots were grainy and distant but others were clear enough that it was easy to see Michiko's face. In some shots, without sunglasses, her eyes were sharp, in control, fiery.

"I had him followed, but I didn't want him to get hurt. I just wanted him to stop having affairs." Her voice was low and plaintive, her face caught between anger and fear.

"It's not your fault," Hiroshi said.

She choked back tears.

"A private investigator took these?" Hiroshi flipped through the photos one by one. "Can you give me his name?"

She looked at Takamatsu, who nodded to her. She dug into her purse and pulled out a name card.

"I didn't believe him when he said his affairs were over. He was working on a case in Roppongi, he said. But that's what he always

231

said. I was sick of his shoddy excuses and cheap alibis," she said, her voice, aggrieved and forgiving at once.

"Did you have him followed for a long time?"

"Off and on for a couple months. It's expensive." She took Takamatsu's hand.

Hiroshi looked through the photographs, imprinting the faces and bodies into his memory. There were several different women, but Michiko was in most.

"When were these taken?" Hiroshi asked, holding up several of Takamatsu and Michiko.

"Two nights ago. They arrived at our home this morning. Before I knew he was in the hospital."

Hiroshi took out three of the photos, shuffled through them again, checking carefully, then handed the three back to her and said in a quiet, even voice, "Can you get rid of these three for me?"

She took them, stifling tears with a hand on her face and nodded her head yes.

"She's wearing a different outfit in those three. And it's a different place and different day. We don't want to complicate things."

He placed the photos back in the envelope and tucked them under his arm. Takamatsu's wife folded the three photos and jammed them into her purse, and then put her hand on the bed rail, steadying herself.

Takamatsu's one eye rolled toward the morphine drip. His wife pressed it, sending him floating away on the relief it offered. She turned away.

Takamatsu bent his fingers to bring Hiroshi closer.

Hiroshi bent low to his lips to listen.

"You can't solve this sitting in your office," Takamatsu whispered, and then drifted off.

Chapter 37

Arranged three tiers high and hundreds wide on rows of crumbling stone, the round-headed, child-monk statues looked calmly over the temple grounds of Zojoji Temple. Green and gray moss speckled the older, weather-worn statues, but the newer ones sported neatly knit bibs and bright caps, accenting their cherubic features. Reiko had paid for two and Michiko for four. They had to stoop over to tie the red bibs and caps on the small, stone Jizo statues.

"Why four, Michiko? You were always so careful."

"It's not for that," Michiko answered, arranging flowers they had bought nearby. "The priests will do a *mizuko* memorial service for anyone. If you pay."

"What do you mean?" Reiko asked. "You never explain anything anymore."

Michiko hugged her best friend tight with both arms and kissed her on the top of her head. "These will take care of their souls. And ours, too."

"They look so cute, don't they?" Reiko said.

"Compassionate."

"The monk said something about waiting for all humans to be saved, but I don't quite get that."

"It just means, stay calm and be patient."

The rows of squat little statues lined a rectangular area in the lower garden of the temple. From there, steep, wide steps led up to the imposing main building, above which sprang Tokyo Tower. The tower's orange and white lattice of bolted prefab steel loomed skyward above the temple's earthy, wooden elegance.

"Do you still think about them?" Michiko asked.

Reiko shook her head. "It upset me at the time. But I couldn't do what Natsumi did and settle down as a mom."

"Stay in Kawasaki and open a fruit and vegetable store?"

"You have to see her before you leave," Reiko said.

"If I have time." Michiko shook her head. "I've been sending her money. She stopped sending it back finally."

"That's not the same as seeing her," Reiko said.

"She doesn't want me around her daughter."

"That's not true. She's a good student, Natsumi told me. Like you were."

"I set something up for her to go to college."

"What do you mean?"

"A trust fund. It will help pay for her college when she gets in."

"You can do that?"

"I would have set one up for you, too, if you'd let me."

"I'm doing fine. Really. You deserve your money."

"Why don't you move in to my apartment at least?"

"I'm fine where I am. How long are you going to be gone?"

"I don't know. Couple years. Maybe longer."

"Don't say that," Reiko said and took Michiko's arm.

They looked up at the main temple building and Tokyo Tower slicing the sky behind it.

"Did you ever go up there?" Reiko asked.

"No. What about you?"

"I'm scared of heights. I'd pee my pants!" Reiko said.

"Maybe that's what turned the tower orange!"

They laughed and hugged.

"Ready for shopping?"

"Let's go!"

They picked up their purses and designer bags, and slung them over their elbows, hands in the air, Tokyo style.

At the temple gate, they hopped into a taxi to Venus Fort, a huge shopping complex in Odaiba Bay that was devoted exclusively to women. Every female fantasy, need and whim was catered to: cosmetics, jewelry, accessories, lifestyle goods, designer clothing, and shoes and shoes and shoes. Everything, from artisanal chocolate to sex toys, was offered with women in mind.

Inside the sprawling floors of shops, faux-sunlight fell over lovingly replicated imitations of European streets—the Rue de Rivoli, Fifth Avenue, Bond Street and Via Montenapoleone. The lighting delivered the illusion of a sunny day, every day, before the lights dimmed later to recreate an evening sunset and later again a night stroll.

Along the streets, travel consultants offered special tour packages for women. Handsome maître d's stood smiling outside theme restaurants. Even the restroom facilities were designed for women, with double the number of stalls and mirrors so there was never any wait. Though the original design had been altered to welcome boyfriends, husbands and lovers, and a new section for families was added, Venus Fort was still a place of, by and for women.

"Where to first?" Reiko asked. "This is a long way from Takeshita Dori."

"Is it?" Michiko asked. "Maybe we're just getting older."

Reiko stopped and smiled. "How did they find me at Les Chats Gris?"

Michiko stopped and looked back at her. "I don't know how they found you there," Michiko said. "However they did it, you really saved me."

"When that first cop found me, I figured I'd lead him to you and let you handle him."

"Him, I could understand. I knew him before."

"But the second one, the younger handsome one, made me worry something was wrong."

Michiko thought it through again, how they knew that coffee shop.

"Is it?" Reiko asked.

"Is what?"

"Is something wrong?"

Michiko smiled and shook her head. "Cops are always easy to track down, but you saved me a lot of time—the one thing I'm running out of."

"I'm not that naïve," Reiko said in a serious voice. "I know you're in trouble."

Michiko said, "I'm getting out of trouble."

Reiko looked her friend in the eyes, searching—as she always had—for a sign that everything really was all right.

"I still have a couple of things left to do." Michiko started walking again, but Reiko stood still.

"Reiko, really. I'm just finishing up a few things. You can come and visit after I get settled in Europe. Promise?"

Reiko nodded, but didn't say anything more. She took Michiko's arm in hers as they walked to the end of the imitation Venetian street in silence.

Finally, Reiko said, "Are you hungry?"

"Starving."

"Crepe? Like in Harajuku!" Reiko started talking like the young girl she used to be, in excited, singing tones.

"That's the best thing Natsumi ever taught us!"

"Well, almost!"

They snickered, hurrying toward the crepe stand.

"You used to be able to eat three in a row! I could only finish two."

"Remember when Natsumi threw up her whole crepe on that guy? It smelled sugary!"

They both laughed.

At the crepe shop, they hungrily watched the young guy behind the counter load a round crepe with a mound of ice cream, spoonfuls of strawberry jelly and a heap of whipped cream with sprinkles. They sat down on a bench by a scale-model fountain from the Jardin de Luxembourg. The two women clutched their fully loaded crepes in one hand and spooned in big bites with the other.

"How will I contact you over there?"

"It's better if I don't tell you for now. In case another cop finds you!"

Reiko was quiet as she chewed the last bites of her crepe. "If you're in trouble, let me help."

"You can't."

"I can do something."

"You're doing something already. You're taking me shopping." Michiko jumped up and tossed the paper wrapping from her crepe into the trash.

"Come on! Let's go!" Reiko whooped in accented English.

They walked arm in arm, looking in store windows. The air-brushed clouds and the painted-blue sky felt as wide and high as a real sky on the nicest day of the year.

"Is this how it really looks?" Reiko asked.

"Europe? You'll have to come and see for yourself."

"Don't think I won't!"

"I think you will!"

"Where do I get a passport?"

"Oh, Reiko. There's an office, in Ginza."

Reiko nodded her head. Michiko was her main source of useful information.

They kept walking until they got to a luggage shop on a narrow medieval-looking street. They went in, and a saleswoman came right over to help. She explained the features of the bags, kneeling down to demonstrate. Another saleswoman wheeled over more choices, until the center of the shop was filled with bags.

All four women compared the bags, point by point, opening one then the other, turning pieces of luggage over to look inside, then righting and rolling each back and forth. They rejected them one by one until a mid-sized maroon bag with dark blue straps won them over for originality, functionality and design.

"I'm buying it for you!" Reiko shouted and did a little jump of joy. She followed the sales woman to the counter where she pulled out her wallet and handed over several fresh bills.

Michiko gave Reiko a hug as they walked out, Michiko pulling the new suitcase behind. "Thanks, Reiko. I really needed this."

"You seem to have everything already."

"Now I'll have room for the trophy from the English contest."

"You're taking that?"

"It's the best thing anyone ever gave me," Michiko said.

"You mean stole for you?"

"You also stole that video camera. That was useful."

Reiko laughed. "You mean that time we were making those videos and that guy slipped—"

"And had to go to the hospital—"

"His head was bleeding so much!" They both laughed.

"You're the one who pushed him!" Michiko pushed Reiko.

"You're the one who bit him."

"I couldn't help it, I was choking!" Both of them collapsed in laughter.

"And then the cameraman."

"He couldn't operate anything!"

"Wonder where those guys are now."

"I saw one of them—" Michiko said and went quiet.

"You mean, that year?"

Michiko nodded her head, suddenly serious.

Reiko took her arm and pulled her close. "In Kobe? The one who pretended to be a director?"

"Yeah, him."

"You never told me. Was that what it was?" Reiko hesitated to probe, not wanting to bring up Michiko's pain again.

After a long pause, Michiko said, "That wasn't what it was. What it was, was I learned how things really are."

* * *

It was endless humiliation and pain. After the penthouse where they first took her, they weren't so careful of her looks. She stayed for a long time in one room, a long drive from the first place—and lost track of where she was.

She ate what they gave her, but she knew it was filled with sedatives. She couldn't move, couldn't think. She would fall asleep after eating, and sleep for hours, perhaps days, only to wake up, again and again, unsure of where, and then who, she was.

The men told the *kinbaku*-bi rope tying master to leave her strung up for hours at first, coming at her in shifts, between which she was left bound in hemp rope *shibari*, alone for a time on the tatami or a thin futon until they wanted her again. Then, back to the same room at night, same food, same sedative.

She could hear the men's voices, even when she could no longer feel them. The drugs put her beyond pain, beyond caring, her eyes always closed against the lights. She floated through days, unable to muster the energy, the will, to try again to kill one of them. They beat her badly the first two times she tried. After that, they increased whatever it was they put in the food.

When they wanted her cleaned up, they let her bathe, which cleared her head and helped her to come back to herself. But then, when she was clean, it was always worse.

When Shibata finally got her released, it took her half a year to sweat the drugs out of her system. The rope burns on her wrists and ankles left smooth, hard callouses. She had them surgically removed.

* * *

Reiko held her friend close, wondering how bad it could have been, but not wanting to ask. Michiko had told her almost nothing, but Reiko knew one day she could confide it all.

"Money's the only thing that can keep you safe." Michiko said.

"That's what your father always told us," Reiko said. "But it's friends, too."

Michiko came back from where her mind had gone and looked at Reiko. "The trust of friends."

Reiko waited for Michiko to calm down, knowing her inner storms no longer lasted as long as they used to. When it seemed the rage had passed, Reiko urged Michiko on.

"Let's not get old," Michiko said.

"Isn't that what we're doing?" Reiko asked.

Chapter 38

"The monks are free between one and three today. And you mentioned photos in last night's text, but I don't see any here."

Hiroshi blinked his eyes and looked around his apartment. He rose to an elbow and tuned in to Akiko's voice. "Thanks for waking me. I have the photos with me."

He wanted to keep them in his own hands, to hear what Sakaguchi would say.

"Are you coming here or going straight to the temple?"

"Depends on how soon I can start moving. Any news on Takamatsu?"

"Sleeping, but stable."

Hiroshi hummed.

"Anything else?" Akiko asked, much more softly than usual.

"I can't think of anything. But, I can't think."

Hiroshi swung his legs over his sofa and stared at Linda's boxes stacked against the wall. He needed to seal them and send them. He wanted to get rid of the clutter and to sleep on the bed again. More boxes were piled there. Sleeping on the couch and his office futon-chair was draining him. Linda was right: work was procrastination for life, and life was an excuse for not focusing on work.

Hiroshi stumbled to the shower, kicking aside the scrubbers, sponges, buckets and stool—all the bath things he bought for her. He could picture Linda's skin steaming and flushed from the hot water. The bath was his only real cultural success with Linda. She took to it like a tropical fish. Afterwards, she always stood with her hip cocked, a towel around her, another towel in hand, drying her hair to the side.

He opened his eyes. Mold was spreading along the tile and around the drain.

He dressed in a hurry and stopped in the Chinese chukka restaurant wedged into the outside corner rooms of his apartment building. The cook no longer asked what he wanted. He ordered the same every time: shrimp fried rice and pork dumplings. They had no reason to speak. The silent predictability of it left him time to be with himself, to prepare for a noisy, rush-around, people-filled day.

* * *

Akiko and Sakaguchi were waiting in his office when Hiroshi arrived.

"The monks are waiting. You ready?"

"Just need a quick coffee," Hiroshi said.

"Are those the photos?" Sakaguchi asked.

Hiroshi handed them over. There were photos of Takamatsu and Michiko huddling in a doorway, walking and laughing, standing on a train platform. Most were grainy and distant, a long lens at night, but clear enough.

"When were you going to tell me?" Hiroshi asked Sakaguchi.

"Tell you what?" Sakaguchi replied, looking through them again slowly.

"About Takamatsu. Your former investigation. The money. Knowing her before."

"Who knew if it was connected? Takamatsu went to find out."

"You must have known when you saw her photo."

"I could guess, but I didn't know."

"And the money? From before?"

"That was Takamatsu. I'm the one that got demoted."

Akiko went back to her desk, shuffling papers but listening closely.

Hiroshi stood over Sakaguchi, whose bulk filled the chair. "So, Takamatsu dragged me into this as his surrogate?"

Sakaguchi shrugged. "We got tripped up on the English before. The investigations were almost done, a solid case, but the English was holding us back. We were missing something in the documents and messages."

242

"So, you just need me as a translator? That's what this is all about?"

"No, it's more than that."

"You want me to take care of the money for you? A little trick accounting?"

Sakaguchi spoke calmly. "We had trouble with that, too. Takamatsu couldn't handle it."

"He took some of it?"

"No, he had too much. It was going to be used as bait. If we hadn't done what we needed to do to get the cash in hand, we'd never have gotten as far as we did."

"Where did they find it?"

"Takamatsu had it in a locker at a train station. Stupid, I know, but safer than anywhere else. The chief sent someone to follow him one day."

"So, I'm cleaning up your mess."

Sakaguchi eased himself forward and pushed himself up from the chair. "There's no cleaning up that mess. Let's focus on this one."

"Takamatsu almost got killed."

"He's the one who did things that way."

"Did you know what he was doing?"

"No," Sakaguchi said. "I wouldn't have let him if I did."

Hiroshi stared at the floor, angry, but no longer sure about why or at whom. "What was he thinking?"

"Making up for before."

"Wrong way to do it."

"He makes fewer mistakes than most."

"That was almost his last one."

"Almost." Sakaguchi moved toward the door. "The monks are waiting."

* * *

At Yushima Tenjin Shrine, Sakaguchi explained to the young detectives what needed to be done. Akiko followed Hiroshi to the rack of wooden *ema*, the prayers swaying on the wire frames. Hiroshi started examining the wood plaques, which clicked as they swung side to side.

"What are you looking for?" asked Akiko.

Hiroshi looked where he thought the *ema* had been. "Ah!" He said and pulled it off the rack.

Akiko leaned over to read it.

Kamisama, Kigan. I had a moment of weakness and I felt human again. Thank you for that. Let me leave this city of pain, this city of men. I'll let you punish those who deserve it, save those who need saving. Please, transport me safely, away, from this, from here, never to return.

Sakaguchi and the young detectives came over. "Don't touch them. Fingerprints. The ones surrounding hers may have dates. Keep them in order. And bag them carefully." Sakaguchi was starting to sound like Takamatsu. "You two look for the same handwriting. You two take photos of everything. And wear your gloves."

Hiroshi noticed an old monk with a bald head and a long, wispy beard and mustache walking beside a young, thin monk near the side halls. Hiroshi pulled out his ID and flashed it at the older monk, who, he assumed was the abbot of the temple.

"I am Detective Shimizu. Thank you for your cooperation. These may be very important. We won't disturb you, but we need to take all that could be evidence."

"Where will you take them?" asked the older monk—the abbot— his only self-introduction a piercing gaze that made Hiroshi look away.

"We need fingerprints, photos, and time to decode the messages."

"Will you return them?"

"We'll return the ones we don't need."

"We have an obligation to protect the sanctity of the temple space and purify the prayers with fire," the monk said, catching Hiroshi's eyes again.

"You burn them?"

The monk nodded.

"I understand. But Tokyo is a sacred space, too, that should be rid of murder and crime."

The abbot hmm'ed and spoke quietly to the younger monk, who hurried off. "We burn them according to the lunar calendar. I will give you the exact dates so you can find when these were written."

"That's important," Hiroshi answered, and then bowed and set to work. The young detectives looked through the racks with white-gloved hands.

Akiko said, "We only have two hours. We'll never finish."

Hiroshi looked over the hundreds, maybe thousands, of *ema* and sighed. He walked to where the abbot was standing calmly counting his thick, wooden prayer beads.

"If we don't finish today," Hiroshi said to the abbot, "can we come back? And are there other shrines close by? We need to check them also."

The abbot's eyes were milky, his eyebrows long and white. He spoke calmly. "My assistant is already calling the ones close by."

"You're one step ahead of me."

"Maybe more steps than that," said the abbot, the skin around his eyes crinkling, as if smiling inwardly at a joke Hiroshi wouldn't understand.

A group of four young monks came around the side of the main shrine in single file. They stopped in front of the older monk. They all had white gloves that stood out against their brown robes. Another monk hurried over to a locked door, fiddled with the chain, and pulled open a large wooden door on its wooden hinges. A couple of monks busied themselves inside the dark room. A light bulb came on inside.

The young monks came over to the rack of *ema* and began to reach up for them.

Sakaguchi hurried over, shouting, "No, don't touch them!"

The younger monk with the abbot stepped over, "You want photos of all of them, in order, and you want to take the ones that may be evidence, so we are helping."

Sakaguchi and Hiroshi hesitated, but the force of his words, and his tone of voice, made them give in.

With a wave of the abbot's hand the monks proceeded to take the rows of *ema* off the racks, holding them by their strings. Inside the room, the monks placed the *ema* in order from top to bottom. Akiko and the two detectives took close-up photos of each, the camera flashes lighting up the room.

"Here's another one!" Hiroshi shouted and everyone stopped to read it:

Kamisama, Kigan. My supplication, Lord. Please let his soul go free and not wander. Protect me from others and from myself. Purify my actions with your wisdom and power. Nature takes its course and only the half-living follow unnatural paths. The rest has yet to be done. Take care of their souls.

Sakaguchi put the suspected *ema* in a special bag and set it to the side. He felt out of place—ponderous while they scurried—and yet, he was one with their care and focus.

After they finished each row, the abbot wordlessly signaled the young monks to place the *ema* back on the racks in the same order as before.

Two racks later, Hiroshi waved Akiko over. "Here's another one!" Akiko took several shots then stooped down with the detectives and monks to read:

Kamisama, Kigan. Protect me and grant me justice in this life. The material world ensnares us with desire for justice, but without justice we cannot move toward the spiritual. The time is always now, the action is always direct, the result is always right.

Within an hour, all of the *ema* had been photographed and the evidence bagged. The young monks closed up the room and stood patiently counting the prayer beads encircling their wrists.

The young detectives looked around waiting for Hiroshi's or Sakaguchi's orders. Akiko wrote notes on everything, as the detectives with the cameras packed them in carrying cases.

Akiko said, "We have more evidence now."

Sakaguchi said, "But we don't have the connections among them."

"And we don't have her," Hiroshi said. "We better get to that photographer who took the shots of Takamatsu before she does."

While the young detectives carried everything to the vans, Hiroshi said, "I'll be along in a minute, I just want to thank the abbot for his help."

Hiroshi bowed when he approached the venerable old man, who stood impassively by the racks of *ema*, reading them as if for the first time.

The abbot said, "These *ema* help people handle the anguish of everyday life."

"There's a lot of anguish, judging by the numbers."

"Anguish rules most people's lives. With their troubles as their main focus, they live off-balance and disordered."

Hiroshi looked down at the gravel. "I guess that's why people become detectives. They want balance and order."

"That's why people become monks, too!" The abbot smiled. "Only here, we know that balance and order often arise from our desiring mind. And when it comes from there, it's an illusion."

Being an accountant was putting things in order, but where did order lead? When she killed those men, did she think she was putting things in order, rebalancing the world?

Looking across the courtyard, the abbot continued, "I instructed the young monks today to contemplate death as they worked."

"You wanted them to learn about death?"

"I wanted them to learn *from* death." The abbot looked at Hiroshi with an intensity that made him turn away. "Death is a strict teacher, but the lessons are crucial."

Hiroshi managed to look up at him again and replied, "It's hard to learn about death, about desire."

"It's harder not to," the abbot said, and turned and walked away.

Hiroshi bowed to the abbot's receding figure. He stood there and felt the wind—moist with impending rain—blow across the temple grounds. He stood listening to the rustle of tree leaves and the clack of the *ema* swinging into place, wondering if his senses—the feel and sound and look of the world—were all an illusion, too.

Chapter 39

Ryo Shibata, Michiko's photographer accomplice, came down the outside stairwell of his concrete and glass studio and stopped to light a cigarette, cupping it with his head down. He reset his two camera bags like crisscross bandoliers, pulled on his gray ponytail, and looked both ways, up and down the lane of shops.

He headed uphill on a small side street of Harajuku. The area was crowded with young fashionistas and intense hipsters loaded with subculture brands and outlandish accessories, prowling the latest, coolest shops for more. The side streets offered a calmer, slower pace, with studios—like Shibata's—and coffee shops, upscale boutiques and private homes.

Sakaguchi stood at the corner of the tree-lined Omotesando Dori and the small lane up to Shibata's studio. Hiroshi waited uphill, on the other side of his studio, pretending to look into the window of an imported hat store. Ueno sat at the wheel of the car parked downhill, with Osaki, in the other seat, ready to get out.

Hiroshi watched Shibata's reflection pass behind him in the window and then turned casually to follow. Seeing Hiroshi turn, Sakaguchi, too big to hide, lumbered uphill after them. Once they went over the crest of the hill out of sight, Osaki got out of the car and followed.

At the top end of the lane, far from the wide street, Shibata stopped by a tall rack of vacation pamphlets outside a travel agency and crushed out his unfinished cigarette. The pretense of not noticing he was being followed lasted only a few seconds.

As Hiroshi stepped closer, Shibata grabbed the top of the pamphlet rack and yanked it down, the metal edge just missing Hiroshi's head. The vacation pamphlets flew over the street like big, bright-colored confetti.

Hiroshi lunged forward and snagged one of Shibata's camera bag straps, but Shibata grabbed Hiroshi's wrist and shouted, "Hahhh!" before twisting and toppling him.

Hiroshi landed on the edge of the metal rack and Shibata took off running. Standing up clutching his ribs, Hiroshi could hardly breathe. "Shit, shit, shit—," he cursed in English as he stood up and got himself going after a few painful steps.

Osaki and Sakaguchi came running. Sakaguchi skirted the thousands of slick adverts, stepping nimbly, and then heaving into a run, but Osaki ran right over the scattered pamphlets, lost his balance and tumbled forward.

The lane was too narrow for even a sidewalk and had few shoppers, but seeing the men race by, those few shoppers quickly dodged to the side, their backs against the shopfronts, watching Shibata and then the detectives disappear into the maze of small lanes.

Osaki and Sakaguchi were ahead of him, but Hiroshi saw Shibata disappear down a narrow set of stairs between two rows of small hair salons, antique stores and one-counter restaurants. There was nowhere to hide, but many places to turn.

Shibata turned as often as he could, each lane only a short sprint, and then finally headed out of the maze of small streets toward the heavy traffic of the large Aoyama Dori.

Sakaguchi dropped down the stairs to Aoyama, losing the pace. Hiroshi lost sight of Sakaguchi, but hoped he could cut Shibata off up ahead. The crowds on Aoyama Dori would slow him down.

Hiroshi saw Shibata ahead where the street curved before he disappeared down a small side lane. He didn't know where Sakaguchi was, but when he turned down the small line, he saw Sakaguchi had cut through a small side street ahead of him.

At the dead-end of the side street, Hiroshi saw Sakaguchi several steps away from Shibata, both of them contemplating a chest-high stack of paving stones, a back hoe and temporary metal dividers, on which hung a large banner apologizing for the construction. The stairs leading out of the narrow street were blocked.

Penned in by construction ahead and housing on both sides—Sakaguchi and Hiroshi behind—Shibata got ready to fight.

Osaki ambled up behind Hiroshi, and everyone paused, breathing hard. Shibata set down his camera bag and positioned himself, as Hiroshi held out his badge, trying to catch his breath. "We just want to talk," he finally wheezed.

Shibata's stance—balanced, yet as tight as if spring-loaded—indicated he knew just how to defend himself.

Hiroshi walked closer, his ribs aching with every breath, wary after being so neatly flipped onto the pamphlet rack a few minutes earlier. "We want to know about some photos you took," he said.

Osaki and Sakaguchi stepped to the side to block any possible way past them.

"You took these, right?" Hiroshi continued, trying not to clutch at his ribs. "All we need to know is where we can find her. Can we talk back at your office?"

"Let's talk here," Shibata said. "It's safer."

"It's safe for us either place."

"You should have identified yourself," Shibata said, pushing his gray hair behind his ears and smoothing his ponytail. "Men in divorce cases get angry. They take it out on me."

"You know her?" Hiroshi asked. Shibata nodded his head once, quickly, in acknowledgement. "And you're Ryo Shibata?"

Shibata nodded again and looked off in the distance, saying, "What do you want with her?"

"We just want to talk with her."

Shibata sighed and held up his cigarettes, wiggling them as a question. Hiroshi nodded, okay, and Sakaguchi and Osaki stepped closer.

Shibata lit up and took a drag, looking past the detectives. "I can guess what you know, so let's skip the dance." He inhaled deeply and exhaled. "It was an accident."

"You were close enough to see?"

"Through the camera, you see things better."

"What did your camera see?"

"He was drunk. She was helping him. He slipped."

"Why were you even there?"

"I'm a photographer."

"Blackmail?"

"We had an arrangement. I took photos for her."

251

"Your arrangement could get you a murder charge."

Shibata fidgeted.

"We need to find her," Hiroshi said again.

"We could make the next twenty days go by very slowly at the station," Sakaguchi interjected.

Shibata said, "I have a license to investigate. I do divorces mainly. Pays the bills."

"But, don't tell me, you're really an artistic photographer?"

"You saw my work online before you came."

"She hired you before? Michiko Suzuki?"

"You know her name?" Shibata looked surprised. "You know everything then."

"But tell me again."

"The plan was to double the take. Investigate one side, blackmail the other. All I did was document it all." Shibata crushed out his cigarette under his running shoes and looked at the detectives with resignation.

Osaki waved to Ueno, who pulled the car down the narrow street, maneuvering it into a spot that entirely blocked traffic.

"She met men and set them up. Not hard to do if you look like her. All I had to do was get one shot. You ever see your loved one with someone else? Naked or not, it's a shock."

"That's not all of it, though, is it?"

"No, that's pretty much it."

"You know what happened to the men?" Hiroshi asked.

"Which men?"

"They're dead."

Shibata fixed his gaze at the horizon, above their heads.

"Those who get close to her don't seem to last long," Hiroshi said. "Take a look at these." He held up a photo of Takamatsu.

Shibata focused on the photo and then Hiroshi's eyes.

"I guess you're immune," Hiroshi said. "So, you must know where she is."

"She's gone. Or will be."

"Where is she going?"

"Paris, she said."

"Paris?"

"She saved enough money, she told me."

Hiroshi let that sink in for a second, trying to decide if Shibata was telling the truth. "So, how did she set up the photo sessions?"

"She blackmailed the husband, and I charged the wife for investigating. She got hush money from the men. The wives paid in advance."

"But that's not all she did."

Shibata sighed, looked away. "The businessmen told her about investments, real estate deals, new products, company plans. It was info she could sell. And for a lot more money."

"Where did you meet Michiko?"

"We met at an aikido dojo, in Shinjuku, years ago. I needed self-defense because so many angry husbands came after me. She was the highest-ranked woman in the dojo, won competitions. She was beautiful. One thing led to another."

"What led to what?"

"We talked every night after training. When she found out I was an investigator, she asked me to help."

"And you didn't hesitate?"

"She's hard to refuse," Shibata said. "Look, these guys," Shibata added, "these wheeler-dealers are not good people, any of them."

"This guy was," Hiroshi said, holding up Takamatsu's photo.

"Michiko told me different. She worked with him before, to steal information. He was a dirty cop." Sakaguchi stepped forward and Shibata stepped back. "The corporate world is even dirtier. Photographs are simple. I just document what happens."

"If he dies," Hiroshi said, "it might not be so simple."

Shibata lit another cigarette. "It was all pretty simple, until she changed."

"Changed?"

* * *

Shibata had never been as terrified as when he pulled up to the massive gate of the compound in the hills above Kobe to get Michiko back. He had enlisted Sono, the accountant, to help locate Michiko's whereabouts through his many crime world connections. It took almost a year to find someone who would help him, and then, only with a large cash payment of Michiko's money that Sono kept in his safe. Sono refused to go to Kobe, so Shibata went alone.

The contact said he should wait in a hotel in downtown Kobe and they would find him. He waited for two days in the business hotel, terrified to go out. When he went out to the convenience store to get some food, they were waiting in front of the hotel, inviting him into a black Toyota Crown with tinted windows at the curb.

The compound had bodyguards positioned like trees at points along the driveway up to the Japanese style house. Normally curious about every visual detail, Shibata kept his eyes down and followed them inside the house, where more bodyguards—big guys in black suits—stood passively in the entranceway.

Whoever he was—Shibata didn't dare ask his name—who came out to talk with him on the tatami mat room was obviously someone of importance. He wore a black shirt with frog buttons and a mandarin collar, all very expensive silk, Shibata noticed, but that was as high as he allowed his eyes to go.

The boss lit a cigarette and had one of the bodyguards give one to Shibata, who was glad for something to help stop him from trembling.

"She's caused us a lot of trouble, this girl," the boss said, kneeling down on a *zabuton* cushion on the tatami. One of the bodyguards put his hand on Shibata's shoulder for him to sit down. "Lost a lot of money because of what she did."

Shibata bowed and said, "I understand. I am very sorry for the inconvenience she caused. It won't happen again."

"It seems from her attitude now it won't happen again." The boss pulled on his cigarette and scoffed as he exhaled. "But how can I know that?"

"You have my word," Shibata said, bowing deeply onto the tatami. It was the only time in his life he had bowed so low his head actually touched the floor.

"That's not much good to me. Neither is the word of that accountant—what's his name, Sono?" He sighed. "Everything in Tokyo causes problems for us down here."

A couple of the bodyguards let out a low chuckle, so Shibata assumed this was supposed to be a joke of some kind. He kept his eyes low and only let them up when the boss nodded his head to one of the bodyguards at the side of the room. The guard walked off through the shoji sliding doors—covered in a large painting of a crane—into the next room.

When he came back, Michiko was with him. She was dressed in a simple, indigo-dyed *hakama* with her hair pulled behind her head tightly and simply. Her face was swollen and her eyes downcast. She walked with delicate, mincing steps and kneeled down on the tatami and bowed.

The boss spoke in a big voice. "We taught her some manners, how to be more Japanese. So, you'll find she's a changed girl, I think." The sarcasm in his voice made the bodyguards snicker. "No more money games, OK?" he said to Michiko, and she bowed again.

The bodyguards waved him up and another stood behind Michiko. They walked them to the door, without another word from the boss, and after they slipped on their shoes, they were led back to the Toyota Crown.

The driver and two bodyguards took them to the *shinkansen* entrance of Shin-Kobe train station and said, "Go directly back to Tokyo."

Shibata was about to say he had left his things at the hotel, but there was no room for argument. He led Michiko to the train station ticket counter and bought them both tickets back to Tokyo.

* * *

Hiroshi asked again, "How was she changed?"

"When she disappeared. For a year. In Kobe." Shibata looked off at the distance. "I tried to help her that day but I couldn't get across the street in time. If I had, none of this would have happened. One of the men she got information from figured out she was smarter than she acted. Some people lost a lot of money and decided it was her fault."

"Was it?"

"I don't know. Maybe. I wouldn't be surprised. There were properties, in Kawasaki and Azabu. Any building involves a lot of cash, but the Azabu one was billions of yen. Even a small percentage comes to a lot."

"So, the people who lost money wanted her to pay it back?"

"She said Paris would close the circle."

"What circle?"

Shibata shrugged.

"We need to stop her," Hiroshi said, "before she gets out of the country. To Paris or wherever."

Shibata said, "She has an accountant. Somewhere in Akasaka. I met her near there once, after she came back from that year away. I thought everything was going to be all right. She was taking accounting classes."

"Was she?"

"She said a lot of things."

"What's his name, the accountant?"

"She never says things like that."

"What happened that year?"

"Before, she could have been a model. I thought she was the one I'd make my name with. But after that year, she never let me take any more photos of her."

"Except for business."

"Except for business," Shibata pulled his cigarette pack out and turned it in his hands, then put it away. "She was still so beautiful, but her beauty was too far inside. I couldn't get to it, and she wouldn't let it out."

"So, it was you who pushed the emergency stop button last night?" Shibata nodded, yes. "So," Hiroshi continued, "where do we find her?"

"You don't. She's leaving, or has left." Shibata picked up his camera bags by their straps and placed them over each shoulder. "I tried to stop her years ago, to get her to ease out of it, to let go a bit, but—" He shook his head and looked off in the distance again. "Is he all right, that cop?" Shibata asked.

"It could have been worse. They had to pick the other guy up with chopsticks."

256

Chapter 40

"Pull over here, can you?" Hiroshi said to Ueno. He came back out of the convenience store where they'd stopped holding an ice pack for his ribs. Easing into the front seat with a groan, he put the ice pack under his shirt.

Sakaguchi said, "I told you to be careful."

"That was in the game center in Shibuya."

"Just breathe through it."

"I'd stop breathing if I could."

"Once it bruises up, you'll be all right."

"It's not far from here," Hiroshi told Ueno, breathing in hard when he pointed the direction.

"First lesson in sumo is where to land," Sakaguchi said.

The lime-green building of Sono Accountancy looked grimy in the false twilight created by the taller buildings around it. Ueno parked nearby, and Osaki walked toward a convenience store, searching for something to eat. Hiroshi left the ice pack in the car, testing his ribs gently before tucking in his shirt.

Sakaguchi and Hiroshi squeezed into the rickety elevator up to Sono's accountant office. The elevator moved slower than Hiroshi remembered, probably due to Sakaguchi's weight.

The same secretary unlocked the door, peeking out, meek and confused, holding a lap blanket.

Sakaguchi pushed in, with Hiroshi right behind.

"Where's Sono?" Hiroshi demanded.

She looked to the back of the cubicle-filled office and stepped out of the way.

Sono, peering out from behind a partition at the far back of the office, sighed when he saw Hiroshi. Hiroshi and Sakaguchi stood in the partitioned meeting area, which was bathed in an unsettling green tint from the flickering bulb in the back. The secretary brought tea, which spilled into the saucers, and gave a curt bow. Sakaguchi barely fit into the low chair, his huge knees bumping the coffee table. Hiroshi sat up straight to keep the pressure off his ribs.

Sono fiddled with papers in his cubicle and then came forward and sat down. Before Sono could say anything, Sakaguchi placed a photo of Michiko on the table.

"Is this one of the women you made payments to? For Wakayama?" Hiroshi asked.

"I sent the payments to bank accounts." Sono put on his glasses, leaned over and studied the photograph, finally pulling off his glasses. "I never see their faces."

"Never?" Hiroshi persisted.

"I sometimes meet clients the first time. After that, few clients come in person again. It's phone or email."

"Let me remind you: Michiko Suzuki."

"A common name."

"Not a common person."

Sono worked the hinge of his glasses back and forth. Sakaguchi wiggled forward in his chair. "If you're sure you don't recognize her, we can get a squad of detectives in here to look through your files."

"That could take a week or more," Hiroshi added.

"I can check my records, but I doubt it," Sono said.

"So, go check your records."

"You'll need a court order for anything more than a verbal confirmation." Sakaguchi shook his head. He could have a dozen detectives here in twenty minutes to confiscate every file in the place. Sono knew that, too. He got up and ducked behind the partitions. They heard him lighting a cigarette and smelled the smoke floating over the partition, heard him burrowing through papers.

In a few minutes, he was back. He opened a file folder, put on his glasses, and looked at them. "I was thinking of someone else. I remember her now. What do you need to know?"

"Did you send money from Wakayama to this woman?"

"She was one of the women. Yes."

"We need to find her," Hiroshi said.

"All I have is a bank account number," Sono said.

"Don't tell me. She contacts you," Hiroshi said, his voice drenched in sarcasm.

"She showed up here from time to time. Unexpectedly," Sono said. "But that was years ago."

"If you handle accounts for her, you must have an address."

"I'd have to look in another file."

"Did Wakayama put any buildings in her name?"

"Wakayama owned property only in his name." Sono folded and unfolded his glasses.

Sakaguchi moved forward, "If we have your files impounded, it could take our accountants years to get through them all."

"I used to work in a government office. I never leave my books vulnerable."

"That just means it will take longer."

Sono allowed himself a small snort.

"You worked as a government accountant?" Hiroshi asked.

"Finance Ministry."

"No one quits government work," Sakaguchi said.

"During the bubble years. I got tired of making things work for a bunch of spoiled bureaucrats who went to college together. The Japanese economy was one bubble after the next. As soon as one burst, another was floated in its place. I got tired of it."

"So, now you use that technique yourself."

"No bubbles. I make sure everything has no air inside."

Hiroshi said, "Even if all's aboveboard, our looking through them will chase away most of your clients. Especially the foreign ones."

"The foreigners aren't afraid of that. And they need my expertise even more than Japanese."

Hiroshi's guess was right: Sono handled foreigners needing Japanese accounting. That was enough to connect Sono to Bentley, he hoped. He looked up at the flickering bulb, his ribs aching with each breath. "What is it your clients need from you?" Hiroshi asked, trying to bring Sono closer to Bentley. "They have their own accountants."

"They don't know bureaucrats on the inside," Sono said. "I do. Before the economic reforms, it was hard for foreign firms to get a foot in the door. After the reforms, everything was up for grabs."

"And you grabbed what you could?"

"I helped others negotiate bureaucratic tangles across the two economies."

"Two economies?"

"Outer and inner. Transparency is not a Japanese concept." The flickering bulb went into a longer off cycle, before buzzing and snapping back on. Sono lit another cigarette.

"And Michiko. Where is her money?" Hiroshi asked.

"Mostly overseas."

"And where did it come from?"

"That's not my job."

Sakaguchi sat forward to the end of his chair, his belly over the top of the table. He started drumming his fingers on his huge knee.

Hiroshi had followed the trails of offshore accounts, faked investments and embezzled funds from his office, but now he was hearing it all in person. Takamatsu was right—he couldn't solve this case from his office. Hiroshi continued, "If you did her taxes, you had to write something down."

"Hostesses make a lot of money. Especially with her looks and her smarts," Sono answered.

"Did she have more than one source of income?" Hiroshi asked.

Sono smoked and nodded, yes.

"Several men on the hook or a few on the hook in different ways?"

"I don't investigate clients. That's your job, isn't it?"

"Our job is to find out who committed murder," Sakaguchi said, pushing forward over the table.

Sono looked at the file folder in front of him. "As far as I know, all she did was make money. Roppongi has plenty of it."

"How much did you put away for her?" Hiroshi asked.

"I'd have to look."

"Enough to live on for a long time? Overseas?"

Sono nodded. "I'd say a good long time."

"She's not coming back to Japan?"

"She doesn't need to return for money. Maybe in a couple years."

"If her money is already moved, she won't need you anymore," Sakaguchi said. "You know that, don't you?"

"Give us her address. We know you've got it," Hiroshi said.

Sono stared at the two investigators, and then leaned back, smiling. "You two don't really know what you're doing, do you?"

Hiroshi's ribs hurt as he leaned forward. He had to stop his hands from moving to them.

"You don't know where or how to find her, do you?" Sono said, shaking his head.

"We know this," Sakaguchi said, his thick fingers tapping the photograph. "The girl's cleaning house. She's already killed several men. What makes you think she'll spare you?"

"She needs me."

"That's what the others thought, too," Hiroshi said. "Things have changed in the last few hours. She might not need you anymore."

Sakaguchi leaned forward. "You're a sitting duck. She'll be back for you." He put a photo of Steve's body on the train tracks in front of Sono and tapped it with his thick fingers. "See this? That's what happens."

Sono looked under his glasses at the broken, bloody body in the photo, and then looked back and forth at them.

"You better hope we find her before she finds you," Sakaguchi added. He pushed the photo close toward Sono. The photo was graphic and close up. The dead man's head was smashed into the "I" of the steel rail of the track, his eyes turned up and away. His thigh bone jutted out jagged and sharp from the meat of his thigh, and his hip bone collapsed inward.

Sono looked away.

Hiroshi leaned toward him. "You know who ends up testifying in every fraud and murder case we handle?"

Sono folded his arms and stared silently at the two detectives.

"The accountant. You know why?" Hiroshi stood up. Sono crushed his cigarette out in the ashtray. "Because they want to stay alive."

Looking back at the detectives, Sono pulled a form from a file folder and passed it over to Hiroshi, pointing out one box.

Hiroshi took out his cell phone, sucking in the pain when he moved, and photographed the address. "That's one. Where're the others?"

"That's the only one I have."

"She lived in Kawasaki?"

"That's the address she uses for taxes. It's a factory."

"A factory?"

"Small one. Her father's."

"She lives with him?"

"He died some time ago. That's all I know," Sono said.

"We'll see if that's all you know," Hiroshi said.

Chapter 41

The outdoor stairs of her father's factory always grabbed at Michiko's shoes because of the cross-tread pattern of the metal steps. The welded pipe handrails had surface rust, but the cross-beams and support poles were sturdy and solid. The office and living space had been built by workers who didn't need to skimp or hurry.

In the musty office, only a sliver of light came through the window from the workshop floor. Michiko went to the small sink and washed her hands. She opened the hanging key case and took out a large key ring for her father's desk. The top drawer clanked into her hands as she pulled it all the way out and set it on the floor.

She took five well-wrapped packets of cash from her black leather duffel bag and spun a round of duct tape over them. Squinting into the desk, she taped them inside. She set the heavy drawer back on its tracks, hammered it down, and slid it in place. She looked over the window at Uncle Ono in the factory below. For years, he had kept the machines in shape, even though no orders came in.

Sensing her presence, Uncle Ono spun the hand-wheels and flipped the spindle control until the lathe slowed, patient as any machinist. He pushed the overhead socket to the side and hung up his safety goggles.

"*O-kaeri nasai*, welcome home," Uncle Ono called out to her.

"*Tadaima*, I'm back," she answered.

Neither could hear the other, but they didn't need to.

Uncle Ono latched the front door with an extender arm that let air circulate but kept the entrance from opening wider. His compact, wiry body bristled with energy, though his coveralls and *jika-tabi* toed work shoes were worn soft.

Michiko climbed down the ladder from the office, her duffel bag dangling and bouncing on her back. From the large pegboard rack she loved organizing when she was a girl, she took down a long ratchet handle and socket. She knelt down at the lathe in the middle of the floor, and set to ratcheting off the bolts that held the lathe in place by pulling with her whole body as if sculling a boat.

Uncle Ono came over with a push-button box control for the overhead crane. Uncle Ono had always been in charge of cleaning the motors and oiling the hoists, blocks and chains. The load limit of 20,000 kilograms was more than needed, but Michiko's father never skimped. The crane slid along I-beam tracks forming an overhead lattice capable of moving heavy loads in any direction.

Michiko stepped back and watched him run a thick chain under the central bed of the lathe and hook the safety latches. He pushed the button once to tighten the chains, and checked to be sure they were set, then pushed again and the lathe creaked up from the floor. With the push of another button, the crane pulled the huge, heavy lathe so it hung just an arm's length to the side.

Beneath the base of the lathe was an in-floor door that Michiko leaned down to pull up on its hinges. Inside was a vault lined with thick sheets of tin, filled with sealed, taped bags of 10,000-yen notes stacked carefully in rows. Michiko took the new wrapped bags of money from the duffel bag and added them to the stacks, leaning deep into the vault.

When she was done, she shut the door and waited while Uncle Ono used the motor overhead to maneuver the lathe and lower it down. Michiko spray-oiled the bolts, and tightened them while Uncle Ono undid the chain and moved the whole mechanism back to where he kept it ready. He rubbed down the lathe and the floor with a rag. When Michiko stood back to look at their handiwork, she could see no trace of the vault door, only a lathe that looked well-used, well-kept, and never moved.

"The fish store closed." Uncle Ono said, picking up the tools to put away.

"Did someone die?"

"They hung a sign, 'closed shop,' nothing else."

"You'll just have to walk to the new supermarket."

"It's not the same. No one talks there. And it's crowded."

"That's why this place will be worth something someday."

Michiko went to take a shower in the add-on bathing area she and Reiko used as girls. Uncle Ono grilled fish and put on the rice and miso soup, filling the air with the seaside humidity and salty aroma of home cooking. Michiko, in sweatpants and T-shirt, came out rubbing her long, wet hair with a towel until it was dry enough that it didn't drip, and draped a fresh towel over her shoulders under her hair.

She got chopsticks for them both, and her favorite *furikake* topping of seaweed, sesame seed, and dry wasabi. Uncle Ono served the grilled fish, its skin crackling brown, on long thin plates with shaved daikon and grated ginger. Michiko scooped miso soup into small lacquer bowls. They both said "*Itadakimasu*," and Michiko poured *furikake* all over her rice.

* * *

After the year in Kobe, they spent every day like this. Uncle Ono had no need to talk. He kept the lathe humming, which put her to sleep, and made sure meals were cooked, even when she didn't sleep or eat, or even leave her room.

After that year of confinement and torture, she took long baths every day, soaking for hours, sweating out the drugs. The shaking chills and brutal nightmares took a long time to ease up. Some mornings she woke with her old school books and manga and the wooden *kokeshi* dolls strewn over the bed, unsure of whether there'd been an earthquake or if she'd shaken them off the shelves herself. Her nightmares were gut-clawing, mind-thrashing streams of panic. It soothed her to spend the day reorganizing the shelves.

Reiko visited her often, but was too worried and frightened to ask questions. Michiko stretched out listening to Reiko chat about her customers and the other hostesses until she fell asleep with her head in Reiko's lap. Shibuya came to see Michiko, bringing cash, but Michiko just stared at him in silence until he found an excuse to leave.

Natsumi, who combed Michiko's and Reiko's hair when they all lived together so many years earlier, brought fresh fruits and vegetables every day, like the surrogate mother she had always been.

Michiko listened to Natsumi talk about what a good student her daughter was and about the fresh produce stand Michiko helped Natsumi buy.

In October, when the weather cooled, six months of detox took hold and Michiko finally felt like jogging.

Her route led her past the old dojo training hall for aikido and the cries of youngsters drew her to the open door of the small wooden hall. She was surprised to find Sato sensei, with his loose clothing and long gray hair, teaching a group of children, just as he had taught Michiko when she was a child. She had heard he'd moved to Hawaii to set up a dojo hall there.

She walked into the dojo and stood at the door. The children gradually slowed their practice to a halt when they noticed Sato sensei and Michiko looking at each other across the hall. When Michiko turned and left, they slowly started back up.

The next morning, Michiko was inside the dojo in the early morning. Sato sensei said nothing, but stood calmly in the middle of the hall and waited for her to mirror his motions. She could follow very little of it the first day, but over the next few months, she built herself up.

Michiko said yes when he invited her to help with the children. She felt strange with them in the afternoons because she had never been around children, and had hardly been a child herself. "Maybe you'll take over the dojo," he suggested to her. "Falling leaves return to their roots," he said, quoting a Chinese saying.

As she rebuilt her technique and stamina, Michiko started to talk with Sato sensei, though he was always allusive and abstract. He never asked what happened to her father, or to her. They worked out together in the mornings, and then after the children's workout in the afternoons, they talked over tea before she went home.

Sato sensei liked to talk about the Japanese spirit—part of the falling leaves returning to roots, he said—in old stories like the *Chushingura* with the 47 *ronin*, master-less samurai who avenged their master's honor after waiting for years. He talked about how the soul of modern civilization—not just in Japan, but in America, too—had lost direction.

"Honorable revenge was necessary. It was a form of justice. But now," he shook his head. "Now, who would notice?"

"Justice is still a matter of honor, isn't it?"

"For those *ronin*, it was more important than death. They knew how to suffer small disgraces in pursuit of their goal."

"But sensei," Michiko protested. "In Japan, women have always been *ronin*."

Sato sensei grunted, "Times have changed."

"But that's stayed the same," she insisted. "Women are still in exile, enduring their suffering, waiting for their moment."

When Sato sensei died a year later—a year in which he showed no signs of fatigue or age or sickness while helping develop Michiko's aikido—Michiko was too bereft to grieve. She organized the funeral, and his students poured in from all over the country, and from Hawaii, to pay their respects at the shrine. When the funeral was over, she knew she was ready.

* * *

Michiko scooped in a mouthful of rice loaded with *furikake*. After she fully chewed the rice, another lesson from Sato sensei, she started to explain things to Uncle Ono. "You need to take some of the money to the shrine at *Obon* ancestor festival and at New Year's, too."

"I do that every year," Uncle Ono answered, using his chopsticks to neatly stack fish bones on the edge of his plate. "And buy a plaque in the factory's name."

"A big one."

"The priest turned over the shrine to his son."

"He wasn't that old, was he?"

"I don't know. Maybe he was tired."

"Take the money inside the desk first. Use the money in the lathe later."

She stripped the big bones out of the fish in one smooth motion and dug into the underside of flaky white meat. When they were done, Michiko poured tea. Uncle Ono sliced watermelon by the sink, and Michiko came over to eat it. They chomped into the slices, spitting the seeds into the sink and setting the rinds there, too.

"Last watermelon for the year," Uncle Ono said.

"Season always ends too soon," Michiko said.

Michiko went to her room and came back with a file of documents inside a large envelope. Uncle Ono got his reading glasses as she spread the purchase agreements, transaction documents, escrow instructions, inspection findings, mortgage papers and closing statements out on the table. She was not sure how to begin to explain it all to him, but she wanted to at least make sure he knew the importance of keeping them safe.

"This one shows the debt on the factory is paid off," Michiko said. "So the hold on ownership is lifted. It now moves to you. The red stamp here means it's finalized, in case you need to show anyone."

He took the document in his hand, peering at it carefully. "How did you get it all paid off? Your father never could. Did you talk to them?"

"I didn't have to. I sent them all their money."

"They won't come back?"

"No, they won't come back. You don't need to worry."

He nodded, hesitantly, and put down the document.

She pulled out another document.

"These deeds are for the storage and warehouse buildings by the Tama River. There are a lot of them here, so don't get these out of order. It's all set up, so keep them like this, OK?"

"Those are the ones that were in your mother's family, before?"

"That's why I got them back."

"There's no business now to make them worth anything."

"They aren't worth anything for storing metal parts. The whole area is being turned into apartments, so—"

"Who wants to live there? The river stinks."

"It does now, but once the factories are gone, it'll become fashionable. We own the land they'll need. I've bought a checkerboard of—"

"Checkerboard?"

"It just means I don't own all of the land, but just pieces in between the large tracts. They'll have to buy those in order to develop the entire riverfront area." Michiko didn't tell Uncle Ono who the developers were and worried that they might come to the factory looking for her, but she didn't have time to explain all that to Uncle Ono now.

"How do you know they're building there?" Uncle Ono asked. "It doesn't seem like a place people want to live."

"I just know," Michiko said, and looked away. She needed to tell him enough, but not too much. "The entire area is being developed, though nothing's been announced yet. We'll start negotiating after the official, public approval notice." That negotiation would be tricky, and dangerous, but she already had the accountant Sono prepare the offers in advance. That way, she could get the sales concluded quietly before they launched any strong-arm tactics.

"When will that be?" Uncle Ono asked. "Soon?"

"A couple years maybe. I'll be back when it's time." Michiko said, carefully turning each document—there were over a dozen different deeds with supporting papers—to be sure they were in order.

"How will you know the right time when you're in another country?" Uncle Ono asked.

Outside, a car door slammed. Michiko stood up and quickly put all the documents into two files—one for him and one for her—and said, "Put these deeds away in the safe in the office. I've got to go."

"Who's that?" Uncle Ono asked.

"It's not them. But I don't know who it is."

Together, they listened together for a minute. The front door on the factory floor rattled.

"I better go," Michiko said. Uncle Ono watched as Michiko hurried back to her room. The doorbell to the living quarters rang, but Uncle Ono waited for Michiko to get her things, change her clothes, and head out through the back.

He tucked the deeds she'd left behind into a stack of papers on a small desk beside the dining table and arranged the dishes so it looked like there was only one person eating.

The doorbell sounded again.

After hearing her soft footsteps descending the back stairs, he climbed down to the workshop floor. Working in the dark, he picked out an arm-length crescent wrench, took the push-button box in hand, and stood in place, ready for whoever came inside.

Chapter 42

Hiroshi stood at the bottom of the stairs outside the factory building and pressed the doorbell. He heard a faint clonk upstairs. He pressed the doorbell again as Sakaguchi pulled at the large rolling doors into the workroom to no effect, hammering on the metal so the sound echoed back from inside.

Hiroshi went around the side of the building, but his way was blocked by metal drums full of discarded parts and an unplugged vending machine leaning just sideways.

Hiroshi walked back to the front and glanced over at Ueno and Osaki waiting by the car parked on the other side of the small canal. Kudzu grasped at frayed canvas awnings and clung to signs lettered in chipped paint. It coiled up and over the sides of the abandoned buildings, windows taped up or boarded over. Along the row of once-upon-a-time factories walled with sheets of rusted-thin, corrugated metal, only this one factory showed signs of life.

"Let's go in," Hiroshi said in a low voice. Hiroshi stood back as Sakaguchi pulled out an expandable baton and a small flashlight. He looked up inside the rolling doors to where a bar rested snugly on two bolts. He poked at it with the baton and ducked back as the heavy cross-arm swung down from the bolt.

With Sakaguchi's help, Hiroshi pulled open the sliding door and stepped in, letting his eyes roam over the vast interior of drill presses and lathes—a steel forest for the skilled labor that built Japan after the war. Even with the door open, it was dark. Sakaguchi pulled out a flashlight as Hiroshi touched the machines, one of which was warm from recent use.

Hiroshi's eyes had barely adjusted when he made out the figure of a small, wiry man, barely as tall as the machinery by a tool rack at the back of the space. Hiroshi squinted and moved his head to see more clearly what he was holding in his hands—a long wrench of some kind and something connected to a thick wire up to the ceiling.

And then Hiroshi heard a motor grinding and a metal chain pulling overhead.

Simultaneously, Hiroshi and Sakaguchi looked up in the dim light. Sakaguchi flicked the flashlight around, but neither could see what was up there, their eyes still adjusting. Hiroshi could see the short man reach for another dangling object, a box of some kind, connected like the other one to a thick wire looping up toward the ceiling. The grinding suddenly stopped and the lights clicked on.

A thick silver bolt clattered to the floor by their feet. Hiroshi and Sakaguchi looked up at a large clamshell bucket filled with heavy pieces of discarded metal swaying right over their heads. As the bucket creaked to a stop on the overhead track, another bolt, round as a fist and twice as heavy, toppled over the edge and slammed into the concrete at their feet.

When the man pressed the push-button on the box, the motor—or maybe it was another one—started grinding again. Hiroshi could hear the motor glide along the overhead runway toward him and Sakaguchi. He looked up at a second clamshell bucket swaying right above their heads.

Hiroshi and Sakaguchi waited for the man to speak, but he just stood there, watching them with a long-handled crescent wrench set against his leg ready to be snatched up if needed. His thumbs hovered over the smooth green release buttons that could send two full buckets of misshapen metal parts onto their heads with a quick push.

Hiroshi cleared his throat and said, "We need to ask you a few questions." The man stared intently at Hiroshi and then at Sakaguchi. Hiroshi tried not to look up at the buckets dangling over their heads, high enough for a quick, fatal rain of metal. He could tell Sakaguchi was getting ready to dive out of the way. For some reason, Hiroshi couldn't move, but listened intently for the click of a button or the rattle of a chain.

Hiroshi said, "We're looking for Michiko Suzuki. This is her address, isn't it? We're detectives."

"You're all the same to me."

"Do you know where we can find Michiko?"

"It's all paid off."

"What's all paid off?"

"It's on an official document."

"We're not here about the factory. We're here about Michiko. We're police detectives."

"You're all the same to me," he said again and reset the motor and release mechanism just a little bit to underscore his point. Hiroshi flinched and looked up at the swaying clamshell buckets. Sakaguchi didn't move.

"Have you seen her recently?" Hiroshi asked.

"She doesn't come here anymore."

"This is her father's shop, isn't it? Michiko's father? Suzuki, right?"

"He's long since dead. He was killed."

"We're not going to hurt her or bother you."

"How do I know that?"

"We have badges," Hiroshi said. "Can I pull mine out for you to see?"

He held his up and Sakaguchi fumbled his out, fingering his collapsible baton.

"Last time put me in hospital," the man said.

"Last time?"

"Last time you came."

Hiroshi answered quickly to keep him talking. "This is the first time we've ever been here and you're right to be careful here all alone. But we just need to ask Michiko what she knows."

"She's not here, that's all I know."

"You work here?"

"Forty years."

"Are you related?"

"I was cousin to her father. I keep things running."

"You must have known Michiko since she was a baby?"

He nodded.

273

"We're not here about money. We're here about information. We can push your badges over to you, so you can see them," Hiroshi said. He put Sakaguchi's badge on top of his, stooped over, and slid them along the rough floor. They only made it halfway. The man didn't move to get them.

Sakaguchi switched to his thick Osaka accent and said, "This place reminds me of my uncle's shop. Shops like this built this country. You still machine parts here? For automobiles, appliances, furniture, precision parts, I guess?"

"We made everything in our time," the man said, his focus shifting toward Sakaguchi. "Until the big companies cut our orders and let us rust to death."

"My uncle went broke, too, had to let all his workers go."

"I'm the last one left," the man said.

"You still get orders?"

"Replacement pieces."

"Enough to live on?"

"Not really." The man changed his tone, "Michiko's not in any trouble, is she?"

"We want to get her out of trouble."

He shook his head. "She said it was all paid off."

"If she said so, it must be. We'll be able to help her if we can find her," Sakaguchi said.

"If you're police, you can look. But I don't intend to take a beating ever again, though."

He let the push-button box swing free on its wires and picked up the long-handled crescent wrench. Sakaguchi and Hiroshi quickly stepped out from under the buckets.

"We just want to look at her room."

He said, "It's upstairs."

"Can you show me?"

The man started up the ladder to the rooms above, still clutching the wrench firmly in hand, and Hiroshi followed. He winced because his ribs still ached from when he fell chasing the photographer.

Seeing how steep the ladder was, and that the man seemed to be no threat, Sakaguchi said. "I'll wait for you in front."

Outside, Sakaguchi told Osaki to take a jog around the block and for Ueno to drive around the area and then come back. He then went around the side of the building bellying past metal drums filled with scrap. He whacked at the kudzu with his baton to get to a chain link fence topped with barbed wire. Below the fence was a canal that gave off the smell of toxic algae, clogging the water, mixed with the stench of used machine oil. He stopped and sniffed the air, and then sniffed again.

It was the unmistakable scent of lotus.

He looked down at the bank running beside the canal. A thick metal slab formed a footbridge over to the other bank where a set of concrete stairs led up to the street on the far side of the canal. The only way in was through a cut section of the fence. Sakaguchi pulled it back, but there was no way he could fit through. He called Hiroshi. "We've got to go. She was just here."

Chapter 43

Hiroshi came running down the stairs to the front of the factory where Sakaguchi was already getting in the car with Ueno at the wheel.

"Where's Osaki?" Hiroshi asked.

"We'll pick him up on the way," Sakaguchi said.

"Are you sure she was here?" Hiroshi asked.

"Smelled her perfume. She slipped out the back."

"Perfume?"

"Lotus."

Hiroshi turned to him. "I smelled that upstairs in her room, too, but outside means she was there. The shower floor was still wet."

They got in the car and Ueno pulled off, asking, "Where to?"

"She has a cousin, or older sister, or someone, who runs a fruit and vegetable stand near the station," Hiroshi said.

Around the next corner, they stopped for Osaki, whose weight tipped the entire car when he got in, but righted itself as they drove off.

Hiroshi couldn't imagine how the room he looked through was the room of someone capable of murder. The shelves in the room held English grammar books, entrance exam study guides, a how-to book on translation and manga in English, lined up neatly above her handmade desk. Posters of girlish-looking, big-eyed boy bands and happy-end anime covered the walls. A small shelf held her ribbons, medals, and prizes in aikido. Even the hundreds of *kokeshi* dolls— the armless, legless bodies formed and painted by skilled craftsmen— were nothing out of the ordinary. The racks and racks of clothes were expensive designer brands—strapless one-pieces, silk blouses, satin dresses and leather skirts and pants—but plenty of Japanese women were similarly obsessed with clothes.

"Hurry up," Hiroshi said to Ueno. "It's a little shop at the end of the street leading to the train station, he told me."

As Michiko's father's cousin had said, Suzuki Fruits and Vegetables was at the intersection of two narrow streets on the factory side of the station. The shop's yellow awning was rolled down on one side and on the other, a soiled awning hung down with just enough space for a grown man to stoop under. Yellow light splashed out over the plywood and milk crates that served as shelves.

After Hiroshi and Sakaguchi got out of the car, Hiroshi went over to the plastic nets of *mikan* oranges—400 yen a bag. Sakaguchi wandered to the daikon radishes—50 yen each.

A tall woman in a thick, indigo apron ducked under the awning and pulled up short and skittish at the sight of Hiroshi and Sakaguchi. She wiped her face with the back of her hand and pushed back her long ponytail. She was young and turned to shout, "Mother!"

In a second, an older woman with the same apron and same ponytail came out from under the awning and stood next to her daughter. They could have been twins: lean, calm, and attentive to whomever might be at their shop after it closed.

In a loud voice, the mother said, "We're closed."

Hiroshi asked, "Are you the sister of Michiko Suzuki?"

The mother whispered to her daughter with a small push to go inside, but the girl stood her ground, holding the nets of *mikan* like boxing gloves. The mother didn't insist and straightened up, re-tucking the white towel around her head. The sleeves of her white T-shirt were rolled up over her shoulders exposing her arms, muscled from moving boxes and crates of fruits and vegetables. "I haven't seen her in a long time," the mother finally said as her daughter fidgeted.

"We just have a few questions," Hiroshi said. The front light of the house next door to the fruit and vegetable stand clicked on and a second-story window slid open two doors down the narrow shopping street.

Hiroshi and Sakaguchi pulled out their badges and held them up without moving closer. "We're detectives," Sakaguchi yelled in a voice loud enough that he could be heard through the open windows.

"Is she in trouble?" The mother asked.

Hiroshi said, "We're not sure. Can we come inside?"

"We can talk here," the mother said. The girl set down the *mikan* on a stack of plastic crates.

"OK, but could you pull up that shutter? I can't see anything," Hiroshi said in a lighter tone. "I want to show you something."

Neither woman said anything more, deciding what to do. A window in the next house slid open, and Hiroshi could hear whispering. Hiroshi stepped closer, holding out the photo of Michiko and Natsumi. "This is you, isn't it? You're Natsumi?"

The two women stepped closer to look, and in the brighter light, Hiroshi could see that they both had the same lively eyes and the same way of nodding their heads while pushing back their hair.

"Where did you get this photo?"

"From the old man at the factory. He told us where you were and said you might know."

"He told you that only because he knows I don't know where she is either."

A door opened in the small, two-story house behind Hiroshi, and a man and a woman in their seventies stepped out. The woman had her cell phone open in her hand, and the man stood with his arms crossed, watching intently. Natsumi bowed to the old couple. Another older man slid his front door open and came and stood beside the old couple.

Seeing that the neighborhood was getting involved, Hiroshi spoke in a softer voice. Natsumi's face became prettier as she lost her nervous, for-strangers mask, and started to believe they really were detectives. Hiroshi could see a resemblance to Michiko's photos. He continued, "Actually, she might be related to a case we're investigating, and we need to find her."

"I haven't seen her in a long time. I told you."

"You had a falling out?"

"Not exactly. She's not my real sister."

"What do you mean?"

"Michiko's father took me in after my father died. We're cousins, actually. Her father was going to officially adopt me, but the paperwork never got finished. I lived there, until I had her." She pointed at her daughter. "This is Shie." Shie bowed and wiped her long hair out of her face.

"This is your fresh produce stand?"

"It is now. It was the only one around here, for this community. I took it over when Shie started school."

"When was the last time you talked with Michiko?"

"In person? It's been a while."

"She came by here?"

"The last time, I had to go find her. She lived in Roppongi. It wasn't easy."

"Why did you need to find her?"

"Uncle Ono got beaten up and put in the hospital."

"Who beat him up?"

"People who knew her father, said he owed them money."

"Do you know who they were?" Hiroshi glanced over at Sakaguchi, who was listening closely.

Natsumi shook her head, no, and looked down at the ground. "People like them, it doesn't matter whether you really owe them money or not. They take it either way."

"How did you find her that time?"

"I went in the middle of the night to a club, the David, where she used to hang out. We talked in the club next door, where it was quieter."

"Do you remember what it was called, the club?"

"Some flower's name."

"That was the last time you saw her?"

Natsumi frowned, trying to remember. "She came by one other time." Natsumi turned to her daughter. "Why don't you run upstairs and get supper ready so you can get back to studying?"

Shie looked at Natsumi to be sure everything was all right. The mother gave her a soft push, but before she went inside, she walked over to one of the old couples standing in the street and whispered with them. The couple nodded, patted her shoulder, and she scampered under the awning, out of sight inside. Natsumi nodded to the neighbors who collected in the shaded street outside the ring of light.

"Do you know this woman, too?" Hiroshi asked, holding up the photo of Reiko, Michiko and Mark.

Natsumi snorted. "This is Reiko. She's the cause of it all."

"All what?"

"Michiko's going to work there, getting in trouble."

"She was in trouble when she was young?"

"Michiko got kicked out of school. Broke her father's heart. She was a great student, but couldn't stand the rules."

"So, she ran away and—"

"She came back when her father was killed. The police never found the person who ran into him. She searched a long time on her own trying to find who did it."

"You were friends with Reiko, too?"

"Reiko's parents both drank. They beat her. Her father worked for Michiko's dad until he collapsed from the alcohol. She had nowhere else to go. We all three slept in the same room for years like sisters. Then things fell apart, like they always do."

A door opened somewhere on the street and another two men, in their sixties or seventies, joined those already congregating on the street. They whispered together and the men moved closer to the stand. Hiroshi wondered why they were so suspicious, and so protective of Natsumi.

Natsumi smiled at the men and raised her voice to explain, "These men are detectives, from Tokyo."

"We'll wait here until they're gone," one of the men said.

Hiroshi bowed to them politely, and fingered his badge, wanting to use it to get some privacy with Natsumi. Sakaguchi didn't seem bothered by the situation in the least. Hiroshi turned back to Natsumi. "So, you have no idea why they beat up Uncle Ono, that's his name isn't it?"

Natsumi nodded, yes, and then said. "I assume it had to do with money. I ran the office for a few years, and there were losses, but never anything amiss."

Hiroshi nodded. "And Michiko's mother?"

"She died when Michiko was young. She was a beauty. Everyone loved her."

"She died from...?"

"Cancer. Michiko didn't handle it well. It made her rebel in all the worst ways."

"Michiko helped you with the store?" Hiroshi gestured at the store.

"She gave me enough to get started. More when she moved back all of a sudden."

"Moved back from where?"

"I don't know. She was just gone for a long time."

"She disappeared?"

"It's hard to explain." Natsumi cocked her head, as if still confused. "It took a lot of fruits and vegetables to heal her. Once she got better, there was no reason to ask. She changed, but she insisted on paying for Shie's private high school, set up a college fund, and paid off my business loan."

"You have a nice setup here," Hiroshi said. The stand was larger than most, with second-floor windows on two sides. It took up the corner building on a street that led directly to the station. Foot traffic would be big if this side of the station was ever developed like the other side.

"With a daughter, and no husband, I didn't want to work in an office. I wasn't going to work as a hostess. I know everyone in the neighborhood," Natsumi pointed to the neighbors gathered in the shadows around the stand, "I don't have to flatter anyone or listen to a boss. I'm free here. Not many women can say that."

"You want this photo?" Hiroshi held out the photo he'd taken from Michiko's room. Natsumi looked at the picture of Michiko standing and smiling next to Natsumi when they were still in high school. Natsumi nodded once, yes, tears welling up in her eyes. She took the photo from him, wiping her eyes, and said, "If you find her, tell her to just come home. We'll be here."

The group of elderly men, and one woman—eight or nine of them now standing in the street—watched silently. Two of the older men hobbled over and started carrying trays and cartons inside. They looked frail when they stood still, but they moved with neat, efficient motions.

Hiroshi bowed to them as he and Sakaguchi walked to the car where Ueno and Osaki were waiting.

Inside the car, Sakaguchi asked, "You think Michiko was inside the store?"

"The sister'd have to be quite an actress," Hiroshi said. "But, Ueno, drop us off at the station, then pull around and wait with Osaki to see if Michiko comes out. We'll take the train to Roppongi, try the David Lounge and the Tulip. That's all we got."

Chapter 44

The twenty-story building of clubs, offices and apartments that housed the David and Tulip was not far from Roppongi station. The dark brown tile of the building was as clean as if it had been put up the day before. Across from the building, Hiroshi unwrapped the ice pack from his handkerchief and checked his aching ribs. Sakaguchi took a call.

"Sugamo," Sakaguchi said, holding up his cell phone. "He's coming in a car. His son won his sumo match." Sakaguchi and Hiroshi wiped the sweat off their faces, necks and forearms. It was humid outside, and ready to rain.

Hiroshi wrung the water from the ice pack out of his shirt and tossed it into a trash can by a vending machine. He squeezed his handkerchief as dry as he could and tucked in his shirt.

"Was it the David Lounge where Takamatsu got drugged?" Sakaguchi asked.

"We should have pushed more the first time we went," Hiroshi said.

"Stepping to the side wins as often as heading straight ahead. Use the opponent's momentum."

"But pushing forward works, too?"

"If it's hard, fast and steady."

They got into the elevator, and Hiroshi pressed the button for the twelfth floor.

Inside the darkness of the Tulip, the quiet, empty room was exactly the same as before. The bartender's face was sliced by shadows, the pallid skin stretched taut over his bones. He ignored Hiroshi and

285

Sakaguchi when they entered. Soft jazz played from the speakers. No one else was in the place.

Just like the time before, the bartender held an ice pick in one hand, and in the other, a ball of half-chipped ice, which he deftly tossed in rotation as he took off one small flake after the next. He wore a fresh, purple tulip on the lapel of his black vest. The light from below the bar gleamed on the white pleats of his shirt and reflected off the immaculate rows of bottles along the glass wall behind.

Hiroshi said, "You might remember me and one of my colleagues. We stopped in here a couple of days ago." The bartender looked up briefly as Sakaguchi settled onto the stool and leaned forward onto the sleek black lacquer of the bar.

The bartender chunk-chunked the ice, small slivers flying off and melting quickly in the sink below.

"I need to know about that window over there," Hiroshi said, pointing at the small opening in the backside wall.

The bartender swiveled his head to see where Hiroshi pointed, but went back to his ice ball without missing a chip.

"Answer him!" Sakaguchi bellowed, the sound echoing off the black walls. The bartender briefly stopped chipping at the ice, sighed, and then went back to work as if they weren't there.

"Does that door go to the David?" Hiroshi asked. The bartender hoisted the ball so that he could appraise its roundness, twisting it back and forth, ignoring Hiroshi's question. "I'll take that as a 'yes.' And you can send drinks through there, right?"

"Another 'yes,' sounds like," Sakaguchi growled.

Hiroshi said, "You provide special drinks from time to time."

The bartender rinsed the ball under the tap until it was luminous and smooth.

"Another 'yes,'" Sakaguchi said, his voice drained of patience.

"Where do you keep the stuff?" The bartender put the ice ball in a highball glass and twirled it to be sure it fit. Then he squatted down to put it in a freezer cabinet under the counter.

"You keep it under there?"

The bartender stood up from his squat, laying a rectangular slab of ice onto a cutting board where he sliced off a cube with a serrated knife. He then filed down the corners of the cube and appraised it like a sculptor. He took up the pick and got back to work.

"I don't think he's going to answer," Hiroshi said to Sakaguchi.

"Oh, he will," Sakaguchi said. The rhythmic picking was louder than the jazz through the speakers.

Sakaguchi said, "How much do you get paid for the drugged drinks?" The bartender kept up his steady chipping while Hiroshi's eyes followed the bits and pieces of ice sailing up and off the counter as silver flickers before they fell to the floor and sink and melted away.

Hiroshi pulled out the photo of Michiko and flopped it on the gleaming, black counter. Still picking at the ice, the bartender looked down but did not respond.

"When was the last time you saw this woman?" Hiroshi said. "Was she here last night? And the night before?" Sakaguchi sighed. Hiroshi could tell it was a preparatory sigh. Hiroshi continued: "Well, as Takamatsu used to say, questions sometimes get in the way of action."

In one quick lunge, Sakaguchi grabbed the hand holding the ice pick and yanked the bartender down hard across the counter. Hiroshi snagged the bartender's other wrist and twisted it until the ice cube rolled into the sink. Sakaguchi pushed down until the ice pick rolled away so Hiroshi could elbow it and the serrated knife down the bar.

Sakaguchi pushed the bartender's arm into the middle of his back, shredding his fresh tulip, and pulled him forward across the bar top until his toes barely touched the floor on the other side. The bartender did not squirm and did not say a word. His eyes stared as sullenly as before, only now to the side without being able to see their faces, or much of anything else.

"Let's try those questions again," said Sakaguchi.

"I think he remembers them, but let me help. The drinks are drugged, right?" The bartender nodded, yes, sideways, his ear smashed into the bar top by Sakaguchi's huge hand.

"Speak up," Sakaguchi commanded.

"Yes."

"And you get paid extra for those?"

"Yes."

"They order from the David?"

"Right."

"Through the window or by phone."

"Both."

"How often do you make them?"

"Not often."

"How not often?"

"Every so often. It's just for fun."

"Fun?"

"The girls do that to their boyfriends. The guys know. When they can't move, it gets them hot, I guess."

"It turned someone cold. This woman killed someone. That makes you an accessory to murder."

Sakaguchi let up his weight enough to let the bartender turn his head the other way and cough.

"You know this woman?" Hiroshi shoved the photo of Michiko in front of him. Thick drops of blood slowly dripped from the bartender's nose to the counter.

"No."

Sakaguchi pressed into him again. "You sure?"

"Maybe she comes in sometimes. They all look alike."

"Look again." Sakaguchi leaned his entire bulk onto the bartenders' head.

The bartender groaned, coughed, and spat out, "She's been in before."

"In here or in there?"

"Both."

"Before someone arrives to arrest you, you better get your story straight."

Hiroshi reached into the bartender's back pocket for his wallet, took out his wallet and ID and read it carefully, memorizing the details before taking a photo of it with his cell phone. He tossed the wallet aside and nodded to Sakaguchi. Hiroshi picked up the ice pick and slammed it straight into the bar top. It quivered in place and cracks radiated through the black lacquer as if it were glass.

Sakaguchi released his grip, and the bartender stood up, stretching. He touched his nose and picked up a white towel to staunch the blood.

Sakaguchi grabbed the half-chipped block of ice from the sink and hurled it at the mirror, splintering it and knocking over bottles. Top-shelf vodka, gin, and single malt spilled everywhere.

"Who's the owner of this bar?"

"You'll see."

"Who pays you?"

"The guy who owns the building."

"Where do I find him?"

"He'll find you," said the bartender, gesturing toward a small black security camera in the corner and wiping the blood from his nose.

"We'll send someone around for you later," Hiroshi said. The bartender stared at them as they walked out the door.

Hiroshi pointed out the David Lounge next door. Sakaguchi tried the door, but it was locked. He pounded with his fist.

Hiroshi said, "They don't open up until later."

"Sugamo should be downstairs by now. We'll post him there to wait for her," Sakaguchi said.

"She has to come up for air sometime."

"Unless she's gone already."

Hiroshi pushed the elevator button, and they got on. When the elevator doors opened on the ground floor, Hiroshi and Sakaguchi looked straight into a solid wall of bulky black silk suits, all big enough to fit Sakaguchi—the men inside them all his size.

Chapter 45

The five-man wall blocking Hiroshi and Sakaguchi's exit wore sunglasses and dressed in black, jackets, shirts, and pants.

Hiroshi reached for his badge, but the three men in front mirrored him by reaching into their jackets, so that Hiroshi put his hand back down.

"We don't need to see your badges," said a shorter guy standing behind the front line. "We know you're cops."

"You'll want to answer our questions then," Hiroshi said.

"Someone will, but not us," the shorter guy said. "Upstairs."

The men stepped forward, and Hiroshi and Sakaguchi stepped backwards to squeeze onto the elevator. There was nothing for Hiroshi and Sakaguchi to do but see what these men would do. The short guy slipped around the door and put a key in the button panel and pressed the top button. The other two men stepped on—the elevator dipping slightly—and the weight limit buzzer sounded.

The two men stepped off, and the buzzer stopped. One of them stepped on again, with no buzzer, but when the other put his foot on, the buzzer went off again.

The short guy, impatient, gestured for the last guy to get off and wait. He stepped back into the hallway and folded his thick, workout arms over his stomach with a dead-black sunglass stare. When the elevator got to the top floor, the door opened into a tri-level penthouse with one entire wall of floor-to-ceiling windows overlooking the lights of Roppongi.

The three men who rode up on the elevator with Hiroshi and Sakaguchi strolled to a U-shaped bar on the upper part of the split-level room and sat down on bar stools. Two women in silver lame dresses stood up from a long, overstuffed sofa by the windows. They brushed their long hair with their hands, rearranged their dresses, and walked to a back room without even a glance at Hiroshi and Sakaguchi.

A stocky man stood up from the sofa and watched the women walk away. He refocused his attention to Hiroshi and Sakaguchi and walked toward them with a limp that made his loose silk pants sway. The mandarin collar of his shirt was pinned with a diamond stud that held it tight around his broad, muscular neck. His face was as rough, wrinkled, and red as that of a rice farmer who worked outdoors every day of his life.

Hiroshi waited patiently by the elevator door, with Sakaguchi by his side.

A tall, gaunt man with a ponytail halfway down the back of his thin leather jacket came striding out of the back room where the women disappeared. An energetic young man with thick-framed glasses and a laptop against his chest bounded out after him.

"Welcome," the rice farmer said, his voice cheery and raspy. With broad gestures, he waved Hiroshi and Sakaguchi over to plush couches surrounding a low table inlaid with a tiger image made from cut, polished stones. The tiger's crouching body and legs were made of artfully arrayed agate and onyx, the claws of polished white coral. The eyes were made from glittering tigers eye stones that caught the light from deep inside.

Hiroshi looked at Sakaguchi, who shrugged and took a step toward the man. Hiroshi hesitated.

"We don't get many visitors up here. Would you like a cup of Gyokuro tea from Fukuoka? I had to give up alcohol a few years ago."

"We won't be here long," Hiroshi said.

"Always time for tea," the rice farmer said, holding out his arms to welcome them over to the sofa before nodding to the men at the bar, one of whom walked to the kitchen.

The rice farmer sat first, gesturing for Hiroshi and Sakaguchi, and then the tall ponytail man to do the same. The young guy with thick-frame glasses stood to the side, clutching his laptop and seesawing slightly from leg to leg. Hiroshi sat on the edge of the sofa.

"I'm Mochida," the rice farmer said.

"I'm Hiroshi Shimizu," Hiroshi said, pushing his *meishi* across the table. The ponytail took it, read it, and put it in a case in his jacket pocket.

Mochida smiled and said, "The police are getting younger all the time. And are you a sumo wrestler?" he asked Sakaguchi.

"I was. Now I'm a homicide detective."

"Investigating in my building, it seems. So, what can I help you with?"

Hiroshi said, "Murder."

The crust that overlay Mochida's face hardened.

The ponytail leaned over the tiger, and the computer guy quit bouncing on the balls of his feet.

"If those clubs are yours, you could be in trouble," Hiroshi said.

"You mean the club you just busted up," Mochida said calmly.

"That was your club? The name on the business papers is not 'Mochida.'"

"Business papers?" Mochida smiled. "If it wasn't my place, why else would I invite you up here?"

One of the men brought the tea from the other room in elegant handmade cups. After the drugged drinks in the Tulip, neither Hiroshi nor Sakaguchi felt like drinking anything. "You can't get this tea very often, you know," Mochida nodded to them both to try it. Mochida sipped his tea with relish, smacking his lips with the delight of a connoisseur. "So, what is it you need exactly?"

"Video from the surveillance cameras."

"Why would I give that to you? After all the expensive imported liquor you wasted?"

"We can investigate the bars the slow way. That'd involve twenty-some people in and out of everything in this building for a week, maybe two. No income plus lawyer fees, it adds up," Hiroshi said. "This looks like a high-tech building."

"That's my tech guy there," he pointed to the laptop guy, who adjusted his glasses. "They're getting younger every year, too."

"We're looking for a woman."

"Who isn't?" Mochida's voice rose in amusement.

"This woman," Hiroshi put the photo of Michiko on the table. Mochida, the ponytail, and the computer guy glanced at the photo.

"Pretty girl," Mochida said.

"Dangerous girl."

"All pretty women are dangerous!" Mochida laughed.

"Not all women commit murder."

"Fortunately," Mochida said and leaned back in his chair. The laptop guy took the photo and began scanning it with a mobile scanner. Mochida tapped the table over the white-stone fangs of the tiger. "You have to understand, people come to my clubs trusting not to be seen."

"We only need the footage for certain dates. Just the twelfth floor, the entrance and elevator." Hiroshi pulled out a pen, jotted down the dates, and pushed the paper over.

The laptop guy took the dates and times and tapped them in. The scan finished. He handed the photo back and started a search for Michiko's image.

"There was no murder in this building," Mochida said. "We would have known."

"Your bartender poured the knockout drugs."

"I can turn him over to you. He'll testify and do the time. You're done."

Mochida turned to the guys at the bar.

"I don't want any sacrifice. I just want the video on specific nights," Hiroshi said. This was the second time he'd been offered a fall guy, or fall girl. The guy outside the club offered to find a hostess to take the rap, and now Mochida was offering up the bartender. Hiroshi couldn't believe that all these low-level people would be so loyal, or maybe so desperate.

"You want to see if she was with the guy who died?" Mochida asked.

"That's all."

He shrugged a wordless "no big deal," his crusty face creasing at the ease of giving an okay to something so simple. The computer guy carried over the laptop to Mochida, who nodded and then turned it to show Hiroshi the screen, re-typing a code and pressing play. A dozen video screens appeared: shots from inside the clubs, the hallways and the elevator.

"You have a lot of video."

"Video is very persuasive. It provides insurance," Mochida explained.

"What time, roughly?" the computer guy asked.

"Midnight," Hiroshi said. The computer guy tapped in the time and the videos raced by on fast forward. When the videos slowed, Michiko and Steve walked into the elevator. Steve leaned his bulky frame over to kiss her as the elevator doors shut.

"Is that them?"

"Yes. Can you copy all the cameras?"

The computer guy zoomed in and let it run as he made a circling gesture to the men at the bar. One of the men disappeared into a back room and brought back a blank DVD.

"I'll put all of them on this. You can see the date there, at the bottom. You'll need a special media player: Winzap. It's used on all security film. Do you have that?"

"Maybe at the station."

"I'll put a copy of it on here with the video."

"We have a tech lab."

"I know. I used to work there," the laptop guy said, repositioning his glasses. "Didn't pay very well."

Mochida picked up Michiko's photo and frowned. "She looks familiar, doesn't she?"

He handed the photo to the ponytail guy who said, "I think this is the girl who beat up Tanigawa."

Mochida pulled a face and shook his head, trying to remember.

"Tanigawa, from Iwate? She sent him to the hospital."

"I remember," Mochida said, chuckling. "Pretty ones like her don't need to be violent usually. Where was she working?"

"She started at the Venus de Milo, but then moved to the Ring, and the Strap and Tie."

"That S&M joint?"

"They make a lot there. Tanigawa tried to shake the girls down for a cut, so she beat him up!"

"And most women are so passive!" Mochida laughed out loud. "If she worked at the Ring, there'll be an address for her. Get that, can you? And look in the Venus database. That mama-san kept good records."

The laptop whirred.

Mochida sipped his tea. "Real estate's so much easier. Fewer personnel problems."

The laptop guy sat back, his eyes moving rapidly over the video footage. He turned the screen to Mochida who watched for a few minutes and laughed. "Oh, her! Now, I remember! I knew I'd seen her somewhere."

The ponytail looked and nodded his inert face, "Yes, that's her. The same one."

"She was in trouble with those guys and now with the cops. She gets around!" Mochida shook his head with a laugh.

"Trouble with what guys?" Hiroshi asked.

"There was a development project in Kawasaki or Shinagawa, I forget the details. That's why I have to hire this guy," Mochida waved at the laptop guy. "She found out ahead of time. In bed, I guess. How it usually happens. Messed up their investment."

"And then tried to blackmail them!" The ponytail guy shook his head.

"When the investment went bust, they asked her to work off the debt."

"Work off the debt?" Hiroshi asked. "What do you mean?"

Mochida and the ponytail guy snorted.

Mochida leaned forward over the tiger's head. "The group she jerked around does not like to lose money. They're not used to it."

The ponytail said, "They're not a forgiving group of investors."

Mochida said, "She's lucky to be alive."

The laptop kept clicking away.

"Were these guys from Kobe?" Hiroshi asked.

Mochida shook his head, smiling at Hiroshi. "I don't bat in the big leagues. I know my place. Learned it the hard way." Mochida pointed to his crippled leg.

"Who did she sell the information to?"

"Foreigners, I heard. That made it even worse."

The ponytail said, "Those Kobe guys like to keep the best deals inside Japan."

"But who knows what really happened. The foreigners are the ones you should be looking into," Mochida sneered. After a few minutes of clicking, the laptop guy turned and waved to one of the guys at the bar—their well-pumped muscles made them all look the same to Hiroshi. The bulky, black-suited guy came back holding two pages of printout and a second DVD.

The laptop guy glanced at the printout and looked at Mochida for an approving nod. Getting it, he slid the printout and the DVD copy over the tiger.

The printout had Michiko's Kawasaki address and another in Roppongi, a clear head shot, her age and birthdate, insurance card info, old work schedules and a list of cell phone and landline numbers. Below that was the address for Bentley Associates in Nishi-Shinjuku and the names Steve Deveaux, Mark Whitlock, and Barbara Harris-Mitford.

"Do you want us to take care of it for you?" Mochida asked, his underlings listening attentively.

"We'll handle it," Hiroshi said, standing up.

"Maybe we can talk again sometime."

"I doubt it," said Sakaguchi, on his feet in one motion.

"You didn't touch your tea." Mochida smiled. "I'll send you some."

Hiroshi put the DVD and printout in his pocket as they walked toward the elevator. The short guy keyed them in and waited to take them down to the ground floor.

"Be careful you don't get beat up!" Mochida called out after them before the doors closed. The laughter from the penthouse echoed through the elevator shaft as Hiroshi and Sakaguchi descended.

Chapter 46

Sugamo was waiting at the corner with the new car, as Ueno and Osaki were still driving back from Kawasaki when no one emerged from Natsumi's fruit and vegetable stand. Hiroshi and Sakaguchi hurried over to the car and hopped in.

"Here's the address," Hiroshi said, popping the numbers from the printout into the car navigation device on the dashboard. "Not far."

"Congratulations on your son's win!" Sakaguchi said as they pulled out.

"The other kid was much bigger, but my son got his hand under the *mawashi* belt and dumped him with a perfect *uwatenage* over-arm throw," Sugamo said, his voice filled with pride.

"That was your specialty, wasn't it?" Sakaguchi asked.

"Yeah, but the funny thing is, I never mentioned it to my son," Sugamo said.

"Must be genetic," Hiroshi said, rubbing his ribs.

Sugamo parked in the circular drive of Michiko's apartment building so that he could see both the front door and the parking garage. At the entrance, Sakaguchi watched from a short distance while Hiroshi buzzed the building manager's call button. When there was no immediate answer, Hiroshi leaned on the button again. Sakaguchi looked over at the parking garage as Hiroshi dialed the manager's security code on the keypad. When the manager answered, Hiroshi told him they were police detectives.

The manager ran to the door, nearly knocking over the large ikebana flower arrangement just inside the security doors. Hiroshi and Sakaguchi showed him their badges and he nervously flipped through the master keys dangling from a coiled nylon string around his neck.

At Michiko's door, the manager fumbled the keys and twisting them in and out of the lock and trying several wrong keys, until Sakaguchi snatched the keys from him, slid the deadbolt back with the right key and opened the latch with a second key.

"Wait here," Hiroshi told him.

"I'll wait downstairs. Call the same number to get me," the manager said before hurrying away.

Sakaguchi whipped off his shoes in two quick motions and stepped inside, braced, picking the bedroom to the left. Hiroshi followed, but headed into the living room.

They moved slowly, listening, and watching. Light from the street below came through the sliding glass doors along the living room. An L-shaped counter marked off the kitchen area. A row of countertop appliances and a large, stainless steel refrigerator twinkled in the dim light. A white sofa spread out past the dining table. The place was immaculate and huge.

Sakaguchi walked into the living room and flipped on a light switch. Off the living room, a ten-mat tatami room held a yoga mat, CD player, and meditation CDs. A brushwork scroll of a single-stroke circle—open at the end—hung on the wall next to an empty cherry bark shelf.

Sakaguchi opened the refrigerator and smelled the milk and yogurt containers. He poked a bag of greens and unscrewed a bottle of *sake*. "All fresh," he growled.

"She could have someone come in to do all this," Hiroshi said.

"Or someone else could be staying here," Sakaguchi said.

"Or we missed her."

Hiroshi checked the locks on the row of sliding glass doors. All six were closed tight. Outside, small bushes grew from planters embedded in the balcony floor. Spotlights pointed down on three rounded worn rocks nestled in gravel. Ten floors up, the apartment commanded a panoramic view of the night streets stretching south from Roppongi's hills all the way to Tokyo Bay.

"What's a place like this go for a month?" Sakaguchi wondered out loud.

"More than your salary and mine combined."

"The bedroom's bigger than your office."

"The living room's bigger than the homicide office."

"Better view, too."

Hiroshi walked over to the bookshelves that lined two walls. On the top shelf were tea ceremony bowls. Filling two shelves were photos of Michiko in stand-up frames: together with Reiko, Steve and Mark in Tokyo, alone at the Eiffel Tower, alone in front of European churches and art museums, and with a young man on the bayside walk in Hong Kong.

The next shelf had photos of Natsumi and her daughter, of Michiko and a handsome young man at an *onsen* hot springs resort, in her aikido outfit next to what was probably her old teacher, in front of the entrance to the Ikenobo School of ikebana flower arrangement, and relaxing in a sash-tied yukata summer kimono.

Behind those, toward the back, were portraits of Michiko nude, leaning back on rounded river boulders in front of a waterfall. In another, she posed in the surf, the tide bubbling sand over the contours of her body. Hiroshi gazed at them, mesmerized.

On the lower shelves were dictionaries and travel guides, for Paris, Hong Kong, and the rest of Asia, Sei Shonagon's *The Pillow Book* and the classic treatise of bushido—*Hagakure, In the Shadow of Leaves*—well marked in pencil. The rest of the shelves held classics in Japanese and English, paperbacks and an e-reader flat on the shelf.

Hiroshi went to the bedroom, when Sakaguchi came out, roaming, observing. A long silver reading lamp arced over the large, western bed. A book of English idioms rested on the antique, Chinese-style bedside table. Hiroshi could not fit this bedroom together with her cramped, claustrophobic childhood bedroom he had seen in Kawasaki. But this bedroom didn't seem to be the bedroom of a killer, either.

Large closets opened behind floor-to-ceiling doors. Hiroshi pulled them open and stepped inside. The clothes were even more lavish than those in Kawasaki, and these were neatly organized by type and length.

Inside the closet stood three suitcases: one, maroon with dark blue straps, the other two, brushed leather with lots of pockets—all locked. Hiroshi picked them up. They were heavy and full. He left them in the exact same place.

301

"Come here," Sakaguchi shouted from the bathroom. He held out a bottle to Hiroshi. "Same scent I caught in Kawasaki."

"Must be her brand."

Hiroshi put the perfume back among the other conditioners, gels and creams. He went back to a Chinese-style antique desk in the living room. He flipped open Michiko's laptop. Sandwiched inside was an airplane ticket. He turned on the laptop, but got a password input icon and turned it off. The airplane ticket was for the next morning. He set it down and looked in the woven trash container below, retrieving a pair of torn-up airplane tickets from Fly A Way Travel Agency, dated two days before. He laid them out on the desk, trying to re-piece the torn parts.

"What did you find?" Sakaguchi asked.

Hiroshi held up the tickets. "In the trash. And look at this. Paris."

"From the same travel agency."

"She missed that flight and has another tomorrow. Paris again."

"Both in her name?"

"The two for two days ago have the names ripped off. Tomorrow's is a single ticket for Michiko Suzuki. I dug around in the trashcan, but nothing."

"See a passport anyplace?"

"No such luck."

"Her bags are packed and waiting in the closet. Now, what?"

Sakaguchi took a big breath and said. "Have Akiko call the airlines. If she's coming back for her luggage and the ticket, we still have a chance. We'll get her here or at Narita."

Hiroshi set the ticket and envelope back where he'd found it, in the laptop. "Let's wait downstairs. Otherwise that manager will scare her off." Hiroshi replaced everything in the desk and called the building manager.

"Could you come lock up for us? We're finished now."

"Finished? What do you mean? Didn't you see her?" the manager sounded like he was strangling on his own words.

"See who?" Hiroshi asked.

"The tenant," the manager whispered.

"The woman who lives here?"

"Yes, I, well, she, I ran into her in the hallway and she said she knew you and I shouldn't worry and—"

302

"When was that?"

"Just a minute ago."

"Did she ride the elevator up?"

"I think so."

Hiroshi hung up. He moved quickly to the genkan and slipped on his shoes. Sakaguchi followed, surmising what the manager had said. As he stepped into the hallway after Hiroshi, Sakaguchi folded two pieces of paper and wedged them into the deadbolt and latch strikes in the doorjamb.

Hiroshi nodded toward the stairs for Sakaguchi and at the elevator for himself. Hiroshi waited at the elevators, but did not press any buttons. One of the elevators went up to the top floor, and the other stopped two floors below. He waited for the one on the top floor to start down before he pressed the button. When the elevator doors opened, Hiroshi quickly apologized to a well-dressed couple—the woman's perfume as strong as her glare—and stepped back into the hall.

The other elevator came up to the floor and stopped. When its doors slowly slid open there was nothing more than empty space. His ribs were aching and he held his sides as he got on and pressed the buttons for every floor. When the doors slid open, he held them, looking up and down the hall. At the first floor, he pushed the button for Michiko's floor. The folded paper Sakaguchi stuffed in Michiko's front doorjamb to keep the apartment open was still there.

He listened for any sound coming from inside and before he pulled the door open, he felt the cool of a breeze wafting through the hallway—perhaps a window at the end of the corridor or the door to the stairwell had been propped open—and then he went inside.

He could not remember if he'd turned off the lights, but the apartment was all shadows. He stood at the door and looked over the living room, ready for Michiko.

He turned around and walked into the bedroom, but could not remember closing the closet. He turned to the closet doors, and with one solid yank, swung them open.

The three suitcases were just where Sakaguchi left them.

"The ticket," he murmured and started back toward the laptop on the Chinese desk in the living room. As he passed the bathroom, though, he noted the perfume that he'd sniffed before. The closer he got to the laptop, the stronger the smell of lotus perfume.

He flipped open the laptop, hoping to see what he'd put back in there only minutes before, but braced for what the lotus scent told him to expect. The scent was right—the ticket was gone.

He fumbled through the papers on the desk, and then dug through the trash can below, but her ticket for tomorrow's flight to Paris was not there. Hiroshi punched Sakaguchi's number into his cell phone. "Did you take her ticket?" he asked, knowing the answer already.

Sakaguchi, out of breath, said, "No. Where are you?" and then he remained silent on the other end.

Hiroshi's mind raced to figure out how it could have happened. The ticket was gone, and so was she.

Chapter 47

Hiroshi came out of the front door and stood in the circular drive in front of Michiko's building and looked at the surrounding apartment buildings of Azabu. Most were larger than they appeared, and had multiple entrances on different levels of the steep hills and hard-to-walk slopes that enforced a certain privacy and quietude that attracted wealthy people and embassies.

Hiroshi looked at Sugamo still waiting in the car under a streetlamp. It was already dark and Osaki and Ueno had still not arrived. If someone had come out, Sugamo would have seen. Sugamo frowned at Hiroshi—thinking he knew where Sakaguchi had gone—and then pointed to the parking garage to clue him in.

Hiroshi hurried down the incline into the dimly lit parking garage. He looked for Sakaguchi up ahead and at both lines of cars as he passed. He thought he smelled a whiff of lotus scent perfume amid the car exhaust and oil drips, but was maybe imagining it. Hiroshi looked under and around the parked cars and kept moving.

At the bottom of two winding floors of parking, Hiroshi vaulted over a low wall into a garden and hurried down to a line of trimmed trees at the edge of a drop-off. A set of switchback stairs led to the road below.

Hiroshi could see Sakaguchi all the way at the bottom looking both ways. Hiroshi peered through the densely packed houses and apartment buildings all around. Through a break between the houses, a tall figure—Michiko, he was sure—flashed by.

Hiroshi tried to point her direction out to Sakaguchi, but Sakaguchi had already taken off down concrete steps that led to a narrow street up a steep slope. Hiroshi clambered down after Sakaguchi—

and hopefully Michiko—and once at the bottom, raced to the nearest intersection. From there, he caught another glimpse of Michiko heading toward Roppongi Hills—a skyscraper complex of offices, apartments, and entertainment spots.

At the end of the next block, he could see her walking quickly up the slope leading to an escalator into the complex. At the top, she turned and looked back.

Hiroshi was not sure whether she had seen him or not, but it no longer mattered. They had to catch her before she got lost in the crowd or ducked into one of the thousands of clubs, restaurants, and bars off the main streets on the other, busier side of Roppongi Hills.

When he looked again, she was gone. He hurried up the stairs and ran under the scraggly ten-meter-tall bronze spider statue, *Maman*, under whose marble eggs people waited to meet. Michiko kept going through the milling crowd and hopped on a long escalator carrying a stream of people slowly down. Hiroshi got on the escalator just as she got off on the street below.

Hiroshi called Sakaguchi and told him, "She's on the street heading down Roppongi Dori." He twisted back and forth to avoid passersby with their shopping bags and narrow focus on cell phone screens.

"I see her," Sakaguchi said. "I went around the other way. I've got her."

Breathless, with his ribs still aching, Hiroshi said, "Don't try to get her on your own. I'll call Sugamo with the car and backup team and Osaki and Ueno will be here soon." He wasn't sure if Sakaguchi heard him or not.

Michiko was far down the street by the time Hiroshi caught sight of Sakaguchi ahead, his large ambling gait easier to spot than Michiko's graceful stride. He looked past Sakaguchi and saw her long, gleaming hair under the lights amid the bustling, nighttime crowd.

At a crosswalk under the elevated highway, Michiko sprinted across just as the light changed to red. Sakaguchi sprinted across just before traffic pulled out. Hiroshi stayed on the opposite side, hurrying to pull even with them, watching Michiko emerge and disappear between people and pillars. Taxis, buses, and cars pulled by in waves, blocking his view across the eight lanes of traffic.

He could see that she took the next crosswalk back to Hiroshi's side as the light changed to red. Sakaguchi held up his hand to the cars to get back across, still ahead of Hiroshi but now on the same side of the street.

Sakaguchi steered his bulk through the crowd more like a football running back than a sumo wrestler, weaving through the clumps of people along the crowded sidewalk, speeding up when Michiko sped up toward the large, five-way Roppongi crossing. Hiroshi started running. They could catch her at the corner. With the heavy traffic, she was trapped.

Hiroshi watched closely as Sakaguchi sprinted toward her, closing the last few steps and springing toward her as if bursting across a sumo ring, his arms reaching forward. Michiko pivoted to the side. In one smooth motion, she slipped her hand under Sakaguchi's huge armpit, blocked his leg, snagged his belt, and sent his momentum headfirst into the plate glass window of Almond Coffee Shop. His speed and weight propelled him straight through it.

The huge window shattered like a bomb, flinging glass in all directions, causing people to cringe, scream and scatter. Sakaguchi landed hard and skidded to a stop against the front counter, his head cracking the metal as angrily as a car crash. Cakes and cookies spilled over him in soft thuds as the counter girls in pink and white lace uniforms shrieked, frozen in place with half-filled cups and just-cut slices of desserts in trembling hands.

Hiroshi saw Michiko take off and took off after her, then stopped himself. He had to be sure Sakaguchi was all right. Hiroshi stepped through the broken window and knelt down beside Sakaguchi. Blood and coffee pooled beside his huge round body, soaking into his bland, summer jacket, his back an arch of sweat. The back of his head was slashed and his legs splayed over glass shards and sponge cake.

Sakaguchi moaned and lifted his blood-drenched face toward Hiroshi, whispering, "Don't let her get away." His legs tried to find purchase, but Hiroshi patted him and told him to stay down.

Two uniformed policemen with long, wooden *keijo* sticks arrived from the nearby station. They looked as startled as the customers and clerks. Hiroshi flipped open his detective badge and ducked back through the window. He spun in all directions looking down the sidewalks and small lanes radiating from the large crossing like spokes.

She was gone.

A small man with round glasses frowned at Hiroshi and pointed with a finger.

"She went over there?" Hiroshi asked. "You saw her?" The small man nodded. "She went down there?" The man pointed to the subway entrance. Hiroshi had to trust him.

Hiroshi ran for the stairs, spinning 180 degrees on the landing and running down the next flight as fast as the crowd allowed. The gate attendant barely gave Hiroshi's badge a glance as Hiroshi shot through the ticket gate and sped down the escalator to the platform.

At the bottom, the platform split in two. To the left, the wall curved in, letting him see to the end of the platform. To the right, the wall curved out, so he could only see part way down. He walked along the curved-out side, pushing and twisting his shoulders to get through the waiting passengers chatting amiably or checking their cell phones.

The rumble of an approaching train drummed loudly from inside the tunnel. He stepped back to the advertisements as a wall of air streamed through the tunnel into the station. He could see the front light of the train coming out of the dark tunnel. He did not see her anywhere. The train pounded closer.

Hiroshi turned into a cut-through that led to the platform on the other side of the wall where she could have slipped through and doubled back. He surveyed the crowd in both directions along the platform as the train burst out of the tunnel into the bright platform area. The metal snarl and shriek of brakes echoed against the tiled concrete walls.

After the train stopped, the rush of exiting passengers turned the platform into a blur, and then the waiting passengers plunged onto the train. Four cars down, a head of long hair, Michiko's, or one just like hers, ducked inside the door. The departure signal sounded. Was it her? He stood with one foot on the train, desperate for another glimpse. When the departure signal stopped and the conductor's announcement finished, Hiroshi followed his instincts and hopped back on just before the doors shut and the train heaved into motion.

He turned sideways to squeeze past the commuters holding the overhead straps, absorbed in their own little worlds of cell phone surfing and text-messaging. He glanced at each person worrying that Michiko had given him the slip once again. He sidled to the end of the car, wearily checking each face he passed, grabbing the overhead bar above their heads for balance and murmuring, "*Sumimasen,* excuse me," as he twisted past.

He pulled the door and passed through the inter-car space, the metal plates grating and screeching below. Inside the next car, he looked for her up and down the rows of sitting and standing passengers. It was too crowded to get very far, even with louder apologies and gentle pushes. He worried he wouldn't even recognize her, but took a breath and told himself to let his gut do some work for a change. There was no Excel spread sheet to help him here.

He thought of Takamatsu in the hospital and kept going, but more warily than before. The next stop came soon. He stepped out onto the platform to move a few doors closer to where he thought she must be. When the inhale-exhale of humans finished, he scrambled on just as the doors closed.

At the end of the next car, the door handle between the cars pushed uselessly up and down, locked. Through the glass, Hiroshi saw her sitting calmly, her long hair falling around her face. That was her, he felt sure. Her hair was the same length, but he could only see her from the side, so he stopped looking and tried to think things through.

The next stop was Shinjuku Station. Thanks to Linda, who had time to look up things like this, he knew that the 3.6 million passengers that used the station every day had a choice of over two hundred possible exits and over fifty platforms. Hiroshi knew this because Linda had recited the numbers to him—repeatedly, out of amazement. Hiroshi joked and laughed with her about that being almost as many people as in the Boston metropolitan area—through just one station—but as the train pulled to a stop he realized that Shinjuku Station was probably the easiest place in the world to lose someone.

If Michiko got a step ahead, he couldn't keep up and she would escape through one of the many permutations of possible escape routes. Hiroshi knew he had to grab her as soon as she got off the train. But he wasn't sure he could take her alone after seeing what she did to Sakaguchi.

The train pulled to a stop. When the doors opened, Michiko raced off the train and up the escalator and Hiroshi hurried after her. She climbed steadily up all three flights of escalators and two half-flights of stairs without slowing. At the top, Hiroshi was breathing hard, his ears buzzing. He pulled his cell phone out, still trailing her, but moving, and called Sugamo.

"Shinjuku Station. Heading for the south exit."

"I'll be there. Fifteen minutes."

"Where's Ueno and Osaki?"

"They're coming, too."

"And—"

"Sakaguchi's on the way to the hospital. Be careful."

Hiroshi spun around like some human toy, before he saw her duck down a passageway to a brightly lit underground shopping mall. The shutters were pulled down over most of the shops, and last-minute shoppers milled around the still-open stores and sale baskets out front. He could see her easily in the underground passageway, and followed her until it spilled into a wide concourse with shiny pillars.

They had circled around to the east entrance, Hiroshi realized, so she must be heading back to the trains. He saw her move quickly across the open area in front of the gates and hurry inside.

Hiroshi ran after her, flipped his badge to the attendant at the gate and saw her going up the stairs to the Yamanote Line, the circular heart of Tokyo's train system.

The platform was packed. He couldn't see her anywhere. The departure signal finished and he slipped onto a train whose doors banged shut as everything leapt forward. He was either completely right or completely wrong. As they passed the end of the platform, he pushed toward the back of the train looking at every person. There were plenty of women with long hair, but most were shorter than Michiko, or stood slumped in dreamy fatigue.

In the third car, he found her, so he stopped a car length away. She stood tall and relaxed, her hair down her back and her eyes looking out the windows. She did not hold the overhead strap, but balanced herself masterfully, staying upright in place through the swaying rhythm and sporadic jolts of the train.

He stopped. Between them was a full carload of people.

She did not look his way.

Hiroshi texted Sugamo: "Heading south from Shinjuku on the Yamanote line." He did not move any closer, and she stayed where she was. Hiroshi wondered if she had seen him, but she gave not the smallest sign that she had. That made him all the more cautious. At the next stop, Yoyogi, she stayed on the train. At the next stop, Harajuku, she glided off with the crowd. Hiroshi texted Sugamo: "Harajuku Station."

Instead of hurrying to the stairs like before, though, Michiko stood stock still on the platform, staring at the steep slope of over-grown vegetation leading up to the grounds of Meiji Jingu Shrine, the largest, most sacred Shinto shrine in Tokyo. On the platform, a cool breeze flowed down from the thick woods that surrounded the shrine.

After departing passengers got on, the train pulled away, leaving only a few people to trundle up the stairs toward the exit. Michiko turned away from the shrine and looked at the large billboards for designer brand clothing lining the fence across the tracks. The trapped-in-time faces of the models looked down on the platform, showing off the latest styles and designs and trendy views, their surface appeal both beckoning and ignoring whoever looked their way while waiting on the platform.

Hiroshi walked toward Michiko and stopped. She turned to him. They stood facing each other. The overhead sign for the next train's arrival started blinking.

Chapter 48

Michiko's long black hair appeared glimmering brown under the harsh overhead lighting of the platform. She stood calmly in the middle of the platform, her tall, muscular body resting and ready, her only movement a quick tug on her black shawl.

"Leave me alone," she hissed.

"I know what happened." Hiroshi said.

She pushed her black leather travel bag behind her and took a step, then another, toward him. Hiroshi could hear the wind through the trees and the rumble of the next train. Her eyes locked on his.

"I know what happened to you. In Kobe," he said over the heightening sound of the train. "Tell me about them, about Bentley, about—"

"You don't have any idea what happened."

"Yes, I do. I know what happened. And why."

"Here's what happened," she said. With a quick jump and spin, she landed a kick into his already-bruised ribs, his tucked-in elbow little defense.

Unprepared for the blow, Hiroshi buckled and dropped to his knees. He pushed up on one knee, clutching his side.

She balanced her weight, tying her shawl tight around her waist.

"I can help you get those guys," Hiroshi gasped. "Even in Paris. We get their cash flow and—"

She spun her leg toward his head. Hiroshi threw up his arms to break her kick. Her leg glanced off his arms, so she leaned down to punch his solar plexus. Hiroshi snatched at his diaphragm, coughing and sucking for air. He felt her snatch his wrist, twist the joint, and his body spun around, totally at her command. He worried she would snap his hands into useless appendages with one more twist as he felt himself being dragged to the edge of the platform.

"How would you like a year of this?" she asked. She looked over her shoulder at the train rocketing toward the platform. Hiroshi pushed backwards, scraping the platform with his shoes for traction, but felt her knee in his back and his hands levered over his head. He flinched at the pain.

The train pulled closer.

He understood just how easy it would have been for her to throw someone drugged into incapacity—she was dragging him against all the sober force he had left. Hearing the sound of the train, he dug his foot into the concrete. As the train approached, he twisted one leg underneath himself and leaned back as hard as he could. The pain in his wrists was excruciating. He made one last effort to pull his center of gravity away from the edge, but she kneed him and pulled back. It was too late.

The train shot past.

Hiroshi managed to splutter, "I can help you get those guys," before she wrapped her arms around his throat and locked them tight at the elbows, cutting off his air. Hiroshi tried to get his fingers inside the vise of her arms, but found no opening. He tried to elbow her, but she easily dodged aside.

He clawed at her arm, desperate for air. "You...get them...you know...invest..."

She whispered in his ear, "When I get them, on my own, I want to see their eyes up close. Not across some courtroom. Even Takamatsu understood that."

She pulled him toward the end of the platform and when her arms loosened for a moment, Hiroshi wheezed and coughed out, "Takamatsu wanted to help you, too."

"He didn't know how." She squeezed tighter. "Neither do you."

Michiko cranked her forearms and dragged Hiroshi along the platform. As he gasped and sucked for air, concentrating to be sure he didn't lose consciousness, he could see a bevy of station attendants talking into their microphone-earphones and passengers being blocked from the platform.

Hiroshi's eyes were watering too much to see any more as he blanked out for a moment when Michiko twisted his neck again, hard, and whispered, "You don't look in shape to help."

The commotion of passengers and station attendants grew more frantic. Police pushed through the crowd and started down the stairs to the platform. Hiroshi blearily tried to focus on them, but they seemed to be receding as he lost breath and awareness of what was happening.

Suddenly, he felt a flood of air into his lungs and blood rushed to his head. Michiko had let him go. He rubbed his neck, then his ribs, but as he pushed himself up, he nearly screamed, his wrists hurt so badly. He looked up just as she leapt off the end of the platform onto the tracks.

Struggling to his feet, Hiroshi saw the police coming down the platform, looking at him. Hiroshi put up a hand to let them know he was all right, held up his badge and called Sugamo. He took a painful breath and saw Michiko's figure far down the tracks. She darted up a steep, grassy slope leading from the train line to the shrine grounds. Michiko pulled herself over a security gate and disappeared into the dark forest encircling the shrine.

Hiroshi's breath came back enough to tell Sugamo, "Meiji Jingu Shrine."

"Inside?" Sugamo asked.

"Yes," Hiroshi said, trying to breathe and focus. "I'll follow her, meet me inside."

Hiroshi told the police to block the main shrine entrance and the smaller entrance that led to Yoyogi Station, and that he would go inside after her.

Hiroshi stumbled to the edge of the platform and eased himself down. He tried to run, but lost his balance on the tracks, ties and gravel underfoot. A fine mist, nearly fog, made him blink. He pulled himself up the wall from the level of the tracks, climbed over a fence, and then headed up the slope into the forested grounds of the shrine.

At the top of the slope, a dirt trail snaked down to the central processional path. The reflected glow from the surrounding city cast a faint light over the forest. Hiroshi moved from tree to tree, steadying himself below the rice-stalk ropes tied around the sacred trunks. His eyes adjusted to the darkness and his lungs gulped in the cool,

315

oxygen-rich air. His hair and shoulders became wet from the tall, dripping trees.

He passed under a wooden, copper-topped *torii* whose gentle curves were strung with leg-thick ropes dangling white paper lightning bolts. Above was a ribbon of sky. All else was shadows and the muffled stirrings from the thick undergrowth and overhead canopy.

He heard far-off steps along the wide gravel path. He followed the sound and stepped onto the mossy earth alongside the path.

The sound of her footfalls stopped, but Hiroshi kept on to a weathered rack of white-painted *sake* barrels stacked six-high. He paused there, listening, trying not to huff so loudly, under the subtle glow of the white paint on the barrels. He peered into the darkness of the cedar trees and bamboo thickets and shouted into the silence. "At least, tell me what you know, so I can get them."

The ripping and creaking of splintering wood was the only warning before the huge white casks of *sake* cascaded over him, burying him completely. As the barrels started to smother him, he realized they were empty. Shouldering the wet casks aside, Hiroshi stood, disoriented, barely able to pull his legs out.

In the immense silence of the surrounding shrine, between the thumping in his head, he heard her footfalls move toward the main shrine. She was moving quickly.

He got himself back into motion, following the sound to the sprawling inner courtyard, a vast area paved with tightly fitted flat stone that stretched to the walls in all directions. It glimmered, wet from the mist.

He felt in his pocket for his cell phone, but it was not there. It must have slipped out when the *sake* barrels buried him. Sugamo should have arrived by now, with Ueno and Osaki. Hiroshi was counting on them coming in to the shrine from the path that led to the entrance, but there was no sound and no sign, only the main shrine roof lifting like wings in flight against the dark sky.

He worked his way along the outer wall and climbed the stairs to the balustrades blocking the shrine's forbidden interior. The floorboards were designed to creak, an old warning system, so his every step made them sing out.

He stopped and listened, his back to the bamboo screen veiling the innermost altar. A faint clack of wood came from an ancient tree, its outstretched branches held up by struts and its broad trunk circled by a rack of wooden *ema* plaques.

He could feel her on the other side of the massive tree, hidden behind the torrent of prayers, hopes, and desires hung up for the Shinto gods. He cautiously circled the rack of *ema*, sure that she was watching him.

"Just listen for a minute," he whispered but when he got to the other side of the rack, he saw her jump and pull herself over the top of a high wooden wall at the edge of the courtyard. He couldn't figure out how she got there so fast. She slipped over and disappeared.

Hiroshi ran as best he could to the gate and stepped on a *shishi* lion-dog statue to get over the top. His ribs dragged painfully over the top beam and he fell onto his hands on the other side. He steadied himself from the pain by leaning back against the wall. The crunch of gravel receding in the distance refocused him and he pushed to a run, wheezing and dizzy. Thick drops of rain fell from the overhead tree branches.

The gravel turned to a moss-covered incline. When Hiroshi got to the top of the rise, sweating and breathless, he realized that Michiko had led him in a circle back to the tracks. She was already over the same fence separating the shrine grounds from the train tracks. It was a long drop from the concrete wall to the tracks below.

Dim light from the station a train's length away fell across the tracks, catching the rain slanting sideways by the wind. Michiko picked her way across the tracks below. Her figure looked small against the two-story billboards covered with smiling models in the latest fashions.

Hiroshi put his fingers and toes into the fence and climbed up. He let himself down from the wall as far as he could. Looking both ways for oncoming trains before letting go, he landed with a thud that shuddered through his body.

He heard the ping-ping-ping warning for an oncoming express train, then the wheeze and grind of a local train from the other direction. Wobbling from fatigue, he ran after Michiko, who was neatly sprinting along the tracks, heading for a low fence that dropped down to the busy streets of Harajuku beyond. The sound of the trains startled him into stopping. He turned and wiped the rain from his eyes.

From the opposite side of the tracks, he could see that the tracks narrowed sharply ahead of her, the wide station distance cut in half by a tall row of large electric circuit boxes and a concrete sluice for electric cables. The oncoming train's headlight temporarily blinded him and he reeled back, unable to cross or to see. The driver blasted the horn long and loud. He didn't hear the second train coming from the other direction until it was almost next to him. Because of its speed, it could only be an express.

When the horn blared again, Hiroshi glimpsed Michiko's head whip around, noticing the express for the first time.

Then, for some reason—Hiroshi could never piece it together no matter how many times he went over it in his mind later—she bolted straight across the tracks right in front of the trains.

The entire track heaved and shook as the express train braked, too late to lessen the force of the speeding wall of metal. From the other direction, the local train bucked and jolted, throwing passengers to the floor inside.

The express train slowed to a crawl, and the local train stopped halfway out of the station. The clunking and screeching of the engine and the brakes fell to a quiet hum. The loud, steady clang of emergency signals blasted through the air.

Hiroshi limped around the back of the express and the front of the local. He found Michiko's body crumpled across the tracks. Her limbs were thrown at odd angles, her neck twisted sideways.

Blood oozed out over the concrete ties wetting her long, thick hair and the gravel below. One of her sandals was torn from her leg, wedged tight into the V of a track switch, her foot still in it, severed.

There was no need to feel for a pulse, but he did anyway, stooping to put his fingers on her neck. Her body was smashed to meat and marrow, her hip crushed and her shoulder pulped.

A small crystal bottle slipped partway out of her bag, broken open so the scent of lotus flowers drifted up as the perfume became diluted with blood and rain.

Her face pointed skyward, untouched, her eyes closed into two gentle brushstrokes and for a moment her lips looked as flushed as if she'd just been kissed, turning pale as they cooled.

Hiroshi leaned over her to push back a bloodied strand of hair. He brushed his fingers over her cheek, a moment's comfort before her soul slipped away. He pulled her shawl over her as the raindrops washed her skin clean.

Hiroshi stood up, his ears buzzing and eyes blurry. He could hear the intercom crackle from the local train, and turned to see the driver climb down from the front compartment. The driver from the express came along the length of his train to talk with the driver of the local in a low, anxious voice. Hiroshi watched them call again on their handheld mics, their caps and shoulders already soaked, listening and nodding, waiting to be told what to do.

The drivers stared uncertainly at Hiroshi, who was barely able to stand as he pulled out his badge. He turned back toward the station, picking his way along the tracks. He did not want to stay and see her picked up with chopsticks and stuffed into a bag.

Chapter 49

The doorbell jolted Hiroshi from sleep. He pulled himself off the sofa and stumbled to the door. He clutched his ribs, his T-shirt wet from where he fell asleep with an ice pack. He pushed open his door and winced at the light and air pouring in to his apartment. He tried to focus on the two men standing there.

"Yes?" He blinked at their blue uniforms and quizzical expressions.

"ABC movers? To pick up some boxes?" A young guy with spiky hair and a dark tan looked at his clipboard, and then at the apartment number and the name beside the door, and then turned back to Hiroshi.

"Boxes?" Hiroshi scratched his head and touched his ribs again. "Oh, the boxes." He pushed the door open a little wider, leaning across the genkan in shorts and a T-shirt.

Both of the movers stood there ready to work, or to leave—either way. The second guy pulled at the white towel tied around his head.

"Come in," Hiroshi said, finally.

The movers sidled into the cramped entryway and toed their shoes off. "Twenty-five boxes, right?" the spiky hair mover said to confirm.

"Something like that. I can't remember." Hiroshi led them from the genkan to the living room. He squinted as he pulled open the curtains above the sofa, squinting and holding his side.

The boxes all had their tops sprung open and stuff poking over the edge.

"I'm not quite done, I guess," Hiroshi said.

The clipboard guy said to his younger colleague, "Go get some tape from the truck." Clearly, it was not the first time they had helped a deserted man send boxes to a departed woman.

Hiroshi tried to lift the first of the boxes but dropped it, wincing with the pain in his ribs and wrists.

"You OK?" the clipboard guy asked, rushing to help him.

"Been better."

"We'll get it. You sit down."

"I can do a little," Hiroshi insisted, though he wasn't so sure.

The younger guy came back with the tape and rolled up his sleeves, revealing a tattoo of the cartoon character, Doraemon. On his bicep, Doraemon's soft blue body, red mouth, and floppy orange tongue stood out in bright, bold colors.

Hiroshi shoved things in and held the boxes shut while the clipboard guy deftly stretched tape over the top. The Doraemon tattoo guy picked up three boxes at a time and carried them to the handcart on the walkway outside. Their calm, workmanlike pace kept Hiroshi focused on the work and not on Linda.

The two movers reminded Hiroshi of the young guys Sakaguchi, Ueno, Osaki and Sugamo had tossed around at the game center in Shibuya—the same tan, dyed hair and earrings—only these guys had energy and integrity, displaying the self-respect Japanese accorded all jobs, high or low. They worked—pure and simple.

Hiroshi went to the bedroom for things piled on the bed and slipped in Linda's things to the still-open boxes wherever they would fit. When the movers were almost done, the clipboard guy stacked all but one of the boxes outside Hiroshi's apartment.

"That everything?" the clipboard guy asked. "People always forget one last, little thing."

Hiroshi said, "Wait a minute," and went back for a handful of framed photos of Linda and him.

But once he had them in his hands, he paused, and set them back on the shelf. "Nothing else, I guess," he shouted.

He looked at the photos, arranged like Michiko's—a forest of memories, each covering over another. For now, it was okay to leave them there. He would call Linda to tell her the boxes were on their way.

He heard the last rip of tape and went to the entryway where the clipboard guy was calculating the bill.

"Twenty-seven boxes, all going to the US. This is the correct address?"

Hiroshi nodded.

"Normally, we charge for helping to pack, but we'll give it to you free."

"Let me get the cash," Hiroshi said and went to the bedroom where he kept cash in a drawer. The clipboard guy counted out the cash out—twice—and then gave Hiroshi a receipt.

"And here, this is for you," Hiroshi said, handing him a five-thousand yen note. "Since I threw off your schedule."

"We don't usually take tips."

"It'll buy you lunch." The other guy with his Doraemon arm came back for the last load of boxes. "Or beer."

"Thanks," the clipboard guy said, tucking the money into his pocket.

Hiroshi watched them take the last load of boxes down the outside walkway on the handcart. He went back inside and let the door shut. His cell phone rang.

Akiko said, "I just got to the office. What happened?"

"I'll tell you about it when I come in. I'm stopping by the hospital to check on my ribs first. How's Sakaguchi?"

"He's asking for you."

"He's up and around already?"

"I won't describe how he looks," Akiko said.

* * *

Akiko was talking with Sakaguchi in Hiroshi's office when Hiroshi arrived, clutching pain pills and ice packs from the clinic. Coffee percolated and the smell filled the room. Sakaguchi's hands were covered in gauze and one side of his face was covered in thin, neat slices, just missing his eye. On his cheek and neck, he had X-stitches holding meaty folds of skin together. The cuts on his face were deep, puffy and purple-red.

"I can't believe you're here today." Hiroshi shook his head.

"Missed all the major things. Would have had to cut pretty deep to get to them, I guess," he laughed.

"I shouldn't have left you," Hiroshi said.

"I missed her side-step. She used my weight against me," Sakaguchi said.

"You could have severed an artery," Hiroshi said, over the tinkling of fresh beans spilling into the grinder.

"One thing you learn in sumo is how to fall."

"Not through plates of glass," Akiko said.

"I'm still not sure all the glass is out. What about you?" Sakaguchi asked.

"Rib fracture. Nothing to do but wait."

"I used to get bruised ribs when I started sumo. Hurts every breath."

"This arrived," Akiko said.

Hiroshi took the envelope and glanced through copies of bank account statements, property mortgages and investment accounts.

Hiroshi started reading. "Where did it come from?"

"Can't you guess?" Sakaguchi chuckled. "He must have listened to us."

"The accountant?"

"Hand-delivered to the office, no return address," Akiko said.

Hiroshi looked through the copied pages and shook his head. "Apartments in Hong Kong, Paris and London. Solid and long-term. Accounts in Switzerland, Hong Kong, and the Cayman Islands. Easy to access. Stock accounts in Japan, the United States and London. Diversified."

"She is one smart girl," Akiko said.

"Was," Hiroshi said. "This is interesting. The factory in Kawasaki and a line of riverside warehouses are in the name of Sadahiko Ono."

"Is that the old guy in the factory?"

"Must be," Hiroshi said, nodding his head. He flipped through the documents to the accounts. "And the names on the accounts are not all Michiko's, either. One of them is Natsumi Takada. Must be the Natsumi at the fruit stand."

"Maybe she doesn't know she's going to get rich?"

"Once the accounts get cleared up," Hiroshi said. "She also owns the building the photographer is in."

"She knew how to work it," Akiko said.

"She knew how to kick," Hiroshi added, as he opened the freezer and exchanged the old ice pack for a new one.

"I'll get the coffee. You two are injured," Akiko said, pouring three cups.

Sakaguchi took his cup without a word. "Why not?" Sakaguchi said, the cup small in his hand.

Hiroshi looked at him strangely and then turned over another document, saying, "Here we go. Bentley. I knew they'd be in here."

"What did she have on them?" Sakaguchi asked.

"It looks like Michiko kept track of Bentley's purchases. It's a long list here, many of them—no, all of them are clouded," Hiroshi said.

"You'll have to translate for me," Sakaguchi added.

"It means there's a dispute about the ownership of properties, so the sale is halted. Costs run up trying to determine if ownership can be clarified, wiping out part of the profit margin," Hiroshi said.

"Why would that happen?"

"It could be another buyer tried to purchase the property and Bentley got in before them. Whatever it is, there's doubt as to ownership. This is quite a list and will take time to get through. I'll run these down later."

"I can do that," Akiko offered, holding her hand up with a smile. Hiroshi handed her the documents.

Sakaguchi swallowed his coffee with a wince and asked Akiko, "Are you going to stay?"

"Where? Here? I don't know. Takamatsu got me transferred for this case."

"It'd be great if you could stay," Hiroshi said.

Sakaguchi said, "Hiroshi, you need someone who speaks English, don't you?" Hiroshi raised his eyebrows.

"There won't be many cases like this one, will there?" Akiko asked.

"They're all like this," Sakaguchi said.

"What about Takamatsu?"

"Sick leave," Sakaguchi said. "After that, administrative leave."

"He'll have time to work out an explanation," Hiroshi said.

"Takamatsu won't get fired, will he?" Akiko asked.

Sakaguchi shrugged. "His case clear rate is still the highest in the department."

"Where are those photos?" Hiroshi asked.

"Here," Akiko handed them to him.

The ones showing Michiko and Takamatsu together on the platform the night he was nearly killed went in one pile. All the others, of Takamatsu with her on other nights, some from years before, he folded over and handed to Akiko.

"Shred these," he told her.

"I'll borrow a shredder from another office. Maybe you should buy your own if you're going to cover up for all your colleagues," Akiko said.

Sakaguchi stood up and steadied himself. "You'll need a heavy-duty one."

They sipped their coffee.

Hiroshi said, "You're not going back to the *chikan* section, are you?"

"With Takamatsu recovering, I'm back at homicide."

"Oh, and also, there's this DVD, postmarked Roppongi, no return address. Maybe more investments?" Akiko said, waving a small mailing pouch.

Hiroshi put the DVD into his computer and pulled the viewing frame larger, expecting to see more data.

After a few seconds of white fuzz, what came on was a video of a naked woman hanging from a ceiling hook by red cord wrapped around and around her midsection. She was tied with *shibori* knots and a *kinbaku-bi* rope. Her breasts popped out between the tight loops. A knotted cord held her arms behind her and a silver rod tied behind her knees kept her legs wide apart.

She swung slowly in place face down and horizontal by a long rope from the ceiling. Her long black hair dangled to the floor. As her face rotated toward them, the camera zoomed in on her eyes—glassy and distant—looking straight at the camera, a ball held firmly in her mouth by a rubber strap around the back of her head.

It was Michiko.

"I can't watch this!" Akiko said, turning away and walking back to her desk.

Hiroshi fast-forwarded and the place he stopped showed Michiko kneeling on the floor of a dark room with a circle of naked men around her, stroking themselves and waiting for their turn with her.

Sakaguchi said, "That's enough for me, too."

Hiroshi clicked eject. "We'll send it to the tech guys. They might find something."

Hiroshi got a plastic bag and dropped the DVD inside. He held it out for Akiko but she looked away, so he set it on his own desk.

Akiko said, "If someone did that to me. I'd kill them, too." Hiroshi got up and poured more coffee. "Why would she be so careful about everything and then kill herself?" Akiko asked.

"Her foot got stuck in a train switch," Hiroshi said in a low voice, the memory flooding in again. "I think. I couldn't see in the rain. The trains—she was trying to get away and I—"

Akiko and Sakaguchi waited in patient, attentive silence.

Hiroshi shook his head. "She must have understood every detail of their whole investing scheme, how they found out ahead, how they worked the payouts, how—"

"Doesn't matter now," Sakaguchi said.

"How are you going to write it up?" Akiko said.

Hiroshi's cell phone rang.

He listened for a minute and nodded. "I'll be there." He clicked off his cell phone. "That's the second thing I've forgotten today. I have to go."

Hiroshi looked at the DVD in the bag. "Akiko, find out how the payments change depending on the ruling. I want to know who gets what if it is ruled suicide, accident or police responsibility."

"You're going to be sure the payouts go to the right people?" she asked.

Sakaguchi said, "She worked for her money."

"Worked hard," Hiroshi said.

Sakaguchi pulled himself up, out of the chair, handed his empty cup to Akiko and touched the stitches along the back of his neck. "It's not bad, coffee, but it doesn't make you feel better like green tea does. *Ja ne*, well then." He walked out the door stiffly, but surely.

Akiko looked away as Hiroshi got ready to go. "Better take an umbrella," she said. "It's supposed to rain today."

Chapter 50

Outside the station, Hiroshi waved down a taxi. Akiko was right—it was drizzling and the humid air smelled like more rain to come. He could catch the express from Tokyo Station, but he would have to hurry.

The buildings grew shorter and shorter, more spread out, the farther the train traveled from Tokyo Station, with each station they shot through becoming less peopled. Sprawling hillside apartments and chunky housing complexes turned into clusters of houses with small yards. Those yielded to wooden farmhouses with rice fields glistening in the rain.

After passport control, he took the spacious elevator, bigger than the hospital's to the high-ceilinged, check-in area. Thousands of people pushed oversized luggage, blabbed into cell phones, and followed tour group leaders, fidgeting with excitement and anxiety.

"Hey, I can't believe you made it!" Hiroshi heard someone say in English. He turned to find Yukari. She looked nothing like she had in the police station. Instead of ashamed and crying, she was dressed in jeans and a T-shirt, smiling in an excited, teenage-girl way. She skipped, sideways, over to him.

"I made it," Hiroshi said. "You look so different from in the police station!"

"Do I? Aren't you glad I called?"

"I've been a bit busy the past couple of days."

"So have we, packing, yuck."

"I wanted to see you off," said Hiroshi, smiling back at her.

"Me or my mom?" Yukari asked, laughing.

"Both of you."

"My mom's over there in line getting us checked in. We're running late, of course. I had to get some things," she said, holding up two bags filled with odd shapes against the plastic.

Hiroshi let his eyes search out Sanae taking care of the tickets at the counter.

"I read that in America I can just take this test and get out of high school, then apply directly to colleges. Of course, I have to take the tests, but they don't seem so bad. My dad said he'd pay for part of any school I could get into, so I think I'll pick the most expensive one just to make him suffer. I'm thinking of a small school on the east coast, maybe a women's school, what do you think?"

Hiroshi smiled. "Women's school? Why not?"

"Well, I wonder. I'll have to pick one where they won't bore me to death. At least the women's schools seem challenging and interesting. Mom says I should see what happens if I try to really apply myself. I'll show her! She says she might go back to school, too, but I don't think she will."

"What will she do, do you think?"

Yukari smiled. "I don't know. What do you think?"

Hiroshi laughed. "I'm not very good at guessing. Sad to say."

"My mom isn't either, but she guessed you'd meet her for coffee."

"That was an easy guess."

Sanae came out of the check-in area, putting the tickets away and looking around for Yukari. She appeared surprised to see Hiroshi, and busied herself with the passports and tickets and carry-on luggage.

"No hardened killers to catch today?" Sanae asked.

"We've got them all taken care of. For now, anyway."

"Yukari, you've made us late."

"You were the one who had to re-pack everything."

"The woman said we have to proceed immediately to the gate or we'll miss our flight."

"If we weren't late, we would have missed him!" Yukari giggled. "I have to get some more of my favorite gum they might not have in Boston since it's so sophisticated there and I have to go to the bathroom again so, you'll just have to wait for me, though I'll be right back," Yukari sang, ignoring Sanae's "*Chotto matte*, wait a second."

"How long will you stay over there?" Hiroshi asked.

"I want to see her get into college. Who knows how long that will take?"

"Not long maybe, with her energy."

"Can you write your address down for me again?" said Sanae, pulling a notebook out of her bag. "With all this packing I feel like I don't know where anything is."

"I have the same feeling, even without packing," Hiroshi said. He took a pen and wrote down all the information he could think of, his phone numbers, work and home addresses, and emails.

"Here's your umbrella by the way," he said.

"I can't take it on the plane. Besides, it's wet."

"Well—" Hiroshi twisted it around awkwardly.

"Keep it. Until I come back."

"Okay. I will. Thank you."

"I like hearing that."

"What?"

" 'Okay. I will. Thank you.' " She lowered her voice to mimic his. Hiroshi smiled.

Yukari came prancing back and in a mock-adult voice said, "Okay, you two, now we can go."

Sanae admonished her as they turned toward the inspection area. "You're making us late."

"Me? You!" Yukari giggled.

"Write to me!" Hiroshi said.

"I will," Sanae answered.

"Who writes anymore? People Skype or text or chat or visit, you know." Yukari laughed.

They all looked away from each other's eyes for a moment until Yukari grabbed Sanae's arm and tugged and said, "Ma-um, let's go-oh."

Hiroshi and Sanae hugged each other quickly. Her bag slipped off her shoulder and swung around against him. Yukari laughed.

Mother and daughter ran off fumbling with their bags and laying them out on the conveyer belt before walking through the X-ray machine. They waved from the other side of the glass, hurrying excitedly.

He watched them disappear and looked up at the huge ceiling high above the departure lounge, thought of Linda's goodbye, watching all the people going to new places. He felt, strangely, as if he had just arrived.

Hiroshi woke groggy from the short snooze when the airport express pulled into Tokyo Station. He took the Yamanote Line to Akihabara Station and caught a taxi. The rain was heavy. After a few minutes of hypnotizing windshield wipers, he was there. The driver looked at him like he was crazy to get out in such heavy rain, but took his money without a word.

Hiroshi opened up Sanae's umbrella. Rain beat down on the nylon in loud, watery slaps. The wind-blown rain quickly soaked his pants, which clung to his legs from the knee down and dripped into his socks, sending a shiver through him.

Inside, bronze gutters channeled streams of rainwater into stone basins set around the bottom of the main building of Kanda Shrine. The overflow from the basins spilled onto the stones and gravel below. He could just make out the smaller buildings and outer walls through the heavy, gray rain.

Under the overhanging roof, he took down his, Sanae's, umbrella, and slipped off his shoes. He couldn't leave them in the rack in the rain, and there was no plastic bag to put them in, so he slipped them inside the umbrella and hurried up the old, wood stairs into the temple.

Inside the main hall, he could see a small light shining where a monk sat reading at a table, flipping thick prayer beads around his wrist, idly watching over a display case of *omamori* protective charms, folding sutras, and *ema*.

The monk looked a little surprised, but acknowledged Hiroshi's presence—the one determined visitor in such a downpour—with a look that took in who Hiroshi was, and why he was there.

Seeing the monk reminded Hiroshi what the temple abbot said about the importance of contemplating death as a force in life. But Hiroshi wanted to contemplate all the other forces, too, the ones that guided and led him forward. He wasn't sure what they were, but he felt them just the same.

Hiroshi tossed coins into the collection box, pulled on the huge rope attached to the bell and clapped his hands. With his head bowed, he held his hands together in front of his chest with his eyes closed and prayed. He wondered what was supposed to happen inside when offering a prayer he truly felt. Only a prayer truly felt had any hope of changing anything, of helping him accept what would never change.

The monk looked up at him again for a few seconds and then went back to his reading, flipping his beads to start another count.

The prayer Hiroshi offered was for the soul of Michiko Suzuki, whoever she might be.

If you enjoyed this book, please consider taking a minute to write a review. If you'd like to read more quality non-fiction and fiction, I'd really appreciate a review on Amazon, Goodreads or whatever site you like best. A review helps others know about your reading experience and lets you express your opinion. It also helps me immensely. Like other readers, I appreciate feedback.

Here's a link to leave a review: viewBook.at/LastTrain

About the author

Michael Pronko is a professor of American Literature and Culture at Meiji Gakuin University in Tokyo and writes about Japanese culture, art, jazz, and politics for *Newsweek Japan, The Japan Times, Artscape Japan* and other publications. He has appeared on NHK Public TV, Tokyo MXTV and Nippon Television. His website, *Jazz in Japan*, can be found at: www.jazzinjapan.com. His award-winning collections of essays about life in Tokyo are: *Beauty and Chaos: Slices and Morsels of Tokyo Life* (2014), *Tokyo's Mystery Deepens: Essays on Tokyo* (2014), and *Motions and Moments: More Essays on Tokyo* (2015), in addition to three essay collections in Japanese. When not teaching or writing, he wanders Tokyo contemplating its intensity and waiting for the stories to come.

For more on the Hiroshi series: www.michaelpronko.com
Follow Michael on Twitter: @pronkomichael
Michael's Facebook page: www.facebook.com/pronkoauthor

Also in the Hiroshi series:
Japan Hand
Thai Girl in Tokyo

Thank you to so many people, but especially to AA, MM, CR, RK, NL for hands on, hands in and great, unrepayable input. You all touched this book and made it better. Thank you to the many editors in my past who so graciously schooled me over the years. You touched my writing and made it better. I learned, if slowly. And thanks to my wife for being there and then some. And then some more. And then still there.

CPSIA information can be obtained
at www.ICGtesting.com
Printed in the USA
FFHW011314121118
49385237-53683FF